PRAISE FOR *PARIS IS*

"A playful, breezy read that I coul[...] [...]*me*

    —Abby Jimenez, *USA To[...]*

"A delightful romance with characters I adored! Jenn McKinlay takes readers along on a fun and charming adventure in *Paris Is Always a Good Idea.*"   —Emily March, *New York Times* bestselling author of *Teardrop Lane*

"*Eat Pray Love* meets *Mamma Mia!* I devoured this clever novel in one sitting!"

    —Lori Nelson Spielman, *New York Times* bestselling author of *The Star-Crossed Sisters of Tuscany*

"Witty, warm, and wonderful . . . an American *Fleabag*, told with heart, hope, and joie de vivre."

    —Lori Wilde, *New York Times* bestselling author of *The Moonglow Sisters*

"McKinlay spins a funny yet poignant tale."

    —Jen DeLuca, author of *Well Met*

"A funny and charming romp of self-discovery. . . . You'll feel like you've been on a European vacation even if you didn't make it out of your own backyard."

    —Kwana Jackson, *USA Today* bestselling author of *Real Men Knit*

"Sparkles with wit yet profoundly humane at its core. You will be rooting for Chelsea through all her travels."

    —Jenny Holiday, *USA Today* bestselling author of *Mermaid Inn*

"*Paris Is Always a Good Idea* made me smile, cry, swoon, and cheer. It's a beautiful, funny, and relatable story about finding yourself."

    —Sarah Smith, author of *Faker*

PRAISE FOR JENN McKINLAY'S ROMANCE NOVELS

"Jenn McKinlay writes sexy, funny romances that will leave you begging for more!"

—Jill Shalvis, *New York Times* bestselling author of *Almost Just Friends*

"Funny, charming, and heart-stoppingly romantic. Jenn McKinlay is a rising star."

—Jaci Burton, *New York Times* bestselling author of *The Best Man Plan*

"McKinlay once again serves up her signature literary cocktail of sassy humor and sexy romance expertly spiked with a surfeit of small-town charm and holiday cheer." —*Booklist* (starred review)

"Witty dialogue and a charming small town filled with warm, loving characters will keep readers coming back to this tender series."

—*Publishers Weekly*

"As cozy as the hero's favorite Christmas sweater, with a warm, home-for-the-holidays feel." —*Library Journal*

"[*Every Dog Has His Day* is] superbly satisfying. . . . A contemporary romance that is practically perfect is every way."

—*Booklist* (starred review)

"[*Every Dog Has His Day*] enchants from the very first page. . . . A sparkling gem of a book that is sure to lift your spirits!"

—RT Book Reviews (top pick)

"McKinlay delivers heartwarming humor at its finest."

—Lori Wilde, *New York Times* bestselling author of *The Moonglow Sisters*

"Clever writing, laugh-out-loud humor, and a sizzling romance. This one is a keeper."

—Delores Fossen, *USA Today* bestselling author of *A Coldwater Christmas*

PARIS IS ALWAYS A GOOD IDEA

Jenn McKinlay

BERKLEY ROMANCE
NEW YORK

BERKLEY ROMANCE
Published by Berkley
An imprint of Penguin Random House LLC
penguinrandomhouse.com

Copyright © 2020 by Jennifer McKinlay
Readers Guide copyright © 2020 by Jennifer McKinlay
Penguin Random House supports copyright. Copyright fuels creativity, encourages diverse
voices, promotes free speech, and creates a vibrant culture. Thank you for buying an authorized
edition of this book and for complying with copyright laws by not reproducing, scanning, or
distributing any part of it in any form without permission. You are supporting writers and
allowing Penguin Random House to continue to publish books for every reader.

BERKLEY and the BERKLEY & B colophon are registered trademarks of
Penguin Random House LLC.

Library of Congress Cataloging-in-Publication Data

Names: McKinlay, Jenn, author.
Title: Paris is always a good idea / Jenn McKinlay.
Description: First edition. | New York: Jove, 2020.
Identifiers: LCCN 2019057298 | ISBN 9780593101353 (trade paperback) |
ISBN 9780593101360 (ebook)
Subjects: GSAFD: Humorous fiction. | Love stories.
Classification: LCC PS3612.A948 P37 2020 | DDC 813/.6— dc23
LC record available at https:// lccn.loc.gov/2019057298

Jove trade paperback edition / July 2020
Berkley Romance trade paperback edition / November 2023

Printed in the United States of America
7th Printing

Book design by Alison Cnockaert
Interior art: European sights by ostudio.ok/Shutterstock

This is a work of fiction. Names, characters, places, and incidents either are the product of the
author's imagination or are used fictitiously, and any resemblance to actual persons, living or dead,
business establishments, events, or locales is entirely coincidental.

For Alyssa Amaturo, my adorable flower girl now a beautiful grown woman. I am so impressed by the amazing person you have become—funny, talented, smart, and with a generous heart! You helped me so much with this book. I can never thank you enough!

chapter one

"I'M GETTING MARRIED."

"Huh?"

"We've already picked our colors, pink and gray."

"Um . . . pink and what?"

"Gray. What do you think, Chelsea? I want your honest opinion. Is that too retro?"

I stared at my middle-aged widowed father. We were standing in a bridal store in central Boston on the corner of Boylston and Berkeley Streets, and he was talking to me about wedding colors. *His* wedding colors.

"I'm sorry—I need a sec," I said. I held up my hand and blinked hard while trying to figure out just what the hell was happening.

I had raced here from my apartment in Cambridge after receiving a text from my dad, asking me to meet him at this address because it was an emergency. I was prepared for heart surgery, not wedding colors!

Suddenly, I couldn't breathe. I wrestled the constricting wool scarf from around my neck, yanked the beanie off my head, and stuffed them in my pockets. I scrubbed my scalp with my fingers in an attempt to make the blood flow to my brain. It didn't help. *Come on, Martin*, I coached myself. *Pull it together.* I unzipped my puffy winter jacket to let some air in, then I focused on my father.

"What did you say?" I asked.

"Pink and gray, too retro?" Glen Martin, a.k.a. Dad, asked. He pushed his wire-frame glasses up on his nose and looked at me as if he was asking a perfectly reasonable question.

"No, before that." I waved my hand in a circular motion to indicate he needed to back it all the way up.

"I'm getting married!" His voice went up when he said it, and I decided my normally staid fifty-five-year-old dad was somehow currently possessed by a twenty-something bridezilla.

"You okay, Dad?" I asked. Not for nothing, because the last time I checked, he hadn't even been dating anyone, never mind thinking about marriage. "Have you recently slipped on some ice and whacked your head? I ask because you don't seem to be yourself."

"Sorry," he said. He reached out and wrapped me in an impulsive hug, another indicator that he was not his usual buttoned-down mathematician self. "I'm just . . . I'm just so happy. What do you think about being a flower girl?"

"Um . . . I'm almost thirty." I tried not to look as bewildered as I felt. What was happening here?

"Yes, but we already have a full wedding party, and you and your sister would be really cute in matching dresses, maybe something sparkly."

"Matching dresses? Sparkly?" I repeated. I struggled to make sense of his words. I couldn't. It was clear. My father had lost his ever-lovin' mind. I should probably call my sister.

I studied his face, trying to determine just how crazy he was. The same hazel eyes I saw in my own mirror every morning held mine, but where my eyes frequently looked flat with a matte finish, his positively glowed. He really looked happy.

"You're serious," I gasped. I glanced around the bridal store, which was stuffed to the rafters with big fluffy white dresses. None of this made any sense, and yet here I was. "You're not pranking me?"

"Nope." He grinned again. "Congratulate me, peanut. I'm getting married."

I felt as if my chest were collapsing into itself. Never, not once, in the past seven years had I ever considered the possibility that my father would remarry.

"To who?" I asked. It couldn't be . . . nah. That would be *insane*.

"Really, Chels?" Dad straightened up. The smile slid from his face, and he cocked his head to the side—his go-to disappointed-parent look.

I had not been on the receiving end of this look very often in life. Not like my younger sister, Annabelle, who seemed to thrive on "the look." Usually, it made me fall right in line but not today.

"Sheri? You're marrying Sheri?" I tried to keep my voice neutral. Major failure, as I stepped backward, tripped on the trailing end of my scarf, and gracelessly sprawled onto one of the cream-colored velvet chairs that were scattered around the ultrafeminine store. I thought it was a good thing I was sitting, because if he answered in the affirmative, I might faint.

"Yes, I asked her to marry me, and to my delight she accepted," he said. Another happy, silly grin spread across his lips as if he just couldn't help it.

"But . . . but . . . she won you in a bachelor auction two weeks ago!" I cried. I closed my mouth before I said more, like pointing out that this was hasty in the extreme.

The store seamstress, who was assisting a bride up on the dais in front of a huge trifold mirror, turned to look at us. Her dark hair was scraped up into a knot on top of her head, and her face was contoured to perfection. She made me feel like a frump in my Sunday no-makeup face. Which, in my defense, was not my fault, because when I'd left the house to meet Dad, I'd had no idea the address he'd sent was for Brianna's Bridal. I'd been expecting an urgent care; in fact, I wasn't sure yet that we didn't need one.

Glen Martin, Harvard mathematician and all-around nerd dad, had been coerced into participating in a silver-fox bachelor auction for prominent Bostonians by my sister, Annabelle, to help raise funds for Boston Children's Hospital. I had gone, of course, to support my sister and my dad, and it had mostly been a total snooze fest.

The highlight of the event was when two socialites got into a bidding war over a surgeon, and the loser slapped the winner across the face with her cardboard paddle. Good thing the guy was a cosmetic surgeon, because there was most definitely some repair work needed on that paper cut.

But my father had not been anywhere near that popular with the ladies. No one wanted a mathematician. No one. After several minutes of excruciating silence, following the MC trying to sell the lonely gals on my dad's attempts to solve the Riemann hypothesis, I had been about to bid on him myself, when Sheri, a petite brunette, had raised her paddle with an initial offer. The smile of gratitude Dad had sent Sheri had been blinding, and the next thing we knew, a flurry of numbered paddles popped up in the air, but Sheri stuck in there and landed the win for $435.50.

"Two weeks is all it took," Dad said. He shrugged and held out his hands like a blackjack dealer showing he had no hidden cards, chips, or cash.

I stared at him with a look that I'm sure was equal parts shock and horror.

"I know it's a surprise, Chels, but when—" he began, but I interrupted him.

"Dad, I don't think a bachelor auction is the basis for a stable, long-lasting relationship."

"You have to admit it makes a great story," he said.

"Um . . . no." I tried to sound reasonable, as if this were a math problem about fitting sixty watermelons into a small car. I spread my hands wide and asked, "What do you even know about Sheri? What's her favorite color?"

"Pink, duh." He looked at me with a know-it-all expression more commonly seen on a teenager than a grown-ass man. Hmm.

"All right, who are you, and what have you done with my father?" I wanted to check him for a fever; maybe he had the flu and he was hallucinating.

"I'm still me, Chels," he said. He gazed at me gently. "I'm just a happy me, for a change."

Was that it? Was that what was so different about him? He was happy? How could he be happy with a woman he hardly knew? Maybe . . . oh dear. My dad hadn't circulated much after my mom's death. Maybe he was finally getting a little something-something, and he had it confused with love. Oh god, how was I supposed to talk about this with him?

I closed my eyes. I took a deep breath. Parents did this all the time. Surely I could manage it. Heck, it would be great practice if I ever popped out a kid. I opened my eyes. Three women were standing in the far corner in the ugliest chartreuse dresses I had ever seen. Clearly, they were the attendants of a bride who hated them. And that might be me in sparkly pink or gray if I didn't put a stop to this madness.

"Sit down, Dad," I said. "I think we need to have a talk."

He took the seat beside mine and looked at me with the same patience he had when he'd taught me to tie my shoes. I looked away. Ugh, this was more awkward than when my gynecologist told me to scoot down, repeatedly. It's like they don't know a woman's ass needs some purchase during an annual. *Focus, Martin!*

"I know that you've been living alone for several years." I cleared my throat. "And I imagine you've had some needs that have gone unmet."

"Chels, no—" he said. "It isn't about that."

I ignored him, forging on while not making eye contact, because, lordy, if I had to have this conversation with him, I absolutely could not look at him.

"And I understand that after such a long dry spell, you might be confused about what you feel, and that's okay," I said. Jeebus, this sounded like a sex talk by Mr. Rogers. "The thing is, you don't have to marry the first person you sleep with after Mom."

There, I said it. And my wise advice and counsel were met with complete silence. I waited for him to express relief that he didn't have to get married. And I waited. Finally, I glanced up at my father, who was staring at me in the same way he had when I discovered *he* was actually the tooth fairy. Chagrin.

"Sheri is not the first," he said.

"She's not?" I was shocked. Shocked, I tell you.

"No."

"But you never told me about anyone before," I said.

"You didn't need to know," he replied. "They were companions, not relationships."

"They?!" I shouted. I didn't mean to. The seamstress sent me another critical look, and I coughed, trying to get it together.

Dad shifted in his seat, sending me a small smile of understanding. "Maybe meeting here wasn't the best idea. I thought you'd be excited to help plan the wedding, but perhaps you're not ready."

"Of course I'm not ready," I said. "But you're not either."

"Yes, I am."

"Oh, really? Answer me this: Does Sheri prefer dogs or cats?"

"I don't—" He blinked.

"Yes, because it's only been two weeks," I said. "You remember that lump on your forehead? It took longer than two weeks to get that biopsied, but you're prepared to marry a woman you haven't even known long enough for a biopsy."

My voice was getting higher, and Dad put his hands out in an *inside voice, please* gesture. I would have tried, but I felt as if I was hitting my stride in making my point. I went for the crushing blow.

"Dad, do you even know whether she's a pie or cake sort of person?"

"I . . . um . . ."

"Do you realize you're contemplating spending the rest of your life with a person who might celebrate birthdays with pie?"

"Chels, I know this is coming at you pretty fast," he said. "I do, but I don't think Sheri liking pie or cake is really that big of a deal. Who knows, she might be an ice cream person, and ice cream goes with everything."

"Mom was a cake person," I said. There. I'd done it. I'd brought in the biggest argument against this whole rushed matrimonial insanity. Mom.

My father's smile vanished as if I'd snuffed it out between my fingers like a match flame. I felt lousy about it, but not quite as lousy as I did at the thought of Sheri—oh, but no—becoming my stepmother.

"Your mother's been gone for seven years, Chels," he said. "That's a long time for a person to be alone."

"But you haven't been alone . . . apparently," I protested. "Besides, you have me and Annabelle."

"I do."

"So why do you need to get married?" I pressed.

Dad sighed. "Because I love Sheri and I want to make her my wife."

I gasped. I felt as if he'd slapped me across the face. Yes, I knew I was reacting badly, but this was my father. The man who had sworn to love my mother until death do them part. But that was the problem, wasn't it? Mom had passed away, and Dad had been alone ever since, right up until he met Sheri Armstrong two weeks ago when she just kept raising her auction paddle for the marginally hot mathematician.

I got it. Really, I did. I'd been known to have bidding fever when a mint pair of Jimmy Choos showed up on eBay. It was hard to let go of something when it was in your grasp, especially when another bidder kept raising the stakes. But this was my dad, not shoes.

One of the bridal-salon employees came by with a tray of mimosas. I grabbed two, double fisting the sparkling beverage. Sweet baby Jesus, I hoped there was more fizz than pulp in them. The bubbles hit the roof of my mouth, and I wished they could wash away the taste of my father's startling news, but they didn't.

"Listen, I know that being the object of desire by a crowd of single, horny women is heady stuff—"

"Really, you know this?" Dad propped his chin in his hand as he studied me with his eyebrows raised and a twinkle in his eye.

"Okay, not exactly, but my point—and I have one—is that you and Sheri aren't operating in the real world here," I said. "I understand that Sheri is feeling quite victorious, having won you, but that doesn't mean she should wed you. I mean, why do you have to marry her? Why can't you just live in sin like other old people?"

"Because we love each other and we want to be married."

"You can't know this so soon," I argued. "It's not possible. Her representative hasn't even left yet."

My dad frowned, clearly not understanding.

"The first six months to a year, you're not really dating a person," I explained. "You're dating their representative. The real person, the one who leaves the seat up and can't find the ketchup in the fridge even when it's right in front of him, doesn't show up until months into the relationship. Trust me."

"What are you talking about? Of course I'm dating a person. I can assure you, Sheri is very much a woman," he said. "Boy howdy, is she." The tips of his ears turned red, and I felt my own face get hot with embarrassment. I forged on.

"Dad, first, *ew*," I said. "And second, a person's representative is their best self. After two weeks, you haven't seen the real Sheri yet. The real Sheri is hiding behind the twenty-four-seven perfect hair and makeup, the placid temper, the woman who thinks your dad jokes are funny. They're not."

"No, no, no." He shook his head. "I've seen her without makeup. She's still beautiful. And she does have a temper—just drive with her sometime. I've learned some new words. Very educational. And my dad jokes are too funny."

I rolled my eyes. I was going to have to do some tough love here. I was going to have to be blunt.

"Dad, I hate to be rude, but you're giving me no choice. She's probably only marrying you for your money," I said. Ugh, I felt like a horrible person for pointing it out, but he needed protection from gold diggers. It was a kindness, really.

To my surprise, he actually laughed. "Sheri is more well off than I am by quite a lot. I'm the charity case in this relationship."

"Then why on earth does she want to marry *you*?" I asked.

The words flew out before I had the brains to stifle them. It was a nasty thing to say. I knew that, but I was freaked out and frantic and not processing very well.

"I didn't mean that the way it sounded," I began, but he cut me off.

"Despite what you think, I'm quite a catch in middle-aged circles."

He stood, retrieving his coat from a nearby coatrack. As he shrugged into it, a flash of hurt crossed his face that made my stomach ache. I loved my father. I wouldn't inflict pain upon him for anything, and yet I had. I'd hurt him very much. I felt lower than sludge.

"I'm sorry, Dad. Really, I didn't mean—" But again he cut me off.

"You did mean it, and, sadly, I'm not even surprised," he said. "Listen, I have mourned the loss of your mother every day since she passed, and I will mourn her every day for the rest of my life, but I have found someone who makes me happy, and I want to spend my life with her. That doesn't take away what I had with your mother."

"Doesn't it?" I argued. This. This was what had been bothering me since his announcement. How could he not see that by replacing my mother, he was absolutely diminishing what they'd had? "Sheri's going to take your name, isn't she? And she's going to move into our house, right? So everything that was once Mom's—the title of Mrs. Glen Martin and the house where she loved and raised her family—you're just giving to another woman. The next thing I know, you'll tell me I have to call her Mom."

A guilty expression flitted across his face.

"No." I shook my head. "Absolutely not."

"I'm not saying you have to call her that. It's just Sheri's never had a family of her own, and she mentioned in passing how much she was looking forward to having daughters. It would be nice if you could think about how good it would be to have a mother figure in your life again."

"I am not her daughter, and I never will be," I said. My chest heaved with indignation. "How can you pretend that all of that isn't erasing Mom?"

Dad stared down at me with his head to the side and his right eyebrow arched, a double whammy of parental disappointment. He wrapped his scarf about his neck and pulled on his gloves.

"You know what? I don't know if Sheri will take my name. We haven't talked about it," he said. "As for the house, I am planning to sell it so we can start our life together somewhere new."

I sucked in a breath. My childhood home. Gone? Sold? To strangers? I thought I might throw up. Instead, I polished off one of the mimosas.

"Sheri and I are getting married in three months," he said. "We're planning a nice June wedding, and we very much want you to be a part of it."

"As a flower girl?" I scoffed. "Whose crazy idea was that?"

"It was Sheri's," he said. His mouth tightened. "She's never been married before, and she's a little excited. It's actually quite lovely to see."

"A thirty-year-old flower girl," I replied, as tenacious as a tailgater in traffic. I just couldn't let it go.

"All right, I get it. Come as anything you want, then," he said. "You can give me away, be my best man, be a bridesmaid, or officiate the damn thing. I don't care. I just want you there. It would mean everything to Sheri and me to have your blessing."

I stared at him. The mild-mannered Harvard math professor who had taught me to throw a curveball, ride a bike, and knee a boy in the junk if he got too fresh had never looked so determined. He meant it. He was going to marry Sheri Armstrong, and there wasn't a damn thing I could do about it.

"I . . . I." My words stalled out. I wanted to say that it was okay, that he deserved to be happy, and that I'd be there in any capacity he wanted, but I choked. I sat there with my mouth opening and closing like a fish on dry land, trying to figure out how to mouth breathe.

My father turned up his collar, bracing for the cold March air. He looked equal parts disappointed and frustrated. "Don't strain yourself."

He turned away as I sat frozen. I hated this. I didn't want us to part company like this, but I was so shocked by this sudden turn of events, I was practically catatonic. I waited, feeling miserable, for him to walk away, but instead he turned back toward me. Rather than being furious with me, which might have caused me to dig in my heels and push back, he looked sad.

"What happened to you, peanut?" he asked. "You used to be the girl with the big heart who was going to save the world."

I didn't say anything. His disappointment and confusion washed over me like a bath of sour milk.

"I grew up," I said. But even to my own ears I sounded defensive.

He shook his head. "No, you didn't. Quite the opposite. You stopped growing at all."

"Are you kidding me? In the past seven years, I've raised millions to help the fight against cancer. How can you say I haven't grown?" I asked. I was working up a nice froth of indignation. "I'm trying to make a difference in the world."

"That's your career," he said. "Being great at your profession doesn't mean you've grown personally. Chels, look at your life. You work seven days a week. You never take time off. You don't date. You have no friends. Heck, if we didn't have a standing brunch date, I doubt I'd ever see you except on holidays. Since your mother passed, you've barricaded yourself emotionally from all of us. What kind of life is that?"

I turned my head to stare out the window at Boylston Street. I couldn't believe my father was dismissing how hard I worked for the American Cancer Coalition. I had busted my butt to become the top corporate fundraiser in the organization, and with the exception of one annoying coworker, my status was unquestioned.

He sighed. I couldn't look at him. "Chels, I'm not saying what you've accomplished isn't important. It's just that you've changed over the past few years. I can't remember the last time you brought someone special home for me to meet. It's as if you've sealed yourself off since your mother—"

I whipped my head in his direction, daring him to talk about my mother in the same conversation in which he'd announced he was re-marrying.

"Chels, you're here!" a voice cried from the fitting room entrance on the opposite side of the store. I glanced away from my dad to see my younger sister, Annabelle, standing there in an explosion of hot-pink satin and tulle trimmed with a wide swath of glittering crystals.

"*What. Is. That?*" I looked from Annabelle to our father and back. The crystals reflected the fluorescent light overhead, making me see spots, or perhaps I was having a stroke. Hard to say.

"It's our dress!" Annabelle squealed. Then she twirled toward us. The long tulle skirt fanned out from the formfitting satin bodice, and Annabelle's long dark curls streamed out around her. She looked like a demented fairy princess. "Do you love it or do you love it?"

"No, I don't love it. It's too pink, too poofy, and too much!" I cried. The seamstress glared at me, looking as if she were going to take some of the pins out of the pin cushion strapped to her wrist and come stab me a few hundred times. I lowered my voice a little. "Have you both gone insane? Seriously, what the hell is happening?"

Annabelle staggered to a stop. The spinning caused her to wobble a bit as she walked toward us, looking more like a drunk princess than a fey one.

"How can you be happy about this?" I snapped at her. I gestured to the dress. "Have you not known me for all of your twenty-seven years? How could you possibly think I would be okay with this?"

Annabelle grabbed the back of a chair to steady herself. "By 'this' do you mean the dress or the whole wedding thing?"

"Of course I mean the whole wedding thing," I growled. "Dad is clearly having some midlife crisis, and there's you just going along with it. Honestly, Annabelle, can't you recognize an emergency when we're having one?"

Annabelle blinked at me, looking perplexed. "What emergency? Dad's getting married. It's awesome. Besides, I feel like I have a vested interest given that it was my auction that brought Dad and Sheri together."

"Because you, like Dad, have gone completely nuts!" I declared. "Two weeks is not long enough to determine whether you should marry someone or not. My god, it takes longer to get a passport. What are you thinking supporting this craziness?"

"Chels, that's not fair and you know it," Dad said.

My expression must have been full-on angry bear, because he changed tack immediately, his expression softening.

"When did you stop letting love into your heart?" he asked. His voice was gentler, full of parental concern that pinched like shoes that were too small, but I ignored the hurt. He didn't get to judge me when he was marrying a person he barely knew. "Is this really how you want to live your life, Chels, with no one special to share it with? Because I don't."

I turned back to the window, refusing to answer. With a sigh weighty with disappointment, he left. I watched his reflection in the glass grow smaller and smaller as he departed. I couldn't remember the last time we had argued, leaving harsh words between us festering like a canker sore. Ever since Mom had died, the awareness of how precious life was had remained ever present, and we always, always, said *I love you* at the end of a conversation, even when we weren't getting along.

I thought about running after him and saying I was sorry, that I was happy for him and Sheri, but it would be a lie, and I knew I wasn't a good enough actress to pull it off. I just couldn't make myself do it. Instead, I tossed back my second mimosa, because mimosas, unlike family, were always reliable.

chapter two

"WAIT HERE," ANNABELLE said. "I'm going to change and we'll talk, okay?"

I didn't answer. Without acknowledging my sister at all, I put my empty glass on a nearby table, walked out of the bridal salon, and went in the opposite direction my father had taken. It was a dick move—I knew that—but I was too emotionally gutted to talk to anyone right now.

The phone calls started shortly after that. Annabelle called twice. I didn't answer. Annabelle texted three times. I didn't read them. Annabelle tried to video chat with me. No, just no. I was too angry—nope, that wasn't quite it. Bewildered? Close, but that wasn't it either.

No, what I was feeling was something in the middle of all the swirling emotions. I couldn't place it. When I tried, it felt like extracting a tapioca ball out of my boba tea with a wide straw. I was afraid if I caught it, I'd choke.

I paused at a crosswalk, feeling March's cold fingers pinch my cheeks like a passive-aggressive auntie. I zipped up my coat, wound my scarf around my neck, and pulled on my beanie. The sneaky brisk air still found ways to slip under my collar and reach my skin. Fortunately, I was too emotionally numb to feel it.

Betrayed. That's what I was feeling. And it cut deep.

I walked the two and a half miles, including a particularly freezing stretch across the Longfellow Bridge, to my apartment, fuming with every step. You'd think my fury would warm me up. It didn't. Mostly because Annabelle was relentless—like a honey badger, she didn't give a shit—and kept calling and texting and calling and texting. I loved my sister like no other. Truly, she was my ride or die, but sometimes her tenacity positively wore me out.

I unlocked the door to my building and stepped into the vestibule, relieved to be out of the biting wind. The door locked automatically behind me as I took the stairs to my apartment. My phone chimed again, and this time, armed with a name for my emotions, I answered Annabelle's call eagerly.

"When did Dad tell you?" I asked.

"Well, hello to you, too, Sis." Annabelle's voice dripped sarcasm but not surprise. "I thought you were never going to answer."

I knew my younger sister was avoiding the question, and it served only to stoke the fire of my indignation. Not only was our father planning to get remarried, I'd bet big money he'd told Annabelle way before me. Shouldn't he have told us together? It seemed a strong enough hook to hang my ire on.

"When?" I took off my winter wear and hung it on the coatrack on the backside of my front door. I paced my apartment, avoiding the squeaky board that ran down the middle. I lived on the second floor of a well-appointed three-story brownstone on Worcester Street in Cambridge. The windows were large, the floors wooden, and the place was as drafty as a train platform, but the view from the lone bedroom of the Dumpster in the alley below was unparalleled.

The buzzer to my apartment sounded, and I said, "Hang on a sec."

I crossed the room and pushed the intercom. "Who is it?"

"Me, actually." My sister's voice came out in stereo from my phone and the intercom. Leave it to Annabelle to be that hi-fi.

"You're here?" I asked.

"Obvy," Annabelle said. "I started over right after you ditched me."

"Oh." I refused to feel bad, and hit the button to unlock the door. "Come on up."

"Thanks." Annabelle ended the call, and I opened my door.

She bounced up the staircase, not even breathing heavily when she arrived. I frowned. I'd lived here for five years, and I still huffed and puffed my way to the second-floor landing. I stepped aside, allowing my sister to enter, and then shut and locked the door. Annabelle slipped off her purple wool coat and tossed it onto an empty chair. Annoying. I picked it up and hung it on the door hook reserved for guests.

When I turned around, Annabelle had flopped onto the couch in full sprawl. Dressed in black leggings, black ankle boots, and an oversized dark-gray tunic sweater, with her long dark curls framing her face, she looked like a spider. I knew this wasn't a nice comparison, but I was still steamed at my sister right now so whatever.

I returned to our conversation. "How long have you known?"

"I helped Dad pick the ring," she said. Her voice was soft, as though if she whispered, then I wouldn't go berserk. Yeah, that was a solid no. Annabelle ran the side of her index finger over her eyelashes, back and forth. It was her tell that she was stressed. I didn't care. Annabelle should be stressed—in fact, she should be downright petrified.

"And when did that happen?" I growled. I turned on my heel and stomped into the kitchenette.

"I don't know." Annabelle dropped her hand and shrugged.

"When?" My teeth were gritted, making my jaw ache. I held up a coffee mug in silent question. Annabelle nodded.

"I think it was a couple of days ago," she said, but her voice went up as if it were a question.

It wasn't a question. She knew what day they'd bought the ring. She was trying to soften the blow, meaning it was going to hurt my feelings. I braced myself. I put the mug under the coffee dispenser and hit the button before turning back to my sister.

"Do you need to check a calendar?" I asked. "Because there's one on the wall."

Annabelle huffed out a breath and glared. "No, it was three days ago."

"And you didn't tell me?" The hurt made my voice rough with jagged edges. I turned away, pulling the milk out of the fridge and grabbing a spoon from the silverware drawer.

"Dad asked me not to."

I glanced up and met my sister's sympathetic gaze, which grated.

"So you didn't? Does our sisterly bond mean nothing to you?"

"Of course it means something to me, but—"

"But what?" I pressed. I was feeling excluded, and I hated it.

Annabelle was silent. I waited a few seconds and then snapped, "But what, Annabelle?"

"Dad's really happy, and I didn't want you to ruin it for him," she said.

The coffee maker beeped, and she pushed off the couch and joined me in the kitchen. She took the mug from the machine, leaving me to replace the little pouch of coffee and put my own mug under the dispenser. So typical.

"Ruin it? Why would you think I would ruin it? Just because they've only known each other for two weeks and this whole thing is stupid and crazy and dumb and ridiculous and—" I ran out of words and absolutely refused to acknowledge Annabelle's point that I had ruined Dad's announcement at the bridal salon with my surlitude.

"How did it go when Dad told you he was getting married?" Annabelle asked. "Sorry I missed that, by the way, as I was busy trying on dresses to celebrate their day." She sounded salty as she slid onto the stool at the counter. It put me on the defensive.

"It was fine," I lied.

"Oh, so when Dad told you he asked Sheri to marry him and she said yes, you jumped for joy and gave him a hug?"

"Not exactly."

"Did you hold up your hand for a high five?" Annabelle narrowed her eyes over the rim of her mug as she took a sip. She drank her coffee black, because of course she did.

"No."

"Fist bump?"

"Stop it."

"Did you congratulate him in any way?" she persisted.

I said nothing. I hated it when she was right.

On the entire planet, there had never been two sisters more different than me and Annabelle. Three years older, I had been the good girl who got straight As, was involved in extracurricular activities, and existed primarily to please our parents. Annabelle, not so much.

Annabelle, now a graphic designer living in a loft on Newbury Street, was the wild child. The impulse-driven, it's-better-to-get-forgiveness-than-permission, miniskirt- and combat-boot-wearing, inappropriate-language-using artsy type who thought rules were merely guidelines.

She got her first tattoo at sixteen, illegally; got arrested for the first time at seventeen, for underage drinking; and now, at the ripe old age of twenty-seven, had recently divorced her second husband, a guy she had known a whole two months before they eloped. It wasn't exactly a huge shock that our father had gone to her first, given that Annabelle seemed to think marriage was meant to last only as long as her running shoes.

I knew the thought was mean, but I refused to feel badly about it. I was too pissed.

"Chels, hello? You in there?" Annabelle waved her hand in front of my face.

"Yes, I'm here." The coffee maker beeped again, and I retrieved my own mug. The ceramic felt hot in my hands, making me realize how chilled I was.

"So, did you congratulate Dad in any way?"

"If by 'congratulate' you mean stood there with my mouth hanging open in shock, then yeah, I nailed it," I said.

"You didn't say anything?" she gasped.

It was virtually impossible to shock Annabelle, and at any other time, I would have felt victorious. Instead, I felt a flicker of shame deep inside, which I dealt with by adding two sugars and a healthy dollop of milk to my coffee.

"I guess you missed that part, too," I said. "Here's a question. Whose brainiac idea was it to spring this on me in a bridal salon? I mean, there was no warning, no prep, no easing me into the idea that Dad's going to throw his life away by marrying a perfect stranger. I mean, really, do you people not know me at all?"

Annabelle nodded. "That's a solid argument. Truthfully, after Dad picked the ring and proposed, we all just got so excited . . ."

Her voice trailed off, so I filled in what I knew my sister didn't want to admit. "You got so excited you completely forgot about me."

"No, we . . . That is to say, okay, yeah," she admitted. "We did."

"Ouch." I dragged the word out for maximum guilt impact. Annabelle blanched, so it was a direct hit.

It didn't make me feel better, and I desperately wished I had two more mimosas in hand. Instead, I went for comfort food, desperately needing a snack to fill the gaping hole of sadness in my soul. I opened the door to my pantry and stared at the neatly stacked boxes of oatmeal, the loaf of bread, and the jar of peanut butter. There were no cookies. Damn it! This was pitiful. I slammed the door.

"I'm sorry, Chels. We should have looped you in sooner," Annabelle said. "But can I ask you something?"

"What?" I asked. I was checking my freezer to see if a pint of Ben & Jerry's Karamel Sutra had miraculously appeared. It hadn't.

"If we had told you a few days ago, would you have reacted any differently?"

I slammed the freezer and stared at my sister. "I guess we'll never know."

"Really?" Annabelle asked. She sipped her coffee. "I think we know."

Her lofty attitude caught me on the raw. "The woman bought our father at a bachelor auction for prominent Bostonians two weeks ago. He doesn't know her well enough to marry her. How can you be okay with this?"

"Because I like her," she said.

"Like her?" I asked. "You don't know her either!"

"I know her better than you do," she said. Her voice was superior. So annoying.

"Right." I rolled my eyes and took a bracing sip of coffee. It chased away any buzz that had been left behind by the mimosas, which was probably a good thing but felt like a shame.

"I still bring my laundry over to Dad's, so we visit on Sunday nights when I'm doing my wash," she said. "Sheri's been there the last two Sundays, and we've hung out. We even hit a show at the Museum of Fine Arts the other day."

"You're friends with her," I accused. *Oh, the betrayal!*

"I'm trying to be," she said. "Honestly, I like Sheri. She's quirky and fun."

"She wants us to be flower girls," I snapped. "That's not quirky—that's weird."

Annabelle frowned. "Well, I think it's fun. She's never been married before. She's excited."

"Ugh," I grunted. Truly, I was beyond words.

"So what if she wants us to wear matching dresses and scatter rose petals? Who cares, so long as she makes Dad happy."

Well, wasn't that some shit. Annabelle sounded like the altruistic one, when I'd always been certain that was my role as the older sibling. Of course it made me even crankier about the whole situation.

"Well, that figures," I said. "It's been you and Dad against me since Mom died. I don't know why I thought you'd suddenly be on my side about him marrying a perfect stranger."

"Chels, come on. That's a load of crap, and you know it. Dad and I have never been against you," she said. "You know, if you'd ever take a day off work and hang out with us, you might be more in the loop."

"Don't patronize me. What I do is very important."

Annabelle was quiet for a moment, and then she said, "So is family."

"I know that," I said, seething. "I know that better than anyone. That's why I do what I do."

"Listen, you aren't the only one who lost Mom." She pushed her mug aside and leaned forward, getting into my space. I refused to back up. "What about the family that's still here, still alive, still wanting you to be a part of it? You've been cutting us out for years, just like you have your friends. You live in this self-imposed solitude, refusing invitations to weddings, parties—life! How much longer do you think we're going to keep reaching out to you?"

"What are you saying?" I asked. Now I did back up, trying to look casual about it. "If I don't go along with Dad's wedding, you're going to disown me?"

"Would you notice if we did? Look, I love you. You're my big sister and you always will be, but you've changed, Chels. You started withdrawing after Mom died, and you never stopped. I don't even recognize you anymore. You shut everyone out."

"No, I don't," I protested. "Besides, this isn't about me."

"Yes, it is. It's one hundred percent about you. Do you realize the only relationships you've had happened before Mom passed?" she asked. "You haven't been on a real date in years."

"What's that got to do with anything?"

"How can you possibly understand how Dad feels about Sheri when you haven't been in love since . . . I don't even know when."

"This is ridiculous," I said. I needed some space. I took a restorative sip of coffee and left the kitchen to go sit on the couch. I pulled my knees up to my chest, pretending it was the cold making me hunker down.

"Look at you!" Annabelle gestured to my curled-up position. "You're doing it right now. You look like a hedgehog, and your posture positively yells, *Don't come any closer!*"

Even though I knew my sister was right, I wasn't ready to surrender. "You know what? I should have known you'd spin all this around in your usual Annabelle way."

"What's that supposed to mean?" She picked up her mug and moved to the far end of the couch.

"I'm trying to discuss Dad's marriage, and you turn it into a monologue about what's wrong with me," I said. "For your information, there is nothing wrong with me."

"Great, then you'll be at the wedding."

Panic hit me like a double punch in the face. "No! I'm not . . . I didn't mean . . ."

"Chels, I'm going to lay it out for you," Annabelle said. "Dad is in love, and he's getting remarried. You can either buck up and be a part of it, or you can continue to slowly fade from the family, as you've been doing, until we are a family in name only. Is that what you want?"

"No, but I can't . . . What about Mom?" My voice cracked, and I took a deep breath, trying to ease the tightness in my throat. I lowered my knees and put my mug down on the coffee table.

"This isn't about Mom," Annabelle said. "This is about you."

"What are you talking about? This is absolutely about Mom."

"Chels, Dad is fifty-five years old. This may be his last shot to find a woman to spend his life with. Are you really going to deny him that because you want him to cling to the memory of Mom as tightly as you do?" she asked. "Mom wouldn't want that for him, and neither should you."

"You don't know what she'd want." Fury pounded through me. I hated this conversation, and I wanted to toss Annabelle out, but my sister wasn't done yet.

"Yes, I do. Mom loved us, and she wanted us to be happy. If you want to honor her memory as much as you say you do, then you should get your shit together and figure out how to move on with your life, just like Dad and I have," Annabelle said. "When was the last time you were happy or had a big, belly-cramping laugh?"

"I laugh all the time," I insisted.

"Really?"

"I'll have you know I follow several online personalities that are hilarious," I said. "There's one that features tiny hamsters eating tiny food, and then there's a whole bunch of kitten videos—oh god."

"To answer your question, yes, it's as pathetic as it sounds."

I dropped my head into my hand.

After a moment, Annabelle said, "I know the last time you were happy."

I lifted my head and looked at my sibling in surprise. "Really? Because I don't."

"Yes, you do." Annabelle put down her mug and rose from her seat. She crossed the living room, her boot heels clacking against the hard-wood floor as she approached the bookcase that stood between the two large living room windows. She squatted down and scanned the books.

"There it is," she said. She pulled out a scrapbook covered in dust from the bottom shelf. She returned and dropped it into my lap. "The last time I saw you smile with your whole heart was in these pictures."

I glanced at the book. It sat like a cinder block on my thighs, holding me down.

"You spent the last three months of Mom's life sitting by her bed, telling her stories about your year abroad, while you pasted this to-gether. She loved your stories."

Annabelle's voice cracked. She swallowed hard, and I could see the grief in her eyes. I wanted to reach out and hug her, but I didn't.

"You promised her you'd go back," Annabelle said. She tapped the white leather cover of the scrapbook. "Aren't you still in touch with some of these people? Maybe it's time."

"I don't . . . I can't," I protested. "I need to think."

"I'm sure you do." She sighed, crossed the room, grabbed her coat off the hook, and shrugged it on. Without saying another word, she left.

Again, it was without saying *I love you*. What was happening to my family? I felt as if we were unraveling and I didn't know how to stop it. I wanted to blame Sheri—I desperately did. If the woman hadn't come into my father's life, there wouldn't be all these conversations, and things would have remained as they'd been. But I knew there was no putting that auction-paddle-wielding genie back in the bottle.

Happy. Annabelle had asked me when I'd last been happy. I knew the exact date and time. May 15, 2013, at 4:20 in the afternoon. The moment right before my father called me when I was in Italy, on my postcollege year abroad, to tell me to come home because my mother had only a few weeks to live. I got on the next plane out of Florence.

Three months later, my mother died with me, Annabelle, and Dad by her side. I had known in that moment that no one would ever love me as much as my mother did, and as the last breath left her lungs, so did the love and happiness leave my world. I didn't know where they had gone, and I didn't know how to get them back. I wished I could find them again, but it wasn't that easy.

I opened the cover of the scrapbook, and my heart squeezed tight. I'd put this book together, a collection of moments from my year abroad, when I'd worked various jobs to pay my way across Europe to celebrate graduating from college. The book had given me something to do while

I tended my mom. The very first picture was of my parents and Annabelle seeing me off at Logan International Airport in Boston.

I traced the photo with the tips of my fingers. I had my dad's eyes and his stubborn chin, but my thick light-brown hair; tall and slender, albeit a bit bottom-heavy, build; and my wide grin were all my mom's. I turned the page. London. Oh, how I had loved it. Big Ben. The Underground. Portobello Market. Next page. Ireland. Working on a sheep farm in County Kerry, I had stayed for the summer. When I closed my eyes, I could smell the sweet grass and feel the mist on my face and the warm sun on my shoulders.

I flipped through the pictures, most of which featured a redheaded boy with a wicked cowlick and a rogue's grin. He beamed at me from the photos, inviting me into his mischief. Colin Donovan. I hadn't thought of him in years, and yet I'd been utterly charmed by him and his shenanigans, like the time he'd convinced our crew to dress the entire flock of sheep in pajamas as a prank on Mr. O'Brien. I laughed at the memory.

I blinked and covered my mouth with my hand. I glanced back down at the book. I thumbed through more pages. There was Jean Claude in Paris. He had made me weak in the knees with his French accent and devastating good looks. I'd been a nanny to the Beauchamp family, and he'd worked as a designer for Monsieur Beauchamp's fashion house. I'd been totally smitten with him, falling deeper in love every day we walked along the Seine, holding hands and sharing dreams.

I flipped through several more countries, the memories coming thick and fast. I'd loved Germany, Sweden, Spain, and Portugal, too, but Italy. Ah, Firenze. That was where I'd met Marcellino DeCapio. A dark-haired young man whose passions had been wine and me and whose chocolate-brown eyes had seen right into my very soul. He was a natural sweet talker who was rumored to be able to coax the grapes on the vines into ripening with a whisper. He'd charmed me into more than that. I could still feel his strong arms about me and the silky feel of his thick dark hair when it slid through my fingers. I sighed.

Marcellino was the only one I'd kept in touch with from my year abroad. Oh, we weren't close. Our contact, which had begun with phone calls during my mom's illness and then her passing, rapidly dwindled to annual Christmas cards once I started working. In fact, I think I just sent him corporate cards from the office because . . . lame.

I slumped back against the couch and closed the book. This. This was the last time I'd been truly happy. My year abroad. It hit me then that I no longer knew the young woman who had fallen in love with Colin and Jean Claude and Marcellino. I couldn't even remember what it felt like to be topsy-turvy, dizzy from a smile, ass-over-teakettle crushing on someone.

Was I even capable of those feelings anymore? I didn't know. But there was only one way to find out. I had to see them again. The thought of leaving, just leaving, everything and everyone to return to Europe and find the three men who'd once meant so much to me was positively terrifying. It was also the first time I had felt fully alive in years. There was no doubt in my mind. I had to go back.

chapter three

THE THING IS, I quit," I said.

"Beg pardon, what?" Aidan Booth removed the earbuds from his ears and held them up for me to see. "I was doing my daily meditation."

"Oh, sorry to interrupt," I said. I glanced around the office, trying to gather the same strength of purpose I'd had a second ago when I uttered the words *I quit*. It had taken me three cups of coffee and a quick sesh of listening to Beyoncé's "Flawless" to get pumped for this. I'd been as ready as I'd ever be, and now I was . . . not.

Aidan was sixty-two with a long gray beard that touched the second button of his Henley. He wore his thick curly hair—also gray—in a ponytail, which started at the nape of his neck and reached down to the middle of his back. He was a vegan who was into the environment, so despite being the general manager in charge of corporate fundraising for the American Cancer Coalition, he shopped at thrift stores, limited his use of plastic, and had a hydroponic tower garden in the corner of his office, where varietals of lettuce grew in front of the window like big leafy flowers on a large metal cylinder that resembled a plant stalk.

"No worries," he said. He said this all the time. It was, in fact, his catchphrase. In all the years I'd worked for Aidan, he'd never seemed to worry about anything. "What was it you needed to tell me, Chelsea?"

"I quit," I said. It came out more abruptly than I'd intended, and I cringed.

Aidan blinked. He jammed a finger in his right ear and wiggled it as if to remove wax, then he nodded. It was a slow bob, as if he was acclimating to the unexpected conversational direction. "I can dig it. Mind if I ask why?"

I blew out a breath. How much did I want to say? I wasn't sure. How could I explain that my father was getting remarried, I was freaking out, and the last time I could remember laughing that didn't involve a video of a pudgy kitten getting stuck in the narrow leg of a pair of tapered pants seemed like a lifetime ago?

"I need to go find myself," I said. It sounded vaguely bohemian, so it was something I figured Aidan could understand.

I reached up and adjusted the tie that held my hair at the nape of my neck, then I fiddled with my earring. I was fidgeting, which made me look nervous and was not how I wanted to present myself. I clasped my hands in my lap to keep from doing it again. I wasn't nervous— really, I wasn't. I knew this was the right thing to do. My life had become as predictable as gravity, and it was time to shake it up.

Aidan stroked his beard. It was a mannerism that had developed with the facial hair. When I had first come to work for the corporate-fundraising arm of the ACC, he'd had short hair and been clean shaven. In the seven years I'd been there, Aidan had been undergoing a slow transformation, like erosion on a beach, except his landscape was more like a reforestation involving beard oil and braids.

I glanced at my reflection in the window behind his desk. It hit me then that I had not changed a bit in seven years. I was wearing my usual slim skirt and tailored blazer over a silk blouse that buttoned to my throat. This was my uniform at the office, paired with narrow-heeled pumps that added two inches to my height, making me five feet nine inches. Today's skirt was navy, as were the pumps, my blazer was sage green, and my blouse was ecru. I wore the same diamond stud earrings and pearl ring, which had both been my mother's, as I did every day. Even my shoulder-length blunt cut was styled exactly the same as it had been seven years ago. I always wore it tied at the nape of my neck, never loose, never styled in any other way.

I suppose it could be that I liked the simplicity of keeping my routine exactly the same. There were never any surprises in the morning. I maintained myself just like I maintained my life: a place for everything, and everything in its place. Oh man, my dad had been right; I really had stopped growing.

Despite the polished look, I was worried. How would Aidan accept my resignation? Would he understand that I had to do this? Or would he try to talk me out of it? I didn't know if I could withstand that. I brought in a lot of money from the corporate sector. It wasn't arrogance to believe my contribution made the department as successful as it was. Aidan said as much at my annual review every single year.

"Enlightenment is what you seek?" he asked. He looked as if he was trying to understand.

Aidan had also become a Buddhist in the years I had known him, leaving his Catholic roots behind as he embraced the teachings of the Dalai Lama. But that right there was why he should understand my need to go. Right? I laced my fingers together, trying not to squeeze too tight. I did not want him to offer to send me to Buddhist camp. It had happened before when he'd feared I was burning out.

"Not enlightenment as much as a general lightening up," I said. I met his kind gaze, took a deep breath, and said, "I need to remember what being happy feels like. I need to find my laughter again."

Aidan's eyes softened. His beard tipped up at the corners, which I knew meant he was smiling, although it was hard to spot through the whiskers. I got the feeling he was trying to think of what my laugh sounded like. When two deep grooves appeared between his eyebrows, I suspected he had no recall of me laughing. That made two of us. Whatever noise I made when amused, it was rusty at best.

Aidan leaned forward. He rested his elbows on the desk and steepled his fingers. He considered me with his steady, pale-blue gaze, and I felt my heart thump hard in my chest. Since I'd been promoted to senior director of major gifts two years ago, a promotion I'd gotten after only five years' experience in corporate fundraising, as opposed to the ten years that were generally required, I'd never called out sick, never taken a vacation day, and in fact, never missed a single day of work, not one.

"You are aware that you're putting in jeopardy all of the work you've done on the ask from Severin Robotics," he said.

I bowed my head. I did know. It was the reason I had slept for only two hours last night and was now operating in a fuzzy half-conscious state where I'd give anything, even my favorite, perfectly worn-in flannel cow pajamas, just to be able to put my head down for a power nap.

"I have every confidence that my team can handle it without me," I said. I met his gaze with assurance. I really did believe in my team. One hundred percent.

Aidan's gaze never wavered from mine. Here was the thing with Aidan. He was absolutely a peace, love, dope kind of guy, but he was also the general manager of a department that raked in millions, and a person didn't get to that level by being a cream puff.

"Your team is without question one of the best," he said. I felt a surge of pride. I had carefully vetted every single person and was damn proud of what we'd accomplished. "But the Severin Robotics account is the largest single corporate gift we've ever tried to negotiate. Are you really willing to leave it to your team to manage without you?"

I leaned back in my seat. I had suspected the Severin account would be a sticking point. I'd spent months developing a relationship with the company's marketing department and philanthropic foundation, and I'd even gone so far as to tap its community-relations people.

When I got a major corporation in my sights, I did my research. If I pursued one, it was because I knew that it was generous in giving back to the community but also that it was sympathetic to the cause because cancer had touched someone prominent in the company in their personal life. In this case, I had read an article in the *New York Times* about the owner, Robbie Severin, who had disclosed in the story that he'd lost his father to prostate cancer because his father had neglected to get checked. I knew that he was passionate about fighting cancer.

Severin was also an eccentric billionaire, and while I had yet to make contact with him directly, his people were responsive to me when I reached out, and so the negotiating for a major gift from Severin Robotics had begun.

"Julia is more than capable of closing the deal," I said. Julia Martinez was my right-hand woman. If anyone could do it besides me—not to sound too full of myself—it would be Julia. "In fact, I was going to recommend her for my position, in the interim for certain but also long term."

"Let's worry about that later," Aidan said. He dropped his hands and leaned back in his chair. "Is there nothing I can do to induce you to stay until Severin's major gift is a done deal?"

"No, I'm sorry, because, as you know, as soon as we confirm one major gift, there's another one on deck. If I keep waiting to finish projects, I'll never leave," I said.

"What's the exact status with Severin?"

"My team is working diligently on the proposal. Our plan is to capitalize on Severin Robotics' history of corporate social responsibility, which is strong. We're also trying to lure them in by offering them exposure to college campuses, using our community-outreach coordinators to set up student events all across the country. The job market for robotics engineers is prime, and this exposure will promote Severin Robotics as a premier employer for those students aiming to work in automation technologies.

"Severin is looking to diversify their tech from manufacturing into the medical field, so they want to increase their candidate pool. They want the best and the brightest working for them. Making their brand more recognizable on a national scale is something their community-relations people were very specific about wanting. Also, the ACC's annual gala is coming up, and we're hoping we can go ad heavy for them there as well. Once the proposal is put together, we'll—excuse me—they'll present it to Robbie Severin and his board of directors."

"Any idea when that will happen?" he asked.

"No," I admitted. "Severin is traveling in Europe presently, and there's no word as to when he'll be back, but I'm hoping for a meeting in late April."

Aidan stroked his beard. He considered me carefully. Then he reached into his desk and pulled out a box of truffles from Teuscher Chocolates of Switzerland, which had a shop over on Newbury Street. Damn it. He knew their truffles were my weakness. He pushed them across the desk toward me.

"I have an idea," he said.

I reached for a chocolate and promised myself that I would not cave. I absolutely would not give in and stay. I bit into the silky smooth confection, hoping it would fortify my resolve. After all, they had loads of chocolate in Europe. If I went, I could try them all.

"I'm listening," I said.

It was a long conversation. Point and counterpoint were made, and in the end, Aidan convinced me to take an extended leave of absence with the caveat that I would remain in contact with the head of my team as needed. If Severin popped up wanting a meeting in the next month, Aidan wanted to be able to count on my input to help see it through.

If I agreed, in return he would keep my position open for me. Should I decide after a month or two that I didn't need to continue the general lightening up I sought, then my job would be waiting for me. It was a generous offer, and I was too smart to turn it down.

While it wasn't the dramatic severing of my old life to start a new one that I had envisioned when I walked into his office, there was no question it was the better move. Despite his old-school hippie exterior, Aidan knew exactly what my contribution to the department was, and he wasn't going to let me leave easily, which I took as the compliment it was. Truthfully, I loved my career, and I had a sweet corner office that overlooked the Boston Common. Despite my quest, I didn't particularly want to give that up either, especially if I failed.

"So, now that that's settled"—Aidan's voice when he spoke was as soft as flannel—"where do you think you might want to start looking for your laughter?"

I felt myself smile when I answered. "Ireland."

chapter four

"MARTIN, WE HAD a meeting scheduled for eleven, or did you—*gasp*—forget?" Jason Knightley, or the bane of my existence, as I thought of him, stood in the open door of my office, looking pointedly at his watch.

At six foot three, he was tall, with broad shoulders and a thick head of dark-brown hair that flopped in a perfect wave over his forehead. Knowing him, he likely spent no time on his hair but simply towel dried and finger combed it into masculine perfection. So annoying. He was dressed in his usual office attire, which consisted of a dress shirt—today's was pale blue—that he wore with the cuffs rolled back, showing off his thick forearms; a geometrically patterned tie in light and dark gray; charcoal-gray trousers; and a pair of black Converse high-tops, as if being an adult ended at his feet.

I loathed him. He had come to work for the ACC three years ago, after a hot-wing-eating challenge he'd thought up for the Children's Leukemia Society went viral. He was all flash and no substance. During Knightley's first month here, Aidan had paired us up to acquire a major gift from Overexposure Media Group, a locally headquartered multimedia corporation. What should have been a slam dunk of an ask turned into one of the most humiliating experiences of my life, and I'd never forgiven Knightley— not a surprise, given that it was all his fault. Looking back, I was stunned that we'd survived the experience without bloodshed.

While I operated on innovative ideas and attention to detail, letting my corporate partners know that they could trust me implicitly to achieve what I promised, Jason relied on that indefinable something about him that made everyone seem to like him immediately—everyone except me. My colleague Julia called it charm, but I had never seen that in him. I found Knightley to be about as charming as a runny nose, which was to say not at all.

I glanced at the clock on my desk, or rather at the spot where the clock on my desk used to be, then looked back at him, meeting his smug expression with a defiant tilt of my chin. I never missed a meeting, ever. My life was ruled by my schedule, and I had never deviated from it until today. Knowing it would vex him, I shrugged, drawing out the gesture by holding my hands up as if to say *whatever.*

His eyes narrowed. He had eyes that switched from blue to gray depending upon what he was wearing. Today they were blue, which was one more reason, on top of his square jaw covered by a thin layer of neatly trimmed scruff, full lips, and perfect arching eyebrows, that I found him to be too much. The other women in the office spent an inordinate amount of time trying to decide if his eyes were blue or gray. It was galling.

"I didn't forget. We'll have to reschedule," I said. I offered no other explanation and turned my back on him and continued packing.

On my way back from Aidan's office, I had snagged an empty box from the mail room so I could pack up the few personal items I had at work, because now that I'd initiated my departure, I was ready to be gone. After a quick visual survey, I realized I could have just used a plastic bag from 7-Eleven. It was amazing to me that I'd been here for seven years, and yet there were very few sentimental items displayed on my desk and bookshelf. Kind of sad for a place that had been my second home.

"Reschedule? I didn't think the itinerary queen—that's you, by the way—even knew that word. Wait," he said. Knightley stepped into my office, a frown creasing his brow. "What are you doing?"

I picked up one of the awards for excellence that sat proudly on the bookshelf by my desk. I had four; Jason had two. I knew it bugged him that I had more, so I took great delight in huffing a breath on the Lucite wedge engraved with my name and lovingly polished it with the sleeve of my jacket. Did it need it? No. Was I being a bitch? Maybe a little.

"I'm packing," I said.

Much to my satisfaction, his eyes went wide. I hoped he thought I'd gotten a fabulous promotion. That would chap his ass. He pressed his lips together and nodded. It was the sort of look one person gave another when they were commiserating with them over bad news, like getting a speeding ticket or finding out your crush liked your best friend instead of you.

"You got sacked," he said.

"What?" I cried. I dropped the award into the box. "No, I didn't!"

"It's okay," he said. "There's no shame in being let go." His voice was infused with an artificial warmth of understanding. I wanted to punch him in the throat.

"I was not let go," I growled.

"Then what are you doing?" he asked. He gestured to the box. "Redecorating? I've got to say, it's about time. Stark white walls with no pictures on them are so 2010."

I glared at him. "This from a man who has a basketball hoop on the back of his door."

"You know you're welcome to play anytime," he said. "I'll even be a sport and spot you ten points."

"No, thank you," I said. "I'd hate to watch a grown man cry when I destroy him with three-pointers."

"You talk big, Martin," he said. His full lips parted in a grin that on any other man might have been sexy. On him, it grated.

Challenge accepted. I straightened my shoulders and ripped a sheet off the legal pad on my desk. I wadded it into a tight ball and tossed it, right past his nose, to land dead center in the wire wastebasket on the far side of my office. The look of surprise on his face was worth the hours I'd spent firing papers into that very can on the off chance I ever had to take him on. I forced myself to stay cool and not do a fist pump. It was a struggle.

"It isn't talk," I said. I turned away and continued packing, hoping he'd go away.

Jason didn't take the hint. Instead, he chuckled and strolled all the way into my office, sat in the cushy chair across from my desk, and nonchalantly propped his feet up on the corner.

"You've got some hidden talents, Martin," he said.

I knew he was trying to get a rise out of me and I should resist. Instead, I smacked his feet off the desk.

"You're mistaking my work space for the frat house you wallow in, Knightley," I said. "Feet stay on the floor."

"You're no fun," he complained.

It was exactly the sort of thing he could have said to me on any other day and I wouldn't have thought anything of it. Not today. Today I felt as if he was speaking my truth, and it hurt.

"Was there something you needed?" I snapped. "Because I really am busy."

He studied my face. Clearly, he'd been expecting a bit more of our usual back-and-forth.

"Busy doing what exactly?" he asked.

"Packing," I said. I gestured to the box and my stuff going inside the box. I really thought I should get points for not adding *duh* to my answer.

He heaved an exasperated sigh. "No kidding, but *why* are you packing?"

"Because I'm leaving," I said. "Not that it's any of your business."

"Wait . . . what?" He rose to his feet, and I found myself staring up at him. "You're serious? You're leaving? For real?"

"Yes," I said. "In two weeks I'm gone."

Jason stared at me, slack jawed. He looked stunned, as if I'd just told him I was pregnant and the baby was his.

"But . . . that's . . . How . . . Why . . ."

I took no small satisfaction in making the usually smooth-talking Jason stutter. I watched as he shook his head as if trying to realign his brain. When he finished, he crossed his arms over his chest and glared at me.

"Martin, you *can't* leave. You can't leave me."

I stared at him. He seemed genuinely upset. Had I misjudged our heated rivalry all these years? I'd thought he couldn't stand me. Had I been wrong? Maybe beneath his flagrant disregard for my organizational skills and his sarcastic asides at meetings when I was speaking, he actually liked me. Was our relationship the professional equivalent of the boy on the playground who showed a girl he liked her by pulling her pigtails or punching her in the arm?

"I mean, who is going to make me look good at the weekly staff meetings if you're not there to bore us all to death with your Power-Points, charts, graphs, and other assorted mind-numbing minutiae?" he asked. He uncrossed his arms and spread his hands wide. "I count on you, Martin, to make me shine."

So that was a negative on him actually liking me. I should have known. Jason Knightley was an arrogant asshat. If I could pick one thing I was not going to miss about working here, it would be him.

"I'll be sure to tell my replacement to load up on the statistical data," I said. "I wouldn't want your lazy little star to go dim."

"Lazy?" His eyebrows rose. "Are you calling me lazy?"

He put his hands on his hips and looked incredulous. Clearly, I'd struck a nerve. Goody.

"Truth hurts?" I asked.

"Truth?" he asked. "What truth? I work just as hard as you do."

I snorted and held up a hand as if he were telling a joke that was too funny. "Please."

"I do," he insisted. "Just because I don't bog it all down with number projections in Excel spreadsheets—"

"Bog it all down?" I gaped at him. "Those projections are what convince the corporations to pony up the major gifts, Knightley. They want to see how their money will be used, how it will impact their business and spread their mission."

"It's all smoke and mirrors," he said. He shook his head. "You make it more task driven than it needs to be. You like busywork because it makes you feel like you're accomplishing something. News flash—you're not. It's the big picture that matters."

That did it! I really was going to brain him with one of my awards.

"Busywork?" I hissed through clenched teeth. My right eyelid started to twitch. I could feel it throb in time to my heartbeat. I wanted to hold it still with my index finger, but I didn't want to betray that he was getting to me.

"Yup," he said. He pantomimed typing on a keyboard with his hands. "Busy, busy, busy. No one wants to read those long-winded reports of yours. They want big ideas; they want something to get excited about; they want to have a campaign that goes viral and makes their company a global presence."

If he kept talking, I suspected my resting bitch face was going to become permanent, like a stone mask that nothing could crack. This. This was precisely why I couldn't stand Jason Knightley. He didn't want to do the work: the grunt work, the hard labor, the number crunching, the projections, the analysis of a corporation's history—oh no, all of that was beneath him. He just wanted to be the idea guy, think the big thoughts, and let the plebs carry out his grandiose plans. It made my fingers itch to slap his smug face.

"Please don't take this the wrong way," I said. "But you're an idiot. No corporation is going to sign off on a major gift for a 'big idea.'"

"No?" Jason asked. He gave me a superior look. "Then why did the sneaker company Soles jump in and match the donations from my hot-wing challenge for the Children's Leukemia Society?"

I closed my eyes. I drew in a long breath, held it, and then carefully let it out. So typical of him to bring up his one significant claim to fundraising fame. I stared at him across my barren desk.

"You got lucky." I carefully enunciated each syllable so that he could hear each drip of disdain in my words.

He tipped his chin up and studied me under half-lowered lids. "Luck had nothing to do with it. What's the matter, Martin? Jealous?"

It was so ridiculous, so outrageous an accusation that I barked out a laugh that sounded more maniacal than I would have liked. "Jealous?" I cried. I stepped out from behind my desk to face him. "You had a hot-wing challenge go viral for a little while. Seriously, BFD."

He grinned at me without humor. "It drives you crazy, doesn't it?"

"Are you referring to your unsubstantiated arrogance?" I asked.

"Unsubstantiated?" He squinted his eyes and cupped his chin with one hand, in a thoughtful pose. "Let me think—what was the grand total of money raised to fight leukemia with the hot-wing challenge? Was it ten million? Nope. Twenty-five million? No, that wasn't it either. Oh yeah, I remember now. Fifty-seven million and change off a genius idea."

"Genius?" I spat. "People challenging each other to eat a Carolina Reaper hot wing or fork up a hundred-dollar donation." I pretended to yawn, patting my open mouth with my hand. "So predictable. If a few celebrities hadn't gotten involved, it would have died a sudden death."

"A few celebrities?" he choked. "I had everyone from Kendrick Lamar to Rachel Maddow participating."

I rolled my eyes. "It was lightning in a bottle."

"Bullshit. It was a well-thought-out campaign that people loved to participate in," he said.

"Well thought out?" I leaned back on my heels and crossed my arms over my chest, trying to look down on him, which was not easy, because he was several inches taller than I was. "Who are you kidding? You cooked it up while killing time at some bar for happy hour where the wings and beer were half price."

He didn't even look embarrassed. He shrugged and winked at me and said, "Inspiration strikes where it strikes, plus it made millions. How much have you ever managed to wrestle as a major gift? One million? Five million?"

"I'm sorry, are we comparing dick size here?" I asked. "Because I can assure you while my anatomy is different, if it's a pissing contest you want, I'll win."

"Admit it, Martin." He leaned down so our faces were just inches apart. "You don't have my reach."

"Ugh." I curled my lip. That was it. I was leaving my job. Why was I even speaking to this Neanderthal? I turned on my heel and crossed to the open door of my office. I raised my hands and gestured for him to leave. "I think we're done here."

"Is that how you deal with losing a debate?" he asked. He turned to face me. "You just throw the person out?"

"First, this wasn't a debate. It was a waste of fifteen minutes of my life that I'll never get back," I said.

I reached forward and grabbed his arm, pulling him toward the door. Normally, I would never touch another employee, as I was hyper-aware of the rules put forth by our human resources person, Michelle Fernando, who was downright scary, about encroaching on my colleagues' personal space, but at the moment, I had no fucks left to give. If Jason Knightley didn't leave my office right now, I was going to put my foot in his backside and kick him out the door.

"Second, I'm not throwing you out but merely assisting your overly swollen head through the doorway so that it doesn't get stuck," I said.

"Aw, sweet." Jason chuckled as I propelled him forward. In an innuendo-laden voice, he wagged his eyebrows and asked, "So, you like my big frontal lobe?"

"Get. Out." I gave him a firm but what I hoped would be construed as friendly—it wasn't—shove through the opening. I stepped back and grabbed the door, slamming it in his face. Then I huffed out an exasperated breath, trying to find my Zen.

"I take it that's a no on the sexy frontal lobe?" he called through the door.

In spite of myself, my lips twitched.

chapter five

I T TOOK ME every second of the following week to clear my desk and pack, but I did it. On the day of my departure, my plan had been to catch an Uber to the airport and leave with as little fuss as possible, but Annabelle insisted that she would take me. Which proved to be a big, fat lie when my father pulled up in front of my apartment in his dadmobile, an ancient green Subaru station wagon that Annabelle and I had been begging him to sell for at least a decade. Despite the peeling paint, rumbling muffler, and general air of exhaustion about the vehicle, he refused.

He bounced out of the driver's seat and circled the hood, coming to meet me on the steps, where I stood, looking for Annabelle's sleek BMW, which was supposed to be my airport ride.

"Dad, what are you doing here?" I asked.

"We wanted to give you our full support," he said.

"We?" I glanced at the car just as Annabelle popped out of the back seat and Sheri got out of the front. What was *she* doing here?

"Oh," I said. I was instantly uncomfortable. This should have been me saying goodbye to my family, and despite this crazy impending marriage to my father, Sheri was not family. She never would be. Not wanting to have any drama when I really needed to get to the airport, I forced my lips up at the corners and said, "Great."

Dad stuffed my suitcase into the back of the station wagon, and we all piled back into the car, with me and Annabelle in back and Dad and Sheri up front. It was so much like the last time my family had seen me off at the airport that I felt as if I were in a dream in which I knew the people but they looked nothing like who they were supposed to be, as if the role of my mother in this dream were being played by Sheri Armstrong. Weird.

"Are you excited for your trip, Chelsea?" Sheri asked. Her tone was polite but cautious. I suspected my father had told her about my freakout at the bridal salon. I wasn't sure how I felt about that. Guilty? Embarrassed? Defensive? All of the above?

"Yes," I said, my voice as guarded as hers. "Very excited."

"Great," she said. She smiled at me, but it didn't reach her eyes. Clearly, she found this forced conversation to be as painful as I did, and that actually made me warm to her about a degree and a half.

"You have to text me every day and tell me what's happening," Annabelle said. "And I want pictures of all the sights." She wagged her eyebrows at me, and I knew that meant she wanted to see what my old boyfriends looked like. "Especially Italy."

"Definitely," Dad agreed from the front seat. "Lots of pictures. We want to see everything."

Annabelle snorted, and I elbowed her in the side, which only made her laugh harder.

The traffic was light at this time of night. We made it to the Callahan Tunnel, which ran under Boston Harbor, in record time. As we moved through it, Dad went over his usual list of travel advice, beginning with "don't lose your passport" and ending with "look out for pickpockets."

Sheri smiled at him as if he was just the cutest thing, while I tuned him out and wished the car could go faster. This right here was why I was leaving. Because my father had managed to move forward in his life, while I was stuck, stuck, stuck.

Dad and I had made up, sort of, after our disagreement at the bridal salon. I had stopped by his house on a night when I knew Sheri wasn't there, because of her evening Pilates class, and I'd apologized for my rudeness. Then I'd told him about my plan to revisit my year abroad.

Surprisingly, Dad had taken the news of my sudden trip with great equanimity. As a math professor, he favored logic and reason and wasn't one to promote leaving a high-paying job with almost no notice to take off for parts unknown. But when I explained to him that I wanted to remember what it felt like to be in love again, he'd nodded his approval with a sheen of emotion in his eyes that he never verbalized, and that was it. No questions, no arguments, he'd just slipped me a wad of cash and told me he loved me.

Terminal E loomed ahead, and Dad wedged his car right up against the curb. Small surprise, as other cars and drivers were giving the dad-mobile a wide berth as if its dents and corrosion were contagious. We all piled out of the car while Dad grabbed my suitcase.

"Do you have everything?" he asked.

I looked at my rolling carry-on and my big purse and said, "Yes. Checked and rechecked. I'm good."

"All right, then, we won't keep you." He studied my face for a moment as if committing it to memory. Then he jerked his head in Sheri's direction, and his meaning was clear. I was to offer a proper goodbye to his intended.

She was standing on the curb beside my suitcase, looking as if she wasn't quite certain of her place in this moment. That made two of us. Did I hug her? Half hug her? Shake her hand? Ugh, this was misery.

I stepped closer, wanting to get it over with. Sheri glanced up at me with a nervous smile. She was a petite brunette with large brown eyes and a pointy chin that gave her a gamine appeal. I opened my arms, signaling, I hoped, that I was coming in for a hug.

She perked up at that, and we closed in on each other. Unfortunately, I zigged when I should have zagged, and when I hunkered down, we almost bonked heads. We reared back at the same time and ended up awkwardly patting each other's shoulders. It was a colossal failure, and we both looked pained, but judging by my dad's grin, he was so pleased by our efforts that it didn't matter that we looked like we were breaking out of a football huddle.

Dad scooped me close and bear-hugged me, giving me a smacking kiss on my cheek. "I love you, peanut."

"I love you, too, Dad," I said. My throat got tight, and I felt the sting of tears in my eyes. I refused to cry. I didn't want to upset anyone.

Instead, I turned to hug Annabelle, who was zipping the front pocket of my suitcase closed. I narrowed my eyes. "What did you do?"

"Nothing," she cried. She leaped away from my bag as if it had zapped her.

"I know you," I said. "I know that face. You're up to something." I strode forward and unzipped the front pocket, grabbing a brown paper sack that I had *not* packed out of the bag. With a glare at Annabelle, I opened it.

"No, don't—" she cried.

Too late. A brightly colored box of condoms fell out of the bag and landed on the ground at my feet. We all stood there, looking at the box that declared itself a pleasure pack, in absolute horror. Well, all of us except Annabelle, who laughed, bent down to retrieve the box, and shoved it into the paper sack, which she stuffed back into my suitcase.

"Yes, well." Dad coughed. "Nice to know you're prepared."

"For anything," Sheri agreed.

They didn't look at each other when they spoke, as if they were afraid they would laugh if they did. Mortified, I couldn't make eye contact with either of them.

Annabelle caught me in a hug that knocked the breath out of me.

"Don't come home until they're all gone," she said.

My eyes went round. If my quick glance was correct, the box held thirty-six condoms. Given the current dormant state of my love life, if I followed Annabelle's directive, I might never come home. I didn't admit this, however.

Instead, I grabbed the handle on my suitcase and headed toward the sliding glass doors. I paused to wave before I disappeared inside, yelling, "Bye! I love you!"

"I love you, too," Annabelle cried, jumping up and down, her long dark hair bouncing around her shoulders.

"Love you, peanut," Dad said. He slipped his arm around Sheri as if it was the most natural thing in the world. My entire system rejected the picture they made as they waved goodbye, looking for all the world like a pair of doting parents.

I forced a smile, pretending that everything was great, when deep inside it felt as if everything was so very wrong and nothing could fix it—not even a giant box of condoms.

FROM THE DUBLIN airport, I had to catch an Airlink bus to Heuston train station. It took an hour to wind our way through the city, allowing me a power nap as I tried to combat the jet lag, which was making me droop. Then it was a three-hour train ride, which ended in the famously colorful town of Killarney late in the morning.

At the Killarney station, I checked my phone to see whether my dad had gotten my text telling him I'd arrived in Ireland. He had, and his response was full of happy emojis blowing kisses, which was so not my buttoned-down dad. Glen Martin in love was taking some getting used to. There was also a text from a number I didn't recognize. It was a Boston area code, so I opened it. I felt my mood plummet as soon as I read the message.

Martin, call me.

There was only one person on the entire blue marble that we all inhabit who called me by my last name, and that was Knightley. How he'd gotten my number and why he'd be texting me, I couldn't fathom, but I had zero interest in finding out. *Call me.* So bossy! Who did he think I was, his personal assistant? If there was something happening at the ACC, Julia would reach out.

I shoved my phone into my bag, leaving the message status as read, which I knew he'd see. Let him chew on that. I then trudged from the station to the hotel where the car-rental place was located, keeping one eye on the sky, as it looked as if it was about to rain at any moment.

I'd been afraid that after so many years away, driving on the left side of the road would be weird and possibly dangerous, but because I was sitting on the right side of the car, something clicked in my brain that made the adjustment easier than I would have thought.

Although I ground the gears once—okay, twice—using the stick shift in the Opel Corsa on my way out of the rental place and swiped the curb with my back tire, I still felt confident enough to take on the narrow roads and rolling hills ahead of me. I purposefully didn't look back to see if the car-rental guy had clutched his chest and keeled over when I left. Best not to know.

The start of my route took me through Killarney National Park. The sun popped out of the clouds, which I took as a good sign. I switched the radio dial to Radio Kerry, which was broadcast out of Tralee and served the surrounding counties. There was some lively fiddle music happening, and I tapped my fingers on the steering wheel as I cruised over the narrow stretch of road.

I gingerly passed a tour bus that was pulled over to the side, and then a second, then I had to brake hard for a goat, who seemed in no hurry to move out of the road at all. In fact, when I honked, she definitely moved even slower. Lovely, a goat with oppositional defiant disorder. I hoped it wasn't an omen for my trip. Finally, I was off the tourist route and onto a narrower and rougher patch of road that cut through the middle of the Ring of Kerry, the tourist loop that took visitors all around County Kerry, and well on my way to the village of Finn's Hollow.

The rugged path wound up through the craggy hills. Sweeps of velvet green were studded with gray granite rocks jutting up through the earth like fists punching up to reach the sky. Despite the cold, I rolled down my window a few inches to bring in the fresh air while the car's heater kicked out a steady stream of warmth, keeping my feet toasty. The sweet cool air from outside was thick and lush and scented with the smell of fresh grass and damp earth. I felt something inside of me shift as my memories of this place filled me up with a sense of joy. I hadn't realized how much I'd missed Ireland until this very moment. It felt like coming home.

It was early afternoon before I reached the turnoff onto an even smaller and narrower road that would take me to my ultimate destination—a bed. The midday coffee was wearing off, and I was feeling a little shaky as I turned down the steep hill, took a long curve, climbed up another hill, and came to a stop at a four-way intersection where there was not a single soul in sight. I paused to take in the vista of the village below.

A cluster of stone buildings were nestled in the valley as if they'd been planted there. It was exactly as I remembered it, and I was surprised at how little Finn's Hollow had changed in seven years. But then I realized my impression was from a distance. The town, like me, might appear the same on the outside, but significant changes had likely happened within, possibly not noticeable until I was in the heart of it. I stepped on the gas.

Finn's Hollow was small, even for a village, with one church, a post office, a modest grocery, three bed-and-breakfasts, and a pub called the Top of the Hill, which seemed to be a bit of a misnomer, since it actually sat at the very bottom of the hill at the end of the road.

Michael Stewart, who'd owned the pub when I'd last been here, liked to tell the tale of how the pub had started at the top of the hill but one year a horrible rainy season had come upon Finn's Hollow. It rained and rained and rained some more. It rained so much that the townspeople had to use boats to get around instead of cars, the sheep began to grow gills and fins, and then one night, during the heaviest rain of them all, the pub slipped down from its foundation at the top of the hill and landed at the bottom. The townspeople were happy because they hadn't been able to get up the hill for their usual nip, and the bar owner was as well, and he announced to one and all that he wasn't going to change the name, because anyone who went looking for the pub on the top of the hill would surely be able to find it at the bottom.

I smiled when I thought of the many hours I'd spent at the pub with Colin and the other summer workers. We'd been a motley crew, with Colin, being local, taking the role of our leader. He'd kept us out of trouble for the most part, but he'd also gotten us into some ridiculous scrapes as well. In addition to his natural ability to lead, Colin Donovan had been quite a mischief maker.

I'd spent as much time online as I could trying to find Colin, but I hadn't found a presence for him on any social media. I hoped that someone at the farm still remembered him and knew how I could locate him.

I felt a flutter of nerves in my belly. It had been seven years since I'd seen Colin. Would he remember me? Would he mind that I was popping up in his life after so much radio silence? I felt as if I were living out an Adele song and the potential for pain and humiliation was spectacularly high.

Colin Finley Donovan. I tried to picture what he'd look like now. Would he still have his thick thatch of red hair with the crazy cowlick and the smattering of freckles across his nose? Were his eyes still the pretty blue of the common field speedwell that bloomed all over the farm between craggy rocks and along the roadsides? When we'd last been together, he'd begged me not to go on to my next post but to stay with him in Ireland. He'd tried to convince me that Finn's Hollow was where I belonged—with him. It had been tempting, so tempting.

But I had made commitments for different jobs all over Europe that I felt honor bound to keep. Plus, I'd wanted to see as much as I could during my year abroad, and staying in the first place I landed wasn't a part of the plan. When I kissed Colin goodbye, I promised to stay in touch, but, of course, I hadn't. I wondered how he'd felt about that, if he'd felt anything at all.

I hadn't kept up with Jean Claude either, which made me question whether my plan to visit Paris was wise. Eh, who was I kidding? Paris was always a good idea!

My itinerary was vague at best. I didn't know if I'd be retracing my footsteps from my year abroad for a week, a month, or a year. That's why I'd taken a leave of absence. I simply had no idea what was going to happen, which was both exhilarating and terrifying and reminded me so much of how I'd felt during my year abroad.

Life was an adventure! For now, I'd deal with Ireland and worry about Paris when I got there. No matter what happened here or there, I had heard from Marcellino in Italy, via email, and he was looking forward to seeing me when I arrived. The thought made me smile.

Right now, my mission was to find Colin. For the first time since I'd conceived this trip, I wondered what exactly I was going to say to him if and when I found him. I decided to practice just like I did for my important meetings.

"Hi, Colin, do you remember me?" I said it out loud, trying it on. No, it was too desperate. It didn't fit, like a pair of jeans that were too tight in the crotch. I tried again.

"Hey, aren't you Colin Donovan?" I shook my head. Nope. I was a lousy fibber and would never be able to pretend I just happened to be in Finn's Hollow, the backside of nowhere, without a purpose, like stalking my ex-boyfriend.

I lowered my voice as I shifted into a higher gear, picking up speed down the hill toward town. In my sultriest tone, I said, "Well, hello, Colin."

Yeah, no, that was awful. I sounded like I had a horrible head cold and was likely contagious. I sighed. What was I going to say? How was I supposed to approach a man I hadn't seen in seven years?

The panic began to thrum in my chest. What if he didn't remember me? What if he rejected me? That would be levels of embarrassing I wasn't sure I could handle. I shook it off, thinking of the sparkly pink flower girl dress waiting for me back in Boston. Right, so it could always be worse.

I turned my car onto the main road through town. There were a few people out and about, and I caught myself looking for a thick head of red hair with an unruly cowlick. Of course none of the men were him. That would make things entirely too easy. Although, if I actually did spot him, I didn't suppose it would be good form to stop my car and run him to the ground right then and there, so perhaps it was for the best.

Since I hadn't been able to find any information about Colin online, I knew he might have moved on to greener pastures, as it were, but I found that hard to believe. Colin had loved the outdoor life Finn's Hollow offered. Hiking the Kerry Way and angling in Lough Caragh and the Caragh River had been his favorite ways to spend his days off. I couldn't picture him anywhere outside the Iveragh Peninsula, but then again, I was here, and I'd never expected to be back, so there was that.

The Finn's Hollow Cottages were conveniently located on a side street just past the Top of the Hill. I passed the pub, took a sharp turn, and arrived at a large, cheery yellow house with white trim with several smaller versions of the same off to the side, forming a short row. If I remembered my reservation right, my cottage was number five, the last one in the line.

I parked in the small lot, beside several other vehicles, and switched off the car. I grabbed my shoulder bag and stepped outside, taking a deep breath while admiring the view of the countryside. Despite the gray sky overhead, the landscape was beautiful, rolling hills divided by thick hedgerows with big brown mountains looming in the distance.

Mrs. Darby O'Shea, the woman who owned the cottages, had seemed very friendly in her email. It wasn't peak tourist season, so she had a cabin available. She'd told me to come knock on her door no matter the time to collect the key to my cottage. I pictured Mrs. O'Shea in my mind's eye as a sort of grandmotherly type who enjoyed baking and knitting and had one too many cats, basically the sort of person I was destined to become if I didn't get back out there and find myself. Not that there was anything wrong with the quiet cat-lady life. I just wasn't ready to embrace it fully quite yet.

My phone chimed again, and I pulled it out of my purse. I glanced at the display. It was a text. Again, from Knightley.

Martin, I know you're getting my messages. Call me.

Hmm. I considered my options as I stared at my phone. It chimed again.

Please.

Ooh, manners! Well, that was a game changer. I started to text back when the first fat plop of a raindrop splashed the side of my face, and I glanced up, assessing the likelihood of more rain. This was a bad move, as the droplet had been a warning shot, and in the next instant the sky opened up as if someone had ripped through the bottom of a cloud with a knife blade. The deluge hit so fast, it soaked me through before I even had a chance to grab my umbrella from the back seat. With a yelp, I shoved my phone in my bag and ran for the main house at top speed.

I yanked open the door and stepped into the glassed-in porch, which also appeared to serve as an office, as there was a small wooden desk at the far end. Unfortunately, no one was there. Brown wicker furniture with plump blue-and-white-striped cushions filled the other side of the porch, but those were vacant, too. Hmm.

A bass beat sounded over the steady pounding of the rain on the roof. I stood on the doormat, dripping a big puddle onto the floor, while I tried to identify the noise. It was definitely music—I could hear a guitar and singing coming from inside the house. Should I knock? Was

Mrs. O'Shea having a party? I glanced at the door, the empty desk, and then my car.

Well, standing here was doing a whole lot of nothing. I shook off as much of the rain as I could and strode to the front door of the house. I knocked. No one answered. Undoubtedly, they couldn't hear me over the music. I sighed. I was wet and tired and becoming rapidly cranky. I tried the doorknob. It turned, so I opened the door and went inside.

The music was infinitely louder in the foyer. I recognized the song "Bellyache" by Billie Eilish. Maybe Mrs. O'Shea had some teenage grandchildren who were visiting. I listened, trying to determine if the music was coming from upstairs. It wasn't. I walked down a short hall, poked my head into the front room, and came face to rump with, not kidding, a glittery pink bottom.

"Ah!" I cried and fell backward with my hand over my heart.

The front room was bare of furniture except for three stripper poles placed in a line in the center of the room. All three of the poles had women draped on them in various poses, and all three of the women were spinning to the music.

"Well, hello, dear," the owner of the pink tush yelled over the music as she twirled with her head down and her posterior high, the pole clasped by one hand and one leg. "You must be Chelsea Martin."

I nodded. I stood frozen, unblinking, as the woman uncoiled herself from the pole and landed in a split on the ground. Her long gray hair and gently lined face put her in her sixties at least. I wondered if she'd hurt herself. Should I give her a hand? I glanced at the other two women, still on their poles, who did not seem concerned in the least.

The woman in front of me popped up to her feet, reached over to a small Bluetooth speaker, and turned down the music. She had on a black sports bra with the bedazzled pink boy shorts, and that was it. I glanced at her arms, legs, and abs—they were all muscle. Wow.

"I'm Darby," the woman said. She used a hair band from around her wrist to tie her hair into a high ponytail. "Welcome to the cottages."

My mouth opened and then closed. So much for a knitting cat lover. I tried to shake off my shock and said, "Thanks."

Darby's brown eyes sparkled as she took in my expression. "Fancy a go?" she asked and jerked her thumb at a pole.

"Uh, no." I shook my head. "But thank you."

"You change your mind, you let me know. I teach pole dancing. I can show you how." She turned to the other two women and said, "Keep practicing."

The women continued twirling. They were considerably younger than Darby, and I noted that one of them had an orangey glow to her skin, the sort that looked like it came from a can of spray-on tan.

"Follow me," Darby said. She grabbed a blue towel and draped it around her neck. I fell in behind her, completely entranced by the way her muscles bunched and released beneath her skin as she walked to the porch.

"Sorry to interrupt your class," I said. "I knocked but no one answered."

Darby waved her hand at me. "It's no trouble. I teach classes all day long, so most people know where to find me."

So many questions. I felt as if I were going to bust if I didn't say something. "So, pole dancing, huh?"

Darby moved behind the small desk and smiled at me. Her entire face lit up, and she said, "Isn't it wonderful?"

"Amazing, for sure," I said. "How did you happen to take it up?"

"Oh, that's a story," Darby said. "The short version is that I found my lying, cheating, no-good husband in bed with another woman, so I kicked him out."

I nodded.

"He had the bloody nerve to tell me it was my fault that he'd cheated, because I'd gone soft." Darby patted her ripped abs. "This after I'd borne him two sons."

"Bastard," I said. Maybe I was overtired, but I was really in sync with Darby's rage toward her ex.

"Then my boys tried to tell me that I should sell the cottages. My father built these cottages. They said it was too much work for an old lady, and I was feeling old and achy in my heart and in my bones. I was this close to selling and moving in with my sister." She held up her thumb and her index finger. "But then a young lass from the States came to stay for the summer, and she was a pole dancer. She took me to a studio in Killarney to try it, yeah, and I loved it.

"I started taking classes, and I was getting stronger and stronger, and I was feeling so sexy. Then my ex, he came sniffing around, wanting me back, and you know what I told him?"

I shook my head. I was grinning. How could I not?

Darby leaned close and said, "I told him to fuck off." She threw back her head and laughed, and I laughed with her. "It was like unloading twelve stone of negativity just like that." She snapped her fingers.

I glanced at the woman before me. Darby looked like she could open a can of whoop ass anytime she felt the need, which was all kinds of awesome. "Well, you look incredible."

"Thank you, pet." Darby handed me a key with the number five on it and said, "Anytime you want to try the pole, you let me know. First lesson's free."

My first thought was to give it a hard pass, but my second one was a solid maybe. The Chelsea who had been here seven years ago would have jumped at the chance to try something new, and I was trying to be more like her. I nodded. "I may just take you up on that, Darby."

"Breakfast is served in the dining room from six in the morning until nine. I do the fry-up myself, and it's a full Irish breakfast, with bacon and sausages, black and white puddings, and potatoes all cooked in butter, with soda bread on the side." She gave me an assessing stare. "You don't have any dietary issues, do you?"

"No, ma'am," I said. "That sounds terrific." It sure beat the plain yogurt and mango slices I'd had this morning.

"For the rest of your meals, you're on your own, but the pub does a nice stew served in a Yorkshire pudding bowl, and I suppose their bangers and mash aren't terrible either," Darby said. Her praise was faint and grudging at best. I wondered if there was a rivalry of sorts there.

"I'll be sure to try it," I said. I didn't mention that I'd been to Finn's Hollow before and enjoyed the bangers and mash at the Top of the Hill. No need to go there. The reasons for coming back were too personal to share, so I opted to say nothing.

"Do you need help getting settled?" Darby asked. "There's a peat block in your fireplace that's all ready. You just need to strike the match."

"No, I think I've got it," I said. "Thank you."

"I'm here if you need me," Darby said. With that, she left me on the porch and went back to her class.

I took a moment to gather my scattered wits before I headed back out into the rain. I debated leaving my bag in the car, but the lure of clean clothes was too much to resist. The wind pulled the front door out of my hand, and it took an effort to shut it. The gusts were fierce, and the rain was going sideways as I lifted my suitcase out of the trunk. Thankfully, my clothes were already as soaked as they could possibly get, so there was that.

I dashed down the gravel walkway along the row of cottages. The tiny yellow houses had front porches just big enough for two chairs and a window box of flowers. The boxes were barren at the moment, but the chairs remained. I hurried up the two steps to the front door. I turned the knob, which thankfully wasn't locked. With the rain pelting my back, I opened the door and stepped into what Annabelle would have described as the cutest little room.

The interior was done in green and cream. A table and two chairs were placed in front of the window that overlooked the tiny porch, the fireplace was set in the far wall, and a peat log was waiting, just as

Darby had said. It was chilly, so I quickly lit the fire with the matches I found on the mantel, thrilled when the peat caught and filled the air with its earthy aroma.

As the fire warmed the room, I checked out the rest of the cottage. A door led into a modern bathroom with a tub-shower combination that made me want to weep—I was so desperate for a shower. There was a dresser with a small television on top of it and a very efficient kitchenette with a mini-refrigerator, a stove top, a sink, and a few cupboards. It was charming.

I hung up my coat and quickly stripped down to my skin, taking a long hot shower to slough off the grit of every mile I'd traveled. It felt heavenly. The heat from the shower and the fire was so lovely and relaxing that my jet lag reared up and walloped me. I let out a jaw-cracking yawn as I pulled on my favorite pajamas—a set Annabelle had given to me as a gag gift for my birthday—which made me look like a dairy cow, as they were white with big black spots all over them, with a pouch in the front that looked like udders. The joke was on Annabelle since I loved these soft, warm flannel jammies. Deciding a power nap wasn't out of order, I climbed into the crisp white sheets, pulled up the heavy blanket and quilt, and fell into a deep slumber of the sort enjoyed only by drunks and babies.

WHEN I AWOKE, it took me a moment to remember where I was and what I was doing. Ireland. Colin. I was stalking—er, tracking down—my old boyfriend. *That's right.* I snuggled under my blanket, thinking about our first meeting.

I could see Colin striding down the hillside of the O'Brien farm, looking as rugged and ruddy as the terrain around him. The sun would shine on his auburn hair, highlighting strands of gold and copper. He'd see me waiting, the breeze tousling my loose hair and the hem of my long skirt.

Wait, had I packed a skirt? I knew I had my little black dress, but that wasn't the same. No, I was sure I didn't have a skirt. Shoot. Scratch that—I pictured myself in jeans and a sweater. He'd see me and stumble to a halt. We'd stare at each other for a heartbeat, no more, before we recognized each other as our one true love, and then we'd race into each other's arms, and he'd hold me close and kiss me—

My phone went off, interrupting my daydream just when I was getting to the good part. Damn it. I picked it up and noticed there were several text messages, all from Aidan, sent while I was showering, in addition to another from Jason. I got a weird feeling in my belly. This could not be good.

chapter six

SLID MY thumb across the screen and answered him.

"What's on fire, Aidan?" I asked. "You never text me, and you've texted me six times and now you're calling. Is something wrong?"

"Hey, world traveler," Aidan said. He sounded chipper, but was it a little forced? I couldn't tell. "How goes the trip?"

I thought about Darby and her pole. "Um . . . interesting, very interesting. But you haven't answered my question. What's going on?" I sat on the edge of my bed and pushed my hair out of my eyes.

"Nothing," Aidan said. "I just wanted to touch base with you before you talked to anyone else."

I went still. My heart started to pound. Had something happened to someone at work? Was that why Jason had been texting me? Had something happened to someone on my team? "Is everyone okay?"

"Everyone is fine," Aidan said. "It's just—"

"Just?" I prompted. I felt a knot twist in my stomach. I knew I shouldn't care this much. I was technically on leave, but still. I tried to keep my voice normal when I asked, "Is everything all right with the Severin Robotics account?"

"I'm glad you asked," Aidan said. "Hey, let's switch over to video mode. I much prefer to see people when I talk to them."

I glanced down in dismay. I had no makeup on, my hair looked like a home for wayward critters, and I was still in my cow pajamas. I quickly pinched my cheeks, finger combed my hair, and grabbed the blue chenille throw off the end of the bed and threw it around my shoulders like a shawl. I made sure I was backlit and the lighting was dim before I hit the button to accept Aidan's video call.

"There she is!" Aidan's big bearded face grinned at me.

Despite my annoyance at having to be on video, I grinned back at him. Although our personalities were very different, Aidan really was one of my favorite people. I could tell he was sitting in his office, with the lettuce tower behind him and the Boston skyline just visible through the window beyond that. I felt a pang of homesickness that I immediately squashed.

"Hi, Aidan," I said. "So, what's happening?"

"Nothing, really. Can't a boss just check on one of his favorite people?" he asked.

His gaze skidded away from the screen. Uh-oh. I sat up straighter. "Aidan, what did you want to tell me before I talked to anyone else?"

"I've made a decision about the Severin Robotics account," he said. "I know we talked about having Julia step in, but in light of the magnitude of the major gift, I think we need someone a little more seasoned."

"I disagree," I said. "Julia is more than ready for this. She's been with me every step of the way in the planning and execution. Who else could—"

I froze. A feeling of dread began to swirl in my belly. I held my phone up to my face, trying to get a good look at Aidan's expression. Sure enough, there was guilt in those eyes. I could only imagine what he was making of my crazy face staring back at him. He had to see how upset I was.

"You didn't," I said.

"Didn't what?" he asked.

"You didn't give the Severin Robotics campaign to Knightley."

Aidan didn't answer, which was all the answer I needed. I jumped to my feet. The throw fell off my shoulders as I began to pace. I dropped the arm holding my phone, which meant Aidan was getting a fantastic look at the lovely hardwood floor of my cottage. I didn't care. I needed a minute to regroup.

Months and weeks of work flew through my mind. The meetings, the proposals, the bending over backward to get through Severin's people to get directly to him, which I still hadn't managed, all to convince him to consider offering a major gift of $10 million to the American Cancer Coalition. I had killed myself for this ask.

I held my phone up and glared at Aidan, who seemed to be meditating while I processed the bomb he'd just dropped on me.

"How could you?" I asked. Aidan opened his mouth to speak, but I didn't give him a chance. "He isn't qualified," I said. "He doesn't have the skill set. You could have put anyone in this role, but you chose him. Is this some white-male-privilege thing?"

"Chelsea, you know me better than that," Aidan said. His tone was reproving, and I knew it was deserved. Aidan had an incredibly diverse staff, and he promoted on merit, which was why putting Jason in charge of the Severin account made no sense to me. He simply didn't have the chops, in my not-so-humble opinion.

"You're right," I said. "I apologize. I just don't understand why him."

"Quite frankly, because Jason is the only other person I have on the same pay grade as you. Besides, he has a knack for making people work together who normally can't," Aidan said. "This is a huge ask we're going for, and it's going to take a wide variety of talent to accomplish it all, and Jason can manage people in a way that Julia can't. She's too tentative. I need a leader, and you and Jason are the best I've got, and you're gone."

"I disagree. This ask needs someone who is extremely detail and task oriented," I argued. "That's not Jason. He's more of an idea guy."

"Chels—" Aidan tried to interrupt me.

"No, I'm serious," I said. "He's a total Tom Sawyer. I have it on good authority that he gets Liz from Accounting to spreadsheet the numbers for him, because math is hard. And Nicole in Marketing adds the graphics so it's pretty, and his assistant slash henchman, Blake, writes it up and puts the whole thing together for him. All Knightley does is put his name on it and present it with panache."

"Chels—" Aidan tried again.

"Aidan, I can assure you that sort of overgrown-frat-boy-slacker approach is not going to work with Severin," I said. "The man is a certified genius, and while Knightley can use his good looks and charm on most people and get results, Severin is going to see right through the handsome façade and—"

"Chelsea!" Aidan interrupted. "Enough."

He looked pained, and I felt my stomach drop. *Uh-oh.*

"He's there with you, isn't he?" I asked.

Aidan reached forward and spun his computer monitor so that it faced the visitor side of his desk. Jason grinned at me and gave me a little finger wave.

"Tom Sawyer, huh?" he asked. He tipped his head to the side and drawled, "And here I always thought I was more of a Huckleberry."

"Turn me back to Aidan, please," I said. I refused to apologize, even though my face was hot and I was completely mortified. At least he'd mentioned only the insults and not the—

"What's that? Were you calling me handsome again? Or was it charming?" Jason cupped his ear. "I couldn't make it out through those gritted teeth." He took a moment to study me. "Dayum, Martin, you look rough." He squinted. "Are those . . ." He pressed his lips together. It didn't work. Like a dam bursting, a laugh boomed out of him. "Seriously? Cow pajamas? I mean, you've always had the sex appeal of yesterday's leftovers, but this is a sad state of affairs even for you."

"Feel better?" I asked. "Does insulting me help you deal with my accurate assessment of your capabilities?"

"Accurate?" His eyes went wide and then narrowed. "Just because I know how to delegate and you don't doesn't mean I don't work just as hard as you do. I'm just better with my time management."

"When Friday happy hour is your most important meeting of the week, I guess you have to be."

"Don't judge me just because I have a life and you don't," he said. "You should try it sometime. It might get the stick out of your—"

"Jason! Chelsea!" Aidan interrupted. "That's enough."

The monitor spun, and I was looking at Aidan again. For a guy who maintained a positive Zen at all times, he looked a bit wild eyed and red faced. I would have felt badly about it, but Knightley, really? On my campaign? I refused to feel guilty for calling Knightley out, and when the idiot screwed it all up, I wasn't going to feel bad then either. No, I wouldn't feel bad; I'd be furious.

"All right." Aidan pinched the bridge of his nose. "I understand that you two don't see eye to eye all of the time, but the thing to remember is that we're all on the same team and this is the biggest corporate gift we've ever gone after. Ten million. It could set a precedent, and I do not want to lose it because you two can't buck up and work together."

I huffed out a pent-up breath, and I heard what sounded to be the same coming from Knightley in the background. Aidan sighed.

"Listen, I am asking you two, as professionals, to put your personal feelings aside until the Severin Robotics campaign is a go. I'd step in and do it myself, but I just can't right now."

There was something in his tone. I felt the hair on the back of my neck prickle. Aidan was never one to back down from anything. He'd managed corporate gifts and campaigns for years, pulling millions from seemingly unreachable corporations. This wasn't like him.

"What is it, Aidan?" I asked. "You can tell me and it will go no further—you know that."

"Same here," Jason agreed.

The computer monitor swiveled again, and I now had a view of both Aidan and Jason. I glanced at Jason and noted he was wearing a charcoal-gray shirt today, making his eyes a stormy shade of gray. Whatever. He wasn't looking at me, however, but frowning at Aidan with a quiet intensity that made me even more nervous.

"I'm going to hold you both to that. The truth is . . . I've been diagnosed with stage-two lung cancer—damn cigarettes of my youth—and I just don't know how things are going to roll out for me for the next few months. So I'm asking you two to take this on together—for me."

There was a beat of silence as we absorbed the news. Shock rendered me speechless, and I imagined it did the same to Jason. He recovered first.

"You can count on me," he said. "I'll do whatever it takes."

I stared at my mentor's face on the tiny screen of my phone. Aidan had lung cancer. Stage two. That meant it had traveled to either his chest cavity or his lymph nodes. Not good. But only stage two. That was better than three or four, right? Still treatable, still beatable.

"Breathe, Chelsea," Aidan said.

I exhaled a breath I hadn't even known I'd been holding.

"How long have you known?" I asked. I supposed it didn't really matter, but if he'd told me that day in his office, the day I'd tried to quit, I likely wouldn't have left. Had he known that?

"A few weeks," he said. So he had known, and he'd still let me go. "And yes, the irony of working for the ACC and getting diagnosed with cancer is not lost on me."

I studied his face. Did he look thinner? Yes, he did. How had I not noticed? The beard. It was hard to get a sense of his health behind all that hair.

"Can I count on you, Chelsea?" he asked. "Will you continue to work in an advisory capacity with Jason on the ask?"

"Of course," I said. "I'm available whenever you need me."

"Thank you." Aidan let out an undisguised sigh of relief. He grinned at me through the phone and then at Jason. "And hey, who knows, maybe you two will learn to enjoy working together."

I glanced at Jason. The look of doubt on his face mirrored mine. Oh, we'd do this for Aidan and it'd be amazing, because I would make damn sure it was, but there was no way either of us was going to enjoy it.

"I received the Severin files from Julia," Jason said. "I'll review them tonight, and we can talk tomorrow. I have some questions about how you're quantifying the return on investment to Severin."

I opened my mouth to ask what questions, since it was meticulously accounted for in my documentation, but I didn't. Instead, I nodded and said, "Great. I'll talk to you tomorrow . . . Huckleberry."

To Knightley's credit, he laughed. It was a good laugh, deep and resonant. Then he winked at me and, with his usual swagger, rose from his seat. He shook Aidan's hand before he left the office, telling him to let him know if he needed anything. Aidan waited until the door closed after him before turning the monitor so that it was just him and me.

"Jason will be a good fit for this," he said. "You'll see."

I doubted it, but I wasn't going to say anything, not now that I knew Aidan was ill. That was the most important thing, taking any worries off Aidan's desk that didn't need to be there.

"I'm sure we'll be fine," I said. "We've got this—don't you worry."

"Thanks, Chelsea. I knew I could count on you," he said. "So, cow pajamas, huh?"

"Don't start," I said. "They were a gag gift from my sister, but they're really comfy."

He laughed, and the sound made my chest ache. "Aidan, you'd tell me if I needed to come home right away, wouldn't you?"

He gave me a sweet smile. "Of course I would."

I stared at him. Hard.

"I promise. Now go have a pint at a pub—or even better, a shot of whiskey—get into some trouble, and find your laughter again. I miss you."

"I've only been gone from the office for a few days," I said.

"Yes, well, it's not the same without you here," he said. He sounded grumpy. "So find yourself and then come home, okay?"

I smiled. "Okay."

I ended the call and tossed my phone onto the bed. I put my hand over my face, trying to take in the news of Aidan's illness. I felt my throat get tight and my eyes water up, but I refused to cry. I pushed my feelings down deep. He was going to be okay. It was early stages. And Aidan wasn't an idiot. He'd get the very best of care, and he'd fight this with everything he had.

I crossed the small cottage to the windows facing away from the village. I pushed back the thick white cotton curtain with the decorative cutouts and noted that the heavy rain had stopped, but there was a thick fog hanging down from the sky. The hills rolled all the way to the horizon like a sea of green, and somewhere out there was the woman I used to be. I just had to find her—quickly.

At the moment, it felt impossible. Aidan's news had rocked me, and I started to fret and worry. What if Aidan was actually sicker than he'd said? What if his treatments didn't work? What if I didn't get back to him in time? What if I was off gallivanting around Europe when he needed me? What if he died on me, just like my mother had?

The thought made me gasp. It was all hitting a bit too close to home.

A sob choked me. I was an idiot to come here. I needed to get back to Boston and help Aidan through the next few months. I could always return afterward. Of course that meant that I would have to embrace my father's hasty marriage without the benefit of reconnecting to my old happy self. Could I do it? Maybe. Was it the right choice? I didn't know.

My phone chimed, and I almost ignored it. I wasn't in any shape to talk to anyone. But maybe Aidan had forgotten something. I hurried across the cottage and scooped my phone off the bed. I hit the green button, opening the video call, expecting Aidan and not noticing that it was an unknown number until Jason Knightley's annoyingly hand-some face filled my screen. Great.

"Martin," he said.

"Knightley," I replied, immediately irritated. "What's wrong? Was there an insult you forgot to zing me with?"

"This from the woman who said I was an overgrown frat boy."

"You called me as sexy as leftovers."

His grin was rueful. It made him look endearing. And he scratched the scruff of closely trimmed beard that covered his jaw, adding to the charm.

"Admittedly, that was . . . inaccurate," he said. His gaze met mine, and I wondered what he was thinking. "Honestly, I'm calling to see if you're okay after Aidan's news. Are you?"

I gave my phone side-eye. "Jason Knightley, expressing concern for me? I'm touched."

I sank slowly onto the edge of the bed. My heart rate was slowing, so that was something. Still, I was suspicious. What was Knightley's angle?

"Yeah, well." He glanced away, out the windows of his office, and then turned back. His eyes met mine, and I could see they were clouded with concern. "I know Aidan is a mentor to you, like me, and I'm just—shit, I'm struggling a bit with the news, and I thought maybe you were, too."

I was surprised. I hadn't expected this level of honesty from Jason. He'd always seemed like the sort of guy's guy who buried anything that involved real emotions down deep, preferably six feet under and with a weighty headstone.

"I'm worried," I said. "I mean, lung cancer is one of the big baddies."

"But he's only stage two."

"Which is better than three or four."

"But worse than one."

"Right. I thought about canceling my trip and coming back, but I suspect Aidan didn't tell me before I left because he didn't want me to change my plans for him," I said. "I'm feeling conflicted."

"I thought you might be," he said. "I mean, it's Aidan, our hard-core lettuce eater. He's supposed to outlive us all."

I smiled. "He has always seemed like a force of nature."

We were both quiet for a moment. I was full of thoughts about Aidan, and I suspected Jason was, too.

"Is that why you texted me earlier?" I asked. "To tell me about the change with the Severin ask?"

"I thought a warning might be in order," he said. "But now that I know you think I'm handsome and charming—"

"Shut up," I said. My words lacked heat, and I was thankful for the dim lighting, hoping it hid the blush I could feel heating my face.

He chuckled, and an awkward silence echoed between us, becoming more uncomfortable with each second. I didn't want to admit how worried I was, and I suspected Knightley didn't either.

"I'll keep an eye on him for you," he said. It was the first time I could ever remember him offering to do anything for me. "If there's any change in his condition, I'll let you know immediately. Wait, where are you exactly?"

I had to admit I was pleasantly surprised by his thoughtfulness. "Thank you," I said. "I'm staying in a cottage in Finn's Hollow, Ireland."

"Ireland, huh?"

"Yeah."

I bent over to grab the blanket that had landed on the floor. I dropped the spread onto the bed and pushed my hair out of my face with my free hand. I glanced at the phone and saw Jason watching me. The look in his eyes was one I didn't recognize.

"Hey, Martin, I've never seen you with your hair down before," he said. "You should wear it like that more often."

I lifted one eyebrow, feeling annoyed. Next he'd be telling me I ought to smile more. "Because how I wear my hair matters why? Am I more 'likable' with my hair loose?"

His lips twitched as if he was trying to control a smile. "Um, no, actually. You're still as lovable as a feral cat, but I gotta tell ya, Martin, the hair down . . ."

"What about it?" I glowered.

"It's dead sexy," he said. He gave me a little finger wave and a wink. "Until tomorrow."

The call ended, and I stared at my phone. What a jackass.

Okay, that wasn't fair. He had been decent and called me to see if I was okay after Aidan's news. So perhaps he wasn't 100 percent jackass— more like 75 percent, with the remaining 25 percent being a cubbyhole in his soul that housed his compassion and empathy. If I got lucky, I'd have to deal with only the 25 percent for the next few months. In the meantime, I absolutely planned to ignore the part of me that had been just the teeniest, tiniest bit flattered that he'd noticed my hair and called me sexy.

I stretched my arms over my head, trying to get the kinks out. I wondered if I should go hit Darby up for a spin on the pole. The mere idea made me smile. As if.

The nap had helped to clear my head, and now, after that unexpected conference call and Aidan's news, I felt compelled to take action. I was on a mission to find Colin Donovan and look him right in his pretty blue eyes and see if I remembered what it felt like to feel all the feels again, even the ones that terrified me.

chapter seven

THE PUB WAS packed. A tourist bus was parked out front, and groups of people filled every table, forcing me to sit at the bar. Not that I minded, since I wanted to see if Michael Stewart still owned the Top of the Hill, but they were an awfully loud group, and I had to shout over the conversations to be heard.

"What can I get ya?" A woman was behind the bar, and she looked at me expectantly.

"Um . . ." I stared at the taps, trying to read the names on the handles in a mild panic, as I didn't want to keep the busy woman waiting and really just wanted to know if Michael was around, but wasn't sure how to ask.

"Was that going to be today or Thursday?" the woman teased. Her accent was a soft lilt, and she pronounced *Thursday* with a hard *T*, which I thought was just charming, even though she was looking more exasperated by the second.

"She'll have a pint of the Golden Spear, Sarah." I turned to see a man walking up behind the bar, carrying a full keg on one shoulder. He set it down on the ground and grinned at me. It was the full grin that did it.

"Michael," I said. I leaned over the bar to give him a hug, and he met me halfway.

"Chelsea Martin," he said. He squeezed me tight and then released me. "What are you doing here?"

Well, that was the million-dollar question, wasn't it? Instead of giving him a rundown on my father's impending nuptials and how they had sent me into a panicked downward spiral, I opted to be vague.

"Just passing through."

His gaze narrowed. He clearly suspected there was more to it, but he didn't press.

"And how are you?" I asked.

"I've no complaints," he said.

"I can't believe you remember me. It's been seven years," I said with a grin.

"You haven't aged a day," he said. "But you and your crew did make quite an impression." He jerked his thumb at the wall behind him, and I saw that it was full of photographs. He tapped one with his forefinger, and my eyes went wide. There I was, sitting in this very bar with Colin and our other friends in a snug over in the corner, and Colin had his arm about me.

Sarah slid a pint of blonde ale in front of me, and I took a long sip. So many memories were coming back thick and fast.

"Oh, look," I said. I squinted at the picture and hoped I sounded more casual than I felt. "That's Colin Donovan, isn't it? He was quite the troublemaker."

"Still is," Michael said.

I felt my heart pound. Did that mean that Colin still lived in Finn's Hollow? I wasn't sure how to ask, so I just went for it.

"Is he still in the area, then?" I tried to sound mildly curious instead of desperately hopeful. No small feat. "I lost touch with him over the years."

"Oh, yeah," Michael said. "He manages the O'Brien farm since Mr. O'Brien passed four years ago."

That was an unexpected blow. I took a moment to remember the man who had been so kind to me when I was fresh out of college and on my own in a foreign country. Mr. O'Brien didn't need to have a pack of twenty-somethings running amok on his farm, but he loved his life, and he wanted to expose as many young people as he could to the rewards of sheep farming.

My best memory of Mr. O'Brien was of him striding across the green pastures with Fiona, his border collie, at his side. He'd give a command, and Fiona would run the sheep in any direction he asked. They'd had an uncanny ability to communicate with just a few terse words. Mrs. O'Brien used to joke that the only woman she had to share her man with was Fiona.

"I'm sorry to hear that," I said. "He was such a good man."

"Timmy O'Brien was at that," Michael said. His voice sounded resigned to the loss. Another customer arrived at the bar, and he turned away to serve him. "Give me a wave if you need me, and welcome back, Chelsea."

I lifted my glass in a silent toast to the man who'd had a hearty laugh, a rogue's grin, and a love of Ireland that ran deep into his soul. "Godspeed, Mr. O'Brien," I said and then finished my pint and ordered some dinner to take back to my cottage.

Now that I knew Colin was here, at the farm no less, I realized I had to follow through and go see him. Tomorrow I would drive out to the O'Brien farm and find my old friend. I was nervous, no question, but I was also excited. I tried to remember the last time I'd felt this sort of thrill. I couldn't. Was this it, then? The feeling I was looking for? I certainly hoped so.

A GLANCE OUT the window the next morning, and I was pleasantly surprised to see the sun beginning to lighten the sky. Maybe my luck was turning. The peat in the fireplace had burned out, and the room was chilly. I hurriedly took a hot shower to warm up, wanting to get to breakfast, as I was starving.

I took a bit longer with my appearance than usual. This was a reunion, after all, and I didn't want to look too dowdy. I kept my hair loose, not because Jason had said it looked dead sexy, but because it was cold out and my hair would keep my head warm. I put on mascara and lipstick and a thick black turtleneck sweater to fight the March chill.

The O'Brien farm was only a few miles—er, kilometers—away, and I could be there in fifteen minutes. The thought was tempting, but I knew I needed to eat and get myself together first, meaning coffee, I needed coffee. I walked up to the main house to find the door open and the smell of sausage and bacon coming from the dining room, where the large table was loaded with food, and two other guests, a husband and wife by the look of them, were already seated, sharing the newspaper over coffee.

"Mornin', Chelsea." Darby greeted me from the doorway to the kitchen with a wide warm smile. There were no sparkly boy shorts today. Instead, she wore a large apron over jeans and a sweater and was carrying a spatula. "I'm frying up another batch of bacon and sausage, if you don't mind waiting a bit."

"Not at all," I said. "I'll just get myself some coffee, thanks."

Darby nodded. "These are the Parks, Mary and Jerry, visiting from Nova Scotia, Canada."

"Really?" I said. "My mother was from Pocologan, New Brunswick, but moved to the States when she married my father. I'm just south of you, in Massachusetts."

"Practically neighbors," Jerry said. His round face broke into a smile.

"Indeed. Nice to meet you, dear," Mary said. She had curly white hair and a smile as friendly as her husband's.

Jerry pushed a few sections of the *Irish Times* my way. I poured myself a cup of coffee and slid into a seat.

"Do you come to Ireland often?" Mary asked.

"No, it's only my second trip," I said. "I came for the first time about seven years ago while living and working for a year abroad after college."

"Tried to put off being a grown-up?" Jerry teased.

"Exactly." I smiled. "I toured most of Europe and had planned to head on to Asia, Africa, and South America, but life changed my plans."

"As it does," Mary said. I suspected there was a world of living packed into that sentence.

"We're here to drive the Ring of Kerry but also to check out the border collie demonstration at the O'Brien farm," Jerry said. "I've always liked the breed, and I want to see them in action."

"Border collie demonstration?" I asked. I felt my face get warm at the mention of the farm. What were the odds? They hadn't done any dog demonstrations back in the day, which was surprising because Fiona would have done anything for Mr. O'Brien. "That sounds fascinating."

"It is if you like dogs, eh," Jerry said.

"We're going after breakfast. You should join us," Mary said. "Unless, of course, you're here to take classes with Darby."

"Uh, no," I said. "I don't think I bend that well."

"I hear that," Jerry said with a laugh.

"But I am a dog lover," I said.

Just because I didn't have a dog didn't mean I didn't love them. Going to the farm with the Parks could really work for me. It would give me cover if Colin didn't recognize or remember me or if I lost my nerve. I could just cling to the Parks and pretend I'd never been to the O'Brien farm before. And if he did remember me but everything was awkward and weird, the Parks would be my out. I'd be leaving with them, one way or another, so it was perfect.

"Then it's all settled," Mary said. "We'll go together."

IN HINDSIGHT, CARPOOLING might not have been my best idea. The drive to the farm was steep and treacherous, but Jerry didn't drive like caution was warranted along the winding road. Oh, no, the eighty-something Canadian drove like he was a cow in a race to get to the barn.

I buckled myself into my seat in the back, and as Jerry stomped on the gas pedal, I wished for a set of rosary beads to pray on. Which was new for me, because I wasn't generally a praying type. But *Jaysus*, as the locals said, when Jerry took a curve too fast and the car felt as if it was going to go up on two wheels, I found myself digging deep for some dusty bits of a Hail Mary, particularly *Holy Mary, Mother of God, pray for us sinners now, and at the hour of death.*

And please don't let that be right now, I added. I hadn't even found Colin yet. I resisted the urge to cross myself but only just. The car leveled out, and I was just catching my breath when Jerry crested a hill and saw something that caught his interest in the distance. He pointed and both he and Mary looked, and of course the car veered precariously toward the edge. I had to bite back a shriek for fear it would startle him and cause us to go over the drop.

So while I wasn't very religious, at the moment, I would have prayed on a banana to arrive safely and in one piece. Mary, for her part, didn't bat an eyelash at her husband's driving. A sharp curve, a hairpin turn, a double-back, Jerry navigated it all without reducing his speed even a little. Upon arrival, he swerved into a parking spot between a tour bus and a minivan without slowing down.

I wanted to leap from the car and kiss the ground, but the damage was done. Darby's fry-up roiled in my stomach, staging a full-on rebellion. I was sweating, panting, and, I suspected, as green as the hills surrounding us. It was taking everything I had not to throw up.

"Chelsea, come on—you're going to miss it!" Mary called to me from the platform where she and Jerry joined a busload of tourists.

"Be right there," I said. It was a lie. The vomit-inducing drive over here had taken the starch right out of me, and now I was in the thick of an existential crisis.

What had I been thinking? I couldn't face Colin. It had been seven years! He was going to think I was some crazy ex-girlfriend, assuming he remembered me at all. My potential for complete and utter humiliation was at an all-time personal high.

I must have been out of my mind to think I could do this. Had I really fantasized that he and I would spot each other across a field and rush into each other's arms? That was never going to happen!

The reality was I was standing in the frigid cold on the side of a hill on a freaking sheep farm, trying desperately not to throw up on my own shoes. This was not how romance fantasies were supposed to play out! God, I was an idiot.

And with that crack of vulnerability, I realized I couldn't do this. I couldn't face him. I just wanted to curl up in the back seat and pull a blanket over my head until it was time to go. I didn't even care that Jerry would likely get us killed on the ride home. I yanked on the door handle of the car. It was locked. Damn it.

The bleating of sheep broke into my panic, and I glanced up the hillside to see a flock scurrying out of the low-hanging fog, heading toward us with two dogs and a handler following them. Was that Colin? He was too far away. I couldn't tell. Suddenly, my palms were sweaty and my breathing short. I was ridiculously nervous. Either he'd remember me or he wouldn't. It was no big deal. Right?

I stepped away from the car. My curiosity about whether it was him momentarily pushed aside my nerves, and I moved closer to the platform just to take a better look. Once I knew if it was Colin or not, I reasoned, I could always run back and hide behind the car. So mature, I know.

Halfway to the observation deck, disaster struck. One of the sheep broke away from the flock, heading straight for me. Instead of jumping out of the way, like a perfectly functional normal person, I stood frozen, even as I saw one of the dogs peel away to run down the sheep, who was now bleating in a frenzied terror that seemed perfectly understandable to me.

The sheep's eyes were wide with fright, and the black-and-white dog looked more like a wolf, with teeth bared, as it closed in on its prey. The sheep sideswiped me, knocking me to the ground as if I were a human shield that would protect it from the dog, which would have bounded past me in hot pursuit if not for the voice of command that broke through the cacophony of the tourists' gasps and cries, the bleating sheep, and the panting dog.

"Lie low, Seamus, lie low," the handler I'd seen on the hill ordered, and Seamus dropped to the ground beside me. I glared at him, but he showed not one bit of remorse.

It was then that I felt the cold seep into my hands and knees. I glanced down to see I'd been knocked into a mud puddle. Great. I pulled my hands out of the muck. They were dripping mud and water—I sincerely hoped it was water—and I tried to find a patch of grass so I could push myself up to my feet. I flailed a bit just before two strong hands grabbed me under the arms and hauled me up to standing.

I glanced over my shoulder, and my breath caught. I'd know those blue eyes, those deep dimples, and that particular cowlick in that thatch of dark-red hair anywhere. Colin Donovan!

chapter eight

"ALL RIGHT, MISS?" he asked.

I ducked my head, letting my hair fall over my face. For the nanosecond that our eyes met, I didn't see startled recognition in his gaze, just the polite inquiry of a stranger making certain I hadn't hurt myself.

"Fine," I said. "I'm perfectly fine."

"Sure, if wet, muddy, and cold is your definition of fine," he replied. There was laughter in his voice. It was so achingly familiar, I wanted to tip my head back and laugh, too, but a hot case of shyness kept me from looking up. "Thomas, take our guest here to the washroom and ask Mrs. O'Brien if she has a change of clothes for her."

"Yes, sir," Thomas said.

"That's not necessary," I protested.

"I insist," Colin said. He was talking to the top of my head, as I kept my face averted—like a weirdo—while I brushed at my knees as if I were trying to get clean, although what I was actually doing was avoiding his gaze. I simply couldn't reconnect with him like this. It wasn't at all like I had imagined it, and the control freak in me was having a hissy fit of epic proportions. I wondered if I could slink off the property without anyone noticing and walk back to the cottages.

"This way, miss," Thomas—I presumed it was him, since I had yet to look up—said.

I turned away from Colin and followed the voice. Tall and skinny, with the open face of a boy rather than a man, Thomas looked to be about eighteen, and he smiled at me with kindness and not mockery, which I appreciated.

We left the platform behind, and there it was. The old white farmhouse with black trim and shutters; flower boxes on all the lower windows; and a big garden, barren now, that ran along the side of the house. Beyond that was the barn, where I had learned to shear sheep, and in between the two was the long low-slung bunkhouse, also white with black shutters, just like the big house. It was there we'd all bunked down during our time on the farm. I smiled, remembering late nights of laughter, big breakfasts, and days spent out in the mountains, tending the various flocks of sheep. My heart swelled at the memories.

Thomas let me into the bunkhouse. It hadn't changed much. The same utilitarian bunk beds stacked on each side of the room with a random collection of dressers between them.

"I'll just run up to the house and ask about some clothes," Thomas said.

I glanced down. "There's no need. It's just my knees. A towel will do the trick."

Thomas fetched one from a nearby cupboard and gestured to the bathroom. I went inside, hoping to repair the worst of the damage. I used the towel to scrub at the drying mud on my knees and washed my face and hands. I tossed the towel into a nearby hamper.

I wondered if I could hide in here until the exhibition was over. Probably not. Both Thomas and Colin knew where I was. They were sure to come looking for me if I didn't turn up soon.

Leaving the bunkhouse behind, I walked back up the trail. I was huffing and puffing as I reached the deck. The crowd was applauding, so it was clear I had missed most of the demonstration. I was disappointed by that. I would have liked to have seen Colin with the dogs.

Colin was standing on the ground below. He grinned at the crowd's applause and then turned to open the gate. The sheep pressed forward into the pen in a nervous mob. It was clearly a general admission situation here, and I was surprised none of them were trampled in their hurry to get away from the dogs.

"Have you ever had a dog kill one of the sheep?" a young boy asked. His eyes were huge and he looked concerned.

Colin latched the gate and turned back to the group. His bright-blue eyes moved over the crowd and rested on the boy with a friendly gaze.

"Not to date, but it could happen easily enough," Colin said. His lilting accent curled around me like a soft, woolly blanket. "The hunter spirit of their ancestors, the wolves, is still in them, so if they killed one sheep, they'd kill them all. That's why you never leave them alone with the sheep. It'd be a massacre, and it wouldn't be the dog's fault but the master's."

The boy nodded. There were a few more questions. Someone else asked about the red, blue, and black markings on the sheep's coats, and Colin explained what I already knew, that the colors designated which farm the sheep belonged to, which ones had been dipped, meaning inoculated against disease, and which females had been serviced, so to speak.

I was riveted. How had I forgotten his killer dimples and the wicked twinkle in his eyes when he teased? The man was full-on Irish hottie, and I had come so far to see him. Could I really skulk away now? Not a chance.

How I was going to approach Colin, I had no idea, so instead, I watched him, indulging in the moment. I recognized the way he carried himself with his back straight, his broad shoulders strong, and his head tipped ever so slightly to the side, as if he was just looking for a bit of mischief to make the day fun. Oh, how I had missed him.

With a wave of his arm, he signaled for the crowd to start down the gravel path to the shearing shack. Colin was busy. He was working. I knew I should leave the man alone, but I didn't. Adhering my courage to the sticking place, which at the moment felt more like a preschooler's paste than the superstrength glue I used as an adult, I stepped forward into his line of sight.

"And don't let Seamus bamboozle you into thinking he needs extra food now," Colin instructed. He clapped Thomas on the shoulder. "He's goin' to get fat if everyone keeps believin' those big sad eyes of his."

"Aye, sir, I know better than to fall for his beggin'." Thomas whistled, and the dogs jumped to their feet. They followed him, crowding his legs as they left the area.

"Sir?" I said. "You've certainly come up in the world, Colin Donovan."

He turned to face me. His face was kindly polite. "Are you all right, miss? You weren't hurt, were you?"

He didn't recognize me. It shouldn't have been the crushing blow that it was. It had been seven years. Clearly, I was not as memorable to Colin as he was to me. The mature thing to do would be to introduce myself and tell him we'd met before, but I just couldn't make myself do it.

The truth was, I'd built him up so much in my mind that I was bitterly disappointed that I was no more than a stranger to him. I gently tucked my pride and my dignity into my pocket and forced a smile.

"No, I'm fine," I said. "After all, a little mud never hurt anyone."

His smile slipped off the side of his face, and his eyes narrowed as he stared at me with an intensity that made me nervous. Was he worried I was going to sue the farm? I would never. I was about to reassure him of that when his frown faded into a look of pure astonishment.

"Chelsea Martin, as I live and breathe, is that you?" he asked.

He remembered! My heart swelled and I found I had no words, so I just nodded with a grin parting my lips. The next thing I knew, he was climbing up the front of the platform, not even bothering to go around to the stairs. He vaulted over the railing and landed in front of me.

"I can't believe it. It's been donkey's years since I've seen you," he said. He grabbed my arms to hold me in place while he studied my face. "Pinch me. Am I dreamin'?"

Obligingly, I pinched the tender skin between his glove and his sleeve.

"Ouch!" he cried.

"You said . . ."

"Aye, and you're still a literal girl and a very fine thing," he growled, which made me blush. Then he laughed and pulled me into a rib crusher of a hug, lifting me off my feet.

"And you're still a charmer," I said, hugging him back with all my strength. He smelled of fresh air and peat smoke, warm wool and sunshine, everything that was clean and good. When he set me back on my heels, I missed his warmth immediately.

"Colin, you're still givin' the tour, yeah?" a voice called from the barn down the hill.

"Blast, I have to go," he said. He waved to the man to signal he was on his way, but then he turned back to me. "We need to visit. What are your plans? Where are you staying? How long are you here?"

The flurry of questions had me blinking.

"I don't have any plans. I'm at the cottages. I don't know how long I'll be here," I said. I didn't add that it depended upon him. "Did you want to have dinner tonight?"

"Brilliant, let's do that," he said. "I'll meet you at the Top of the Hill, say, at six?"

"I'd like that," I said. Impulsively, I stood up on my toes and kissed his cheek.

Colin flushed a pale pink and grinned at me. "What was that for?"

"For remembering me," I said.

"Oy, I could never forget you, Chelsea, love," he said. He kissed my forehead and then turned and reached back to take my hand to pull me along behind him as if he didn't want me to get away as he strode down the hill toward the barn. He didn't let go until he stepped into the shed to give his demonstration. It was no exaggeration to say I was halfway to smitten.

THE PARKS WERE exhausted by the end of the tour. I had no doubt it was because Jerry had volunteered to try his hand at shearing. Suffice to say, he'd gotten one of the wigglier young sheep, and much hilarity had ensued as the ewe had outmaneuvered him at every turn.

"Come here, you stubborn girl," Jerry cried as she slipped through his hold. When he got a grip on her again, he looked to be in control of the situation, but then she slipped right through his legs. "I think I'd have better luck with a greased pig!"

"Bacon would be a bigger incentive for you—that's for certain," Mary teased her husband.

Colin stepped up and muscled the sheep into submission, managing to shear her in a matter of moments. I watched in fascination. He'd thrown off his coat, and his tight gray sweater hugged his muscular form. Gone was the slender young man I'd known before, and in his place was this burly man's man. It was easy to see when he hefted the sheep, as if it weighed nothing, where those powerful shoulders of his had come from.

Despite the chill wind that greeted us outside, I was relieved by the bite in the air, as I felt a bit overheated by the whole morning. As impossible as it seemed, Colin was even more attractive now than he'd been in our youth, and that was saying something, 'cause he'd been smokin' hot then, too.

I offered to drive the Parks back to the cottages, and to my relief, Jerry was happy to let me, which was good because I didn't fancy the idea of wrestling an octogenarian to the ground and forcibly taking the keys, but I would have. As we climbed into the car, my gaze met Colin's. He mouthed the word *six* and I nodded, feeling a thrill course through me. The tingle started at the top of my head and ran all the way to my toes. Had he had that much of an impact on me seven years ago? Or was it years of pent-up emotion just looking for an outlet? Hard to say.

On the drive back, Mary and Jerry talked about the dogs, particularly the one called Seamus, wondering if they could have a dog like that running around their cottage in Nova Scotia or if it would get into too much trouble with the local farms. I listened, but my mind was elsewhere, wondering what Colin's life was like outside the farm. Well, I supposed I'd get my chance to ask him at the pub tonight. I felt my heart race in anticipation as I contemplated all my body parts that needed some landscaping. Finn's Hollow did not boast a beauty salon. This was going to be a DIY project of major proportions.

JET LAG AND nerves overwhelmed me, so I took a nap until midafternoon and then began to prep for my date. It was a date, I reasoned. I'd asked and he'd said yes. Two consenting adults meeting for dinner in a public place was a date. Absolutely.

Because I had packed so minimally, I chose to go bold and wore my clingy red tunic sweater over black jeans and half boots. I styled my hair in big loose waves and decided to put on a little extra makeup. Was the cat eye thing with eyeliner still happening? I frowned at my reflection. Could I even manage it?

I opened up YouTube on my phone and watched a quick tutorial. It didn't seem that hard. I'd just finished one eye, which came out okay, and was working on the other when my phone chimed. The noise startled me, and I stabbed myself in the eye, because of course I did. I closed my eye as the tears started, and slid my thumb across the display, unable to see the number through my tears.

"Hello," I answered. I tried to sound chipper while I grabbed a tissue out of the holder on the top of the toilet and attempted to wipe my eye without smudging the liner and ruining the rest of my face. That was a fail. My eye was watering so much I looked as if I were bleeding black out of my eyeball. "Damn it."

"Well, hello to you, too."

I glanced at my phone. Jason's annoying face smiled at me through the display, and then his eyes went wide. "What happened, Martin? Did you piss someone off with an overzealous itinerary and they popped you in the eye?"

"Ha ha, you're hilarious. It's a makeup malfunction," I said. "Can I call you back?"

"No can do, I have a conference call with the community-outreach team at Severin Robotics in ten minutes, so it's now or never," he said.

"Fine," I growled. Leave it to Knightley to catch me at my worst. I propped the phone up on a nearby shelf while I tried to wipe the thick black trails off my cheek.

"Makeup, huh?" he asked. "I've never seen you wear that much makeup."

"Well, you've never seen me on a date," I pointed out. I finished cleaning off the mess that was formerly my eyeliner and frowned.

"Oh, someone's got a hot date tonight?" he asked. "Do tell. Did you bag yourself a leprechaun at the end of the rainbow?"

I frowned at the phone and said, "Shut up." He smirked.

I turned back to my reflection and wondered if I should wash my other eye and just go with mascara or if another attempt at a cat eye with the eyeliner would be worth it.

"Martin, the clock is ticking here," he said.

"Yeah, yeah, give me a second," I said.

He sighed and propped his chin on his hand while he watched me. I decided to go for the cat eye.

"They say less is more," he said. "If that helps."

"It doesn't," I snapped. "I watched a YouTube tutorial to get this right, but I don't think my eyes match to begin with."

He studied me. "What are you talking about?"

I turned to face the phone. "I think my right eye droops a little in the corner."

"What, like you've had a stroke?" he asked. He stared at me hard.

I glared. "No, Knightley, it's the corner of your mouth that droops after a stroke."

"I think it's both," he said. "And your eyes are perfectly matched. It's just that one is all gooped up and the other isn't. You have pretty eyes—you don't need to make yourself look like a cat or smoky or glittery or whatever it is you girls think is trending."

I hesitated. "Are you sure? Because this is a very important date."

"I'm positive," he said. "But lipstick is important. No pressure, but make it a good color, like cherry red."

"What? How is lipstick important but eyeliner isn't?" I asked.

"Men don't think about kissing your eyeball," he said. "But lips? Lips will stay on a man's mind for days, weeks, possibly years."

"Gotcha." I washed the liner off my other eye and patted my face dry. "Okay, what did you call about?"

"In anticipation of my conference call, I was going over your proposal," he said. "It's good, but the fundraising incentives you've come up with for the employees—you know, the weekend-getaway prizes, the free dinners, the cancer screenings—it's all very . . ."

"What?" I pumped my mascara wand and looked at him. "What were you going to say?"

"Pedestrian," he said. "Movie tickets or a new television as prizes for getting donations to support them in a bike-a-thon or have them sell raffle tickets is so *meh*."

I rolled my eyes. "Those are all tried-and-true methods for employee engagement, especially as the company departments will be competing against each other for the yet-to-be-named grand prize."

He didn't say anything, and when I glanced over at my phone, he was yawning a big fakey yawn.

I gritted my teeth. "Listen, I am not going to have this go the way of the Overexposure Media Group ask."

He winced. That was the only time we'd ever worked together, and it had been an unmitigated disaster. Frankly, I was still surprised that Aidan had kept us on after losing that ask.

"Overexposure Media Group tanked because we didn't appreciate each other's unique working styles," he said.

"Among other things," I said. I refused to mention "the incident."

"In anticipation of this, I did some reading up on workplace personalities."

Oh, this should be good. I gave my phone side-eye. "Really? And what personality am I?"

"You're a guardian," he said. "You like meticulously detailed, strategic plans executed with precision."

"Because they work," I retorted.

"Whereas I am a pioneer," he said, ignoring me. "We're all about the big idea, more theory, less detail, and imagination is the key."

"Agreed," I said. "Except that's not why our ask from Overexposure Media Group failed." He opened his mouth to speak, but I plowed on. "It failed because you thought doing videos of our staff rapping about cancer prevention while getting cancer screenings in the ACC mobile unit was a great idea."

"It was a great idea," he argued. "It could have gone viral."

"Yeah, except you neglected to tell me that's what we were doing. I thought it was supposed to be an ensemble piece where I said one line while standing by the machine. News flash—I can't rap, especially not while getting a mammogram!" All right, fine, I brought up "the incident."

"No, you really can't," he agreed. He pressed his lips together as if trying not to laugh. "In my defense, I thought mammograms were just like an X-ray. I figured you could rap the lines I'd given you while getting a chest X-ray like Davis on my team did for lung cancer. I had no idea they smashed your, you know, between plates of glass." He looked pained.

"Do not make light of this," I said. "Imagine my shock when you appeared from behind the curtain while I was in a hospital johnny with a boob on the loose."

"I swear I didn't see anything." He blinked, the picture of innocence.

"So you said . . . repeatedly." I hadn't believed him. To his credit, he'd never spoken of "the incident" to anyone and neither had the technician, but for months afterward just seeing Knightley across the room had caused me to suffer a hot-faced case of extreme mortification. I couldn't look the man in the eye for months. "Honestly, do men really not know what's entailed in a mammogram?"

"Well, I do now," Knightley said. His voice sounded strangled, and he lost the battle and started laughing. Looking back on that unfortunate day, I really couldn't blame him. I must have made quite the picture. I wasn't sure who had been more horrified—me, the technician, or Knightley. I snorted, almost laughed, but then frowned.

"We lost twenty-five thousand dollars on your big idea because of your lack of proper planning and communication skills. The videos that you did manage to produce were . . . not good." I felt I should get points for not saying they were terrible. They really were.

"We were just doing a pilot. I still say Overexposure Media Group could have taken that rapping video idea and run with it," he said.

"Instead, they ran away from it."

"Brutal."

I sighed. I wasn't trying to bust him down, truly. Although I was still mad about the Overexposure Media Group debacle. Knightley was imaginative, and his team had come up with some terrific campaigns, but Severin's was just too big to treat lightly. Still, we were stuck working together. I glanced at his face and asked, "Okay, Knightley, what would you do to engage Severin?"

He immediately perked up. "Play to the company's strengths," he said.

"Such as?" I leaned toward the mirror as I used the wand to apply my mascara. I pressed my tongue to my upper lip as I concentrated on coating each lash.

"They're a robotics company," he said.

"Um. No duh."

"BattleBots!" he yelled, and I stabbed myself in the eye with my mascara wand.

"Ow!" I blinked and put the side of my finger under my lashes so I wouldn't smudge my makeup again. "Damn it! Really, Knightley? Really?"

"Sorry," he said. "But I get excited thinking about it. This could be huge. Company-wide robots battling for domination. It could raise money for charity by having people sponsor their favorite bot, which could cause a social media frenzy as we livestream the battles built by different departments in the company."

"How do you figure? Isn't it just tech nerds who enjoy that stuff?"

He didn't say anything, and I glanced at my phone again. He looked offended. "Tech nerds? I'll have you know I was the captain of my robotics team in college."

"Of course you were," I said. Then I snorted.

"And I was cool," he insisted.

"If you say so." I shrugged. A small smile curved my lips as I reached for my lipstick, which just happened to be in a deep red that matched my sweater, not cherry red but close. I made my lips into an O and slid the creamy color first over my top lip and then over the bottom, then I grabbed a tissue and blotted them, making a pucker in the mirror and then smiling to make sure the shade complemented me but didn't get on my teeth. It was perfect.

I turned back to my phone to find Jason staring at me as if he was actually enjoying looking at me, a first. "Good choice, Martin. You look very . . . nice."

"Nice?" I raised an eyebrow. "Thanks, Knightley. Very nice was exactly what I was going for."

"You look good, Martin, and you know it," he said. "I'm not going to tell you that you're a heart attack in red, or it'll go to your head and there'll be no working with you."

"Thank you," I said. I felt my face get a little warm at the compliment, and I smiled. It was the first time I'd ever actually smiled at him with anything other than malice.

He blinked. Then he frowned. "Just who is it that you're going on this date with?"

"None of your business."

"Does anyone know you're going?"

"Yes, the person I'm going with."

"Martin, you're alone in a foreign country," he said. "What if the guy is a serial killer or a rapist or a drunk?"

I laughed. "He's not. He's an old friend, and we're getting together for dinner. There's no need to worry."

"I'm not worried."

"You sound worried."

"Nope, not me," he said. "But Aidan might be when I tell him you're on a date."

"Aidan doesn't worry about anything," I said. "He believes in the power of the universe. Speaking of Aidan, how is he?"

"He believes in the power of the universe," Jason said, repeating my words as an answer, and I laughed. "He seems all right. He's signing on for a fairly aggressive treatment. The toughest part will likely be losing his hair."

"Oh, poor Aidan, I've watched that hair grow for seven years," I said. "I can't really picture him without it."

"I know, but he's making the best choice."

"Keep me posted?"

"Promise," he said. He hesitated and then asked, "Listen, not to be a badger, but does anyone over there know you're going on a date?"

"And we're back to that," I said.

"I just think it's always good to have a backup plan, in case the date goes badly," he said. "I always have my friends check on me about an hour or two into a date to make sure I don't need an emergency excuse to leave because my hookup turned into a raging psychopath."

"You are a horrible person."

"I prefer realistic. It's a war out there, and you need a wingman," he said. He glanced at the watch on his wrist. "Tell you what, I'll call you in exactly two hours to give you an out if you need one."

"You don't have to," I said. "He really is an old friend. I'll be fine."

"I'm calling," he said. "And you'd better answer, or I'll call the local police. Finn's Hollow, right?"

"Are you always this bossy?" I asked. "Because I have to say, it's not working for me."

"I prefer pushy and overbearing," he said. "And no, I'm never like this, but I need your help on the Severin campaign, so it's in my best interest to make certain you don't get left for dead in a bog in the wilds of Ireland."

"Ah, now it's all coming into focus," I said. "You need me."

"I don't need you," he said. "I need your help in understanding your incredibly long-winded campaign proposal. There's a difference."

"If you say so."

"I do. Now go take yourself out on your hot date, but you'd better answer your phone," he said. "Trust me, if the guy tries to get you to join a druid cult or something, you'll want to hear from me."

"Good night, Jason," I said. I held up my finger, indicating I was about to hang up.

"Bye—"

I pressed END CALL. Druid cult? I laughed. Then I thought about his BattleBots idea. No, we were not doing that. I'd have to call Aidan and have him squash that idea. I had meticulously planned out the next three years of fundraising opportunities for the employees of Severin Robotics, and they did not include battling robots. Honestly, it was like Knightley was a middle schooler trapped inside a grown man's body.

I stepped back from the mirror and checked my appearance one more time. Hair was properly curled, mascara was on and not smudged, lipstick was on point. Sweater was warm and hugged my curves, and my jeans and boots were casual but flattering. I pulled on my thick wool coat and grabbed my shoulder bag, tucking my phone inside as I went.

I locked the cottage door behind me, feeling a dizzying combo of excited and nervous but mostly the former. It was the same fluttery feeling I'd had when Colin recognized me. That was what I was looking for, what I wanted to remember: that feeling of being wholly alive.

Was that how my dad felt when he looked at Sheri? If so, I could understand why he'd been drawn in. The law of attraction. It was impossible to resist. Feeling as if I might understand my father's hasty marriage—just a little, not a lot, because really, a proposal after two weeks was still bonkers—I headed to the pub.

I arrived at six o'clock on the dot because that was my nature. I always got antsy if I was late. I hoped Colin was on time, as I didn't want to look too eager. I couldn't remember if he was a timely sort of guy or not, but I dreaded the idea of sitting in the pub, waiting for him, wondering if he would show up. I needn't have worried. As I walked in the door, he swooped down on me with a giant bear hug.

"You're here!" he cried. "Brilliant. I'd half convinced myself that I'd imagined you."

I laughed as the cold air pushed me into the warm pub full of chatter and laughter, the rich smell of a peat fire, and something delicious frying in the back kitchen.

"Come on—I've got a snug for us in the back," he said. He took my hand and led me through the tables.

It was obvious that most of the patrons were tourists, with a sprinkling of locals thrown in to keep the place authentic.

"Oy, Colin," Michael called from behind the bar. "I see you found our fair Chelsea."

I waved and Michael smiled, but his gaze darted to Colin with concern. I wondered what that was about.

"Aye, I did," Colin called. He turned to me. "What can I bring you?"

"Whatever you're having, or a pint of the black stuff is fine."

"Guinness it is. I'll be right back," he said as he handed me into the booth, kissing me on the head as he did so. I thought it was a ridiculously sweet gesture, as if I was something rare and precious. There hadn't been a lot of that in my life over the past few years, and it touched me.

He returned with a pint for each of us, but instead of sliding into the opposite side of the booth, he sat with me so we were side by side. He lifted his glass and held it up, waiting for me to do the same.

"There are good ships, there are wood ships, there are ships that sail the sea, but the best ships are friendships, and may they ever be," he said. We clinked glasses.

"Sláinte," I said. Then I took a fortifying gulp of beer.

"You remembered." He looked pleased. "What other words that I taught you do you still know?"

"Not much. *Dia dhuit*," I said. I was hesitant about my pronunciation of the greeting after all this time. "That's about all I remember, honestly. Well, that and a few swears. For some reason those stuck with me."

Colin laughed. It was a deep rumble that came up from his belly and made me laugh, too. "That's about all you need, I expect."

We were both silent, smiling at each other, taking in the subtle differences the years had made.

"I ordered fish-and-chips for us," he said. "I remembered that was your favorite. I hope you haven't gone vegetarian on me."

"Well, actually," I said. He looked alarmed, and I couldn't keep up the pretense. I grinned. "I'm kidding. Fish-and-chips is still my favorite."

Colin blew out a breath. His blue eyes when they met mine glinted with the same mischievous twinkle I remembered from our youth.

"You look amazing," he said.

"You do, too. You haven't aged a day, and you're working for Mrs. O'Brien—I want to hear all about it," I said. "Are you happy on the farm? Is life good?"

" 'Tis grand," he said. "Better than I ever expected it could be. I have so many blessings, which I'm dyin' to tell you about, but you're the visitor. I want to hear about you first."

"I don't know where to start," I said. It was true. It felt as if a lifetime had passed during the last seven years.

Michael stopped by our table with two plates loaded with fish-and-chips: lightly battered slabs of fish piled on top of a heap of chips, a.k.a. French fries, with a mound of mashed peas on the side. I realized I was starving and reached for the bottle of malt vinegar to douse my fish with while draping my napkin in my lap.

"This looks amazing," I said to Michael. "There's nothing like pub grub."

"That's the truth of it," Michael agreed with an easy smile. "Can I get you anythin' else?"

"Two more pints," Colin said.

Michael glanced between us, and I nodded. I figured we might as well settle in. Seven years was a lot of catching up to do.

"Comin' up," Michael said. He turned and headed back to the bar.

"So, what happened on your grand tour after you left Ireland?" Colin asked. "Where did you go? Who did you meet? And most important, why didn't you come back?"

"Well." I took a deep breath. Where should I start? Did I start with my mom? No, that was the end. I began with the countries I visited after I left Ireland. There was London, which was amazing; Germany, beautiful; France—that was tricky. I told him I was a nanny, but I didn't mention Jean Claude. I wasn't sure why—it just seemed like bad form. I talked more about Sweden instead.

Colin listened and asked insightful questions. I'd forgotten that about him. What a good listener he was, as if he could hear the subtext in my words. I gave quick details about the rest of my trip, not mentioning Marcellino either, and then I came to the news about my mother. When I told him about the call I'd received on that fateful day, my throat got tight. Colin put his hand over mine and gave my fingers a gentle squeeze.

"I felt that way when Mr. O'Brien died. He was like a father to me in the truest sense of the word."

"I'm so sorry," I said. "How did he die?"

"Fuckin' cancer," he said. "He was a smoker his whole life. I suppose it was to be expected, but it came for him fast. Three months after the first diagnosis, and he was gone."

"Fucking cancer is right," I agreed. Then I told him about how losing my mom had caused me to take a job with the American Cancer Coalition.

"Isn't that something?" he asked. "Look at you, making a difference in the world. I always knew you would."

"You knew no such thing, you big charmer," I said.

Michael came by and took our empty plates and brought us fresh pints. We toasted one another again, and I felt myself, my old self, poke her head out of the closet I'd kept her in for the past seven years. I was feeling attraction, affection, and, frankly, a little lust. Warmed by the good food and better company, I put my hand on Colin's arm. I pressed closer, wanting to feel connected to someone in an intimate way, a way I hadn't felt in a very long time. It occurred to me that I'd been lonely over the past few years, but I'd just rolled it up with my grief and poured it into my work. But now I wanted more.

"It's your turn. Tell me what's happened to you over the past seven years," I said.

"Well, I hardly know where to start," he said. He was staring into my eyes, and I smiled. I could tell he was feeling the same rekindling of our old relationship that I was. Would it be too pushy to invite him back to the cottage? Probably. Was I ready for that sort of thing? Probably not. I still wanted to.

"Aye, Colin, do tell the fine young lass what you've been up to." A woman came to stand at the end of our booth. She held a baby in her arms and had two young children, who looked to be about three and five years old, holding on to the hem of her coat. "I'm sure we'd all enjoy the tellin', and you might want to start by introducin' her to this tiny fella and his cohorts in crime."

"Uh." Colin's eyes went wide. He glanced from the woman to me and back.

I heard my phone buzz inside my purse. Not now! I pulled my phone out of my bag and glanced at the display. Knightley! Two hours had passed since I'd spoken with him, and here he was, calling just like he'd said he would. Of all the times to be responsible!

I went to mute it. Then I hesitated. He'd said he'd call the local authorities if I didn't answer. Would he? Oh god, he might! Which was about the only thing that could make this insanely uncomfortable moment even more awkward.

"Hi," I answered, overly bright and cheery. "Now is really not a good time. Thanks for the call. Bye."

Colin looked at me askance as I ended the call. I wondered if I'd offended him by answering. I mouthed the word *sorry* and then glanced back at the woman. She looked familiar, but I couldn't place her. I could tell from the look on her face, whoever she was, she was not happy.

My phone started to ring again. I looked at the display—Knightley! Argh! I suspected he would just keep calling and calling. I answered, "What?"

"Maverick, this is Goose," he said. "What's your twenty?"

"My what?" I asked. "Who's Maverick? Wait, are you using a *Top Gun* reference?"

"Well, Goose is the greatest wingman ever," he said. "I figured it was appropriate."

"No, it's not. I don't need a wingman," I hissed. "What do you not understand about this is not a good time?"

"Is everything all right?" he asked. His voice was abruptly serious.

I glanced back at Colin and the woman. No, everything was not all right. The woman was smiling, sort of—it was a brittle curve of her lips—while Colin was looking decidedly ill at ease. It hit me then. I'd never even thought to ask if he was married. I glanced at his hand. There was no ring on his finger, but the vibe here was definitely not good between him and the woman.

"Colin," I asked, forgetting about Jason on the phone. "Are you married—to her?"

chapter nine

I N A MANNER of speaking," he said. He had to raise his voice as a trio of musicians began to warm up in the corner.

"That's a yes," the woman clarified.

"Oh man, your old boyfriend is married, and he didn't tell you," Jason said in my ear. Then he sang, "Awkward."

"Shut up," I said. Colin's eyes went wide, and I shook my head. "Not you. Him." I gestured to the phone.

"Him?" Colin asked. "Who's him?"

"A coworker," I said.

"Hey, I'm more than that—I'm your wingman," Jason protested. I ignored him.

"And he's calling you all the way in Ireland at night?" Colin sounded outraged.

"Seriously?" I asked. "You're offended when you neglected to mention that you have a wife . . . and kids? They are yours, I presume."

"I was just about to tell you about them," he said. He glanced at his wife. "I swear."

"Uh-huh." The woman and I spoke together.

"Ooh, man, I'm glad I'm not him," Jason said. "One angry woman is bad enough, but two? He's a dead man walking."

"Good night, Jason," I said.

"What? No!" he cried. "It's just getting good. Switch to video so I can watch."

"Not likely."

"Pretty please?"

"No, and if word leaks out about this at the office, I will cut you," I said.

"You sound fierce," he said. "That's hot."

Ugh. I ended the call. I was not going to let Jason listen to any more of my complete and utter humiliation at finding out my old boyfriend was married by having his wife and kids crash our "date."

"I was about to tell Chelsea about the lot of you," Colin insisted. The baby started to fuss, and he reached out and plucked it from its mother's arms. "Give him here. Chelsea, you remember Aoife O'Hare from our summer work program?"

"Aoife Donovan, thank you very much." The woman frowned at Colin as he hugged the baby to his shoulder and patted the little one's back in a well-practiced gesture that showed his parental skill as the baby immediately snuggled into his dad's warmth.

I studied the woman's face. Aoife. My jaw dropped. Aoife was a few years younger than we were. Pleasantly rounded with thick, long, wavy black hair, creamy skin, and eyes as blue as Lough Caragh. She'd been a lovely girl but painfully shy. This woman standing in front of me now looked neither plump nor shy. Aoife, pronounced *E-fah*, had matured into a real beauty.

"I remember you," I said. It felt like an achievement to bring her back to mind. I smiled and held out a hand. "You were a lovely girl, but you are a stunning woman."

Aoife squinted at me as if trying to decide if I was full of bullshit or not. I wasn't. That wasn't my way—lying was just too exhausting, plus she really was a knockout. Aoife must have come to that very conclusion, because she shook my hand and nodded once.

"I'm not surprised you didn't recognize me. I've dropped two stone and finally grew some baps." She gestured to her breasts, and I snorted.

"Really, Aoife," Colin said. "Is that appropriate talk in a pub?"

"Says the man who is known for lightin' his farts on fire after a few too many pints." Aoife rolled her eyes as she absently put her arms around the two children, one on each side of her, and pulled them in close like a mother hen spreading her wings over her chicks.

"I was with me lads, and it only happened the one time," he said.

"Aye, the one time you lit your backside on fire," Aoife said. She laughed, and her eyes twinkled with mirth.

"Woman, you're going to be the death of me," he said. He looked disgruntled, but it soon gave way to a smile.

"So you keep saying, and yet here you sit," she retorted.

I felt a laugh well up at their good-natured teasing. It was clear there was a lot of love between Aoife and Colin, and I was surprised to find it made me joyous rather than envious. Okay, maybe there was a pinch of envy when I saw the love so evident between them, but mostly they made me happy and . . . hopeful.

"I'll have you know," Colin said, "that I was about to tell my *friend* Chelsea about the beautiful girl I married, who is the love of my life, who has given me my three greatest blessings," he said. His eyes shone when he looked at his wife and children.

"Oh, were you now?" Aoife asked. A pretty pink blush stained her cheeks.

"I was," he said. "I sent you a message to meet me at the pub after you were done at your mother's. Didn't you get it?"

"Of course I got it. That's why I'm here, but imagine my surprise at seeing you with your former girlfriend in a snug," she said.

"Oh." He frowned. "But I'm married."

"Which you clearly neglected to mention," Aoife said.

Colin turned to me with an embarrassed face. "Oy, you didn't think this was a date, did you?"

"Of course not," I lied. I waved my hand in an awkward *don't be silly* flap, hoping to combat the heat I could feel filling my face, but judging by the pitying expression on his, he did not believe me for one second. Damn it.

I wondered exactly how many Guinnesses would be required for me to drown my mortification. Maybe getting sucked into a bog on the walk home wouldn't be such a bad thing. But then why wait? I could happily go full human combustion with the heat of my embarrassment, turn to ash, and blow away on the wind. Yeah, that would do.

"Now you've embarrassed her, you eejit," Aoife hissed. "Honestly, you're makin' a right bags out of it."

"Right," Colin agreed. "But this is actually great, because now I can introduce you all, which is grand. This here's our oldest, Amelia." He gestured to the girl on Aoife's right side, who had enormous blue eyes and the deep red hair of her father. She stared at me with curiosity as she hugged a stuffed sea turtle to her chest. "And there's Connor." He pointed to the dark-haired boy on Aoife's other side. "And this sleepy fella is Jack."

I pushed aside my mortification and smiled at each of the children, amused to see that Jack was already out cold on his father's shoulder. "You have a beautiful family," I said. "You should be very proud."

"I am," Colin said. "The greatest day of my life was when Aoife, the loveliest girl in all of Ireland, agreed to be my wife," he said. The grin he cast Aoife was full of roguish charm, and she shook her head and sighed.

"You're incorrigible," she said. "And you're still an eejit."

"I am at that," he agreed. His grin deepened. "But you love me."

"With all that I am." She sighed. She leaned forward and kissed him. It wasn't a chaste kiss.

I wasn't sure where to look, but my gaze was caught by Amelia's.

The young girl whispered, in a voice that wasn't a whisper at all, "They do that all the time."

The couple broke apart, and Aoife ruffled her husband's hair and said, "All right, my dearest husband, you've had your fun. Now it's my turn for some craic. Off you pop."

"What?" Colin protested.

"The children are yours," she said. "While I stay and get reacquainted with Chelsea. It's been, what, seven years? We're due for a catch-up."

Oh boy. I wondered if it was going to be a catch-up or an ass chewing, although Aoife *had* said it was her turn for "craic," which in Ireland meant *fun*. Then again, ripping me a new one might be a great good time for her.

I glanced at Colin, looking for help, but he shrugged in resignation and slid out of the booth. Amelia and Connor happily released their mom and latched onto their dad. Aoife kissed baby Jack and each of the children and then slid into the booth across from me. She raised her arm to flag down Michael while Colin leaned in and kissed me on the cheek.

"It was grand to see you again, Chelsea," he said. "Come back out to the farm if you've got time, or better yet, come to the house for dinner."

"We'll see," I said. More accurately, that would happen on the twelfth of never. I lowered my voice and asked, "Aoife doesn't hold grudges, does she?"

"Hide the knives," he said. "You'll be fine."

My eyes went wide, and then I caught the twinkle in his eye and laughed. I took a lingering glance at his square-jawed, handsome face, knowing it was likely the last time I'd ever see him. "It really was great to see you."

Colin glanced at his wife and gave her a wicked wink. "I'll be waiting for you, missus, at home."

"Just make sure it's worth my trouble to come home," she said. Her look was sly.

"Oh, it'll be worth it." He kissed her quick and then hugged the baby close as he strolled out of the pub with his children gathered around him as if he were the pied piper.

The musicians were playing softly in the corner, clearly still warming up, but Colin took the thread of one of their songs and twined it with his rich baritone. He started singing the Irish tune "Whiskey in the Jar," which I hadn't heard since I'd last been here. The rest of the pub regulars joined in as Colin passed by.

Aoife was singing softly under her breath as she watched her man and her children head for home. She blew a kiss in their direction, and Colin caught it with his free hand just before he slipped out the door.

Michael stopped by our booth with two shots of whiskey and two more pints. I glanced at Aoife in alarm. I wasn't sure what to expect from the pretty Irishwoman, so I figured I'd best be blunt.

"Is this where you smash a glass and threaten to go for my throat for going after your man?" I asked. I hoped it sounded like I was kidding, because I was . . . mostly.

Aoife tossed her head back and laughed. "You Americans, you're so dramatic. I have no ill will for you, Chelsea."

"Even though I was having dinner with Colin?" I asked. "I mean, even I know it looked pretty bad."

"I'm not a jealous woman," Aoife said. "It's such a wasted emotion. If Colin did me wrong, then he's not the man I thought he was, and getting jealous certainly wouldn't change that. I'd be the one feeling badly with the twisting snake in my belly, not him."

"True enough."

"Besides, despite his mischievous nature, my Colin is an altar boy all the way through, which is why he sent me the message inviting me to join you," Aoife said. She seemed pleased by this. "He was happy to see you and may have even fancied a bit of a flirt to remember his youth, but if you'd made a play for him, he'd have run so far and fast, you'd not have been able to catch him."

I laughed. I knew Aoife spoke the truth. That was one of the things I'd loved most about Colin. He was good and kind and loyal all the way down to his toes.

"I've no need to fight for what's mine," Aoife said. "He's a steady man, and I'm grateful for it."

"You seem very well suited and happy together," I said. "I'm glad. He deserves a good wife and a happy life."

"Thank you," she said.

She raised her shot of whiskey, and I did the same. We clinked glasses and knocked back the shots. Mine burned a path down my throat, and my eyes smarted as I fought not to cough. Instead, I took a long swig of my beer to wash it down.

"That'll cure what ails you," Aoife said. "At least for the evening."

"Or it'll burn it right out of you," I said. I studied my drinking companion. "When did you and Colin get together?"

"About a year after you left," she said. "He pined for you for a long while."

"I'm sorry about that," I said. I shrugged. "I had to go."

"No need to apologize to me," Aoife said. "I wasn't ready for him the summer I met him, but a year later I was, and because you hadn't come back, so was he. I did wonder why you never returned. You seemed so happy on the farm."

"I was, but I had committed to other jobs, and I knew it was likely my only chance to see the world, and I didn't want to miss it. Then I was called home because . . . my mother was dying," I said. "Everything changed for me after she passed."

"Oh, I'm sorry," Aoife said. She sounded like she genuinely meant it. She reached across the table and put her hand over mine. It comforted me, and I welcomed it. "That's a crushing blow to lose a parent so young."

I nodded. It had been a crusher.

Aoife wasn't one for melancholy, however, and the next thing I knew, she had me up and out of the booth, dancing a reel. The four men were locals, but the other two women were tourists as hopelessly lost at dancing as I was, which made me feel immensely better. There were stubbed toes and people moving in the wrong direction, and occasionally the wrong partner was grabbed. Such as when Aoife grabbed me and danced me out and around the circle to much hilarity.

When the song was over, I was panting and gasping and felt a trickle of sweat run down the side of my face.

"I can't breathe, in the best possible way," I said, wheezing. Then I laughed.

Aoife looked at me, and her eyes were kind. "That laugh. That's the sound my Colin pined for. He always said your laugh made him laugh, too. He was right. It's a good one."

I wiped the sweat off my face with a napkin. I smiled at Aoife and confessed, "I haven't laughed like that in a really long time."

She raised her glass and said, "Then you were overdue. May love and laughter light your days."

"And warm your heart and home," I returned and clinked my glass to hers.

Just before midnight a cabbie appeared, probably the only one in Finn's Hollow and the surrounding area. Colin had sent him to collect his wife. Aoife laughed and insisted that the cabbie drop me off at my cottage first, even though it was a short walk and I could have gotten there in minutes.

Aoife and I hugged each other goodbye like long-lost sisters while the cab driver waited. As I walked to my door, I tripped over a paving stone but caught myself before I fell. I looked at Aoife and asked, "Who put that there?"

She laughed and cried, "Come visit us again, Chelsea Martin. You've got friends in Finn's Hollow!"

I found myself grinning as I unlocked the door to my cottage and stepped inside. Ireland had certainly not lived up to my expectations in any way, and yet I was okay. Surprisingly okay, in fact. Of course it could be the whiskey.

I shrugged off my coat and kicked off my half boots. The cottage was chilly, so I set another peat log in the fireplace and lit it. I sat on the stone hearth and let the fire's heat warm me. My phone chimed and I frowned. It was awfully late for texting, unless it was coming from the States.

I took out my phone and opened the messages. The first one that popped up was a GIF from Jason of Maverick and Goose from *Top Gun* exchanging a high five. I snorted and saw that he'd also left a text message.

Maverick, don't leave me hanging. What's happening? I am dying here. Literally dying.

I wasn't sure why, but I opened his number in my contacts and then paused, staring at it. What was I doing? I didn't want to call him, did I? I was shocked to find I did. Huh. Then again, he'd had a conference call with Severin's community-outreach team. I was definitely curious about how that had gone. Without giving myself a moment for second thoughts, I pressed CALL.

chapter ten

"MARTIN, I WAS about to send out a search-and-rescue party,"
Jason answered on the second ring. "What happened? Was there
a catfight? Did the wife try to take you out? Are you in the hospital?"

"No, no, no," I said. I chuckled. "Aoife—the wife—and I sent Colin
home with the children, and we had a girls' night. Turns out, I'd met
her before."

"Well, that's an unexpected twist," he said. "I'm not sure if I'm more
relieved or disappointed. Unless of course 'girls' night' is a euphemism
for something naughty."

"It's not."

"Pity."

I laughed.

"Let's switch to video," Jason said.

"No, I'm tired, possibly drunk, and—"

"Precisely why I need to get a look at schnockered Martin," he said.
"I don't think I've ever seen you drunk."

"I don't get drunk," I said.

"Thus my point," he said.

"Okay, fine," I agreed. Although I wasn't sure why I was going along with this. I was definitely still the worse for the shots of whiskey, which meant no good decisions were being made.

"Hello." I squinted at my phone when the video link came through.

"Hi there." Jason's face popped up, and I smiled in recognition.

It hit me that I was happy to see someone from home, even Knightley, my resident pain in the ass. I glanced past him and saw his office window and through it the nighttime skyline of Boston.

"You're at work?"

He held up a bound stack of paper. "Severin Robotics, the dossier." Then he yawned.

"Nice, really nice," I said.

"I honestly didn't do that on purpose," he said. "It's just been a long day, and my god, the spreadsheet numbers in this thing could only get an accountant hard."

I snorted. "I like spreadsheets."

"Clearly."

"I tried to warn you that my style and your style don't mesh, but you were so sure you could distill my plan, no problem."

"Yeah, I might have been a bit overconfident there," he said. His tone was rueful. "Don't be mad."

"I'm not. I like that you admitted you were overconfident." I smiled, then waved my hand dismissively. "Besides, I've had too much whiskey to be mad. Brace yourself—I might start singing any minute."

"Ah, so you're one of those cheerful drunks," he said. His eyes were twinkling as he met my gaze.

"True that," I admitted. Then I frowned. "You'd think I'd drink more often."

Jason laughed, and I noticed his eyes appeared to be blue tonight. In the silence that followed, I reached for my conversational fallback. Work. "How did your conference call go?"

"Excellent. I had Eleanor eating out of the palm of my hand."

"Eleanor Curtain?" I asked. "Unibrow Eleanor?" I clapped my hand over my mouth.

"You did *not* just call her that," he said. His delighted laughter boomed out of the phone.

"I didn't mean . . . It's just . . . she can be rather blunt."

"Like her Frida Kahlo brow?" he asked.

"Please forget I said that."

"Oh no, I'm not forgetting," he said. "Since our call wasn't video, I didn't see her or any of the team members, but I consider myself duly warned."

I sighed, hoping that this conversation did not come back to bite me on the behind. I changed the subject. "Have you finished reading my proposal?"

"You left me a lot of reading material," he said. "In fact, I'm only halfway through your very extensive plan for the rollout."

"You'll note the lack of BattleBots," I said.

"Clearly an oversight."

I laughed. He looked at me, and his head tipped to the side as he laughed, too.

"I don't think I've ever heard you laugh before, Martin," he said.

"Probably not," I agreed.

"Which is a shame, because you have a great laugh."

"Thank you," I said. He was the second person to say that tonight. My head was muddled, but I felt there was a significant message here. I studied him. His tie was loose. His hair was mussed, as if he'd run his fingers through it. He looked friendlier than usual. I found myself confiding, "It's one of the reasons I came to Ireland."

"Okay, I feel like I missed a sentence in there," he said. He leaned back in his chair and put his feet on the corner of his desk. "Explain."

I propped the phone up on the coffee table so I didn't have to hold it. The lighting in the cottage was mercifully dim, and the fire was to my back. It felt weirdly intimate to be talking to Jason in the middle of the night. I wondered if I'd regret it in the morning. Probably. I thought about it for a moment and decided I didn't care.

"I don't know if you've noticed, but I am potentially a bit of a workaholic."

He choked on a surprised laugh, which made me laugh, too. It was definitely the whiskey.

"That's the understatement of the century, Martin," he said. "When did you get hit with this sudden epiphany?"

"Someone close to me pointed out that perhaps I'd forgotten how to be happy." I turned around to gaze at the turf log. It was putting out a delicious heat, and I felt like a cat as I stretched and let it bake into my skin and bones.

"That's harsh," he said, bringing my attention back to him. "But I'm still not clear on why that sent you to Ireland."

"It was also suggested to me that revisiting my past might reconnect me with my laughter."

"Your past is Ireland?"

"Among other places."

"And has it worked?"

I could feel the intensity of his gaze coming at me even from the small display window of my phone. I chewed my lower lip, stalling. What could I say?

"I came back, looking for an old friend, and I found him," I said. "I'm glad that I did, but . . ."

"But he's married?"

"Yeah, I mean, I knew that was a distinct possibility," I said. "I figured at the very least he'd have a girlfriend, but I wasn't prepared."

"To see him happy with someone else?"

"Not that so much as the discovery that his life has gone on in such a major way since I saw him, and mine hasn't," I said. I looked at Jason.

"I mean, he's married and with three of the cutest kids. He's put deep roots into the community. It made me feel like I've just been treading water. You know what I mean?"

Jason picked a pencil up off his desk and tapped the palm of his hand with it. It was a gesture of agitation, and I wondered if I'd struck a nerve.

"It's not like you've spent the past several years eating tacos and streaming Netflix," he said. "You've brought in millions of dollars from corporations to help fund the fight against cancer."

"I know, but—"

"I'm not finished," he said. "You've also, through your efforts, raised the level of awareness about preventing cancer. Who knows how many women got screened for breast cancer just because you had the genius idea to have the mobile mammogram bus park outside various corporations and offer free screenings? How many people now put on a hat or sunscreen just because you showed up with your graphs and charts and free gifts as incentives to take better care of themselves? I don't think you're giving yourself enough credit here, Martin."

"Perhaps," I said. I felt a burst of warmth at his use of the word *genius*, but I ignored it. "It's all anecdotal. There's no way to quantify how many lives we've impacted, and I just wonder if I'm not missing the bigger picture in my life."

He narrowed his eyes as he studied me. "Forgive me, but is your biological clock ticking or something?"

"No." I wrinkled my nose at him. "Why do men always think that?"

He shrugged. "Women of a certain age . . ."

"I'm twenty-nine."

"The impending big three-oh sends a lot of people into a tailspin."

"Not me," I insisted. "But maybe I want my weekends to be more than Color Runs, silent auctions, walkathons, cocktail parties, fashion shows, raffles, and wine tastings."

"BattleBots, I'm just sayin'," he said.

I laughed and he did, too.

"I get it," he said. "I do. It's an all-consuming thing that we do, and it's important to make time in your life for more."

"Says the guy who's at the office at eight o'clock at night," I said.

"It's almost nine," he corrected me. "Which means it's close to two o'clock your time. You should cash out, Martin."

I nodded. "You should, too. I'll call you tomorrow, and we can talk more about your conference call with Eleanor if you want, and I can break down my spreadsheets for you. I know you're more of an idea guy than a numbers guy."

"That would be helpful," he said. "See? We make a great team, Martin."

"Whatever," I said. I rolled my eyes, but when I looked at him, he was giving me a lopsided smile that I couldn't interpret. "What? Do I have food in my teeth?"

He chuckled. "No, I'm just . . . This was a pleasant conversation."

"It was, wasn't it?" I asked. I blinked. "You know something, Knightley? You're not so bad when I'm an ocean away from you."

"Sadly, you're not the first woman to say that," he said.

I laughed. "G'night, Goose."

He grinned. "G'night, Maverick."

I ended the call and went to plug in my phone to charge it. The thought of the supersoft mattress awaiting me made me hurriedly brush my teeth and pull on my cow pajamas. Thankfully, I hadn't put those on before I called Jason.

Although I wondered. It was a different Jason who had answered the phone tonight. Or maybe I was a different Chelsea. I was Chelsea who'd consumed several shots and beers, so there was no question I was a much mellower version of myself. I considered the amount of alcohol I'd had, and decided an enormous glass of water and two ibuprofen would not be out of order.

Once I was properly medicated and hydrated, I climbed into bed. I didn't expect to sleep, knowing that I had so many mixed emotions about seeing Colin again to sift through. But a weariness I wasn't prepared for hit me hard and fast as I lay down, and before the breath left my lungs in a big old sigh, I was dead asleep face first in the down-filled pillow. Bless their hearts, the hangover gods had decided to be kind. I woke up with a mild case of cottonmouth, but that was it. No headache, no queasiness—in fact, I was starving. I glanced at the clock. I had just enough time to toss on some clothes and get up to the main house for Darby's Irish breakfast.

I rolled out of bed and hit the ground running, throwing on yoga pants and a sweatshirt. For the first time since I'd arrived, there was not a cloud in the sky, and I paused to marvel at the brilliant jewel-green hills all around me.

The trees were still mostly bare, but their branches were thick with buds. A magpie flitted by in a flash of black and white with a swish of green tail feathers, no doubt looking for something to eat or pilfer. I remembered during my summer in Ireland that I'd learned a group of magpies was called a parliament. I wondered if it was because they always sounded like they were yelling at each other. The thought made me smile.

I climbed the steps to the main house. The smell of sausages and bacon made my mouth water. I hurried into the dining room to find Darby just clearing away the serving dishes.

"And here I was just wondering if we'd see you today, Chelsea," she said. Her smile was wide and warm. "Had a good time at Top of the Hill with Aoife Donovan, did you?"

"I'm not even going to ask how you knew that," I said. I took the plate she offered, and loaded it with what remained of the buffet. When I was satisfied with the meat and potatoes, I topped it with a thick slice of Irish soda bread that was stuffed with caraway seeds and raisins.

"Finn's Hollow is not a large village," Darby said. She waved for me to follow her into the kitchen, where she had me sit at the counter while she poured me a cup of coffee. "I knew you were kicking up your heels before you even got home last night. Did you have a good time?"

"We had great craic," I said, and Darby laughed.

I ate while she did the dishes. For the first time in forever, I felt as if my day was wide open. This was not a feeling I ever had back home as I raced from one meeting to the next, my weekends full of events and my life in a constant state of hurry up and wait. The only thing on my agenda was to pack my meager possessions and hit the road—oh, and to check in with Jason. With the five-hour time difference in my favor, I had plenty of time.

Amazingly, the thought of calling him didn't fill me with the usual dread, so that was something. Maybe we'd managed to build a bridge between our very different personalities last night. It would be nice to be able to work together on the Severin account for Aidan without the usual animosity between us. I wondered if I should be embarrassed that I'd called him while intoxicated. Nah. I was 95 percent sure I hadn't said anything stupid.

I rose from my seat and washed my plate as Darby had moved on to scrub down the counter. Once it sparkled, I put it in the drying rack with the others.

"Darby, if you have some time this morning, could you show me some pole-dance moves?" I asked, surprising myself. I wondered if I was still a little drunk.

Darby turned from the counter and considered me. "What are you doing right now?"

"Nothing," I said.

"Let's go." Darby led the way out of the kitchen, and I followed, thinking, *What have I done?*

"Pick a pole," Darby said.

I chose the one at the back of the room. On the off chance anyone popped by, I wanted to be as far from the door as possible.

"Let's start with the basics," Darby said. "You want to stand on your toes and extend your dominant hand up high and grasp the pole in a firm grip." She demonstrated. "Keep your weight leaning out away from the pole, leaving an arm's length of space from you to the pole. Otherwise, you'll smash into it, which is unpleasant."

"And bad form," I said. So far this all seemed logical.

"Precisely. Take three steps, and on the fourth step, you'll kick off into your spin."

Darby demonstrated. I watched as she stepped around the pole, then grabbed it with her other hand and hooked one ankle around the pole while bending her other leg. She did two revolutions, sliding down the pole as she went, and ended by gliding to a standing position. "This is called the pinwheel. You try it."

I grasped the bar. Darby adjusted my position. She counted the steps while I walked around the pole. And then I grabbed the pole with my other hand and began my swing, tucking one ankle behind the pole while the other leg was bent. Inexplicably, I picked up speed and circled the pole two, three, then four times, spinning faster each time. Oh man, how did I get it to stop? I was hauling ass, literally.

"Loosen your grip," Darby said. "You'll slide down."

"I can't!" I cried. "This is not sexy! I feel like a cabbage in a salad spinner."

Darby laughed. "Unclench your hands!"

I forced my fingers to relax, and sure enough, I slid down the pole, finally landing in a heap on the floor. I looked like a felled gazelle that had some extra junk in the trunk.

"That's the way," Darby said.

I gave her a dubious look.

"It was an excellent start," she insisted.

The lesson continued until I finally managed to spin and slide down the pole without dropping like a rock. We went on to the fireman and the scissor sit. By the time I'd gotten a handle on those, my arms were shaking, my core was wrecked, I had a blister, and I was drenched in sweat. It felt amazing!

When I swiveled down from the final hold, I slapped the floor twice and breathlessly announced, "I'm tapping out."

Darby leaned over me and asked, "You all right?"

"Sure," I said. "Don't I look all right?"

"Take some Nurofen," she said. She gave me a knowing look. "You're going to be sore tomorrow, but on the upside, you have new skills."

I used the pole to pull myself to my feet. "It's a bit like flying, you know, when you're not flailing."

"That's why I fell in love with it," Darby said. "And if I can do it, anyone can, and now I'm teaching it to others."

"In other words, you're living the dream," I said.

"Aye, I've always believed that if I can think it, I can do it," she said. "And I've yet to see any evidence that that's not true."

"You're an amazing woman, Darby O'Shea," I said. I went to hug her and only whimpered a little when I lifted my arms.

chapter eleven

I **T WAS EARLY** afternoon when I drove off with a wave, watching the pretty house and the cottages get smaller and smaller as I went. I motored slowly through the town of Finn's Hollow, smiling as I passed the Top of the Hill where it sat at the bottom.

I wasn't sure where I wanted to land that night. I knew I needed to make my way back to Dublin, but there was no rush, as my flight to Paris wasn't until tomorrow. I decided to take my time and soak in the beautiful countryside of the west counties, not knowing when I'd ever be back this way again.

I was just outside of Limerick and headed into County Clare when the mercurial Irish weather decided to make a mockery of my life choices. I'd gotten a wild hair to go see the famed Cliffs of Moher before heading to Dublin, and I was almost there when a fierce storm blew in, blotting out the colors of the landscape with a blanket of ominous gray.

My small car was buffeted by the wind as the rain came at me sideways, making my wipers practically useless as they tried to swish the rain off the glass. My knuckles gripped the steering wheel until they cramped, and my heart started keeping time with the beat of the wipers.

I squinted through the storm, hoping I didn't surprise any cows or sheep on the roadway, because with the rain this thick, I doubted I'd see them until I was on top of them.

I cursed myself for not checking the weather. Then I double-cursed myself for leaving Darby's delightful cottages. Why had I been in such a hurry to leave? Quite simply, because I was on a quest and Colin's part in it was over.

Had I bothered to check the weather, I'd have chosen differently, but now I was probably going to die on some back road in Ireland. My car would be swept off the road and into a bog, to be sucked into the earth and exhumed hundreds of years from now. My body just a skeleton labeled rando female X, who was smothered by gobs of mud in her car because she was too stupid to live.

A strange noise gurgled out of my throat, something between a whine and a whimper. I was alone in the middle of nowhere, leaving me just vulnerable enough for a scorching case of nerves to come rushing at me, jostling me just like the wind rocked my car.

What if I died out here? I'd never get to see my dad or Annabelle again. I'd never remember what falling in love, laughing wholeheartedly, or being happy felt like.

Panic was making my head buzz, my skin itch, and my breath raspy. My heart was speeding up and slowing down in a weird rhythm that was making it hard to focus on anything except not passing out. My grand adventure, my new start, my search to find myself was going to be cut short when I had a freaking heart attack!

Desperately, I started making deals with the universe. *Shelter*, I bargained. *Give me shelter, and I'll forge on with my journey. I'll find Jean Claude in Paris and reconnect with Marcellino in Italy. I'll do everything I can to find the lighthearted, fearless me of my youth, as opposed to the sweaty, panicked, borderline-hysterical woman I am right now.*

Kilometer after kilometer, I bargained, pleaded with the fates, and wheedled the powers that be for mercy. Darkness, pouring rain, and wind were the only response. I was certain the universe had forsaken me, and I was about to pull over and start planning my trip home—why had I thought this solo trip was a good idea?—when I spotted a very faint light up ahead. Half-afraid I was hallucinating, I stepped on the gas.

I had reached the outskirts of Ennis when a large stone building two stories high appeared on my right. In the encroaching darkness, I could see every window illuminated from within. A stylized sign at the edge of the road announced the place as the Bee and Thistle Inn. I turned my rental car into the drive, not caring that I was lurching through puddles or that the lot looked alarmingly full.

My compact umbrella was helpfully packed in my suitcase in the trunk of the car. I pulled into the lone empty spot at the edge of the parking lot and knew I'd have to make a run for it. I looked down at my favorite black leather boots. If I ran quickly, maybe they would survive. I switched off the engine, grabbed my shoulder bag, and bolted for the door.

Loud music poured out of the inn, waving me in with the promise of happy people, hot food, and a dry bed. I was almost to the front door when my legs, exhausted from this morning's workout, slipped on some mud, and I didn't have the strength to keep my balance. Instead, I flailed and failed, and my heels shot out from under me. I went down with a horrific splash and a smack of my behind on the gravel below that smarted enough to make my eyes water. For a nanosecond, I thought about just sitting there and having a good cry.

A shout sounded, and the next thing I knew, two strong arms were lifting me out of the mud and helping me to the door. The pouring rain soaked me and my rescuer, a man who looked to be about the same age as my father, and when I turned to thank him, my voice was lost in the downpour. Once we stepped inside the inn, my teeth began to chatter, and I turned to thank my hero properly. To my dismay, he was in a tuxedo, and the pink rose pinned to his lapel looked wilted by the blast of the wind and rain.

"I hope I didn't interrupt your swim, lass," he said.

I stood still as the water sluiced off me, forming a small personal reservoir in the lobby, while my butt bone throbbed. I looked at the man in front of me, and the ridiculousness of the moment hit me. I laughed.

"It was my best dive of the night, too," I joked in return, and he grinned. I gestured to his suit. "But I am sorry about your tuxedo and your poor flower."

He grinned at me with a smile so like my father's it made my heart pinch. "Don't you worry about it. Another pint or two, and I won't even feel the damp. Come along—let's get you settled."

The lobby was crowded, and I turned sideways to follow my new friend as we navigated our way through the small groups of people who were all dressed up. The man I followed greeted everyone he passed, and I wondered what was happening to warrant such a celebration.

When we approached the desk, we were joined by another man, who looked remarkably like the first, except instead of touches of gray in his hair, his was fully silver.

"You're a bit late for the party, miss," the older man said to me. He handed each of us a thick, fluffy white towel.

I smiled. "My boat was delayed. I had to swim for it." I began to dry my sodden hair and blot my face, gratefully wrapping my fingers in the towel's warmth.

Both men laughed. The younger of the two said, "I'm Joseph Connor, and this is my father, Niall."

"Nice to meet you both," I said. I offered my freezing cold hand, and it spoke well that neither of them flinched when they shook it.

My rescuer, Joseph, turned to the counter and said, "Elliot, my lad, my new friend is in need of a room."

"Yes, Mr. Connor."

Tall and skinny, Elliot had big ears and an even bigger smile. His brown hair fell over his forehead into his eyes, and he tossed his head to move it out of the way. He looked young, early twenties maybe, but his grin was infectious, and I found myself smiling back at him.

A burst of music came from the big room at the far end of the lobby. I glanced over my shoulder at the boisterous party. A woman in a puffy white gown danced by the open door with a man in a tuxedo. Her head was tipped back as she laughed, and he looked at her as if he was the luckiest man in the world. A wedding. That explained my rescuer's fancy duds. I had a feeling my quest for a room was going to die a quick and painful death right here. Damn.

Elliot tapped at the keys of his computer and said, "We have exactly one room left, but—"

"I'll take it." I was so cold. I didn't care if it was a closet wedged between a noisy kitchen and a smelly bathroom. I was positive I'd sleep through anything, even an all-night wedding reception, if I could just put my weary head down. I handed Elliot my credit card.

"Brilliant." He began to tap on his computer, and I turned to watch the reception in progress. The music and laughter were pouring out unrestrained, and I found myself tapping my toe to the lively beat. I glanced at my phone and noted that it was Thursday. What an odd day for a wedding. I wondered if that was an Irish thing, to have the wedding midweek.

"You're all set," Elliot said. "We do have room service, but the kitchen is a bit busy at the moment. I'd be happy to have them send a tea tray up to you as soon as possible. It may just take a bit. Your room is on the second floor. Room twenty-two, right above us. To give you fair warning, it's a bit on the small side."

Elliot looked at me as if expecting me to complain. I didn't. I took the keycard and said, "Thank you. You can hold off on the tea tray, though. I think I'll be all right."

"Nonsense, you have to eat," Niall said. The Connors looked at each other.

"How do you feel about cake?" Joseph asked.

"I love cake," I said.

"Who doesn't?" Niall asked.

"Exactly," I agreed.

"We'll have some sent to your room," Joseph said. "With a whiskey on the side to warm you up."

I grinned. There really was no beating Irish hospitality. "That would be grand."

My new friends returned to the wedding, and I went up the stairs, happy to let Elliot take my car keys and retrieve my bag for me. Letting people help me was always a struggle for me. Control freak! Also, I didn't like to put people out, okay, and perhaps I felt that no one did things the way I would, meaning the correct way, but I was so tired and sore, I just didn't care.

Elliot had not exaggerated. The room was tiny, barely more than a closet, really, with just enough space for a twin bed, a nightstand with a lamp, and a very small washroom. The lamp was on, so I could see, and the calming blues and greens of the room soothed me. I knew I was going to crash as hard as a bear in hibernation.

Elliot arrived a few minutes after me with my bag and a tray that held a gloriously rich piece of wedding cake, which was the traditional Irish fruitcake, soaked in whiskey and stuffed with sultanas, raisins, and cherries, and slathered in a thick buttercream frosting. It was quite possibly the most decadent dinner I'd ever had, and I was completely here for it.

I thanked him and then maneuvered around my suitcase to put the tray on the small dresser. I settled back on my bed, listening to the sounds of the party below. Every now and again a laugh boomed, but the music was muted to a nice background noise that accompanied the wind and rain that continued to pelt against the window. I drew the thick comforter over myself, planning to rest my eyes, just for a moment, before changing into my pajamas.

It was my phone that woke me out of a deep slumber. I blinked. I'd left the lamp on, so it wasn't dark, but it still took me a moment to remember where I was and how I'd gotten here. The Bee and Thistle Inn outside Ennis.

I listened for a moment, but the rain and wind had stopped, and only the muted sound of the party below and the chime of my phone interrupted the quiet. I checked the clock as I grabbed my phone. It was just after eleven.

I glanced at the display. It was a text from Jason. I winced. I'd told him I'd call him back today, but with the long drive in the storm, I'd forgotten. Feeling a pang of guilt, I called him immediately.

"Martin," he said. "There you are. I called earlier but there was no answer, so I thought I'd send a follow-up text."

"Sorry, I was caught in a surprise storm," I said. "I didn't hear my phone ring."

"Are you all right?"

The concern in his voice sounded genuine, and I couldn't help but think how odd it was that the guy who had driven me nuts for the better part of three years was feeling more like an ally. Weird. Cool but weird.

I could hear noise in the background, like a busy restaurant or maybe a bar. Oh no! Had I called him when he was on a date? Awkward.

"You sound like you're out of the office, Knightley," I said. "Please tell me I'm not interrupting something."

"Define *something*," he said.

"Like a date," I said. I ran a hand through my hair. "Seriously, you should just hang up on me if it's a date. For that matter, what are you doing answering the phone on a date? Rude."

He laughed. "Relax. I've got to say, you are wicked high strung, Martin."

It occurred to me that I liked the way his light Boston accent dropped the *R* in my name, making it *Mahtin*. I shook my head. Everyone said my name like that in Massachusetts—heck, I said my name like that. This was not charming. I was not charmed.

"I'm not high strung," I protested. "I'm just making sure you observe the niceties."

"Appreciate it, but I'm not on a date, as I'm not dating anyone right now. In fact, I just left my bros at a bar, and I'm freezing my tail off as I walk to the T."

"Oh, well, at least you're not chatting on your phone on a date," I said. "That's the worst."

"Noted," he said. "And for the record, I happen to agree."

"Did you call me earlier to discuss the spreadsheet or to strategize a meeting with Severin?" I asked.

"Both," he said. "But given that I'm out of the office and don't have any of my notes with me, it'll have to wait."

"Sorry." I sighed. I hated that I'd missed his call, and now I felt like a screwup. This was not normal for me.

"Don't be," he said. "You're doing me a favor. There's no need to apologize."

"Except that I promised to help you for Aidan, and I'm not much help if I don't answer my phone," I said.

"Seriously, not a big deal," he said. "We can hash it out tomorrow."

"All right. How is Aidan, by the way?" I asked. I was hit with a sudden pang of missing my boss. I hadn't had much time to think about him since I'd heard the news, and when I did, it was with a mild blast of panic that I was so far away and couldn't do anything.

"He's fine," Jason said. "You know him. He plans to meditate right through his treatment and come out the other side."

I could see Aidan doing just that. "That's good to hear. Well, I'll let you go—"

"Hang on," he said. "I can't feel my feet. I'm catching a cab."

I waited until I heard a car door slam and Jason gave the driver his address.

"Wild guess here," I said. "You're wearing your black high-tops, and it probably snowed."

"How did you know?"

"Because you always wear those and you always complain about your feet being wet and cold when it snows."

"So what you're saying is you've noticed me." His voice was amused.

"No, what I'm saying is you're an overgrown man-boy who needs to buy some decent footwear," I said.

"But you have noticed me."

I rubbed my forehead with my fingers. "Why is talking to you always like trying to communicate with a fourteen-year-old? I think I liked you better when I was drunk."

"Everyone likes me better when they're drunk," he said. "It's part of my charm."

Despite myself, I laughed.

"So, where are you right now?"

"At an inn in Ennis," I said. "There's a wedding happening, so it's loud, but I did manage to score a room, some cake, and a whiskey."

"You're living large, Martin."

I chuckled. "Actually, I fell in a puddle, and a lovely man in a tux came to my rescue. I think he's the bride's father but maybe the groom's. I'm not sure. I only know he ruined his tux to help me up and then gave me cake."

"Not all heroes wear capes."

"Indeed."

His voice was amused when he asked, "Why do I think this could only happen to you?"

"I've no idea," I said. "I can assure you my life is not that exciting normally."

"Hang on a sec—I'm at my place," he said.

I listened as he settled up with his cab driver. There was the sound of a door closing, some street noise, and then silence.

"You still there?" he asked.

"Yup."

"Great," he said. "I'm at my building."

"Oh, I should let you go," I said. "We can talk—"

"What?" he asked. "No way. Don't you dare hang up. I want to hear about the rest of your day."

"Why?" I asked.

"Because it sounds way more interesting than my happy hour with the guys," he said. "Besides, I have some office gossip that I'd be willing to share, but you have to bring something to the table."

"Are you holding out on me, Knightley?"

"Oh yeah."

"Switch to video when you get into your apartment," I said. "I want to look you in the eye when you divulge your secrets."

I heard a door shut and keys being tossed, and I imagined he was toeing off his black high-tops. I took a moment to grab the tray off the dresser and sat back against the headboard with my cake and whiskey in my lap. I heard a refrigerator open and shut, and then there was the distinct hiss of a beer bottle cap being twisted open.

"Okay, Martin," he said. "I'm approaching my landing pad, also known as my couch. Let's switch to video."

I waited until my phone signaled that it was him, then I answered. I propped the phone up on the tray so I could talk to him while I nibbled my cake. Now that I was finally warm, I found I was starving. When he appeared on the screen, he was in a similar position on a leather couch with a fleecy blanket pulled up across his chest.

There was an intimacy to the connection, seeing each other in our relaxed positions with the cares of the world held at bay by the cover of our blankets. I glanced away from the picture of him with his dark hair flopping over his forehead and the mischievous glint in his eye. It suddenly felt a little too personal.

"Okay, tell me about your day," he said. "What did you do? Who did you meet? All of it. Don't skimp."

I shook my head, reminding myself that this was Knightley. No need to make it uncomfortable. We were colleagues, after all.

"Well, since you asked, I started my day with a rigorous pole-dancing class," I said.

I caught him on a sip, and beer spewed out of his mouth and all over the phone.

"Shit! Hang on." He jumped up from the couch and hurried to the kitchen for paper towels. He came back and wiped down himself, his phone, and his couch. I managed three solid bites of cake while he was busy. I'm not gonna lie—I took a perverse pleasure out of shocking Knightley.

"Pole dancing? As in exotic dancing? As in stripper pole dancing?"

"It's a form of fitness," I replied, very primly.

"Yeah, sure, fitness," he said. He flopped back onto his couch. There was a delighted glint in his eye. "Any chance there is video of this rigorous class?"

It was my turn to choke on my beverage. "Hell to the no," I said. "And even if there was, you're never going to see it."

"Buzzkill."

"Like I said, talking with you is like chatting with a fourteen-year-old."

"Yeah, yeah, on with the deets." He waved his beer bottle in a *continue* gesture and took a big sip.

"There are no more deets. After that it was a white-knuckle drive to this inn, where I am now enjoying cake," I said. I held up my fork before taking a bite.

He watched me chew in silence for a moment, then his eyes narrowed.

"Martin, I have a very specific question for you," he said. I met his gaze, curious. "Exactly what the hell are you doing in Ireland?"

chapter twelve

TOLD YOU, I'm looking up old friends and stuff," I said. I offered nothing more, even though that wasn't entirely accurate.

"No, actually, you haven't," he said. "You told me you were there because you're a workaholic—no surprise there—and you needed to reconnect with your past, but I know there's something bigger going on, so spill it. Because no one here is talking. Whenever I ask Aidan or your right hand, Julia, they flee the room as if I've set it on fire. So tell me, why did you have to drop everything and race to Ireland? And I don't believe any hokum about finding happiness, because when you were torturing me here in Boston, you looked plenty happy to me."

"That's because I enjoy causing you pain," I replied. Not a total lie either.

"Martin." His voice was low. "Talk to me. Tell me what you're doing."

"Well, tomorrow I'm driving out to the Cliffs of Moher," I said. Truth. "And then I'll drive back to Dublin and fly to Paris."

"France?" he asked.

"Well, I didn't mean Texas."

"So, now you're off to France. Why?"

"It's the next stop on my quest," I said.

He put down his beer and rubbed his hands together. "Now we're getting somewhere. What's the quest, and why are you on it?"

"I'm trying to find myself," I said. He stared at me, waiting, and I found myself adding, "I'm trying to remember what it felt like to—oh god, if you mock me, I'll kill you dead."

"There will be no mockery, I promise." He made some sort of two-finger Boy Scout salute. Whatever.

I stared at him for a second and then said, "I'm trying to remember what it felt like to be in love."

To my eternal relief, he didn't mock. Instead, he tipped his head to the side, curious. "What do you mean, 'trying to remember'? Has it been that long? And why do you need to be across the ocean to do this?"

And then, as if he'd poked a poorly made dam with a stick, what began as a trickle of random words with little meaning suddenly gathered force inside my chest and came out in a deluge of information that I couldn't have held back if I'd tried.

"My father is getting remarried," I said. "To a woman he met just a few weeks ago, because they think they're madly in love. They want me to be in their wedding, but I can't . . . I never . . . I've never even thought about my dad remarrying, and I just . . ."

He waited, not interrupting, not telling me what I should do or feel. He just listened.

"When my father told me he was getting remarried, I couldn't find it in myself to be happy for him," I said. "I just kept thinking, *Why?*"

"Why what?"

"Why did he want to get married, why now, why her, why not just live together, and why did he want me to be a part of it—you know, *all* the whys," I said.

"I'm guessing that didn't go very well."

"Now who's the master of understatement?" I asked. "My father was hurt, and then he asked me when I'd stopped letting love into my heart."

"*Oof*, that had to be tough," he said.

I nodded. I met his gaze, saw the sympathy there, and quickly looked away. "It was. And of course my younger sister, Annabelle, thinks it's all great, and she's all over me because why can't I be happy for Dad, blah, blah, blah. It got a little ugly, especially when she pointed out that I haven't been in a real relationship since my year abroad seven years ago."

"Seven years?" he asked. He sounded flabbergasted, and his eyes were huge. Like seeing-a-flying-saucer huge.

"Yeah," I said. "During my postcollege gap year, before my mom passed away, I fell in love three times, with Colin in Ireland, Jean Claude in Paris, and Marcellino in Italy. Annabelle thought if I went back and found these guys, then maybe I'd remember what it felt like to fall in love, and I'd be okay with my dad getting remarried. It's crazy, I know, but I didn't know what else to do." I shoveled more cake into my mouth.

"Whoa, whoa, whoa." Jason picked up his beer and took a long gulp. When he finished, he lowered the bottle and leveled his gaze on me. "Are you telling me you had three different men in your life in one year and no one since?"

"Do not slut shame me," I said. I pointed the empty fork at him as if I'd stab him with it. "I was twenty-two, it was a year abroad, and I loved every one of them."

He made an annoyed face. "What? I would never. Three in a year is completely respectable. It's the seven-year dry spell that has me boggled."

"It wasn't totally dry," I said. "There just wasn't anyone who was relationship material."

"No, I refuse to accept that in all of Boston, you couldn't find one man who was shaggable on a semipermanent basis."

"I couldn't," I insisted.

"Really?" he asked. "And you're not even going to pretend to consider me for a moment? I'm hurt, Martin, really hurt."

I laughed, knowing he was teasing me, and he grinned in return.

"So, that's my story, and I don't want to talk about it anymore. Now, what's the office gossip?" I asked. "I feel so disconnected from everyone."

"Well, it started as a major brouhaha over the staff-room refrigerator," he said.

"Why?" I asked. "And also, I was really looking for more of a who spatted with whom."

"Oh, this is even better than a spat," he said. "Because it involves a mystery."

"I'm listening."

"You know Michelle Fernando from Human Resources?" he asked.

"Yup." I tried not to make a face, but it slipped out.

"I can see you *do* know her," he said.

I bit my lip. "She's just a bit rigid, you know? And coming from me, that's saying something."

He laughed. "Indeed. Well, someone got into the turkey club sandwich she brought for lunch a few days ago and took a quarter of it."

"A quarter? Why not take the whole thing?"

"Exactly," he said. He raised one eyebrow. "Needless to say, the signs went up immediately. She positively papered the place, calling out the culprit and demanding reimbursement."

"Michelle does love her copy machine signs," I said. "Let me guess, the font was Helvetica."

Jason laughed. "As in give them hell-vetica? Yes, it was—in bold. And yesterday she had a personal pizza in the fridge, and someone took one slice, or again, one quarter of the pie."

"No way."

I knew I shouldn't laugh, but I did anyway. It was hard to feel badly for Michelle. The woman had a well-deserved reputation for being a jerk, which had proven true when one of my team members wanted to take an extended maternity leave and Michelle refused. We'd almost come to blows over it because of the sheer unreasonableness on Michelle's part in not letting the new mom attach her accumulated vacation time to her leave.

And as for me personally, she had positively vibrated with disapproval when Aidan and I filled out the paperwork for my leave of absence. She was one of those people who should never be given any sort of power. Ever. I couldn't help but admire whoever was messing with her.

"Picture, if you will, Michelle, arms straight, hands balled into fists, stomping through the office, demanding to smell everyone's breath to see who had eaten her pizza," he said.

"She didn't!"

"She did."

I howled. "I am dying."

"I know. It's been as entertaining as all get-out," he said. "Honestly, I can't wait to see what the Quarter Thief does next."

"Is that what everyone is calling him?"

"For now."

"I like it." I met his gaze and found a warmth in his eyes that I hadn't seen before. I wondered if I'd been too hard on him over the past few years. Maybe Aidan was right and Knightley wasn't so bad after all.

"So, Paris tomorrow?" he asked, breaking the silence.

"*Oui*, and then I'm going to meet up with my friend Marcellino in Italy, hopefully for the annual wine festival at his vineyard, Castello di Luce—depending upon how things go in Paris, of course." It made me feel vulnerable to share this much with Knightley, but I refused to be embarrassed that he knew about my quest. I'd made the decision to share, and there was no going back now.

"Well, now I'm jealous. Bon voyage, and this time, Martin, find out if he's married first."

I picked up my phone, preparing to finish the call. "Never going to hear the end of that, am I?"

"Nope," he said.

I rolled my eyes and smiled before hanging up.

. . . .

RETURNING MY RENTAL car took longer than I'd anticipated, because of course it did. I got lost on my way to the Dublin airport from the Cliffs of Moher—totally worth it—and ended up at the wrong gate with a big old poster of John F. Kennedy smiling down at me while I tried to figure out where I was supposed to be. Naturally, my phone began to ring.

I checked the display. It was Aidan. Worried that it was some dire news about his cancer, I answered as I sprinted across the terminal, dragging my bag behind me.

"Aidan, hi, how are you?" I dodged a toddler who'd stopped for no apparent reason, zipped around a man in a wheelchair, and passed a couple who, guessing by their body language, were in the midst of a tear-fueled breakup. Judging by her lack of tears and his quivering lip, it was her doing the breaking, not him.

"Never better," he said. He sounded chipper. "Listen, I know you're busy, but I wanted to ask a favor of you."

"Sure, what do you need?" I checked my boarding pass and read the gate number. I needed to be at sixteen. "Not to rush you, but I'm just about to board my plane to Paris."

"Yes, I know," Aidan said. "Jason mentioned you were headed to Paris and Italy, which is coincidentally where Robbie Severin is going to be. Severin reached out to us, Chelsea, and he'd like to meet with you in Tuscany. Can you do that?"

"What?" I dashed to the gate. I was going to kill Jason. Why had he told Aidan about Paris and Italy, and how had it come up with Severin? I mean, not that where I was going was a big secret, but what else had he told Aidan about my trip? Who else had he told? I had a sudden vision of Jason yukking it up at the water cooler as he told everyone at the ACC about my ex-boyfriend in Ireland being married. Argh.

I couldn't hear Aidan over the airport noise and switched the phone to my other ear, hoping it was clearer. The flight display board behind the person at the counter read *Paris* with the correct departure time and flight number. Phew. I moved to the end of the boarding line.

"So, the wine festival in Tuscany next week," Aidan said, raising his voice. "Can you meet Severin there?"

"Next week? Why does he want to meet there?" I stalled. I'd been in touch with Marcellino online. He was the only one of the three I'd been able to connect with, and I'd been looking forward to visiting him, but we hadn't nailed down a specific date. My travel plans were pretty fluid, since I was retracing my steps and not knowing what I'd find—like a married Colin. Now if I had to hurry to Italy to entertain Severin, who was notoriously odd, it could ruin everything in Paris.

"He just wants to meet you," Aidan said.

"But I don't have my laptop or my files or anything," I protested. Several people got in line behind me, looking as harried as I felt. "It's not like I can give a presentation or anything."

"This is more social than business," he said. "I think he's just looking to make sure his contribution is in capable hands. Can you do this?"

I had no idea what was going to happen in Paris with Jean Claude, and I hated promising to be in Italy when it might prove to be ill timed or really inconvenient, but this was Aidan. He was my mentor and my friend, and he needed me. There was no choice to be made.

"Of course, I'll do it," I said.

"That's my Chelsea," Aidan said. I could just picture his crooked grin behind his beard.

The line moved. I was next up.

"Your passport and boarding pass, miss?" asked the airline representative. She glanced at my bag with a frown. "We'll have to check that here at the gate, as the overhead bins are already full. You almost missed your flight."

"Sorry, Aidan, I have to go," I said. I was feeling frantic and rushed, two emotions that always put me on edge. "I'll be in touch when I land."

I ended the call, hearing Aidan say goodbye as I shuffled my things, trying to hand the airline rep my boarding pass while managing my passport—I could hear my dad's voice in my head, saying, *Don't lose your passport*—my phone, and my bags. I must have looked like a hot mess as the woman smiled at me in a reassuring way, handing my pass back once the machine registered it with a beep.

"Have a nice flight," she said.

"Thank you," I replied.

I hurried down the gangway, relieved to be on my way, only to stop at the end, where people were still waiting to board. Hurry up and wait, hurry up and wait. The joys of travel.

THE FLIGHT WAS mercifully short. We were barely up, then we were down. When the plane had landed, I reached for my phone, only to discover that it wasn't in my purse. I checked everywhere in and around my seat as my panic slowly built. Suddenly, the top of my head went cold. And as the chill spread down through my body, I remembered with a flash that I had stuffed my phone into the outside pouch of my carry-on bag while carefully putting my passport in the zippered pocket inside my shoulder bag.

Like a nut, I raced down to baggage and watched with increasing dismay as my cute little carry-on did not appear on the carousel. I gave it a half hour, and only when all the bags had been claimed did I finally accept the truth. There was no bag for me.

"I am so sorry, mademoiselle. I will need you to fill out this property irregularity report," said the middle-aged man with a name tag that read *Daniel* behind the customer service desk at the Charles de Gaulle Airport.

The same carry-on that the airline person had told me would have to be loaded onto the plane after the passengers boarded, because the overhead bins were full. And now here I was with no phone and no bag. Argh, this was a nightmare.

It was taking everything I had not to have a complete and total stress meltdown. How was I supposed to contact anyone without my phone? My father and sister were going to freak out if they didn't hear from me. Thankfully, when I had booked the studio apartment in Paris from the Bee and Thistle Inn in Ennis, I'd had the foresight, or sheer dumb luck, to text the name and address to my father. Worst-case scenario, he'd be able to find me through the owner.

Right now, the best I could hope for would be to find an Internet café and send a follow-up email. That would tide my family over, but what about all the other things I used my phone for, starting with stalking my ex-boyfriend in Paris? How was I supposed to track down Jean Claude now?

I filled out the form with the pen Daniel gave me, grateful that I remembered the address of the apartment I had rented. I'd chosen a place in the same neighborhood I'd lived in before, so I knew the area quite well, or at least, I had seven years ago.

Daniel, with the close-cropped gray hair, kind eyes, and lovely French accent, assured me that they would be in touch about my suitcase. When I pressed him for specifics, he stated that as soon as my bag was located, it would be hand delivered to my apartment. He almost made it sound like having my bag delivered was the best possible outcome. Sure, but not nearly as convenient as having my bag in hand right now.

It wasn't his fault—I knew that. So I smiled and thanked him and wished him a nice day. He seemed grateful that I didn't rip into him, and repeated his promise to have my bag reunited with me as soon as possible. I left the counter with nothing but the clothes on my back, my purse, and the vague feeling that I was forgetting something big. But I wasn't; I was just *missing* something big.

What if they never found my bag? What if my phone was lost for good? What if it was never recovered? What was I going to do? I gave myself a mental shake. People had lived for thousands of years without cell phones; I could survive a day or two, even if the thought of it made me slightly queasy.

A quick survey of my handbag revealed I had my wallet, passport, sunglasses, a brush, and a pack of breath mints. Surely I could survive on that for a day. Calmer, I went in search of the train that would take me into the city, hoping that the inauspicious start to my Paris adventure was not an indicator of worse things to come.

Since my plane had landed at Terminal One, I needed to catch the free shuttle to Terminal Three, where I could pick up the blue-line train, which would take me into the city center, since the airport was twenty-five kilometers outside of Paris. Normally while traveling, I could switch off my expectations and downshift into a sort of travel Zen; things would happen when they happened, and there was no need to get upset. Of course this was mostly because I spent weeks and weeks preparing for every possible contingency.

Still, it was a giving-up-control sort of mind-set that usually served me well when I was out of my comfort zone, but today, that feeling was gone. I knew it was because I didn't have my phone or my cow pajamas or even a toothbrush. It was easy to feel all *que será, será* when you could reach out to anyone anytime and anywhere, but now I felt cut off and abandoned, and I hated it.

The only upside to not having my carry-on bag was that I navigated the thick crowds with a cheetah-like speed and grace, maneuvering in and around people and their stuff, unencumbered. I knew I was really going to miss my cow pajamas tonight, however.

I leaped from the shuttle to the platform with the blue-line ticket dispenser. I waited for the train with a crush of travelers and then hopped aboard as soon as the departing passengers got off. I had to check the colorful diagram on the inside of the train to figure out what my stop was. It looked like I'd have to do some train hopping to get there. Online, I'd found a sweet studio apartment above a café in Paris 8, the eighth arrondissement, which was one of the numbered neighborhoods of Paris.

I wondered if the family I'd worked for still lived in the same area. It had been a swank apartment off the Avenue Montaigne. The girls, Vanessa and Alyssa, had been four and five when I'd been charged with their care, and we'd spent gorgeous autumn days roaming around the city parks, eating fresh bread and drinking thick hot chocolate, while I people watched and the girls ran out their wiggles in between their dance lessons, which had been many. Madame Beauchamp had loved the ballet, and nothing would have pleased her more than to have one of the girls pursue her dream.

Monsieur Beauchamp had worked long hours, and Madame Beauchamp had been a socialite, always busy with one glamorous event or another. I had been one in a parade of young women hired to care for the sisters until they were old enough to be sent to an elite boarding school in Switzerland. When I had expressed dismay to the housekeeper about the girls spending so little time with their parents, Madame Bernard had shrugged. This was how the children of the wealthy were raised. To me, it had felt so distant and cold. I'd tried my best to make my time with the girls as magical as I could. Jean Claude, charmed by my concern for the girls, had helped.

I remembered one day in particular, when we'd taken the girls on a picnic on the banks of the Seine. The sisters had worn matching dresses and tights, per usual. I did this not because I thought it was cute— although it was—but because I figured if I lost one child, all I had to do was look at the remaining one to know exactly what the missing one had been wearing. Thankfully, I'd never had to use this trick.

It had been early autumn at the time. The chestnut trees had been just turning gold, and to me, the day had felt like a postimpressionistic painting by Georges Seurat. I'd sat on the blanket with our food, watching Jean Claude and the girls run in the grass as he taught them how to fly kites, thinking what a wonderful father he'd make. He'd caught me watching him and winked, as if letting me know he knew what I was thinking. I'd blushed so hard, I'd feared I might pass out. That. That was the sort of feeling I wanted to feel again.

I hopped off the RER train at Châtelet–Les Halles and switched to the Metro line that would bring me into the Golden Triangle, the wealthy section of Paris made up of the Avenue des Champs-Élysées, the Avenue Montaigne, and the Avenue George V, which was the beating heart for shoppers in Paris. It had been a long time since I'd navigated public transportation in the city, but it all came rushing back.

I inhaled deeply as I left the white brick tunnel of the Alma-Marceau stop and climbed the stairs up to the street. I was always struck by the distinctively sweet smell that was Paris. Fresh-baked bread intertwined with the bouquets from the flower vendors on the corners and with subtle notes of tobacco smoke that blended with the pungent fumes of the Metro and the overlying scent of the towering chestnut trees. It was uniquely Paris, and breathing the sweetness in, much like I had the brine- and peat-laced aroma of Ireland, brought me roaring back to my time here seven years ago.

I walked the three blocks to the quiet neighborhood street where I had rented a tiny studio apartment. The sidewalk was crowded, but I didn't mind. Despite the lack of my phone or my luggage, there was something so magical about being in the City of Light that I just couldn't be glum.

I wound my way past a Franprix, a *boulangerie*, a tobacco store, and a *pharmacie*, all with their awnings out. I noted the window displays, as I suspected I'd be doubling back to buy necessities, since I didn't even have deodorant. Finally, on the corner, Café Zoe appeared. I remembered from the instructions in the rental agreement that I was to pick up the keys at the café, because Zoe Fabron owned the café and the apartments above as well.

The circular tables of the small eatery spilled out onto the sidewalk, arranged in rows facing the street, as if watching the world go by was the preferred way to enjoy a meal. I ducked to the side as a waiter carrying a full tray on his shoulder came out the wide door of the restaurant. Dressed in black pants and a white shirt, he had a burgundy half apron tied around his waist. The same pinot noir color was the accent color for the window trim. It all looked very put together.

An older gentleman with white hair and a cane hooked on his forearm held open the door for me. I said thank you in French—"*Merci,*" not the hardest word in the language—and stepped inside. Although a touch warmer than Ireland, the day was still brisk, and I appreciated the heat of the café.

The interior was traditional, with a black-and-white tile floor, burgundy half curtains on the windows, and small silver café tables and chairs with rounded backs, filling all the available space. The walls were papered in a lovely black-and-white toile with repeating scenes of ladies in big gowns and gents in knee-length breeches, strolling under tall trees, riding horses, or playing with puppies. Ornately framed mirrors were hung at random, along with vintage posters of Paris. A service counter was at the far end of the room, bracketed by two large pastry cases, one of which was filled with croissants and breads and the other with enormous meringues, cream tarts with fresh raspberries, and several bowls of chocolate mousse decorated with chocolate curls.

I felt my stomach rumble, and I put my hand over my belly, hoping no one else had heard. I realized I hadn't eaten since I'd left the west counties of Ireland that morning, and that had been a quick and rather soggy sandwich while making a gas stop on my way into Dublin.

The woman taking orders behind the counter was tall and slender. Her dark skin was complemented by the pale-blue blouse she wore with the collar up and the sleeves rolled back to her elbows. Her shoulder-length braids were held back with a wide white headband of eyelet lace, which framed her heart-shaped face becomingly. Her smile was genuine as she gave her customer their change and called their order over her shoulder, back into the kitchen. The chef, who was just visible through a small window, was wearing a toque with many pleats and chef's whites, and he waved a hand, letting her know he'd heard her.

As I approached, I watched the woman assess the happenings in the café with a sweeping glance, and I noticed she had an air of command to which the rest of the staff deferred. Perhaps this was Zoe?

"*Bonjour, vous désirez?*" the woman asked.

"*Bonjour,*" I answered and promptly ran out of French. I shrugged and added, "I'm Chelsea Martin. Are you Zoe Fabron?"

The woman clapped her hands and smiled in delight. Her English had the most beautiful lilt as she said, "I am. And you are my guest for apartment two, *oui*?"

"Yes," I said. I gestured to my windblown and wrinkled self. "I'm sorry—I'm a bit of a mess. My suitcase went missing, and my phone was in it. In fact, has the airport called to say they found my bag? I told them to call here."

"*Oh, non non.*" Zoe clucked her tongue in sympathy. "They have not called, but I am sure they will." She turned to the young woman working beside her and spoke rapidly in French. It was clear she was instructing her about the airport and my bag. Then she turned back to me and said, "Follow me, *s'il vous plaît*. We will get you settled."

She opened a drawer and grabbed a key on a small chain, then she came around the counter and gestured for me to follow her. We walked—well, I walked and Zoe glided—back through the café and out onto the sidewalk. In her tailored capri pants and black leather flats with pale-blue forget-me-nots embroidered on the toes, Zoe cut a perfectly elegant figure, which by comparison made me feel even more schlumpy and gross, if that was even possible.

There was a bright-blue door on the side of the café. Zoe unlocked it, and it opened into a small vestibule with mailboxes. Stairs ran up one side of the foyer to a floor above. She gestured for me to follow her, and we climbed the steps until we were in a narrow hallway.

Zoe turned to me and said, "This floor used to be one very large apartment for a family, but I turned it into four small apartments. It was too difficult to rent the big one, but I always have travelers for the small ones. I hope you will be comfortable here."

"I'm sure it will be fine," I said. I wasn't sure if it was because I'd reached my destination or if the time change was catching up to me or what, but suddenly I was so tired, I was certain I could have bunked down on a windowsill and slept happily through the night.

Zoe passed the first apartment door and then stopped in front of apartment number two. She unlocked the door and then stepped back, allowing me to enter first. I stepped inside and caught my breath. It was lovely.

Directly across from the entrance was a set of French doors, which opened onto a narrow terrace that overlooked the street. A fireplace was on one side of the room, with a small couch in front of it and two armchairs. Tucked into the corner was a kitchenette with the smallest stovetop range and microwave I had ever seen. It was like being in a microhouse. A bathroom was off the kitchen, and it was equally compact, with room for a toilet, sink, and stand-up shower. They were wedged in so tight I was convinced I could use all three at one time. A wide wooden ladder was in the corner, and I glanced up to see that it led to a narrow loft where a bed, a small dresser, and a lamp filled the space.

The room was painted creamy white, as were the fireplace and mantel and the ornate crown molding that ran along the top of the walls where they met the ceiling. The furniture was done in shades of charcoal gray, accented by an apple-green pillow and a matching hand-knit afghan, which caught my eye and broke up the monotony of the gray. A white faux-fur rug and a glass coffee table completed the living area, and the only dining space I could see was the two barstools at the counter that separated the kitchenette from the rest of the apartment. It was perfect, absolutely perfect.

"You look fatigued, Mademoiselle Martin," Zoe said. "May I send some food up from the café for you?"

"Thank you, that is so kind of you," I said. "And please call me Chelsea."

"And you must call me Zoe—everyone does," she said. "There is shampoo, soap, and what do you say, um, *brosse à dents*?" She mimicked brushing her teeth. "In the *toilette*."

"Oh, thank you," I said. I was so relieved I wouldn't have to go out that night and track down the basics, I might have wept. "That is very helpful."

"So many people forget to pack them. I make sure we keep them in every apartment," Zoe said with a shrug. "Make yourself at home."

"*Merci beaucoup.*" I was so hungry there was quite literally nothing I wouldn't eat right now, even the more exotic French foods, like snails, pig's feet, beef tongue, or calf's head—I did not care. That expression *hungry enough to eat a bear*? I was there.

"*Bienvenue à Paris, Chelsea,*" Zoe said. She kissed me once on each cheek and pressed the key to the apartment into my hand. "I will let you know if the airport calls about your luggage."

"Thank you," I said.

When the door closed after Zoe, I crossed to the window and watched as the sun began to set and the lights of the city blinked on one after another. I hugged myself tight. I wanted quite desperately to be brave, to be a better, stronger version of myself, but without a decent change of clothes or fresh underwear, it was hard to feel like anything other than a sad bedraggled waif. I could feel the DJ of the pity party starting to ramp up the "Why Me?" tune in my soul. I shut that shit right down.

Having met so many cancer survivors during my years with the ACC, I never allowed myself to whine over minor misfortunes, because the truth of it was "Why Not Me?" Bad things happened to everyone. Full stop. The only grace to be found was in how you handled it. And so I took in the amazing lights rolling out to the horizon and the blue strobe light sweeping across the cityscape from the peak of the Eiffel Tower, and I thought that of all the places I might find my old self, Paris seemed the most likely. At least, I hoped so.

chapter thirteen

AWOKE TO the feel of downy feathers crunched under my cheek. The light was wrong for my apartment in Boston, which would be a dreary gray at best, given that my bedroom overlooked an alley and any incoming sun was blocked by the building next door. It was also wrong for Ireland. Mornings there began with a thick fog that had to be burned away layer by layer before the sun could light up the green hills.

This light was different. It was bright and stark, illuminating all the cobwebs in my mind and scaring the spiders away. Or maybe it was just that I'd been so stupid tired that I'd forgotten to draw the curtains and the light was blasting into the small apartment like God's flashlight, waking me up at . . . I reached for my phone to check the time. Oh yeah.

The smell of fresh-baked bread was the final nudge I needed to get out of bed and face the day. Surely the café would be open and serving breakfast by now, no matter what time it was. Without a change of clothes, I'd had to rinse out my underthings and let them dry on the heated towel rack in the bathroom. The rest of my clothes, minus the T-shirt I'd slept in, I'd hung up so they could air out. This had taken the absolute final bit of my energy last night.

I climbed down from the loft and pulled on my mostly dry underthings and yesterday's clothes. When I arrived downstairs, the café
was already doing a brisk business. People were standing in line, voices
were engaged in rapid-fire conversations that I couldn't have followed
with a translator at my elbow, and the smell of cinnamon pastries and
coffee hung in the air like the most delectable perfume.

There was no sign of Zoe behind the counter, so I assumed she came
in later. I ordered an espresso and a *pain aux raisins*, which melted in my
mouth and made me long to eat four more. I resisted. The lure of Paris
and a desperately needed change of clothes called to me like a siren to a
sailor. The woman working at the counter—her name tag read *Annalisse*—
had been there the night before, and I asked her if the airline had called
about my missing luggage. Annalisse shook her head regretfully with a
look of pained sympathy. At least, I hoped it was sympathy.

I wondered if she was merely reacting to me because my clothes
appeared distressed, as if they'd arrived in Paris under their own power,
swimming down the Seine, perhaps. Despite my overnight airing out,
both my pants and shirt felt as if they had a lot of miles on them. I did
the sly stretch and sniff to see if my top was offensive. I didn't smell
anything, but that didn't necessarily mean I was okay. I had once heard
that people become immune to their own funk. Fabulous. I'd probably
offended the entire restaurant.

Mercifully, the café offered coffee to go, a fairly recent development
in Paris, so I finished my pastry and espresso and ordered a steaming
hot coffee in a paper cup for my journey. The sun was out, but the
morning air was brisk. I burrowed into my wool coat as I walked away
from the Golden Triangle, knowing that the prices of clothing in this
district were going to be well out of my range. Instead, I kept my eye
out for three things: an Internet café, a pharmacy, and a reasonably
priced clothing store.

The hustle and the bustle of the city soon had me moving faster
than I was ready for, but that was all right. I loved walking along the

Avenue George V. There was almost more eye candy than a person could take in. Men in suits, women in dresses, au pairs walking children to one of the city parks, tourists gawking at the tall cream-colored Lutetian-limestone Haussmann buildings that lined the streets in this part of Paris, and the endless boutiques, salons, antique stores, and restaurants that filled the bottom floors.

I stepped around a row of scooters, which were parked in clusters up on the wide sidewalks, keeping them out of the road, and saw the green plus sign that indicated a *pharmacie* up ahead. Excellent. It looked like the hygiene was happening first. Thankfully, the woman in the white lab coat working at the front counter understood my pantomime of putting on deodorant. There wasn't much to choose from, not like the wall of lip glosses, but that was fine. It was a step closer to being civilized.

While the woman rang up my purchase, I asked if she knew where I could find an Internet café. The woman didn't understand at first, but when I mimicked typing, she nodded. Instead of trying to explain, she wrote down the address on a slip of paper and handed it to me. I recognized it as a side street off the Rue de Rivoli. It was a bit of a walk, but that would give me a chance to shop for clothes, too.

I headed back out into the bright day, stuffing the small paper bag into my large handbag. It was a small errand, but the feeling of accomplishment gave me a surge of optimism. Once I was able to send my family a message and buy a new outfit, I'd be ready to tackle seeing Jean Claude again. I hoped.

I found two boutiques on my walk, where I managed to score some essentials—pants and shirts, nothing as comfy as my flannel cow pajamas, but I'd survive. Of course, I still wanted a dress to wear when I saw Jean Claude, but I'd worry about that later.

Right now, I needed to touch base with my team. With any luck, when I returned to my small apartment, my suitcase and phone would have arrived, but in the meantime, I wanted to make sure I let everyone know I'd arrived in Paris safely but was missing my phone.

Naturally, I got lost looking for the cybercafé. Shocker. I popped into a small bar that had a very "locals only" vibe. The only patrons were a cluster of old men sitting at a table in the back. I approached the counter and asked in my admittedly rusty French for help in finding the address the woman had given me at the *pharmacie*.

The short, bald, pasty man on the other side of the bar looked me up and down with a disdainful curl of his lip and then very clearly said, "No."

I blinked. For real? He wasn't even going to point me in the right direction? I opened my mouth to try again, but he walked away. I was dismissed.

Rude! I turned to leave, passing a tall man with dark-brown skin and soft brown eyes, wearing a corduroy coat and a hand-knit beanie. He gave me a friendly smile and asked, "You are lost? May I help?"

My shoulders dropped in relief. "Yes," I said. I showed him the address, and he walked me outside and pointed in the direction I needed to go.

"At the one, two red light, turn right," he said. His accent was thick, but I knew what he meant.

I put my hand on his arm and said, "Thank you. You're very kind."

He smiled. "Enjoy your time in France."

"I will," I said. I walked away, appreciating that it seemed important to him that I think of his country and its people fondly, unlike that other miserable little man.

Instinctively, I reached into my handbag for my phone. I wanted to share this moment with someone. Annabelle, my dad, or maybe Jason, who would get a laugh when I told him France had its own people with the grumpy personality of Michelle Fernando. When my hand grasped nothing, I remembered why I was walking to an Internet café. Snap! With a sigh, I trudged on.

Sure enough, I took the designated right, and the building loomed up ahead like a two-story monster with a trendy exterior and signs announcing that it offered use of the Internet, printing, and an e-sports arena that was open twenty-four hours per day. Good to know that if I got a wild hair to go on a *Zelda* quest at three o'clock in the morning, there was a place for me.

I walked in, surprised to find virtually every computer in use. As I approached the service desk, I took in the bright interior. It was nice to find that the place did not look like some dark, smelly teenage hangout space, but rather it was slick and professional. I asked to use a computer to check and send email. The man, who appeared to be in his twenties and had a perpetual-student air about him, told me the rate was one euro per hour, and when I paid, I was assigned to a vacant computer with a large monitor over in the corner on the far side of the room.

I settled in and opened my nonwork email. I quickly sent a message to my dad and sister, explaining that I'd lost my suitcase and that my phone was in it. I told them to call Café Zoe if they needed me and that Zoe would get the messages to me. I wasn't a big user of social media, so I didn't bother going to those pages.

Lastly, I opened my work email. This was a bad idea. Despite having set it to a "temporarily out of office" auto reply option, the emails had clearly kept coming in like a tsunami of neediness. I scrolled through, glancing at the volume of new messages, which made my rage for order itch like a bad rash. I knew if I opened one, I was done for, and this was not how I wanted to spend my hour. Instead, I sent my colleague Julia a message, asking her to tell everyone the same thing I'd told my family—basically, I'd be in touch. I hoped this would put everyone's mind at ease.

Once that was accomplished, I hunkered down to do an Internet deep dive on Jean Claude Bisset. As Jason had suggested, I wanted to find out if he was married, engaged, or other. I was not going to get caught flat footed again. While I had done some research on him before I left the States, there simply hadn't been time to follow all the references for Jean Claude. Where Colin had been nonexistent, Jean Claude was everywhere. Frankly, it intimidated the heck out of me. This time when I met up with an ex, I wanted to know as much as I could about him before I showed up on his doorstep, potentially making an idiot of myself.

My initial search didn't offer much more information than I'd gotten before, which was pages and pages of his image with all the movers and shakers of the fashion industry. Jean Claude did not have a clothing line of his own, as had been his dream, and he was now listed as a designer at Absalon instead of the House of Beauchamp, where I'd met him. I'd heard of the designer Absalon Brodeur, known just as Absalon to the world at large. He was a hot ticket in the fashion scene, judging by the buzz that was generated after his show, where Anna Wintour had been seated front and center.

As I scrolled through the most recent Absalon shows, I saw several pictures that included the designers currently in-house. I scanned the faces, looking for him, and just like that, my breath caught. There he was, looking out at the camera as if he knew all the secrets of the person taking the picture. I felt a thrill ripple from my head to my feet. That! That was the sizzle and zip I was looking for, and he—*Jean Claude*— was right here in Paris 8.

I checked the date of the picture just to confirm. The calendar had flipped from March to April since I'd left the States, and this picture was from Paris Fashion Week six months ago. He was here. My heart started to beat triple time in my chest, but I couldn't tell if it was excitement or panic. Could I do this? Could I track down this gorgeous man whom I hadn't seen in seven years on the off chance that he remembered me?

I studied the picture. The truth was Jean Claude was so far out of my league, surrounded by models and aristocrats, billionaires and artists, that it was laughable that I'd even attempt to contact him. Still, there was no mention of a wife or girlfriend. Could I just walk away and not see him again? No.

Decision made. I noted the address of the Absalon design house on the Avenue Montaigne and closed the browser windows. Newly resolved, I pushed back from the computer, grabbed my shopping bags, and hurried to the door. If I was going to do this, I was bringing my A game. Calling *"Merci"* to the man at the counter, I dashed from the Internet café.

BACK AT CAFÉ Zoe, I was disappointed to find that my suitcase had not magically appeared. There were no messages from my family or work, so I assumed my emails had arrived and all was well or they had yet to read my emails—it was still morning in Boston, after all, so they might catch up to me later.

I dropped my loot in my apartment and went back downstairs to strategize while fortifying with a good lunch. I was a planner. I needed bullet points, a spreadsheet, or at the very least a mission statement so that I could keep my nerves from taking over and sending me into a spiral of self-doubt. At the moment, I was 100 percent flying by the seat of my pants. This was not my comfort zone.

I sat by the window, brooding over my latte. Zoe appeared at my table with the salmon toast I'd ordered. It looked amazing. A thick slab of bread with slices of avocado and thinly shaved salmon, topped with greens and a soft boiled egg, which was split open, with the runny yolk glazing the food beneath.

"Merci," I said. "This looks amazing."

"Are you well, Chelsea?" Zoe squinted at me with concern. "You look . . . concerned."

I glanced up at the pretty Frenchwoman. She had such a peaceful way about her; maybe she could give me some ideas on how to handle this situation.

"Do you really want to hear my tale of woe?" I asked.

Zoe nodded and pulled out the chair on the other side of the table.

It was then that I noticed she had a latte in hand and had been planning to join me all along. That made me smile.

I took a bite of my salmon toast, enjoying my food for a moment before delving into my story. I explained about my father's wedding, my sister calling me out, which Zoe kindly protested, forcing me to admit that, no, it was actually true. Then I told her about my year abroad and the recent awkward reunion in Ireland.

I was swabbing the last of the egg yolk with my bread when Annalisse came with two fresh coffees. We thanked her, and she took away my empty plate.

"You are here, then, to see a man?" Zoe asked.

"That'd be the short version, yes," I said. "But I'm nervous. What if he doesn't remember me? What if he's married or horrified that someone from his past has shown up out of nowhere?"

Zoe tapped her chin with her index finger, then she snapped her fingers and pointed at me. "You should follow him in disguise. Dress as a server, and then you can watch him and see if he is worth another chance."

"Wouldn't he notice a woman dressed as a server following him around the city?" I asked.

"*Non*, that is why it is perfect," Zoe said. "No one ever notices servers. In France, we keep our distance and try not to be noticed. We are like background scenery that delivers food."

Her French accent made the crazy idea seem so reasonable. I found myself actually considering it until I remembered. "I don't have any clothes."

"I have clothes for you," she said. She studied my figure with a critical eye. "Yes, we can do this."

THIS WAS HOW I found myself outside the Absalon design house, wearing black pants and a white shirt and one of Zoe's burgundy aprons tied about my waist. I felt like a fraud, an imposter, and a little bit of a stalker. Mercifully, Zoe was with me, wearing the same, as we posed as two restaurant workers taking a break at the bistro across the street.

We were sitting in the corner of the patio, behind a bunch of scrupulously groomed topiary trees beneath a heater. We could just see past the thick foliage to the front door of Absalon. I sipped my wine, wondering how long we could realistically stake the place out. Zoe seemed very French about it all, as if it was perfectly normal to drink wine at midday while waiting for a glimpse of a man.

"You're good at this," I said.

"Love makes us do crazy things." She shrugged.

"Does that mean you've done this before?"

A slow smile lit her face. "Perhaps."

I suspected that was all I was going to get out of my new friend.

"Oh boy," I said. "Just promise me there isn't a warrant for your arrest in Paris or elsewhere."

Zoe laughed, tipping her head back, causing her braids to swing. *"Non non.* But I have gotten a proposal or two."

There was a sexy twinkle in her eye, and I wasn't sure I should trust her judgment. I had a feeling Zoe would encourage all sorts of shenanigans, especially of the romantic kind.

"Oh là là, is that him?" Zoe asked. She sat up straight and pointed across the street.

I whipped my head in the direction of Absalon. My heart stopped. It just stopped in my chest, as if I'd taken a punch to the sternum, then it started up with a hard thump while the blood drained from my face. *It was him!*

Jean Claude was just as beautiful as I remembered, with the same unruly dark hair, chiseled features, and lithe build. His clothes, slacks and a dress shirt, fit him to perfection, naturally. He walked with the same restless energy he'd had when I'd known him. I'd always tried to slow him down, ease his journey, and it took everything I had not to run to him and grab his hand in mine and distract him from his course, just like I used to do with hugs and kisses.

"*Il est magnifique.*" Zoe sighed.

I nodded, and Zoe hopped up from her seat. "We must follow him." Having already paid our bill, we headed toward the door.

"Um . . . small problem," I said. I was watching him out of the corner of my eye as Zoe led the way through the tables. "He's walking this way. He's coming *here!*"

We looked at each other, frozen into immobility, as Jean Claude crossed the street, heading right for us.

"Back, go back!" cried Zoe.

We rushed to our seats, almost spilling what remained of our wine as we knocked the table in our hurry.

I sat with my back to the patio, not wanting him to see me. "Act casual," I hissed at Zoe, who nodded.

She relaxed in her chair, the very picture of nonchalance. She lifted her glass and took a sip, but her eyes widened, gradually, as if she were watching a slow-moving collision. I desperately wanted to turn and see what was happening, but I didn't want to give myself away. Not yet.

Zoe lowered her glass and mouthed some words, but I'd never been good at lipreading. I had no idea what she was saying. Was she speaking French? I started to turn around, but Zoe grabbed my hand and shook her head. Did that mean—oh no, was he right behind me? I widened my eyes at her and pointed right behind me. She nodded, and I broke into a light sweat.

Jean Claude was here, mere inches away! I had to pee. No, I didn't. It was nerves. I jogged my knee up and down. Zoe stared at me hard. I stopped. I reached for my wine. A drink would calm me down. I lifted the glass and took a sip just as I heard his voice.

It was the same deep, sweet tone I remembered, and it felt like getting dipped in warm caramel. With a sigh, I leaned back in my chair to hear more. I could catch only every other word. It sounded like he was ordering a glass of wine. I wondered if he was alone. I glanced at Zoe, who was leaning forward, as she, too, was trying to hear what he had to say over the street noise of cars passing and the conversation of the other diners. We exchanged a frustrated look. I leaned back farther, tipping onto the back legs of my chair ever so slightly.

Jean Claude's voice sounded agitated, and I looked at Zoe in concern. She shrugged and then pantomimed holding a phone to her ear, which explained why I heard only him. His tone became frustrated, and I glanced at Zoe, who was frowning in concentration. What was he saying? I was certain I would understand Jean Claude if I could just get a little closer. I tipped my chair back just a teeny bit more.

Of course that's when disaster struck. I overshot, the legs of my chair gave out, and I tipped over! I flailed, trying to save myself, sending my wine raining down on all of us. Zoe leaped out of her seat to grab me, but she was too late. I went over backward, falling onto the cement with a thud.

Lying on the ground, feeling dazed and winded, I glanced up at the shocked expression of Jean Claude.

"*Mon Dieu!*" he cried.

He was staring down at me as if I were deranged. Hard to argue the point at the moment. Wine dripped off his hair, and there were spots on his shirtfront. This was so not how I'd pictured seeing him again. I wondered if I could just roll over onto my belly and slink out of the bistro without anyone noticing. Highly unlikely.

"Chelsea!" cried Zoe.

She raced around the table to help me up at the same time that Jean Claude reached for me. At the mention of my name, he froze. He frowned at me with his hands outstretched, and I panicked. He could not recognize me now. I would die, just die!

I rolled away from him, drinking the last of the wine in my glass, because screw it. I put the glass on the table, wiped my face with my shirtsleeve, and pushed to my feet. Keeping my head down, I muttered, "*Je suis désolé.*"

Then I grabbed Zoe's hand and pulled her toward the door.

We got through the restaurant and out the door. I was just getting up to speed, dragging Zoe behind me, when Jean Claude vaulted over the wrought-iron enclosure and into our path.

He stared at me with red wine staining my shirtfront, making me look like a stabbing victim, and he said, "Chelsea? Chelsea Martin?"

I let go of Zoe and clapped my hands to my face. I felt like weeping. "I didn't want you to see me like this."

That was all I got out before he let out a cry of surprise and then scooped me up into his arms in a hug that lifted my feet off the ground. I grabbed his shoulders in surprise, not sure of how to react.

"Chelsea Martin!" He set me on my feet and cupped my face. He kissed both of my cheeks, stared at me in disbelief, and then kissed my cheeks again, once, twice, three times.

"Is it you? Is it really you?"

Okay, so as greetings went, this one was damn good. Laughing, I stepped back to catch my breath. "You remember me?"

"But of course," he cried. He stared at me as if I was everything, then he gave me a reproachful look. "You broke my heart!"

I knew this should not have thrilled me as much as it did. I certainly hadn't wanted to break anyone's heart, but it was such a relief to find out that he remembered me and was happy to see me that I couldn't stop the grin that spread over my face, making me lose any shred of coolness.

"I'm so sorry," I said.

He laughed. It was a low rumble that came up from his chest. "You do not look the least bit repentant, *mon chou.*"

I felt my heart do a backflip with a triple twist. He had always called me *mon chou,* meaning my sweet bun, and it was so ridiculous that it always made me blush, just as it did right now.

His brown eyes softened, and he ran an index finger gently along the curve of my cheek, as if marveling that he could still make me embarrassed with his endearment. "I was distraught when you left Paris, leaving me to face the cold winter all alone."

"You seem to have survived it," I said gently.

"Barely," he assured me. "I couldn't eat. I couldn't sleep. I missed you so."

"I missed you, too," I said.

Jean Claude had been a lot for twenty-two-year-old me to handle. And looking at him right now, I wasn't sure twenty-nine-year-old me could manage him much better. The truth was, I'd been in deep with him. The world he lived in was passionate and dramatic, and I'd suffered terrible attacks of insecurity as I'd tried to belong.

Being young and a bit naive, I hadn't always liked who I was when I was with him. Jean Claude had seemed to thrive on my attention—okay, more accurately, my fixation with him. While our spats had been the stuff of telenovelas, dramatic and ridiculous, making up had been breathtakingly erotic. While Colin in Ireland had been a kindred spirit who'd made me laugh and feel safe, Jean Claude had introduced me to true passion. He'd made me feel things I wasn't ready for, so when my time with the Beauchamps was up, I'd fled for my next job in Germany during Oktoberfest.

"Ahem." The sound of a throat being forcefully cleared caught my attention, and I saw Zoe standing there with a big grin on her face.

"Oh, I'm sorry," I said. "I . . . We . . ."

"I understand," she said.

"Let me introduce you. Zoe Fabron, this is Jean Claude Bisset. Jean Claude, my friend Zoe."

"*Enchanté, mademoiselle,*" he said.

"*Bonjour,*" she replied. She then switched to English for my sake. Her face was pure innocence when she said, "What a remarkable coincidence that we ran into you."

Jean Claude beamed at me. "I am a very lucky man today."

I smiled at him, feeling guilty for our deception.

"I can see you two have much catching up to do," Zoe said. "Chelsea, I will see you back at the café?"

"Right, yes, I'll be there," I said. "Later."

Zoe stepped forward, kissed me on each cheek, and with a wave, left us to our reunion.

"I can't believe you're here," he said. He pulled me in for another hug. "How long are you in Paris? We must spend every second together."

I laughed and hugged him back. "I have to be in Italy next week for work, but I'm free until then."

"You are not working?" he asked. He gestured to my stained waitress's garb, and I felt my face get hot. I hated lying. It never went well for me. I decided if Jean Claude and I were going to have anything worth having, then I had to tell him the truth.

"Zoe lent me these clothes," I said. He looked at me in confusion. "So that I could sit outside Absalon and look for you."

I paused, wondering how long, with the language barrier, it would take for him to get that I'd been lying in wait for him. If he ditched me now, I would totally understand.

"You are not a waitress?"

"No."

"So you are not working right now?"

"No."

"Then we haven't a moment to lose," he said. "I have a design meeting tonight, but I need a date for a party that is *très élégant* tomorrow. Go with me?"

"You do understand that I was sitting out here, watching for you," I said.

"And you found me."

Okay, clearly he did not care that I was a borderline stalker. Well, okay then.

"What should I wear to this very elegant party?" I asked. Judging by the pictures I'd seen of him on the Internet, this was likely to be rather high end, and I was not fashionably equipped for that at the moment.

"Haute couture, of course," he said.

"Of course," I repeated. Now I was definitely swimming in water over my head. I'd seen the price tags on those garments. A pair of pants could cost more than a month's rent. Eep! Maybe I could talk him into meeting me for coffee instead.

He pursed his lips, and his eyebrows lifted. I had a feeling he knew exactly why I was hesitating. His words confirmed it. "It is too bad you do not know someone who has an entire design house at his disposal, yes?"

"I couldn't," I said. I shook my head. "That is too generous. Besides, I can't go in there looking like this."

"Of course you can," he said. "You are my guest. You can do anything you want."

He didn't wait for me to answer but swooped one arm around me and whisked me into the design house as if it were a perfectly ordinary occurrence to invite a wine-soaked waitress into a high-end atelier.

Jean Claude led me through the showroom floor and up to the second level, where the seamstresses toiled in bright sunny rooms amid rolls and rolls of gorgeous fabrics. No one even looked up at us as we passed. We entered a space that was an immense closet, and I stared at the blouses and pants and dresses, knowing that I likely couldn't afford to even breathe the air in here, never mind wear any of the clothes.

"Jacqueline!" cried Jean Claude, and a woman dressed all in black with silver hair and the most elegant sharp-edged features I'd ever seen appeared.

Jean Claude spoke to her in French too rapidly for me to understand. Jacqueline took a tape and began measuring me while he spoke. She pushed my arms up and sized my bust, waist, and bottom. I tried not to be embarrassed. I failed.

Jacqueline argued a bit with him, and I felt nervous that Jean Claude was crossing a line by asking her for outfits, but then Jacqueline turned and walked away. She came back a moment later with two dresses, one a pretty blue day dress and the other a pewter silk dress with a fit-and-flare skirt that would make me look like an ingénue. Jean Claude looked pleased and chose the pewter dress.

"You must wear this one tonight, *mon chou*, and think of me while you do," he said. His gaze lingered on my stained blouse. I had the feeling he couldn't bear the thought of my walking around Paris in it. "And now that I have your size, I will send something over tomorrow for the party, especially for you."

"Thank you, but this is too much," I said. Jean Claude shook his head, refusing my protest.

Jacqueline led me to a curtained-off area to change, and while I got into the dress, which was a perfect fit and boasted exquisite hand stitching, she found some very smart black-and-silver pumps in my size and a black cashmere wrap. When I glanced at the mirror, I barely recognized myself, which was a good thing.

Jacqueline delivered me back to Jean Claude, who was downstairs in the showroom. He was standing with a group of well-to-do women, all of whom looked like they were about to swoon at his feet. This perturbed me. A possessive streak inside me that had been dormant for years was electrocuted back to life like my own private Frankenstein's monster, and I found myself studying the cluster of women. I had planned to stand off to the side and wait, but as if he could sense my presence, Jean Claude spun around.

The smile on his face when he saw me was blinding in its brilliance, and I blinked. He held his arms wide and said, "*Mon chou, tu es belle et innocente.*"

Beautiful and innocent? I supposed the cut of the dress did make me look younger. Maybe he was looking to find the carefree, adventurous woman he'd known seven years ago. Well, that made two of us.

As I walked down the circular staircase to the main floor, he gestured for me to stop. I clutched the wrought-iron banister and posed on the marble steps, feeling self-conscious but thrilled that he approved. He held up his phone and took several pictures before gesturing for me to continue and giving me lavish words of praise.

The women in the showroom were clearly eavesdropping on our conversation while pretending not to be, but they had the grace to act as if they were discussing the fabric of the gown they were looking at when he said, "Jacqueline, if anyone asks, I will be back shortly."

Jacqueline nodded, as if she had expected as much. She handed me a silk-handled embossed paper bag with my wine-stained clothes inside. *"Au revoir, mademoiselle."*

Jean Claude took my hand and said, *"Allons-y,* Chelsea. I will escort you home."

He swept me toward the door, and we were almost outside when I remembered one significant detail. I stopped, pulling him to a halt.

"Wait," I said. This was it. The moment of truth. "I have one question."

He looked at me expectantly, and I narrowed my eyes at him.

"Are you married?"

chapter fourteen

H IS EYES WENT wide in a look of horror. Then he smiled and
held up his left hand. There was no ring. "*Non*. How could I get
married when all these years I've been waiting for you?"

The ladies across the room audibly sighed, and I laughed. Always
the charmer, Jean Claude was. I felt better, but wanting to be as thorough as an audit, I asked, "Engaged?"

He shook his head. "*Non*."

"Girlfriend?"

"*Non non*," he said. "My heart is yours, *mon chou*."

And with that, he swept me outside and into the gloriously golden
late afternoon. Jean Claude twined my fingers with his as we turned
and walked down the Avenue des Champs-Élysées. People moved
around us, and I found myself pressed closer and closer to him until he
let go of my hand and slid his arm around my back, resting his hand
on my hip.

"It is okay?" he asked.

I could feel the heat of him along my side, and our faces were just
inches apart. It was hard to believe this was real, that he was real. My

heart swelled, and I nodded, unable to find the words to say how very right it all felt.

As I studied his profile—the lush lips, jutting cheekbones, and full brow—I was struck again by how beautiful he was. The man positively took my breath away. And in that breathlessness, I felt it. The flutters not just of physical desire but of the emotions that had lain dormant inside of me for so long.

He turned his head and met my gaze. His eyes glowed with affection. "Tomorrow I will have your party dress delivered in the morning, and then I will pick you up at *sept heures*. What do you say, Chelsea?"

"I say yes," I said.

He grinned at me, a slash of white teeth against the darkening sky, but only I knew that what I was saying yes to was so much more than going to a party. I was saying yes to all of it: to him, to Paris, to feeling all the feels again.

HE LEFT ME at my doorstep, with a kiss on each cheek and a look that scorched the soles of my shoes.

I'd been in my apartment for all of five minutes when Zoe arrived, demanding details and gushing over my Absalon dress. We squealed like middle school girls invited to their first dance when I told her about the party. She insisted I had to visit her salon the next day and promised to set up an appointment.

I would have stayed in and spent the evening daydreaming about him, but Zoe insisted that since I was dressed, I must go out with her and enjoy Paris. She convinced me to let her do my makeup, which she made very bold with glittery eye shadow and vibrant lipstick. She said it wouldn't be healthy to fixate on Jean Claude. It was the sort of advice Annabelle would have given me, so I went.

Zoe took me on a whirlwind tour of all the hot spots. We danced on a party barge on the Seine under the blue glow of a full moon. We climbed to the top of an abandoned building in Marais and found a drag queen dance club on the roof with a DJ, strobe lights that shot out into the night, and a fully stocked bar.

A pretty black man dressed as Marilyn Monroe and killing it was completely taken with me even though we couldn't converse over the loud music. When I took to the floor to dance with Marilyn, Zoe cheered me on, joining us with her own partner, a very tall and muscular Greta Garbo. Tipsy from the cocktails being served, we left in the early hours of the morning, stopping at an underground café for an enormous meringue filled with sweet Chantilly cream.

With a hug, Zoe and I parted ways in front of the apartment, as she had late-night plans to visit a special gentleman friend. I tried not to envy her that.

I jogged up the steps, still hearing the music from the rooftop party in my head. A delicious thrill rippled through me as I thought about my reunion with Jean Claude and the promise of a date with him tomorrow. I felt more certain than ever that this was what I'd been looking for, the thrill of infatuation. I was giddy.

I stepped into the dark hallway and turned toward my apartment. I was almost at my door when I saw a rectangular lump in front of my door. What the hell? I jumped, and then it hit me. My carry-on!

I picked up my pace and rushed down the hall toward the bag. Socks, my favorite hairbrush, my cow pajamas—oh, how I'd missed them all! I was almost on top of my bag when I saw a pair of legs stretched out on the other side of it. I braked hard.

They were a man's legs in jeans and black Converse sneakers. Was it the airport person waiting for me? Was I supposed to pay them for delivery? Or was the guy waiting for a tip? Maybe he was running a scam and would hold my bag for ransom if I didn't pay up. I wondered how much cash I had in euros in my wallet. Would it be enough?

I thought perhaps I should grab my bag just so he wouldn't try to take it if the transaction didn't go to his satisfaction. I bent down, put my hand on the handle, and gave it a gentle tug. With a yelp, the guy turned and grabbed the suitcase with both arms.

"Oh no you don't!" he shouted.

His face was inches from mine, and I blinked. The first thing I noticed was that he spoke American, if that was even a thing, and the second was that I knew that face. In the dimly lit hallway, I couldn't tell if his eyes were gray or blue, but the scruffy beard that always covered his chin was unmistakable.

"Knightley!" I cried. "What the hell are you doing here?"

chapter fifteen

WHAT AM *I* doing here?" he asked. His hair was standing on end, he had dark circles under his eyes, and his clothes looked as if he'd slept in them. A vein was throbbing in his neck, and a frown line was chiseled between his eyebrows. He looked irate. "A more appropriate question is where the hell have you been, Martin?"

"Out."

"Out?"

"Yes, out."

He looked me over, taking in my loose hair, exotic makeup, and overall sexy party-girl appearance. His expression became outraged.

"You look hot, Martin," he said. It sounded like an accusation. "Wait! Were you on a *date*?"

"That's none of your business."

"Um, when I signed for your bag two hours ago and had to bribe a guy from upstairs, who was kind of a dick, by the way, to let me wait by your front door, keeping watch over your stuff, yeah, it became my business," he snapped. "So . . . François?"

"That's not his name." I crossed my arms over my chest, refusing to get sucked into his drama. "But if you must know, yes, I was out—with friends."

He let go of my bag and stood. He put a fist against his back and stretched with a wince. His voice had the full range of sarcasm when he said, "Well, so long as one of us is having a good time."

I glared at him. It was almost daybreak, and here he was, ruining my fun evening as only an overgrown frat boy could. Any warm feelings I had developed for him vanished like a pebble dropped into the Seine.

I unlocked my door and pushed it open, flicking on the light switch. "You didn't answer my question. What are you doing here?"

Jason followed me, grabbing my bag and another small carry-on, presumably his, and stepped into the small apartment. As he entered, he took the place in, from the windows to the fireplace to the loft. "Nice."

"Focus, Knightley," I said. "Why are you here?"

He glanced at me and squinted as if trying to remember what he was doing. Then he kicked off his shoes and shucked his wool coat, draping it over one of the chairs. He moved past me and grabbed the bright-green throw off the back of the couch.

"I'm here because you went off the grid and there's been a change of plans," he said.

"What change?" I asked. I stared at him over the back of the couch.

"Severin wants to meet here in Paris at Le Cinq. We couldn't get in touch with you, and Aidan freaked out, so here I am."

"What?" I shook my head. I couldn't decide if I was more hurt or angry. "We're supposed to meet in Italy next week at the wine festival."

"Well, Severin changed the plan, which you'd know if you'd bothered to check in, which you didn't, causing Aidan to be rightly concerned. The guy has a lot going on, Martin. That was uncool."

He stretched out on the sofa, which was too short for him, letting his feet hang over the armrest while he tucked the decorative pillow under his head. He tossed the blanket over his body, but it didn't fully cover him.

I stared down at him. I was the most reliable person in the depart-ment. I would have checked in again tomorrow from the café if I hadn't gotten my phone back. If I said I'd do something, I'd do it. How could Aidan think . . . Wait just one second. Suddenly, Knightley being here, wagging the proverbial finger at me, made sense.

"Oh, I see how it is," I said.

He had his eyes shut but opened one to look at me. "And how is that?"

"You engineered this whole thing, didn't you?" I asked.

"Because I wanted to go twenty-four hours without sleep?"

"Admit it. You talked Severin into dinner in Paris, knowing I'd lost my phone and this was your chance to swoop in and save the day, show-ing me up."

He folded his arms behind his head and looked at me as if he thought I was a few slices shy of a ham sandwich. "Do you hear your-self? That's crazy talk. Why would I do that?"

"Because you're threatened by me," I said. "You think I'm going to steal your glory, Knightley."

"Oh man, I do not need this shit." He grunted and rubbed his eyes with the heels of his hands as if he could grind the sleep out of his eyes. "Listen, Martin, since the Severin ask isn't a done deal, there's really no glory to be had."

"Which just proves my point," I said. "If I nailed down a commit-ment from Severin in Italy next week, how bad would that make you look?"

"Are you kidding me?" He spread his hands wide and then clasped his fingers together as if to keep himself from strangling me. "You dis-appear without a trace when you're traveling alone in Europe, and you don't think people are going to worry? And now you're twisting it around to make it seem like a work thing where I'm the one at fault for being too ambitious?"

"I didn't disappear. I lost my phone," I said. My phone! I hurried to my suitcase and unzipped the side pocket. I reached in and felt around, relieved when I felt the familiar rectangle. My phone! Praise the cellular gods—I was back. "I accidentally put my phone in my suitcase, and then when I landed in Paris, my bag took the scenic route." I checked the tags. "To Greece, apparently. I did *not* go off the grid on purpose, and I explained all of this in an email to Julia."

"Right. She's been out of the office with the flu for three days. In fact, half the department has been out, and Aidan hasn't been able to come in, because he can't risk the contagion," he said. "I had to get in touch with your dad, who thankfully had gotten a text from you before you left Ireland, telling him where you were planning to stay in Paris."

"My dad?" I asked. "You called my dad? Did he tell you I sent him an email from here? Because I did."

"No, when I talked to him right before jumping on a red-eye, he hadn't heard from you as yet," he said.

"You didn't make him worry, did you?"

"Of course not," he said. "I told him I'd lost the name of the place where you were staying. What do you take me for?"

"A man who's made himself at home on my couch," I said. "You can't sleep here." I whisked the pillow out from under his head and made to grab the blanket, but he was too quick and grabbed a corner and wouldn't let go.

"Oh yes I can," he said. "Trust me—flying all night, wedged in an upright seat between a snorer and a squalling baby, I can absolutely sleep here. In fact, I'm pretty sure I could sleep on the pointy end of a thumbtack if need be."

"No, I mean you're not sleeping in my apartment," I said.

"Oh my god, Martin, re-freaking-lax," he said. He snatched the pillow out of my hand. "Even if I wanted to jump your sudden hotness, I simply don't have the energy. Go to bed. We'll talk in the morning."

"But I . . . You . . . This." I flapped my hands to encompass the entire situation. I was so vexed, I was surprised I didn't achieve liftoff.

A deep breath interrupted my protest. Just like that, Jason Knightley was dead asleep on my couch. I wanted to kick him. I wanted to grab him by the ear and haul him out the door. This was my chance to reconnect with Jean Claude. I simply could not have Knightley messing it up for me. I grabbed my phone charger and stomped up the ladder to the loft.

Jason said we'd talk in the morning. Fine. But it was going to be me doing the talking and him doing the packing and leaving. Honestly, how was I supposed to give all my time and energy to finding my happiness again with *him* underfoot? Jason was the bane of my existence, a complete pain in the ass, and I knew if given half a chance, he would ruin everything!

I AWOKE TO the smell of fresh coffee. Was there a greater scent to be greeted with in the morning? Well, maybe chocolate cake, but coffee was a solid number two.

Again, it took me a moment to remember where I was. Paris. The ceiling above my bed was low, and the light from below was dim. There was no window in the loft, giving it the feel of a snug cocoon. I didn't want to leave the warmth of my blankets, but the lure of the coffee was too potent to ignore. The café downstairs must be open for business and brewing up a storm. Then I heard the whistling.

It was a tuneless melody, but it was most definitely coming from downstairs. There was someone in my apartment! I clutched my covers in a moment of panic. Then I saw a man, the one who was whistling, crossing the living room to my balcony doors. He held a coffee in one hand and opened the door with the other. He strode outside and made himself at home on my veranda. I immediately recognized his loose-limbed walk. Knightley!

I shoved my covers aside. I finger combed my hair, then snatched my silk bathrobe from the foot of my bed. I shrugged it on and belted it tight. I hurried down the ladder to the floor below, striding across the living room and poking my head out the door.

"Martin," he said. "You're up. Excellent. I picked up coffee and pastries from the café downstairs. Have you met Zoe, the owner? She's something else, isn't she?"

I blinked. He bought coffee and pastries? My opposing desires to rip him a new one or shove a pastry in my mouth and wash it down with fabulous French coffee went to war. Coffee and pastry won before the battle lines were even drawn. Shocker.

"We need to talk," I said. I gestured to the balcony. "Don't move—unless it's to jump."

Jason grinned. "You're all heart, Martin."

I examined the contents of the bag he'd left on the counter. He'd gotten the swirly pastry with raisins. Damn it—that was my favorite. How was I supposed to present a formidable front while stuffing my face with pastry? I grabbed the paper cup of coffee. It was warm in my hand. The bitter aroma made me salivate. Clearly it would be considered bad manners to ignore what he'd bought for us, and I certainly didn't want to be rude.

With my pastry lust justified, I took a paper-wrapped Danish and my coffee and joined him on the balcony, taking the seat on the other side of the very small café table, which was just big enough for our coffee cups. The balcony was in full sun, so even though the temperature was in the low sixties, it was pleasant to be outside in the sweet Parisian air. Jason had his phone out and was taking a picture of the street and the top half of the Eiffel Tower, which could just be seen off in the distance, beyond the buildings. He turned to me once he'd snapped the photo.

"Good morning," he said. His thick dark hair was mussed, and he was wearing jeans and an unbuttoned plaid shirt over a plain white T-shirt. His gaze moved over my cow pajamas and pink silk robe. His lips twitched, but he didn't say a word. The restraint was probably killing him.

"Thanks for the coffee and the pastries," I said. I didn't want to start the morning with a spat. "That was nice of you."

A slow grin moved across his lips, and he raised his own cup and took a long sip. "That hurt, didn't it? To thank me?"

"More than a pulled tooth but less than a broken arm," I said.

He laughed. It rumbled up from deep down in his chest, and I found myself chuckling in return. Okay, so maybe he wasn't that bad. Still, I was the sort of girl who valued her privacy, especially when prepping for a big date, so I needed him gone by midafternoon in order to make it to my salon appointment and give myself a solitary moment or two to get in the right headspace.

I pulled my phone out of my robe pocket to check the time. There were about a million texts from my sister and dad. Oh boy. They'd have to wait. I'd overslept. It was already eleven in the morning, and Jean Claude was arriving at seven that evening. I'd been a charity case when he saw me yesterday, so tonight I was absolutely determined to wow him.

"When is this dinner with Severin supposed to happen?" I asked.

"Tomorrow night."

"I take it we're going together?" I asked.

"We're doing this now?" he asked. "I haven't even finished my coffee."

"Yes, now. I have other things to do today," I said.

"Like what? It's my first time in Paris. I thought we could hang out."

"Sorry, you're on your own," I said. "In fact, you need to find your own place to stay."

"Am I cramping your style, Martin?" he asked. He wagged his eyebrows at me, but I refused to play.

I bit into my pastry. The flaky, buttery heaven momentarily distracted me from the man in my space. I closed my eyes and savored the way the pastry melted in my mouth as the cinnamon burst on my tongue and the plump, chewy raisins added just the right amount of gooey sweetness.

"Ahem." Jason cleared his throat. "I don't want to interrupt your amorous moment with your *pain aux raisins*, but about tomorrow night's dinner, I won't go if it's a problem for you."

I opened my eyes. I saw him watching me and self-consciously licked the excess sugar off my lips. Jason hissed out a breath. Then he frowned.

"Aren't you supposed to have your hair pulled back and be wearing a suit with your collar buttoned up to here?" He put his hand at his throat. "This tousled-hair thing you've got going . . ." He paused and waved his hands in my direction. "It's like I don't even know you anymore."

His discomfort made me laugh, and I intentionally tossed my hair over my shoulder, enjoying being the one of us who was at ease for a change. I sipped my coffee, glancing at him over the rim. It hit me then that I could see what our office mates saw in him. He was handsome, in a rebellious way, and he was always smiling. As far as I knew, he never lost his temper or had tantrums, unlike so many of the men we worked with, and he paid attention to the people around him.

He knew everyone's name, what they liked to eat or drink, what their hobbies were, if they were married or had kids. I'd always thought he was just manipulating everyone into doing what he wanted by pretending to be nice, but now I wondered if perhaps he was, quite simply, a nice guy.

"I don't see why having you join me would be a problem. In fact, since I don't know when I'll be returning to the ACC and you've already connected with Eleanor, this would be a great opportunity for you to meet Severin and line you up to take over the account."

"Last night you seemed to think I had ulterior motives," Jason said.

"Upon reflection, I might have been a bit out of order," I said. "I'm sorry about that. The control freak in me is struggling with letting work go. I think this is a good opportunity for you to build a rapport with Severin, since you'll be taking over the account."

Jason's eyes went wide. "You're really not coming back."

I shrugged. "I don't know."

"All right. Should we do some prep now so we can wow Severin with our ideas?"

I glanced at my phone. "I have a couple of hours free that I can spend going over my proposal so you're caught up."

"Great," he agreed. "And I can just tell you what I've been thinking, since I don't have a fancy PowerPoint or anything even written down."

"Fine," I said. I finished my pastry and picked up my coffee. "I need to take a shower before we start. I can't think until after coffee and a shower."

"Reasonable," he said. "What about this afternoon? Want to hit a museum or, even better, tour the catacombs?"

"I can't," I said. "I have plans."

"Another date?"

"None of your business."

"Aw, come on," he wheedled. "You can tell me."

"No."

"What was his name again? Pierre?" he said.

"If you can't remember, why do you want to know?"

"In case you go missing again, I'll know his name if I have to track you down."

"I have my phone again," I said. "I'll be all right."

"So you do have a date! Is Gaston hot?"

"That's not his name, and he's French—of course he's hot. All Frenchmen are hot. It's in their DNA or something."

"So, this date with Louis, how'd it come about?" he asked. "Did you track him down?"

"Louis isn't it either, and again, it's none of your business."

"No, it's not," he agreed. "But I'm curious about the sort of man you'd like." He looked at me from beneath his surprisingly long eyelashes. "Come on, Martin. Enlighten me."

"No. Don't you think you should use this time to see if you can find a place to stay? I have to make some calls to my family. We can meet back here in an hour, okay? Great."

I rose from my seat and left to go make my calls without waiting to hear his answer. Not that it stopped him from shouting after me, "So, was it Henri's sense of humor that lured you in? I feel like you'd go for a guy who makes you laugh."

A smile curved my lips at his relentlessness, but I ignored him. I had to get mentally prepared, as I knew tonight was going to be significant. I was good at corporate parties, because at those gatherings I was on a mission. But this—this was a fashion-industry party where I didn't know anyone except Jean Claude, and I didn't speak the language very well. The potential for disaster was huge, and I wanted to run possible scenarios through my head to be fully prepped.

"Oh, Martin." Knightley poked his head into the apartment from the veranda. "A package was dropped off for you earlier. It's on the coffee table."

Package? That had to be the dress! Excited, I rounded the couch to find a large white box with a navy bow sitting on the low glass table. In cursive the name *Absalon* was scrawled across the top. There was a tiny card attached. In a man's bold handwriting, it read, *For mon chou with love.*

I felt my heart do a giddy cartwheel in my chest. Jason stood in the doorway, watching me, so I kept my face expressionless. I refused to open the box in front of him on the off chance Jean Claude had sent some sexy lingerie along with the dress. Knightley was hard enough to deal with without giving him that sort of ammunition. I made a shooing gesture with my hands. He heaved a put-upon sigh and headed toward the front door.

"Spoilsport," he said.

I ignored him, waiting for the door to shut behind him before I lifted the lid. Tucked inside blue-and-white polka-dot tissue paper was the most exquisite dress I'd ever seen. I gently lifted it out of its nest as if it were made out of moonbeams and gossamer. A sleeveless gown that

178 • JENN MCKINLAY

was high in the front but so very low in the back, it had a thigh-high
slit on the right side. It was bright white and delicately embroidered
with tiny silver beads along the neckline and hem. It was the sort of
gown that looked demure until the wearer moved, and then it became
a sinuous, sexy sheath that made people stop and stare—at least, that
was what I would do if I saw a woman in it. I didn't even want to know
what a gown like this cost. In fact, I refused to think about it, hoping
it was a reject from the collection, a castoff no one wanted. Otherwise
I'd get so nervous wearing it, I'd leave sweat stains.

Realizing the clock was ticking and I needed to call home, I took the
gown upstairs to hang it up properly. Slipping it onto a hanger, I let my
fingers run over the beads at the neckline. It was gorgeous, and I was awed.
I was going to feel like Cinder-freaking-ella tonight, and I couldn't wait.

ANNABELLE DIDN'T ANSWER her phone. Not a big surprise, as she
let everything go to voice mail when she was creating. My call to my
father was even less successful. Not because no one answered his
landline—yes, the man was the last person in the free world to have a
landline, because ever since he'd lost power during the January blizzard
of 2015, he'd refused to discuss having only a cell phone. No, unlike at
Annabelle's, someone did answer. Sheri.

"Hello?" she said.

Startled, I tried to gather my wits. I failed. "Is Glen Martin there?"

"I'm sorry—he isn't," she said. "May I take a message?"

I froze, panicked. Did I admit it was me, his daughter Chelsea?
Would I then have to make conversation with her? What could I possibly say? I wasn't even sure how much my dad had told her about the
reason for my trip. Probably everything, and if he hadn't, Annabelle
likely had. My family was not known for its ability to keep confidences.

"Hello? Are you still there?" she asked.

"Uh, yeah," I said. "It's . . . uh . . . me, Chelsea."

"Oh," she said. There was a ten-volume set of unspoken conversations in that one syllable. "How are you, Chelsea?"

"Good, really good," I said. "I'm just calling to let Dad know that I have my cell phone back, so he can call me anytime."

"Excellent, that will relieve his mind," she said. There were a few beats of silence, and then she continued, "I hope you're okay with me answering his phone. If I'd known it was . . ."

She trailed off, no doubt realizing that what she was about to say—that if she'd known it was me, she wouldn't have answered—would only take us to the basement level of awkward.

"It's fine," I said. "I mean, of course it is. You're going to marry him, after all."

Yes, a teeny tiny part of me threw that out there in the stupid hope that she would say they'd come to their senses and changed their minds. She didn't.

"I'm glad you understand," she said.

I legit had no idea what to say to that, because in truth, I didn't understand. I didn't understand any of it.

"Yes, well, I'll let you go," I said. Seriously, I could not hang up fast enough.

"Chelsea, if you ever want to talk—about anything—I'm a really good listener," she said.

Maybe she was just being polite, but it felt like an overreach. Like something someone who wanted to be your stepmom would say when she wanted you to start calling her Mom and baking cookies with her. That was never going to happen. Still, I kept it cool.

"Thanks, I appreciate that," I said. I ended the call before the conversation could wander off into any other uncharted territory. Once I had showered and slipped on a pair of beige Capris and a black thermal shirt, I decided to let my hair air-dry and didn't bother with makeup, since I had my salon appointment that afternoon. I figured it was better to leave the makeup application to an expert.

I hoped Jason had managed to find a place of his own, even if it was a hotel, because I could not invite Jean Claude back here if there was a man in my teeny tiny efficiency. Of course it could be that we'd go back to Jean Claude's place, and I found myself wondering where he lived and what his place looked like. I imagined it was as beautiful as he was, filled with art and books. The thought made me smile.

I crossed the apartment to the balcony, half expecting to find Jason waiting, as he seemed to always be underfoot. He wasn't there. I stepped outside, taking in the sight of the bustling Parisian streets below. I heard the yip of a dog and glanced over the railing to see a woman in a pencil skirt and high heels, walking a tiny little pooch who yapped at everyone they passed. I smiled. It seemed so Paris.

"That is not a real dog," a man's voice said. I turned to my right to find Jason sitting on the balcony beside mine, enjoying a cheese plate and a bottle of wine.

I frowned. "What are you doing? How did you get over there? If the residents catch you—"

"Relax," he said. He lifted his glass and took an appreciative sip of the white wine. "For the next few days, I am the resident."

"What?" I blinked.

He grinned. It was a wicked, wicked grin that made something in my belly—probably rage—unfurl like a flame licking around a log.

"Hey, neighbor," he said. He gave me a little finger wave.

chapter sixteen

WAS CONSUMED by a flash of anger that burned so hot and bright I was surprised it didn't scorch the earth. I stared at him. "You can't stay there."

He looked around as if trying to figure out what could be wrong with the place. "Why not?"

"Because this is my place," I said.

He nodded. "Yes, and this"—he paused to gesture to his balcony—"is mine."

"But . . . but . . ."

"Shouldn't we get to work?" he asked. "I brought us some fortification."

I was too stymied to reply. He rose and handed me the cheese plate and the bottle of wine. Then with the grace of a cat, he leaped from his balcony to mine with two glasses in his hands.

"I'll just go get my laptop," he said, putting the glasses on the table. He disappeared into my apartment, coming back out with his computer. He put the laptop in his chair and picked up the glasses. I put the cheese plate on the table and took the glass he held out to me. Suddenly, wine seemed like a fine idea.

I poured myself a glass and handed him the bottle. Jason topped off his own and picked up his laptop so he could sit down. We resumed the same seats we'd had earlier, but the sun was warmer and it felt good on my face.

"Cheers," he said and held up his glass.

"Cheers." Reluctantly, I touched my glass to his and took a sip. The wine was crisp, light, and fruity, a perfect complement to the cheese board, which contained a melty Brie, a soft Morbier, and a semifirm Laguiole.

Jason put his glass down and fired up his laptop. To my surprise, he didn't pester me anymore about my plans for the evening. Instead, he opened up my proposal and then started to go over the campaign I'd worked on for months page by page. His questions were smart and insightful, and I was impressed that he'd actually read the document. I'd thought he'd skim it at best.

After an hour and a half, he closed his computer. "All right, I think I'm about ready for anything Severin might throw at us at the dinner. We can go over it some more tomorrow if need be."

"Do you think he's going to grill us?" I asked. I was prepared for that but had assumed it was more of a getting-to-know-you meeting than a business one.

"I don't know," he said. "Raised on a failing Idaho potato farm, he really is a self-made guy. According to all of the stories about him, I have to conclude that Severin is an . . . unusual man."

"That was polite." I snorted. "I mean, I've never met him personally, but I've heard the tales about the crazy stuff he's interested in and his erratic behavior."

"I heard he has a car submarine," he said.

"Really? I read that he owns an original manuscript of Leonardo da Vinci's."

"He also bought a small Hawaiian island."

"Which has an outdoor golden toilet at its highest point," I added.

Jason choked on his wine. A few drops dribbled down his shirt-front, and he wiped them away and said, "You made that up."

I raised my right hand as if making a vow. "That's what I heard."

He shook his head. "Can you imagine having that much money? How much cancer research you could do? How many people you could help? The treatments you could fund? Hell, you could probably cure it."

I studied him. He had caught me off guard. I'd never really thought about why Jason worked for the ACC. I'd assumed he'd just fallen into it after the success of his viral chicken-wing fundraising shenanigans.

"What?" he asked. "Did I miss a spot?" He glanced down, smoothing the front of his shirt with his hand as he did so.

"No," I said. "I just didn't appreciate how committed you are to raising money for the ACC. It's impressive."

He raised one eyebrow. "Martin, are you paying me a compliment?"

"No, definitely not," I said. "I was merely making an observation."

We stared at each other for a moment. The sounds of Paris drifted up over the balcony rail. The hum of motor scooters, the occasional laugh from the café below, the wail of emergency vehicle sirens, a car horn honking, and the rise and fall of voices in conversation on the street below. It all seemed to fade away as we looked at each other.

His eyes were blue today, reflecting the T-shirt he wore. It looked soft and well worn, and it draped over his muscle-hardened shoulders and arms, making me appreciate him as a man in a way I hadn't before. Knightley was fit. Huh.

He was the first to break eye contact. "Well, I'd better let you get ready for your big date?" He raised one eyebrow, looking for confirmation.

To my utter mortification, I blushed. Why? Why would I do such a thing? It was galling. So what if I was nervous about tonight with Jean Claude? There was no reason to be embarrassed. It was a night out with an old friend, no big deal, even if said friend was one of the hottest men I'd ever seen in my life. No big deal, really.

"All right, all right," I said. "Yes, I have a date, and I imagine I can use all the prep time I can get."

His gaze moved over me, cataloging my features, and I now wished I had bothered to style my hair or slap on some makeup.

"Nah." Jason turned his head and looked out at the city when he said, "You look perfect to me just as you are."

With that, he rose and went into my apartment and retrieved his carry-on. This time he exited out my front door to go to his place. With an abrupt wave from him, the door closed and he was gone.

I stared after him, wondering what that had been about. Had Knightley actually been sweet to me? I understood that we had a lot riding on the Severin campaign, and I knew he was probably grateful for my help, but still, that had been a really kind thing to say, and I didn't know how to reconcile it with the guy who had once announced "Not my circus, not my freak" in regards to working with me during a staff meeting.

Maybe the wine and cheese and Paris were mellowing the man or me. I decided not to analyze it too closely. I'd just be grateful we were a united front for dinner with Severin tomorrow instead of our default setting of bickering like siblings.

With that decided, I grabbed my purse and headed down to the café. Zoe had said she would walk me to the salon. With a glance in the mirror, I had to acknowledge there was work to be done here.

WHEN ZOE SAID she knew the perfect beautician, she wasn't exaggerating. Which was how I found myself being plucked, primped, powdered, and polished down to a molecular level at a salon where the stylist, Estelle, did not make small talk but rather fixed me with an impersonal and terrifying stare, with which she assessed what was required to make this American lump—at least, that was what I assumed she considered me—into a cosmopolitan woman worthy of their fair city.

Estelle took charge of my transformation, not asking about my preferences or style or personality but rather focusing on working with what I had to offer, which clearly did not impress her overmuch.

"Your eyes are too close together," she said. "Your upper lip is not even."

I blinked at my reflection in the mirror. No one had ever mentioned these defects to me before. My head was covered in foil, as Estelle had tsked repeatedly at my natural color. Now she was holding my face by the chin and turning my head from side to side, considering how she could make this random collection of features alluring. The expression on her face, one of intense concentration, made it clear she considered it a daunting task. So my self-esteem was rocking.

"You have excellent skin," Estelle said. Her English was very precise. "We begin."

Time ceased to have any meaning. I was ushered from one chair to the next. Creams, potions, and gels were applied and removed. I spent more time turned away from the mirror or with my eyes closed than I did watching the progress of my transformation. When Estelle finally finished blowing out my hair and retouching my makeup, I felt as if I were a snake who'd been forced to shed its skin. Everything tingled, and I was aware of parts of my face and body I'd never noticed before. I sincerely hoped I wasn't about to drop the equivalent of a down payment on a new car on having someone make me look like a tart. That wasn't what I was going for here.

Estelle stepped back and examined me from different angles. She reached up and tousled my newly highlighted and trimmed hair, and then she nodded.

"*Oui, oui*, you will do," she announced. She spun my chair so that I faced the mirror. My jaw dropped.

"I . . . oh . . . well . . . wow," I stammered. I straight-up did not recognize the woman staring back at me.

For the first time all day, Estelle smiled. It was a small smile—just the corners of her lips moved, in an upward trajectory of about a centimeter—but it was a smile. Her voice was pleased when she said, *"Ravissant, oui?"*

Ravishing. Yes, I was. I broke out in a full-on grin and said, *"Merci beaucoup."*

Instead of tarting me up, Estelle had somehow found a layer of pretty as yet untapped by me and my usual minimalist beauty routine. She hadn't slathered the makeup on; rather, she'd been very selective about what she used and where. She'd made my pleasant features pop. Brown eyeliner in the outer corners of my eyes was drawn out a bit and tilted up, making my eyes seem not so close together. Because I had a lot of real estate for eyelids, a muted purple had been used to enhance the green in my eyes and soften the brown. A pencil had been used to even out my lips, which Estelle had colored a soft rose.

My hair had been trimmed and subtle color added. I was fascinated as the light caught the new strands of gold and copper, which enhanced the pale brown. The most shocking change was the blunt-cut bangs that now framed my face, making me look less hair-parted-in-the-middle studious and more winsome-girl-who-should-be-playing-a-ukulele-and-singing-in-the-park adventurous. I loved it.

In a flurry of gratitude and optimism, I bought all the products Estelle had used to make me over, and when my credit card didn't catch on fire, I took it as a sign that the universe approved of my rash decision to suddenly become a girly girl.

When I thanked Estelle again for the transformation, the woman surprised me by kissing both of my cheeks and saying, "Do not worry, *chère*—now he will be yours."

I left the salon, wondering how the stylist had known that this had to do with a man. Then I shook my head. Duh. Of course it had to do with a man. Why else did a woman spend a month's rent at a salon? I laughed at myself as I schlepped my bags back to the apartment. I had never spent this much on trying to get the attention of any dude ever. If Jean Claude didn't notice the effort and fall at my feet, head over heels in love, then at least I could say I'd given it my best shot.

I SUPPOSE I could have played it cool and stayed up in my apartment, letting Jean Claude wait for me as I made a dramatic late entrance, but that wasn't me. He had said *sept heures*, or seven o'clock, and just like when I met Colin at the pub, I couldn't let my desire to be nonchalant override my punctual tendencies.

At two minutes to seven, I left the apartment and headed downstairs. I carried a wrap and a clutch, but I didn't put the wrap on. Instead, I let the cool night air drift down my exposed spine with chilly fingers, making me shiver in the most delicious way. My hair and makeup were perfection, and I was relieved there was no breeze to mess up Estelle's efforts.

My dress hugged my curves, with the slit up the side ending right at midthigh. I hadn't brought much jewelry with me, so I wore my favorite silver-and-abalone earrings with a matching cuff bracelet. I was quite certain that Estelle would have approved—okay, probably not, because Estelle didn't seem like the type to approve of anything, but I believed she wouldn't have thrown up in disgust, so that was something.

When I stepped out of the door to the apartments, I could feel the Paris night pulse all around me. A thrum of excitement, like the low purr of an engine, revved in my belly, and I had the feeling that tonight was the first night in a whole new life for me.

A wolf whistle brought my attention around to the café.

Jason was sitting at one of the tables. He was holding a book—a spy novel—and sipping a glass of wine. His gaze swept over me from head to foot. He mouthed the word *wow*, and I grinned at him. That was exactly the shot of confidence I needed.

"Martin, you look—"

"Je te trouve belle, mon chou."

I spun around to find Jean Claude approaching me with his hands held out to his sides as if he was trying to take me in and simply couldn't. It was very flattering. When he reached me, he kissed both of my cheeks and stared into my eyes as if he couldn't look away.

"Ma belle, to see you in one of my own creations." He pressed his hands over his heart as if he was overcome.

I glanced down. My beautiful gown was a design of Jean Claude's. I was incredibly touched that he had gifted it to me.

"It is beautiful," I said. "Thank you."

"Mon chou, what a night we are going to have."

"How nice. And where exactly is that night going to be, and when will it be ending?"

I turned to look over my right shoulder to find Jason standing behind me with his arms crossed over his chest, his finger holding his place in his book.

"Go away," I said. "Shoo."

"Is this man bothering you, *mon chou*?" Jean Claude asked.

"No, he's fine," I said. I didn't want to start an unnecessary scuffle. "Jean Claude Bisset, this is a coworker of mine, Jason Knightley. He's here because our business meeting in Italy was moved to here tomorrow."

Jean Claude's wary expression cleared, and he held out his hand to Jason. "Ah, a coworker. It is a pleasure to meet you."

Jason hesitated for just a fraction of a second, long enough for me to contemplate kicking him, and then took Jean Claude's hand in a firm handshake.

"You too," he said. He didn't sound like he meant it. "Chelsea's got a big meeting tomorrow, super important, so you might want to make sure she's home by midnight."

I turned so my back was to Jean Claude, and through gritted teeth, I growled, "Shut up."

Jason gave me an innocent look. Then he shrugged and said, "You kids have fun. I'll just be here enjoying my wine all by myself."

He heaved a sigh that was so forlorn, I felt as if I were abandoning a puppy in the middle of the twelve-lane roundabout that circled the Arc de Triomphe. I shook it off. What had gotten into him?

"Good night, Jason," I said firmly. I took the arm Jean Claude offered, noting for the first time how beautiful his suit was. It was immaculately cut and hung on him as if it was bespoke, which it undoubtedly was.

As Jean Claude led me to a waiting car, a sleek black sedan with a driver standing at the rear and holding the door open, he leaned close and asked, "Should we invite your friend to come along?"

"No!" I said. Seeing his surprise, I realized I might have been too sharp and said, "I'm sure Jason would much rather prepare for tomorrow's meeting."

A slow smile spread across Jean Claude's lips. "Excellent, because I really didn't want to share you."

He helped me into the car and slid in beside me. The driver shut the door and walked around the car to the driver's seat. There was a bucket of champagne waiting, and Jean Claude lifted the bottle to uncork it. I was grateful, hoping it would take the edge off my nerves. As the lights of Paris swooped by, I caught a glimpse of the Eiffel Tower all lit up, and I felt the magic of the city slip in under my skin, making me hyperaware of everything around me, in particular the man beside me.

He smelled of an exotic cologne, not overpowering, just hovering over his person. I had to press closer to breathe it in, and I could smell the subtle notes of bergamot and musk. It suited him, being masculine but not overbearing. He wore no tie with his suit, and his shirt collar fell open to reveal the strong column of his throat.

He poured two glasses, handed me one, and said, "*Une nuit inoubliable.*"

The words sounded delightful, but I didn't know what they meant, so I held back my glass and looked at him in question.

"An unforgettable night," he said. Then he touched his glass to mine and moved so that his arm looped through mine, and we drank with our arms entwined. It was ridiculously romantic.

The champagne was delicious as it fizzed against the roof of my mouth, waking up my taste buds and making my lips pucker with its tart sweetness. Jean Claude took this as an invitation to kiss me, and I welcomed it.

His mouth slid gently against mine as if not wanting to smear my rosy lips. I wore a kissable lipstick, but I didn't tell him this, preferring to ease into this new level of intimacy, like cooking a dish by turning up the heat in tiny degrees.

When he leaned in to kiss me again, the car came to a slow stop, interrupting his progress. Jean Claude looked regretful, but I was surprised to find that I wasn't. In fact, I felt a bit relieved. Despite being happy to see Jean Claude again, I didn't want to rush into anything.

The door opened and Jean Claude slid out. He turned and held out his hand, smiling at me as he said, "I promised you an unforgettable night out, and so it begins."

His strong fingers curled around mine, and I let him pull me to my feet. Instead of letting me go, he laced our fingers together and led me across the sidewalk toward the mansion that was ablaze with light ahead of us.

I glanced back and saw our driver weave his way into the line of cars dropping off other guests, to park at the far edge of the long drive. Men in sharp suits and tuxedos and women in glitzy gowns swarmed the walkway.

"Where are we?" I asked, leaning close to Jean Claude.

"We are at the most exclusive party in all of Paris," he said. "This is the home of François Moreau. He is a collector and an investor."

"Home?" I asked. I glanced up at the massive stone building. Each of its five floors had enormous arched windows, all of which glowed brightly in the darkness. I glanced at the roof and noted that there were gargoyles perched at each corner. Well, then. "What does he collect?"

"Whatever strikes his fancy," Jean Claude said. "Everyone here tonight is hoping that they will engage François's interest and he will use his inherited billions to make their dreams come true."

There was a wistfulness in his voice that caught my notice. "And is that what you are hoping, that he will help you open your own design house?"

"You remember my dream?" he asked. He looked truly touched. Then he smiled, glanced at me from beneath his eyelashes, and said, "You will help me, then?"

"Of course," I said. "Anything you need—I'd be honored to help you."

"I knew I could count on you," he said. He kissed the backs of my fingers. "My beautiful girl."

I felt my face get warm. Being called a "girl" by any other man would have peeved me. Okay, perhaps it irked me just a little, but Jean Claude had that deadly French charm that flustered me to the roots of my hair. I was flattered by his attention and quite certain I would do anything I could to assist him.

We climbed the stairs, joining the party, which was already in full swing. A butler greeted us at the open doorway and gestured for us to follow the other guests into the great hall. We crossed the marble foyer and walked through one of the many sets of open doors, into a room that was thick with people. A jazz quintet was playing in the corner, and waiters were hurrying about the room with silver trays loaded with champagne and tapas. Jean Claude grabbed two glasses and handed one to me.

The interior of the mansion didn't disappoint, being just as over the top as I had expected. The ceilings were decorated in ornamental plaster quadrants that each featured a ceiling rose and dentils that drew the eye up toward the center, where a row of enormous chandeliers sparkled, casting shimmers of light throughout the long room. Doors on the opposite side of the room were open to let in the cool night air and allow guests to step out onto the wide terrace that overlooked the immaculate gardens. It was like something out of a novel. I wanted to pinch myself. Was this really my life?

Clusters of men and women chattered all around us, and I watched them, taking in the beautiful clothes, the excited laughter, the hugs and air kisses, and in one case the moue of disapproval from one woman to her man, who simply shrugged and downed his champagne.

"Jean Claude!" A man approached us. He was older, easily in his seventies, with pale-blue eyes and a thick shock of white hair. He wore a black tuxedo, which, much like Jean Claude's suit, was obviously tailor made, as it fit his slender shoulders, round belly, and short legs in a way that an off-the-rack tux never could.

"François," Jean Claude said. He smiled and broke into French so rapid that I had no chance to understand a word until he lifted my hand and said, "*Ma belle*, Chelsea."

I felt François studying me. He was smiling, but it was a calculated smile, accentuated by his very large, very white teeth. I wondered if being a billionaire made him weigh everything in dollars and cents, or in this case euros, and if so, whether he trying to determine what my value was. Despite what I brought in for the ACC, my personal assets were very middle class.

It was a truth that made me feel like a fraud. I was wearing a gown that likely cost more than I earned over several months, and if I took away Estelle's magic, I was not this pretty on an average day. Not even close. There was no way I belonged at this party with all these beautiful, glamorous people. Without a purpose, like working for the ACC, I felt as if I would be more at home in the kitchen.

"Mademoiselle, it is a pleasure to make your acquaintance," François said. "You are as pretty as your picture."

I glanced at Jean Claude. He smiled at me and said, "Forgive me— I shared your photo from the studio yesterday with my friend François. I am just so happy to have you in my life again."

"That's fine," I said. Truly, I was flattered that my abrupt arrival in his life was of such significance to him.

"He is a lucky man," François said. He took the hand that Jean Claude had dropped and kissed the back of it. His lips were soft and fleshy and left a wet spot on my skin. It took all the good manners my parents had drilled into me not to pull my hand away and wipe it on my dress.

"Thank you," I said. I pushed myself to be friendly even though my instincts revolted. "The pleasure is mine."

He released my hand and turned back to Jean Claude, again speaking so rapidly in French that I was lost. Truthfully, I was relieved not to be the focus of his attention anymore. I got a weird feeling about Moreau, and I'd mixed and mingled with enough privileged males to trust my inner voice when it said, *Danger.*

A displeased look crossed Jean Claude's face, but then François pressed his point and Jean Claude nodded. I wondered if Jean Claude had been hoping to have François invest in his clothing line. If that was the case, it did not seem to be going well. I felt badly for witnessing his disappointment, so I turned away, taking the opportunity to examine the room with its towers of fresh flowers. Arrangements as big as small cars stood on pedestals, in an explosion of blue and white blossoms of delphinium, hydrangea, and lily of the valley all nestled by big leafy fern fronds.

The wink and sparkle of the diamonds, rubies, emeralds, and sapphires at the wrists, ears, and throats of the women in attendance caught my eye. I wondered how much money was in this room in jewels alone. I thought of Jason's outrage at how much cancer research could be funded with the money Severin spent on his oddities. I believed Moreau was much like Severin in wealth. It was hard to imagine having so much money and not choosing to pour every dime of it into fighting for the cure, but then, I knew that battling cancer was my issue.

"Chelsea, *mon chou*, have I lost you?" Jean Claude asked.

I turned to find him watching me. He had a speculative look in his eye that I couldn't interpret. I wondered how his conversation had gone, but I didn't want to pry.

"I'm sorry," I said. "I was soaking it all in."

He nodded and surveyed the room. He sipped his champagne, looking as if there was no other place in the world where he belonged. I admired that, because I felt as if there was no other place in the world where I could be more of an imposter. These were the sort of folks I approached in my slim skirt and blazer with a thick file in one hand and a PowerPoint in the other to coax a tax-deductible smidgeon of their wealth out of their coffers. I was not one of them. I did not fit in. These were not my people.

As much as I loved Paris and was enjoying Jean Claude, I was abruptly hit by such a deep longing for my home in Boston that I almost excused myself to go call my sister Annabelle just to hear her voice. As different as we were, Annabelle had the ability to lift me when I started to get gloomy, and right now I really missed that about her. An image of her in that hideous sparkly pink flower girl dress flitted through my mind, and I found myself smiling.

"Come, Chelsea—let me flaunt the most beautiful woman here," Jean Claude said. He slid his arm around my bare back and pulled me close.

"Certainly. Where is she?" I teased, glancing around us as if looking for another woman.

"Beautiful and humble," he said. "You are like a breath of fresh air. François was quite taken with you, as I knew he would be."

I didn't know what to say. "So your talk with him went well?"

Jean Claude stared into my eyes and then shrugged. "We are coming to terms. What did you think of him?"

"He strikes me as a man who doesn't hear the word *no* very often," I said. I was trying to be circumspect and didn't mention the hinky vibe he put off.

Jean Claude raised an eyebrow in surprise. "Could you say no to him?"

My first impulse was to say, *Hell to the yes*—after all, there was nothing that I wanted from him—but tact made me rethink, and I said, "I suppose that would depend upon what he asked of me."

Jean Claude grinned at me as if my answer was what he'd hoped it would be. I felt like I should be pleased by this, to have made him happy, but something about it felt off.

He kissed my cheek and then put my hand on his elbow. He pulled me in the direction of a stocky, bald man who was waving at him. As we walked, I felt the heat of a hard stare upon my bare back, and I glanced over my shoulder to see François watching us, or more accurately me.

The acquisitive expression on his face was one I'd seen before. It was predatory, the sort of look that reduced a woman to a plaything, an accessory, a toy for his amusement. Men who viewed women this way viewed all women this way. It had nothing to do with how attractive a woman was. His gaze met mine, and he held up his champagne glass and blew a kiss at me. It made me shiver and not in a good way.

I had no opportunity to ask Jean Claude what that was all about as we reached the portly man, who it turned out was on the Council of Paris, representing the sixteenth arrondissement.

And so it went. In a flurry of introductions, we met designers, artists, businessmen, musicians, and even a scientist or two. Everyone who was anyone in Paris at the moment was here to enjoy the hospitality of François Moreau. I ran into him twice more during the evening, and each time, I got the creeper vibe off of him. I felt as if he was circling us, keeping watch, but for what?

Jean Claude made certain I was never without a drink in my hand. I drank the first two glasses of champagne but then began to bluff the rest, turning and setting the glasses down when he wasn't looking. I couldn't decide if he was being a solicitous escort or trying to get me drunk. When he pressed the fifth glass on me, I started to get annoyed.

"Drink up, *mon chou*," he said. "We have all night ahead of us."

"Not if I drink this, we don't," I said. I went to put the glass down, but he grabbed it and pushed it more forcefully into my hand.

"Chelsea, you need to learn to live a little," he chided me.

It was the first time I'd felt any criticism coming from him, and I was taken aback that it was in regards to my not wanting to get loaded on champagne. Because a woman sloppily staggering around in a gown was so hot. I frowned.

"I think your definition of *living* and mine might be different," I said. My voice was cool as I stared down into my glass, watching the bubbles break the surface.

He ran an exasperated hand through his air. He took my elbow and led me to the corner of the room. He stared at me for a moment, and then a smile, a real charmer's grin, slowly tipped his lips.

"I'm sorry, *ma belle*," he said. He ran his hand up and down my bare arm. "I just want you to enjoy yourself."

"I am," I said. Although honestly, I was enjoying him much less now than I had seven years ago. There was something off about him tonight that I couldn't put my finger on.

Jean Claude turned away. He sipped his champagne and studied the room. I saw an unexpected hardness to his features that I didn't remember being there before.

"Is everything all right?" I asked. I leaned forward to get his attention and wobbled a bit in my heels. He caught me with a hand at my hip, and this time when he smiled, it looked more genuine.

"Yes, it's good, very good." He searched my eyes for a moment and said, "I was wondering if you could do me a tiny favor?"

I was so relieved to see a hint of his old self back, I said, "Absolutely."

"*Mon chou*, I need you to work your charms on François," he said. "You would do that for me, *non*?"

What? I'd thought a favor would entail getting Jean Claude a fresh drink, maybe a snack, or taking a walk outside to cool off in the night air.

His hand slid down my bare back to rest on my tailbone, his fingers dipping just beneath the edge of my dress. If he was giving me a hand signal, it was not one I wanted to receive. I closed my eyes and took a breath before I turned to face him, forcing his hand away.

"When you say charm François, what do you mean exactly?" I asked. I kept my voice a low purr. I wanted him to think I was on board so that he would detail it for me and there would be no misunderstanding.

"He is quite enchanted by you," he said. "And he would like for the two of you to spend some time alone together."

I was fairly clear about what he meant by *alone*. Hurt and shock made my throat tight, but I pushed through it. I was going to make him spell it out. "Alone?"

Jean Claude gave me a knowing look. Then he hit me with a one-two punch of disrespect and disillusionment. "François just wants some company. Surely, since I have given you this very expensive dress, you would do me the courtesy of being equally generous with my friend."

"You want me to sleep with him. That's why you showed him my picture. You're using me to bargain with him." It wasn't a question and he didn't deny it. I felt queasy, and it wasn't from the champagne. I couldn't believe Jean Claude was asking this of me. "Why?" I demanded. I glanced around the room. "There are much more beautiful women in this room. Why me?"

"Because you are a beautiful woman with a refreshingly innocent air about you," Jean Claude said. He stepped closer to me, looming in a way I didn't like. "You said you would do anything for me. Did you mean it?"

And now I understood why he'd been plying me with champagne. He probably thought if he got me drunk enough, I'd be okay with this. That was a hard no. There wasn't enough champagne in the world to make me prostitute myself, and clearly, Jean Claude was not the man I'd thought he was.

"I meant I'd be happy to rub your back or get you a sandwich," I said. "Whoring myself out to your friends wasn't on my list." I stepped away from him and shook my head. "Find someone else."

His brown eyes went dark, and he grabbed my elbow. "You're wearing my dress. Did you think there was no price attached to it?"

chapter seventeen

"PRICE?" I REPEATED. Fury hot enough to scorch the earth consumed me.

The sheer arrogance, the gall, the nerve of this guy. I had half a mind to rip the dress right off my body and throw it at him, except then I'd be mostly naked, and there was no dignity in that, plus the temperature would be dropping into the forties tonight, so it was a bit too chilly for that much exposure.

Instead, an image of Darby O'Shea pole dancing in Finn's Hollow flitted through my mind, and I thought about how she hadn't settled for less than she was worth. When her man had done her wrong, she'd cut him loose. Determined to follow her example, I took a step back, stared Jean Claude right in the eye, and with a flick of my wrist, flung the contents of my glass right in his face.

Jean Claude sputtered, the champagne dripping down his shocked expression, as the people around us stared in startled amusement. It was gloriously satisfying.

"Don't contact me—ever again," I hissed. With that, I made the dramatic exit of a lifetime. Head held high and back straight, I stormed through the room. People scrambled to get out of my way, and the butler scurried to open the door for me as if he was afraid I'd kick it down.

I strode from the mansion, not knowing where I was or how I was going to get home. I didn't care. I would rather swim in the Seine than have anything to do with Jean Claude Bisset ever again. As far as I was concerned, he was dead to me.

I was furious with him, with myself, with all the stupid Cinderella daydreams I'd had about the two of us. I felt like a complete and utter idiot. Tears welled up, but I refused to let them fall. It was a struggle, but I had a more pressing problem that tears wouldn't solve. I had to get the hell out of here.

"Mademoiselle," a man's voice called, and I glanced up to see the driver who had brought me here, smoking a cigarette as he stood under a tree beside his parked car. "*Ça va?*"

How was I? Not good. Not by a long shot. But here was the light of escape, shining brightly before me.

"*Indisposé*," I said. I heaved a sigh, touched my fingers to my forehead, and winced, not knowing how to say *headache* in French.

"Ah," the man said. He ground his cigarette out beneath his heel and opened the back door for me. Gesturing for me to sit, he said in stilted English, "I take you back."

I gave him the brightest smile I could manage. "*Merci beaucoup.*"

The return seemed much shorter than the drive to the party. I glanced at my phone and noted it was only a little past nine. The night was still young, but not for me. I was going to take a long shower and wash away the entire disgusting evening.

The driver opened the door for me right outside my apartment. I wasn't sure what to pay him. When I fumbled with my purse, he said, "*Non non.*"

I glanced up, and the kindness in his face almost did me in. "Thank you."

He looked at me closely, and I had the feeling he knew exactly how my evening had gone wrong. With a sympathetic sigh, he said, *"Mieux vaut être seul que mal accompagné."*

While my French was not up to a concise translation, I got the gist, which was that it was better to be alone than in poor company. True that. I stood and watched as his taillights disappeared. What a night. I hated that it had ended this way.

On a whim, I walked down the street. I realized I was hungry and wanted to eat something positively French, like steak tartare, escargot, confit de canard, or coq au vin. I felt as if my trip to Paris had been contaminated and I needed to get the magic of my quest back since I couldn't leave, not with the dinner with Severin happening tomorrow night. Too bad. I'd have given anything to be on the next plane headed to Italy and Marcellino.

He was the only one of the three whom I'd maintained contact with over the years. Before I left the States, I'd sent him a brief email telling him that I planned to be in Italy in the near future and would love to see him. To my delight and surprise, he'd written back with an open invitation to stay in one of the cottages on the vineyard grounds. I had happily accepted. Now it seemed as if fate had been pushing me to Italy all along. I didn't know if Severin was still planning to go to Italy, but I would find out at dinner, and if he was, well, that was just more proof that maybe what I sought was in the last place I'd been before I'd been called home.

A brasserie was up ahead. I could smell beef, garlic, and rosemary in the air. It lured me in as if it had hooked right into my belly. There was outside seating under a string of light bulbs and several heaters. I saw a couple of open tables and hoped I wasn't too late to score one for myself. Then I saw a man sitting alone reading a book. *Jason.*

I thought about turning around and running to my apartment to hide, but why? My night had been an epic catastrophe, but it wasn't my fault. Honestly, I could use a friend right now. Since I didn't have one in the city—or the country, for that matter—Knightley would have to do.

I entered the brasserie and found the hostess. I'd noted Jason's wine-glass was almost empty, so I arranged to have another sent from me. I slipped into a seat a few tables behind him with my own glass and waited.

The waitress brought his drink, and Jason looked up in surprise. I got a kick out of watching him look for who had sent the wine. The waitress placed the glass on the table and helped him out by gesturing to me. Jason turned around, and I gave him a little finger wave, the same one he had sent me from his balcony that afternoon.

A smile of genuine delight curved his lips and warmed his eyes. He stood and gestured for me to join him. I rose from my seat and crossed the restaurant to him. I could feel his eyes on me, but I had no idea what he was thinking; the dim lighting made it impossible to see the subtle nuances of his expression. I stopped right in front of him and glanced up.

"I'm not interrupting you, am I?"

"No, not at all." He pulled out a chair for me, and I sat down, letting him push me in just a bit. He resumed his seat and said, "Thanks for the wine."

"You're welcome." I held up my glass in a silent toast and took a sip. He did the same.

When I didn't say anything more, Jason leaned back in his seat and asked, "Want to talk about it?"

"Not really, no," I said. "Let's just say some people are not exactly as you remember them."

Jason nodded. He looked like he wanted to ask a million questions, but he didn't. "I'm sorry."

"No need," I said. "I'm fine. I was just looking to get something to eat when I spotted this brasserie and then I saw you, and I thought you could recommend something from the menu."

"*Excusez-moi.*" Jason raised his arm and waved to the waitress who had just brought the wine. Then in perfect French, he ordered. "*Elle aimerait la bouillabaisse, s'il vous plaît.*"

The waitress nodded, glancing between us with a small smile.

I was stunned. "You speak French? How did I not know this?"

He looked chagrined. "I speak one sentence of French. That was it, and I jazzed it up by saying *she* instead of *I*. Madame LeBlanc, my long-suffering French teacher, would be so proud. In fact, I was so relieved when this brasserie had the one thing I know how to pronounce on their menu, bouillabaisse, that I hunkered down and stayed put."

I laughed. "Well played, Knightley."

"Is seafood stew all right with you? I can testify that it was excellent," he said. He gestured to his empty bowl.

"It's perfect," I said. And it was—something very French, exactly what I'd been looking for. I sipped my wine.

The cool night air swept over my skin, and I pulled on my wrap, draping it around my shoulders. I was surprised to find that the silence between us didn't feel strained or awkward. In fact, it was comfortable.

Jason drank his wine as he watched the people walk by. Some were eagerly headed out for a night of revelry, while others looked as if they were headed home. The waitress brought the stew with a warm loaf of fresh bread. I offered to share with Jason, but he shook his head, saying he was full.

"Have you been in touch with Aidan tonight?" I asked.

"Yes, I let him know that you were on top of things and we needn't have worried. You would have gotten your phone back in time to meet with Severin," he said. "Aidan said, 'Of course she is,' as if he wasn't the one freaking out about your not being in touch. Honestly, I think he was worried about you, not the dinner with Severin."

"Really? Doesn't that seem out of character for a guy who is all live and let live?"

"A bit, but he has started treatment, so he might be feeling powerless and more anxious than usual."

"That makes sense. Have there been any more incidents with the Quarter Thief?" I asked.

Jason informed me that the thief had struck again, this time taking a quarter of a chocolate chip cookie Michelle had been saving for herself. What was even more mysterious was that she had left the cookie wrapped in a napkin on her desk in her office, which she kept locked, and when she unwrapped the cookie, a quarter of it was missing.

I ate with gusto, listening to the gossip. The seafood was perfection, filling me up and warding off the cool evening temperatures. The lobster stock was enhanced with saffron and fennel, and when I finished eating the muscles and scallops, I wanted to drink the remaining broth. Instead, I broke off chunks of bread and swabbed up the remainder.

"How did the Quarter Thief get into her office?" I asked.

"No one knows, but Michelle is on a rampage. She's installed an extra lock on her door, and this was after she bought her own refrigerator to keep her food in her office."

I chewed the last of my bread. "Do you think the Quarter Thief is actually just trying to drive her crazy?"

"That's a solid theory, Martin," he said. "I was thinking the same thing myself."

"I'm not sure if I want to applaud them or not. That sort of evil genius deserves respect, and yet I'm afraid of crossing them."

He laughed. "I'm going with respect. With any luck, they'll drive her out, and her HR reign of terror will end."

I studied him over my glass. "You know who it is, don't you?"

He blinked, the picture of innocence.

"Tell me," I demanded.

"You tell me first," he said.

"But I don't know who it is," I said.

"Not that," he said. "Tell me what happened tonight."

I leaned back in my chair. "Why do you care?"

"I want to know if I need to go punch someone."

"No, you don't," I said. "I can take care of myself."

"Well, I know that, Martin," he said. "Still, you're my colleague—

no, that's not right anymore. You're my friend." He looked at me. There was a sincerity in his gaze when he said, "We're friends. I don't generally stand by when my friends get hurt."

"I wasn't hurt," I said, oddly touched that he considered me a friend. I fingered my dangling earring.

"You're fidgeting like you always do when you're upset."

Self-consciously I dropped my hand. How had he caught on to that? I didn't think anyone else in my life knew that I fidgeted when I was anxious. Trying to lighten the moment, I smiled at him and repeated his previous words to me back to him. "So what you're saying is you've noticed me."

His gaze met mine with an unexpected intensity. "Yeah, I've noticed you."

I glanced away, abruptly feeling overwarm, and it wasn't the wine. "Truly, I'm not upset."

He made a scoffing noise, which mercifully broke the tension between us.

Relieved, I looked back at him and added, "Fine, I might have been a little angry, but no tears were spilled in the making of this disaster of an evening."

"Disaster? Okay, now you have to tell me what happened," he said. "It's simply cruel not to at this point."

"Okay," I said. I took a deep breath and then gave him the abridged version of the evening. I kept it as emotionless as possible, but it was hard to hide my disgust. "Can you believe he actually thought I'd fluff up some rich old man for him? So gross! Can I pick 'em or what?"

Knightley didn't return my smile. Instead, he looked coldly furious. "I don't suppose you have the address of this party?"

"No, why?"

"Because I feel a sudden need to go pummel a skeevy fashion designer."

"Stop," I said. "I don't know what is going on with Jean Claude, but I left and I am fine. There is no pummeling required."

"Chelsea." He said my first name, and it caught me off guard. Had he ever called me that before? I couldn't remember. I liked the way it sounded in his deep voice. "There is most definitely a beatdown required here, and quite possibly a crippling. This guy was trying to trade you like pork bellies to some noxious billionaire—"

"Pork bellies?" I interrupted. "That's the commodity you're comparing me to?"

"What?" he asked. He looked very earnest. "It's bacon. That's better than gold."

I laughed, which I suspected was his intent. "I'd prefer gold."

"Either way, it was a dick move, and he deserves to have a can of whoop ass unloaded on him."

"Maybe," I said. Still, I didn't want to dwell on it. "Can we not talk about it anymore? It makes me feel stupid and icky."

"There's no need for you to feel that way. Him, on the other hand . . ." Jason scowled.

"Also, you're supposed to tell me who you think the Quarter Thief is," I said.

"Fair enough," he said. "I think it's Bill Listrum."

"Bill?" I asked. "But he's sixty-seven years old and the sweetest man alive. It can't be him."

"He also got passed over for the promotion Michelle got, and he's been reporting to her for three years, which has to be unpleasant," he said. "He's about to retire. He has nothing to lose."

"All right, I can see where that makes sense, but Bill?" I shook my head. It couldn't be. Then again, I hadn't proved to be such a stellar judge of character, now had I? "I give your theory a solid maybe."

"I'll take it. More importantly, what should we do now that your evening is free?"

"Climb into bed and pretend today never happened."

"*Non non*," he protested in a perfect French accent, which made me smile. "Look at you. You're stunning. You can't go hide in your room. You need to get back on the saddle."

"Ugh, why is it always a saddle? Saddles bruise your butt bones. Why can't it be 'you need to get back in the bubble bath, little lady'?"

He laughed. "Have it your way, but you and me are going out on the town."

"What? But I'm not—" I was going to say I wasn't dressed, but that was clearly not the case.

"Exactly," he said. He rose to his feet. "Sit here and enjoy your wine. I'm going to change, and then we are hitting the City of Light, baby."

Oh boy.

chapter eighteen

HIS SUIT MIGHT not have been French, but it fit the man spectacularly. Navy blue, it conformed to his broad shoulders and tapered down to his narrow waist. He wore a white dress shirt beneath it, no tie, matching navy slacks, and dark-brown dress shoes—no Converse sneakers. Shocker! Then again, since he'd rushed here to take my place at the dinner with Severin, it made sense that he'd brought his most professional attire.

Truly, the man looked divine. I supposed he'd always been this handsome, even back when I detested him, but now I knew him outside the office and could appreciate that there was more to Jason Knightley than I'd previously acknowledged.

I watched him walk across the patio toward me and felt my spirits lift. I was in Paris, and I had a handsome and, more importantly, nice man to escort me about town. Really, what more could a girl want?

Well, not to have been made a complete fool of, but at least I'd gotten out before I found myself in an untenable situation. And I'd had the great satisfaction of dousing Jean Claude in champagne. That helped.

"Okay, you were smiling, and then your expression slid into a deep dark frown. What happened between me standing over there and arriving here?" he asked.

"Nothing," I said.

"Please." He shook his head. "Your WTF line is so deep"—he paused to gently poke the skin between my eyebrows—"I could go rappelling in there."

I immediately stopped frowning. "Better?"

"Much," he said. He held out a hand and helped me to my feet. "Come on—we're running short on time."

"I thought we had all night," I said.

"Not for our first event," he said. "In fact, we are cutting it very, very close."

He had already paid the bill, and we hurried from the brasserie with Jason keeping my hand in his. He got to the curb, raised his free hand to his mouth, and let out a piercing whistle. A taxi appeared as if out of nowhere. Jason opened the door and none too gently pushed me in.

"Eiffel Tower, *s'il vous plaît*," he said.

"Oh, that's a great idea," I said. "But we need tickets to go up, and I doubt there are any available."

He pulled two tickets out of his suit pocket. My eyes went wide. "What?"

"The couple who had the apartment before me had to leave town unexpectedly. They left the tickets with Zoe, and she offered them to me, for a price, when I rented the place. I had thought I'd be going alone, but then you appeared." He glanced at the time-stamped ticket. "Plus, we get champagne at the bar on the top."

"Drunk on the Eiffel Tower," I said. "This night is looking up."

"Attagirl," he said. He glanced out the window, tracking our progress.

I could see the tower in the distance; we were getting closer. I felt my nerves wind up and my anxiety spike. I'd never been very good at cutting appointments close. What if we didn't make it? It would be a waste of tickets. We'd miss out. I'd never wanted to be on top of the tower, drinking champagne, as much as I did right now.

"Hey." Jason grabbed my hand and gave it a squeeze. "Don't worry—we've got this."

There he was. The guy who never worried about anything and was totally cool with winging it. He always assumed everything was going to work out okay, and even if it didn't, he could manage it. This was the complete and total opposite of how I lived my life, but for once, just this once, I was going to chill out and turn my penchant for punctuality over to the universe. If we were meant to go up in the tower, we would, and if we weren't, we wouldn't.

When our cab driver pulled to a stop near the tower, Jason settled up with him while I climbed out of the car. The night had gotten cold, and I wished I'd thought to bring a coat. I was going to freeze my butt off at the top. Oh well, what did the French say? *C'est la vie.* It was totally worth it.

"Come on." Jason grabbed my hand again. "We have to run for it!"

I was not exactly in running footwear, but at least I wasn't in stilettos. I let him pull me through the crowd, past the carousel, and across the street, toward the entrance. Dashing into the park, we hurried through the darkness and passed the tchotchke sellers with their blankets spread on the ground displaying tiny Eiffel Towers flashing in all colors.

Our time-stamped tickets put us in the fast lane, and we blitzed through security and the metal detectors. Up the stairs we went, pausing to show our tickets to a man at a desk. He gestured for us to go on, and we crossed a small room and got in line with a bunch of other overdressed people for the elevator that would take us to the second floor. The elevator came swiftly, and Jason hustled me into the car. Although we were level, the car moved on a slant up the leg and into the belly of the tower. I noticed that Jason was still holding my hand. I would have pulled away, but my fingers were cold and his were warm.

We climbed out at the second floor, but there was no time to look at the view, as we had to catch the lift to the summit. Up some more stairs and into the queue, which snaked around the platform. The line moved swiftly, as it was near the end of the evening, and we stepped into the narrow hallway to catch the elevator.

There were four elevators in operation, two red and two yellow, and they worked in pairs as a counterweight for each other. When one elevator emptied, Jason hustled me inside. I was pressed up against the glass with him standing behind me, making a cage out of his body to protect me from the swarm of people who pushed into the lift with us.

They could have crushed me, and I wouldn't have cared. Now, after all this time, I understood why Paris was called the City of Light. It wasn't just because of its prominence during the Age of Enlightenment. As we rose up into the sky in a slow glide, I stared out the glass, past the intricate ironwork, at the beautiful golden lights of the city laid out before me. It was breathtaking.

"Wow, it's beautiful," Jason whispered in my ear.

I turned my head and found him staring at me, our faces just inches apart. I studied his long-lashed, pretty eyes and square jaw with just the right amount of scruff and said, "Yes, it is."

An awareness passed between us, and he smiled at me before he looked back out at the city. "When we reach the top, we'll have just a few minutes to wait before the light show. I read that they only illuminate the tower with sparkling lights for five minutes at the top of every hour."

"Good timing," I said. The words were stilted, as I was now excruciatingly aware of the man standing at my back. I wanted to lean into his warmth, but that would be weird, right? I'd started the night on a date with one man, and now I was here, at the most romantic place in the world, with a guy that up until quite recently I had loathed with every molecule I possessed. The whole situation was most definitely bad form, or was it Paris? I had no idea.

The lift stopped and we stepped out. We were in the glassed-in part of the tower. It was crowded, but Jason took my hand and led me up the narrow stairs to outside. The wind hit me right in the face, and I shivered. My wrap was utterly useless. Without a word, Jason shrugged out of his jacket and put it around my shoulders, pulling me close and keeping me protected within the circle of his arm. Well, how about that. Knightley was a gentleman.

We took in the view: the blue beam shining from the top, the bright city lights rolling all the way to the horizon, and just below, the tour boats and dinner cruises on the Seine. It was stunning. Jason excused himself and went to the small window of the Bar à Champagne to fetch our drinks. He returned with two glasses and a big smile.

"What's so funny?" I asked.

"Wouldn't Aidan be proud of us spending time together like this? We haven't even argued."

"I think shock would be a more likely reaction," I said.

"To Aidan," Jason said. He lifted his glass, and I tapped mine against his.

"To Aidan."

We took hearty sips. I wasn't sure whether it was to calm my nerves at being over nine hundred feet in the air with the wind whipping around me or in the hope that the alcohol would warm me up. I just knew that this champagne was the best I'd ever tasted. Maybe it was the altitude; possibly it was the company. All I knew for certain was that I felt, quite literally, on top of the world. People moved around us, but we didn't give up our little patch of real estate.

Jason shivered. He was obviously getting cold in just his dress shirt. I moved close to him and put my arm around his back, pressing myself into his side. When he glanced down in surprise, I said, "Body heat."

He grunted and pulled me in closer. "You keep surprising me, Martin."

"Do I?" I asked. I knew I probably shouldn't be pleased by this, but

I found that I liked that I could surprise him. Honestly, it was nice to surprise myself as well.

"Yeah, in the best possible way." His voice sounded gruff, and he finished his champagne and waited for me to do the same. When I did, he returned our glasses to the bar. Then he took his cell phone and his wireless AirPods out of his pocket. "Tell me, Martin, have you ever danced on the top of the Eiffel Tower?"

"Nope, I can't say that I have," I said.

"Cool."

He handed me one of the earpieces, and I tucked it into my ear. He did the same and then tapped the display on his phone before putting it back into his pants pocket. He held out his arms, and as the distinctive orchestral opening to "La vie en rose" began to play, I slipped into his embrace, and Edith Piaf began to belt out the lyrics, casting a spell around us with her voice singing about her special man whose love made her see life as rosy.

There wasn't much room to move, but that didn't stop Jason from leading me around in a tight circle and then twirling me within his arms, making my dress flare out. I felt like a 1940s film star, beautiful, glamorous, and oh so sexy. It was a balm to my battered soul.

Together we moved as the wind tugged at our clothes and the conversations of the people around us fell away. Jason pulled me in close, and I could feel the heat of him wrap around me as strongly as his arms. I felt my heart soar up in my chest as the scent of him, a low note of amber dusted with cardamom and mint, filled my senses. I wanted to curl up in the smell of him, as if he were my favorite cow pajamas. It was a comforting scent that made me feel . . . at home.

Edith hit a sweet high note just as I pulled back to glance up at his face. My heels gave me an extra two inches of height, making my gaze level with his mouth, and I couldn't help but notice the generous curve of his lips.

"Hey, eyes up here, Martin," he teased.

I glanced up, and the laughter in his gaze made me smile, but the heat in his eyes caused my breath to stutter stop in my lungs. That look. It was the sort that went to a girl's head, making her think a man was consumed by her. It was an impossible look to resist. Throwing common sense and caution off the tower like confetti, I slid my arms around his neck and pulled him down so that I could kiss him.

When my mouth met the warmth of his and tasted the champagne on his lips, the only thought in my head was *More.* I parted my lips and deepened the kiss, vaguely aware that Jason had slid one hand under his jacket and up the middle of my bare back, anchoring me close while his other hand cupped the back of my head as he returned my kiss with equal fervor.

The feel of his mouth against mine was everything. He sipped my lower lip, ran his tongue across my upper lip, and pressed my mouth gently open with his. The rough rub of his closely shaved scruff made my skin tingle. The kiss was hot, smooth, wet, and delicious, and it made my head spin faster than the champagne had. I felt as if I was free-falling into a desire so thick and rich that my entire body was vibrating with want.

I clung to him, trying to get closer. My hands dug into his hair, and I melted against him as he kissed me senseless. His mouth robbed me of reason, and his hands stroked the good sense right out of me. I was at his mercy and couldn't have been happier to be so.

Oohs and aahs broke through my passionate haze, which seemed very appropriate given the impact of his kiss. I pulled away and blinked, expecting to see the world changed. I wasn't disappointed. Bright lights were sparkling all around us as light beams flitted across the metal structure of the Eiffel Tower from top to bottom. The building had been beautiful before, but now it felt as if there were a touch of magic in it. I glanced at Jason, who was gazing wide eyed at the spectacle. Magic, indeed.

He tucked my back against his front and wrapped his arms around me as we stood and watched the five-minute light show. Some people were filming, but most were just taking it in, recognizing that they would most likely never be standing on the top of the Eiffel Tower again during such an extraordinary moment. Pure, undiluted joy beamed through me.

This was the beauty of Paris. When something didn't go as expected, there was always something else to see, do, taste, or feel. I was at the top of the freaking Eiffel Tower! Did it get any better than this? I glanced behind me to see Jason watching the light show. As if he felt my gaze, he turned to look down at me. The same sense of wonder lit his eyes.

"Like I said, you keep surprising me," he said. Then he kissed me quick, tightened his arms around me, and rested his chin on my shoulder as we watched the end of the show.

He kept my hand in his for the entire elevator ride down. When I went to return his jacket, he shook his head. He looped his arm around my waist and pulled me close. We walked to the cabstand on the street in front of the tower. The line was mercifully short, as the tower was now closed, and we were soon in a taxi.

Jason helped me into the back seat and then leaned forward and gave the driver directions. I noticed the address was not the one for our apartments above Café Zoe. When he leaned back, I sent him an inquiring look.

"We need to make one small stop on the way home," he said. "Are you game?"

A ridiculously flirty girl who had heretofore been unknown was inside me, jumping up and down and clapping. I refused to let her out and instead gave the careless shrug that seemed to be a part of the vocabulary of the French, and said, "*Mais oui.*"

"Excellent." He sat back against the seat, and as if it was the most natural thing in the world, he pulled me close and I let him. As if by unspoken agreement, we didn't talk about the kiss on top of the Eiffel

Tower. I supposed it was sort of like a New Year's Eve kiss. The giddiness of the moment had taken over, and we'd kissed. No big deal. Really. Just because it was the most singular kiss of my life, really, no need to dwell.

The city lights moved past the car window in a blur, and I rested my head against his shoulder. I felt as if we were in our own private nest, where it was warm and quiet and safe. A few weeks ago, if someone had told me that I'd feel this way sharing a cab with Knightley in Paris, I'd have thought they were mental. I'd have imagined that any ride with Knightley would be spent with me timing my jump and roll for when the cab slowed down enough that I could escape him. I smiled.

All too soon, the taxi stopped, and we were climbing out again. The neighborhood was quiet. There were no crowds, only a small shop front with its awning still out and a handful of customers sitting at narrow tables inside.

"What is this place?" I asked.

"Le Chocolat de Lucille. I was told it is the only place in Paris to get *chocolat chaud à l'ancienne,*" he said.

"Old-style hot chocolate?" I asked. "Yes, please."

Jason grinned and walked me into the tiny café. We chose a small table by the window, and then he went to the counter and ordered two hot chocolates. I watched the dark-haired woman, who looked to be in her twenties, take his order and flirt with him. Jason seemed completely oblivious to the batted lashes and come-hither smile.

Okay, so that was charming, although it shouldn't matter to me whether he noticed her or not, since we weren't dating. We'd shared a kiss. He was still Knightley, and I was still Martin—i.e., oil and water or fire and gas. Either way, not good. It was just that our lips now knew the shape and taste of each other . . . intimately. These things happened. True, they'd never happened to me before, but I had it on good authority—Annabelle—that they did happen to some people sometimes.

Jason returned with a tray. On it sat two mugs of the thickest, richest-looking hot chocolate I had ever seen. There were also two more plates, each with a pink and a green macaron on it. I glanced up at Jason in delight.

"I don't want this to go to your head," I said. "But right now, holding that tray, you are the most perfect man who ever drew breath."

He laughed and rested the tray on the table, unloading the mugs and plates. "I'll try not to let it swell up my ego, especially since I have the sneaking suspicion that any man carrying a tray of hot chocolate and rose and pistachio macarons would be considered worthy."

"It would certainly weigh in their favor," I agreed. I wrapped my hands around my mug and let the warmth seep into my cold fingers.

I watched as Jason tucked his spoon into the artistically shaped, fresh whipped cream covered in chocolate curls. He managed to get a little of the hot chocolate on his spoon as well. When he tasted it, he closed his eyes as if savoring every nuance of flavor. I had the thought that he would make love like that—he would relish every bit of it.

Oof! My face got hot, and my body temperature spiked at the mental image. This was bad. I should not be having lewd thoughts about a colleague. For that matter, I shouldn't have kissed a coworker. Michelle in HR would have a conniption if she found out.

No fraternizing among employees was a rule she relished enforcing. The thought made me panic just a little. We were in Paris, I rationalized; it was an accident. Yeah, my lips accidently fell on his. Happened all the time. Ugh.

I needed to build some boundaries and fast. I tried to remember all the things Knightley did that drove me nuts. At the moment, I couldn't think of one. Damn it!

Overheated, I let go of my mug and shrugged off his jacket, taking care to drape it over the back of my chair. When I glanced up, he was watching me with an intense look. He pointed to my mug.

"You have to try this. It's . . . Well, it ain't your grandma's powdered hot chocolate—that's for damn sure."

I picked up my spoon. I noted that the hot chocolate visible beneath the dollop of whipped cream was a glossy shade of dark brown. I tucked my spoon in, and it was almost like diving into a dark chocolate mousse. I scooped up some chocolate and whipped cream and a couple of chocolate curls.

When I brought it to my lips, I could feel Jason staring at my mouth. It made me self-conscious, and I kept my gaze down so I wouldn't get rattled and drop hot chocolate all over my white dress. I closed my mouth over my spoon and abruptly forgot to be self-conscious or mannerly—heck, I even forgot my name.

"Ermagawd," I said as the silky texture of the chocolate and the whipped cream slid over my tongue and down my throat in the most exquisite explosion of bittersweet. I felt as if taste buds that had been dormant my entire life were suddenly awake and clamoring for more.

I glanced at Jason and said, "I think I'm having a religious experience here."

He laughed. He spooned up more of his *chocolat chaud* and said, "I know. I love it so much I think I might marry it."

I sipped more chocolate and then decided I was ready for a macaron. I nudged one of the plates toward him and said, "Together?"

"Agreed. Pistachio first?"

I nodded, and we each reached for a pale-green cream-filled meringue shaped like a cookie. At the same time, we took a bite. It was glorious. The crunchy, chewy meringue cookie with the creamy center melted in my mouth, leaving the delightfully delicate aftertaste of pistachio.

"So good," he said. "I may need a box of these to go."

"Don't tempt me," I said. "I don't even want to think about how many calories we're consuming."

"We're in Paris—calories don't count here." He glanced at me, considering. "I never would have guessed you for having a sweet tooth, Martin."

"Oh, I don't have one," I said. "I have many." Then I smiled at him, showing my teeth.

"Well, your restraint at the office is unparalleled," he said. "Whenever the Friday doughnuts appear, I never see you crack. You don't even have one."

"Because if I did, I'd eat five," I said. "I'm a weak, weak woman when tempted."

"Is that so?" he asked. And just like that, we weren't talking about doughnuts anymore.

I met his gaze and felt the awareness roll between us like a ripple on the luscious chocolate in my cup. There was no ignoring it or denying it, but I wasn't sure what to do with it either. Was the attraction real or just a fallout from my bitter disappointment in Jean Claude? Or perhaps it was manufactured out of the magic of being in Paris and had no real substance? Maybe I'd look at Jason tomorrow and feel nothing but my usual exasperation for him.

A man in an apron entered the dining area and began putting up the chairs, breaking the moment. He glanced at us and began to sing. It was not a song I recognized, but his voice was lovely and the tune made me smile. Every now and then, he would glance at us, wag his thick eyebrows, smile, and continue crooning.

"Do you suppose he wants a tip?" Jason asked. "Because truly, I have no idea what he's singing. Do you?"

"Not a clue," I said. "But he's certainly enjoying himself."

The serenade continued, and when the pretty brunette from the counter stopped by our table with the check, she glanced at Jason and asked, "Do you know the song?"

"No," he said.

The woman glanced at him from beneath her eyelashes and said, "It is 'Donnons-nous cette chance.' How you say—give us a chance."

Her invitation could not have been clearer if she'd stripped naked and crooked her finger at him. Knightley was not taking the hint.

"He has an excellent singing voice," he said. He turned to me. "Don't you think?"

"Most definitely," I agreed.

I glanced around the café and realized we were the last ones here. I exchanged an amused look with Jason, and we made quick work of the remaining macarons and our chocolate.

Back out in the night, our cab was still at the curb. As Jason helped me into the back, he explained, "I figured having him wait was smarter than trying to find a taxi when we were finished."

The neighborhood was quiet for being in the middle of the city, and I nodded. "Good plan."

We were silent as we zipped through Paris back to our apartments. I tried not to think about what would happen when we arrived. I knew I was still smarting from my horrible evening with Jean Claude, but the night out with Jason had obliterated the bad memories, and for that I would be ever grateful. But did that mean there was more here? I didn't know. And even if there was, there were serious ramifications to an office romance, and I was uncomfortable even thinking about it.

The cab pulled up in front of our door, and Jason helped me out and then settled the fare. I stood on the sidewalk, shivering in his jacket while waiting and wondering if I should just ghost into my apartment before he noticed. Yeah, because that was so mature.

Jason exchanged a farewell with the driver, who gave us a cheeky grin before tearing off into the night. When he turned to me, there was a flash of uncertainty in his eyes. Here it came, I suspected—either he was going to try to blow off our kiss on the Eiffel Tower as nothing, or he was going to take it as a green light and try to get into my bed. Men were so predictable . . . except Knightley did neither of those things.

As I stood on the curb, shivering, he walked toward me, looking like a big cat stalking its prey. He slid his hands under his coat and held my hips, the warmth of his palms heating my skin. He lowered his forehead to mine, our breath mingled, and he said, "I want to kiss you, just kiss you, for a few hours or possibly a few days."

That sent a flash of pure heat rocketing through my body at the same time it surprised a laugh out of me. I leaned back to study his face. His gaze was tender with a slow-burning desire. Irresistible. To heck with work and its out-of-date policies. Kissing wasn't that egregious of an offense.

"I think that'd be all right," I said.

He grinned and pulled me close. While our earlier kiss had been a friendly exploration that revealed an unexpected connection, there was nothing friendly about this embrace. When his mouth met mine, it was raw with need and want. He kissed me with a ruthlessness that left me gasping. It felt as if he couldn't get enough of me, and I felt the exact same way about him.

It was intoxicating, more potent than any champagne. I wanted to know the taste of his tongue as it twined with mine, the feel of his muscle-hardened body beneath my fingertips, and the scent of his hair and skin as I pressed closer to breathe him in. I wanted to know what made him sigh and moan, curse and grunt, and I wanted to know what he looked like when he went over the edge. Suddenly, I wanted Knightley. Desperately.

When we broke apart, we were both breathing heavily, and with unsteady fingers, he tucked a lock of my hair behind my ear. The gesture made me melt inside, but without his warmth, the chilly night air made me shiver.

"Come on—let's get you warm," he said.

He took my hand and pulled me toward the bright-blue door. He used his key to unlock it and then ushered me inside. He pulled the door shut behind us. I turned, took two steps, and faltered. Sitting on the floor in front of the mailboxes was Jean Claude.

chapter nineteen

JEAN CLAUDE LOOKED terrible. He smelled worse. The stench of stale cigarettes and alcohol surrounded him like a fog of sour stank. I blanched and put my hand over my mouth.

"Jean Claude, what are you doing here?" I asked.

"Mon chou!" he cried. He pushed up to standing. He was wearing the same suit he'd had on at the party, but it was untucked and wrinkled. His hair was disheveled, and his five-o'clock shadow was looking more like some serious past-midnight shade.

I held up my hands to ward him off when he reached for me. I felt Jason step up behind me. He put his hands on my hips and pulled me back against his chest. I didn't have to look at him to know he was glaring at Jean Claude. I could feel the tension radiating out from him in waves.

Jean Claude glared right back. He looked at me with a frown and asked, "What is this? You are with him now?"

"No," I said at the same time Jason said, "Yes."

We looked at each other in surprise.

"What do you mean, 'no'?" Jason asked.

"What do you mean, 'yes'?" I countered.

"We were just kissing as if our lives depended upon it. I kind of figured the being-together thing was implied," he said.

Jean Claude gasped and threw his arms up in outrage. "You kissed him? This, how do you say, *tête de nœud*!"

I gasped. "There is no need for that sort of language."

"What did he call me?" Jason asked. He went to step around me, but I slid in front of him, halting his progress.

"The literal translation is 'knot head,'" I said.

"All right, I've been called worse." He visibly shrugged it off.

"But the slangy French meaning is more like, um, 'dickhead,'" I clarified.

Jason picked me up by the waist, turned, and set me down behind him. Then he charged toward Jean Claude, who met him halfway. Both men had teeth bared and fists clenched, looking like they were going to tear each other apart. They circled each other, looking for the other's vulnerability. First they went one way, then back, then back again. It was like watching a very poor showing on *Dancing with the Stars*.

I shook my head. Why were men so dumb? Was this supposed to be flattering? It wasn't. It just made me think my taste in men was severely lacking.

"All right, you two, don't be idiots," I said. I crossed the vestibule and opened the door to the street. "Jean Claude, I think it's best if you go."

"*Non non*," he said. He turned his back on Jason and approached me. "I came to explain to you about François."

I gestured for him to go through the door, but he shook me off.

"It was just a misunderstanding, *mon chou*," he said. "I didn't express myself very well. I would never ask you to do something you don't want to do."

I leaned against the open door, my arms crossed over my chest. "But you did, and what's worse is that you made it a debt I was to repay you for this dress." I looked at him with all the disappointment I felt. "You are not the man I thought you were, Jean Claude."

He looked crestfallen. He reached for my hand, grabbing my fingers in his and holding them in a grip that was too tight and didn't allow for escape. He pressed the backs of my fingers to his lips and said, "I would never have let any harm come to you. You have to believe me."

I stared at the beautiful man in front of me. A few days ago—heck, a few hours ago—his attention would have meant everything to me, but now I knew he had a love greater than any other, and it was for himself. He would sacrifice anyone or anything at all in the name of his design house. I was nobody's collateral.

I pulled my fingers out of his hand. "I'm sorry, Jean Claude, but we're done here."

"You heard her." Jason stepped forward and grabbed Jean Claude by the arm. "Time for you to go."

"Mind your business," Jean Claude snapped at Jason. The two of them were nose to nose, and I noticed that Jason had a couple of inches and a lot more brawn than Jean Claude.

"She is my business," Jason said. He began to push him out the door.

"Let go!" Jean Claude demanded. He tried to shake Jason off, but the man clung like a burr. "*Ta mère est tellement petite que sa tête pue des pieds!*"

Jason scowled. He glanced at me and asked, "What did he say?"

"I'm not sure," I said. "But it sounded like 'your mother smells like feet.'"

Jason's mouth popped open in outrage. He grabbed Jean Claude by the front of his shirt and growled, "Did you just 'yo mama' me? I am going to drop you, asshole."

He shoved Jean Claude through the door, and they stumbled onto the sidewalk.

It was dark, and there was no one around but me to witness the two men now involved in an intense match of taking wild swings at each other while going insult for insult, which was ridiculous because neither one of them understood a word the other said, but I supposed to them the meanings were clear.

I clapped my hands. I whistled. I stomped my foot. Nothing. The sound of a high-pitched engine cut into the ruckus, and a mint-green Vespa popped up onto the sidewalk beside me. I feared it might be the National Police, but when the driver lifted off the helmet, a headful of thick braids cascaded down her back. Zoe.

"*Mon Dieu!*" she cried.

"Indeed," I agreed.

"You don't deserve her!" Jean Claude declared.

"Maybe not, but at least I'm not trying to sell her to the highest bidder," Jason snapped.

Jean Claude cursed and swung at Jason's head. Jason ducked and came back up in the circle of Jean Claude's arms, connecting his meaty fist to Jean Claude's nose. There was the sound of bones crunching, and then blood was spurting everywhere. Zoe and I winced and squinted our eyes, because that made it so much easier to tolerate. Not really.

"You son of a bitch!" spat Jean Claude.

He came back at Jason with a right hook that clocked Jason under his left eye. Jason staggered back, and Jean Claude jumped him, tackling him to the hard ground. The two men rolled as they tried to land punches and kicks, grunting and swearing as they went.

"I came in extra early to start the bread," Zoe said. "I wasn't expecting a show."

"They're being idiots," I said.

Zoe nodded. "I'll see if I have something to cool their fire." She hurried toward the locked café, leaving me to monitor the morons.

They grappled, they grunted, and I heard someone's clothing tear. Enough!

"Stop! Stop it right now!" I demanded.

"Here." I turned to see Zoe hurrying back with a pitcher of water in her hands. I grabbed it from her and tossed the contents on top of the two men, jumping back as they broke apart, sputtering, dripping, and cursing.

Jason shoved Jean Claude away from him with a look of disgust and rolled to standing. He was filthy. His shirt was ripped, and his eye was beginning to swell. Jean Claude staggered to his feet. He was covered in blood and dirt. He looked like he had officially gotten his ass kicked.

Given what he had been planning for me earlier, I did not feel one bit of sympathy for him. Of course I didn't feel any sympathy for Jason either. He'd had no right to attack Jean Claude like he had. I didn't need him to defend me.

I handed Jean Claude the dish towel Zoe stuffed into my hand. "Go home, Jean Claude. I have nothing to say to you now or ever."

"But, *mon chou*—" he protested, but I held up my hand in a *stop* gesture.

"Goodbye," I said.

He stared at me for a moment before he turned away, looking utterly defeated.

"And good riddance," Jason added.

I grabbed him by the arm and spun him around to face me. "What were you thinking, getting into a brawl when we are hours away from the biggest meeting of our collective careers?"

"He had it coming," Jason protested. I would have continued to argue, but Zoe joined us with a cloth full of ice.

"It's best if you go upstairs," she said. She looked at Jason in sympathy. "Blood on the sidewalk is bad for business."

"Thanks. Sorry," he said. He put the ice on his eye with a grimace.

"What can you do when the heart is involved and the passions are aroused?" Zoe said with a shrug.

I felt my face get hot. The introvert inside me hated that there had been such a public scene, and it was so unnecessary, as there had been no heart involved, just stupidity.

"Keys," I said and held out my hand to Jason.

Jason took his apartment key out of his pocket and put it in my hand. I led the way back into the building and up the stairs. I passed my apartment and unlocked the door to his place. It was laid out exactly like mine, so I headed to the tiny bathroom while he went to the couch.

I grabbed a hand towel and soaked it with hot water and a little soap. When I got back to the living room, he had his head tipped back on the couch with the cloth of ice on his eye. His knuckles were cut up, and he had blood splatter on his shirt, which was done for.

Without a word, I tended his hands. Once the blood was cleaned off, he wasn't as banged up as I'd feared. This did nothing to calm me down. I was so furious with him for getting into a fight, I was practically pulsing with anger.

Jason watched me out of his one good eye. "What's eating you, Martin?"

"Nothing." My voice sounded like the crack of a whip.

"Yeah, when a woman says 'nothing' like that, it's not nothing," he said. "Out with it."

As if he had popped my bubble of calm with a pin, I found myself exploding on him. "Of all the stupid, boneheaded, ridiculous displays of idiocy that I have ever watched from you over the years, that episode downstairs was the absolute limit. What the hell were you thinking?"

"Um, I was thinking that guy tried to use you, and I was going to rearrange his face for it," he said.

"Humph," I huffed. I was not flattered. I was not impressed. I was livid. I stormed out of the living room to rinse out the towel. I returned in a moment and lifted the ice pack off his eye to assess the damage and clean the scrapes on his face.

"No one asked you to defend me," I said. "You had no right."

"That asshole, Jean Claude"—he said his name in a mocking French accent—"got exactly what he deserved. In fact, he got less than he deserved. I wish I'd pounded on him twice as hard."

"If anyone was going to punch him in the face, it should have been me. You behaved like a thug. I won't tolerate that," I said. I finished tending the cuts on his face and put the ice back on his eye. "I can handle my own life, thank you very much. Now I'm going to my place. You might want to take something for that eye."

I dropped the hand towel in the bathroom sink, washed my hands, and headed for the door. Jason was leaning against it with his arms over his chest.

"Martin, you are full of shit," he said.

I raised one eyebrow and put my hands on my hips. "Excuse me?"

"You don't care that I punched Jean Claude in the face. You're just using that fight to put some distance between us." He pointed to me and then himself. "Because you are freaking out about what's happening here."

"Pff," I scoffed. "As if. And for the record, there is nothing happening here."

"Bullshit," he said.

My mouth dropped open in outrage.

"Yes, this is me officially calling you on your bullshit," he said. "I mean, damn, was I alone during our double make-out fest? Nope. I clearly remember you being there, too."

"That doesn't signify." I tossed my head in a dismissive gesture. "It was the Eiffel Tower—everything is romantic on the tower, especially with champagne. And as for the second kiss, we're in Paris in April. These things happen."

Jason looked at me as if I were nuts. I lost my cool. I gestured with my hands, holding them out toward the window as if I were showing a prize on a game show. "April in Paris, surely you've heard of that ridiculously romantic setting? Everyone goes a little crazy in Paris in April, but it doesn't mean anything."

"What?! Of course it means something," he argued. "In fact, it probably means ten times more because magic on the Eiffel Tower doesn't happen for no reason, and how about Paris in April anyway? Pretty freaking great, right?"

Magic? I didn't know what to say. If I said the kisses we'd shared hadn't been all that, he'd know I was lying, but if I admitted it, then he'd win the argument, which could not happen for a variety of reasons, not the least of which was that we were colleagues who never should have been kissing in the first place.

I mean, this was Knightley. We were rivals. Sure, we'd been getting along here, but what happened if we took this further? What happened when we returned to Boston? We were in charge of a ten-million-dollar ask. We weren't supposed to get involved. In fact, I could see Michelle's head exploding at the mere idea that two employees had hooked up on the company dime in Paris. Ack!

Jason ran a hand over his face and winced when he accidentally touched his eye. "Listen, I get that this was unexpected."

"What 'this'?" I balked. Yup, still panicking. "There is no 'this.'"

"Yes, there is," he insisted. "And I know it wasn't on your agenda, and I know how much you hate that, but it's here and it's real, and you can't pretend it isn't."

"Yes, I can," I said. When he lifted his good eyebrow at me, I knew I'd stepped in it. "Not that I'm pretending anything. What happened between us wasn't real. It was conjured up out of champagne and excess emotional baggage, that's all."

"Bullshit."

"Stop saying that!"

"Fine," he said. "Horseshit. How's that? Better?"

"You're impossible."

"And you're kidding yourself," he said. "Do you really think that what happened between us tonight was so hot because of geography?"

"Yes." I tipped my chin up defiantly.

Jason took a step forward so that he was looming over me. It was a power play, and I resented it. I also refused to back up.

"You're lying to yourself. You're so busy trying to find a girl who doesn't exist anymore, you're missing what's right in front of you."

"You don't know what you're talking about," I snapped.

"The girl who went on a gap year seven years ago doesn't exist anymore, and looking for her is futile," he said. His voice was kind, as if he felt bad about delivering such unwelcome news. It made me clench my teeth. "You're not going to find love with one of your exes. You need to find someone suited to who you are today."

"Like you?" I scoffed.

"Yes," he said. He reached out and pulled me close. "Exactly like me."

Then he kissed me. His lips were warm and firm and fit perfectly against mine as he wooed me into responding to him and the scorching chemistry between us. He splayed his hand on my lower back and pulled me in high and tight, our bodies locking together like two puzzle pieces. His tongue teased the seam of my lips until they parted, and then he deepened the kiss and buried his hand in my hair to hold me steady while he wrecked me with his mouth, positively wrecked me.

The kiss was just as magical as the one atop the Eiffel Tower, perhaps even more so, because whether I wanted to admit it or not, Jason had come to mean something to me. He was more than a coworker; he was definitely a friend, and maybe—no. I stopped the thought.

Jason wasn't who I wanted. He was connected to the Chelsea of my present. The cold, lonely, workaholic person I no longer wanted to be. I wanted the old Chelsea, the bighearted, wide-eyed woman of my youth, before my life had become a tragedy.

It took every bit of inner strength I possessed to break the kiss and pull away from him, but I did it. I pushed out of his embrace, putting some distance between us. I was out of breath, and my pulse was erratic. I felt as if I'd just run the Boston Marathon and I needed a bucket of ice or a fan to get my body temperature back down.

"You don't understand," I wheezed. "Seven years ago, I lost someone very dear to me to cancer. And afterward, in my grief, I lost myself." I felt a hot tear streak down my cheek. "You can't understand what it's like if you haven't suffered that sort of pain. It changes you. But I want to be that Chelsea again. I want to be the optimistic, happy, adventurous woman that I once was. I don't want to be the emotionless zombie that I've become."

He stared at me. "You've never been emotionless around me."

"Rage doesn't count."

"Is that all you feel with me, really?"

"No," I admitted. I scrambled to come up with a new definition for us that had built-in barriers. "I think we've become . . . friends."

"Friends?" he asked. He laughed without humor. He shook his head. He stared past me, out the window, and then looked back. "Is that all we are?"

I saw the confusion and disappointment on his face, and I felt my throat get tight. How had everything gotten so complicated?

I met his gaze and held it, refusing to look away when I said, "That's all I have to give you right now." He looked so hurt and bewildered that I glanced away. "Listen, we just have to get through this dinner with Severin, and then we'll go our separate ways. You'll fly back to Boston, and I'll press on to Italy."

"It doesn't have to be that way," he said. He spread his hands wide as if saying, *Give me a chance*. "You can come home with me, and we can figure out what this thing is between us."

"No, I can't," I said. "I'm committed to going to Italy. If I don't, I'll always wonder *what if*, and I don't want to live with that. Besides, for all I know, Severin is still planning to meet me at the wine festival, and I've already made plans."

"With the guy in Italy?"

I nodded.

"So you're willing to throw away something amazing, albeit unexpected, for a memory that may not live up to your expectation?" he asked.

"I have to," I said. "Even if it wasn't because I want to see my journey through to the end. I still have to be there to meet Severin. I promised Aidan."

"He could send someone else."

I stared at him, and I could tell by the flicker in his eyes that he knew that wasn't true.

"You know how much is riding on this ask," I said. "I have to go. Besides, you know the company policy against employees dating. Michelle in HR would love to fire one or both of us for violating the rules. You know that. This"—I paused to gesture between us—"puts everything at risk, especially because you are on company time right now."

"We could fight it," he said. "Rules are meant to be broken."

"Jason." He knew as well as I did that wasn't who I was.

He turned away from me and contemplated the wall for a moment. I waited, wondering if he was going to yell or argue or try to cajole me. I wasn't positive I could resist the charming Jason, but he did none of those things. Instead, he nodded.

"All right," he said. He turned back to me, and when I met his gaze, there was a distance there I hadn't seen before, not even when we didn't like each other. I knew he was protecting himself from getting hurt, and I couldn't fault him, even as I immediately missed the closeness we'd recently shared. "I don't like it, but I understand."

I nodded, wondering why, having won this round, I felt as if I'd lost something precious and rare.

chapter twenty

I HAD NO idea what to expect when I went to meet Jason the next day
for our shared cab ride to the Four Seasons Hotel George V for the
Robbie Severin dinner. Would he try to persuade me to change my
mind? Would we argue? Or would he remain distant? I wasn't sure
which I dreaded more.

Instead of my white gown with the silver beaded trim—I was having it along with the other dress Jean Claude had given me cleaned and
delivered back to him—I wore my standard-issue little black dress that
I always packed no matter where I traveled. I did my hair up in a twist
and accessorized with jet-black earrings and a bracelet. I had a black
clutch purse and strappy black high-heel sandals to complete the look.

The drama the night before had caused me to sleep late, and if I was
honest with myself, I was avoiding Jason. I'd spent most of the afternoon in my apartment, going over my playbook for the Severin campaign, and I'd mentally kept the disaster of my personal life at bay. It
wasn't until I was getting dressed that a few frustrated tears had fallen,
making my face a hot mess with red eyes, blotchy cheeks, and a pink
nose. I was not a pretty crier. I decided to do the smoky-eye thing with

my eyeliner to try to hide the red rims, and I put on my cherry-red lipstick, hoping it would distract from the rest of my red face, which I tried to subdue with powder. When I met Jason in the vestibule at the agreed-upon time, he barely looked at me.

"The cab is here." He gave me a tight nod and opened the door, gesturing for me to go first.

As I passed him, I noted how handsome he looked in a charcoal-gray suit with a pale-gray dress shirt and burgundy tie, although the burgundy did bring out the purple highlights in the dark-blue bruise beneath his left eye, which was still slightly swollen.

"Nice suit," I said.

"Zoe helped me find a replacement this morning since mine was out of commission after last night."

"Ah." I didn't know what else to say. He'd wrecked his suit fighting with Jean Claude. I knew it wasn't my fault. No one had asked him to fight my battles—at least, I certainly hadn't—but I felt a twinge of guilt all the same.

"Sorry about that," I said.

He looked at me now. His gaze was steady when he said, "Don't be. It was my choice, and I'd do it all over again."

There it was. There was the Knightley swagger I knew and loathed so well. I sighed. I felt like we were back in the office, vying for the position of most successful moneymaker. It proved I was right. A couple of kisses hadn't changed anything.

He held the door to the cab open for me, and I climbed in first. He followed and told the driver our destination, the famous Le Cinq restaurant. Once the taxi merged into the crazy Parisian traffic, I relaxed back against the seat and turned to him.

"Do you want to talk about our strategy with Severin tonight?" I asked. "More specifically, what are you going to tell him about your eye?"

Jason was staring out the window, and I followed the line of his gaze. He was looking at the Eiffel Tower, which was all lit up for another night's festivities. The sight of it made my heart sink. Was it really less than twenty-four hours ago that I'd been there with him, drinking champagne, slow dancing to Edith Piaf, and sharing the kiss of a lifetime? How much had changed in a day.

"I don't think we need to go over it," he said. "We're professionals. We know how to chat up a potential donor. As for my eye, he probably won't ask."

His tone was abrupt, and I was surprised by how much it smarted. I missed the rapport we'd begun to share, the teasing, the laughter, and the camaraderie. I knew I could never go back to thinking of him as just an overgrown frat boy. Not now. He'd become more than that to me.

"All right," I said. I didn't pursue any more conversation. I hoped he could unbend enough at dinner with Severin to give the appearance of unity. It wouldn't help our cause to have Severin think we were at odds. I felt my anxiety spike.

One of the ways I controlled my nerves before big meetings was to run scenarios through my head. I envisioned everything from the initial greeting to the casual small talk to the pitch I planned to make. Sometimes one run-through was enough, but other times, like right now, I had to go over and over the meeting, assessing it from every angle, looking for any possible catastrophes.

I closed my eyes and began working through my initial greeting with Severin. I pictured the handshake, what to say, how to maintain eye contact and ask a personal question that was more in depth than the weather but not overly familiar. I figured I'd ask how he was enjoying Paris. I was just getting to the part where I would say something witty when a low voice interrupted my meditation.

"What are you doing, Martin?" Jason asked.

So, I was Martin again. I sighed and opened my eyes.

"I'm mentally running through all of the possible scenarios that could happen tonight and practicing my responses to them."

He lifted one eyebrow as he studied me. "Do you do that for every meeting?"

I could feel my face get warm with embarrassment. "No," I said. I sounded defensive. "Just the really important ones."

"Huh."

I had no idea what he meant by that. Was he impressed? Probably not. Did he think I was mental? Probably. I couldn't fault him. With everything that was happening, I was beginning to wonder if I was mental myself.

Before I could spiral deeper into self-doubt, the taxi pulled up at the curb, and a doorman from the Four Seasons, who was wearing a long dark coat and a short-brimmed cap, opened the door. I stepped out while Jason paid for the cab with his company card. I waited on the curb, and together we entered the hotel through the revolving door.

Flowers. That was my first impression of the posh art deco hotel. Huge clear glass vases of all sizes and shapes filled the center and the perimeter of the lobby, and each one was stuffed to bursting with irises. I gawked as the chandelier above lit the purple flowers to their best advantage. I got the feeling they'd been arranged with the lighting in mind, as each bouquet seemed to glow from within. Truly, it was breathtaking.

We were meeting Robbie Severin at Le Cinq, the swank restaurant known for its three Michelin stars and its chef's famous French cuisine. Together we walked through the beautiful hotel, turning right at the hallway that ran along the courtyard, which led to the entrance of the restaurant. Aidan had said to treat Severin like royalty. Given that he was considering a major gift of $10 million, in my mind he was royalty, and I was happy to do the requisite bowing and scraping.

At the entrance to the restaurant, Jason paused. He looked around, searching for Robbie Severin, whose face was as well known as those of the other celebrity billionaires, like Jeff Bezos, Bill Gates, and Mark Zuckerberg. There was no sign of him. Jason checked his watch.

"We're a few minutes early," he said. "I'll just check with the maître d'."

"Sure." I watched him walk away. The line of his shoulders was
tight, and I could feel the tension pouring off him. Was this because we
were at odds? Or was he nervous about meeting Severin, or both? Either
way, it did not bode well for the dinner. I turned and looked out at the
marble courtyard with its precisely sculpted shrubbery and lone black
fountain.

"Chelsea Martin." A voice called my name, and I turned around to
find a man about the same age as my father approaching with a woman
beside him. He was dressed impeccably in a navy-blue suit, and his
companion, who was close to him in age, wore a purple dress that I
recognized from my very brief visit to the Absalon design house. I wondered if it was one of Jean Claude's. Oh, the irony. Then I looked at her
face and saw the Frida Kahlo unibrow. Eleanor!

Of course I recognized Robbie Severin immediately, but if I hadn't,
Eleanor's presence would have clinched it. Severin was of average height
but built thick and strong. His gray hair was cut short but with side-
burns that framed his angular face. Meanwhile, Eleanor, who was petite,
walked beside him with clipped steps, her thick heels clicking on the
marble floor.

"Mr. Severin, it's good to meet you," I said. I held out my hand in
greeting. Severin looked at it and shook his head. He pushed Eleanor
forward. She shook my hand as if doing it for both of them. I went with
it. "Ms. Curtain, it's nice to see you again."

"It's good to see you, Ms. Martin," she said. She gave my hand a firm
shake and then dropped it.

"Please call me Chelsea," I said.

"Robbie." Severin pointed to himself.

"Eleanor," Ms. Curtain chimed in. Her dark hair was in a ball on the
top of her head, and her rectangular glasses perched on the bridge of her
nose. She reminded me of an inquisitive little bird, one who sported a

very thick brow over both of its eyes. I tried not to stare—in fact, I turned my head away to keep from doing so, but it really was as if someone had attacked the poor woman with a Sharpie and drawn a thick line across her forehead. Wow, just wow.

"Terrific," I said. So far, so good. I tried not to think about the rejection of my handshake. I remembered Severin was a germophobe and wanted to kick myself for forgetting. Did Jason know? I debated how I could signal to Jason not to offer his hand when he joined us. My stomach cramped. All I could think of was the $10 million being snatched out of our grasp if we messed this up.

"My colleague Jason Knightley just went to check on our table. Shall we join him?" I asked.

Robbie gestured for me to lead the way, so I strode forward, keeping my back straight, hoping I didn't look as nervous as I felt. I knew there was no need to be, not really. If anything, I was overprepared. But I had never had to perform my numeric dog and pony show with a coworker who was less than happy with me, a coworker who hadn't held my gaze longer than absolutely necessary since we'd left our apartments. This was the apex of the uncomfortable day after. Maybe I should have slept with him. I gave myself a mental shake. No, if anything, things would have been much, much worse.

Jason was standing with the maître d' when we arrived. I could see from his expression that he recognized Robbie right away. He said something to the master of the house, and the man nodded.

"There he is," I said. I turned and met Jason's gaze, widening my eyes and glancing up, trying to warn him about the incoming unibrow. He wasn't looking at me, however, but at Severin.

I stopped beside Jason and performed the introductions. Robbie insisted on first names again, and I was relieved to see that Jason never offered his hand in greeting.

Instead, he gestured for Robbie to follow our hostess, who had conferred with the maître d' about our table, and we fell in behind Robbie and Eleanor, passing a grand piano where a man played softly, surrounded by more of the towering vases filled with purple irises.

"How did you know?" I whispered.

Jason turned to look at me. "What?"

"That he doesn't shake hands." I leaned close and kept my voice low.

A small smile spread across his full mouth. He winked at me with his good eye. "Research, Martin. Surely you knew he hasn't shaken anyone's hand in over ten years."

"Of course I knew," I lied. "I'm just surprised you did."

"Sure you did." His low laugh sent a ripple of awareness right down my back.

I ignored it, naturally.

The dining room was beautifully done in gold, cream, and mauve, with pristine white tablecloths that draped all the way to the floor, chairs with plush round backs and upholstered arms—the sort of seating that encouraged lingering over your meal—and a thick carpet done in floral swirls that felt like walking on a pillow.

Real palm trees in enormous pots, gilded framed mirrors, and a row of glistening chandeliers overhead competed for my attention. When Jason pulled out my chair at a table beside a large window, I slid onto my seat, feeling agog at my surroundings. I tried not to let it show, while for his part, Jason was as at ease as if he ate at restaurants that had three Michelin stars every day. I envied him that.

I glanced away and discovered Eleanor watching me with a speculative look. I wondered if she could tell there was tension between Jason and me. I forced my lips into the shape of a smile even though it felt as hollow as a broken promise. She returned it and glanced away. I doubted that I'd fooled her one bit.

The meal began with the waiter giving us a warm welcome. There were several options for dinner, but we deferred to Severin when he requested La Balade Gourmande, which consisted of the same eight courses served to everyone at the table.

"It's perfect," Robbie said. "Now I won't feel like someone ordered something better."

At €350 per person, I just hoped my corporate credit card wouldn't explode when I charged the meal. I glanced at Jason, but he maintained his ease. So annoying.

The sommelier and Severin conversed about wine. Le Cinq was known for its fifty-thousand-bottle wine cellar, so there was much to debate.

"If I may make a recommendation," Jason said. I turned my head to look at him as if he'd lost his mind. I'd always assumed he was a beer guy. What was he thinking? "I believe the 2011 Pauillac, Château Pichon-Longueville, would be a good selection with which to start."

Robbie looked at him, clearly impressed, and nodded. The sommelier straightened and said, "Excellent choice, sir."

I glanced at Jason in surprise. Was he bluffing? Or did he know wine? What else didn't I know about him?

After the bottle was opened and Robbie and Jason gave it an approving taste, we shared a toast.

"To new friends and making a difference in the world for those less fortunate," Jason said. Eleanor looked particularly pleased with his humility, and I began to feel as if I was being shut out of the rapport building, particularly since Jason had yet to look in my direction.

I decided to steer the conversation to the purpose of our dinner. "Before we get distracted by the food, which I've heard is amazing, did you have any questions for Jason and me about our ACC proposal?" I asked.

"I'm glad you asked," Robbie said. He leaned forward, bracing himself with an elbow on the table. He held my gaze and asked, "What do you think about Mars?"

"Mars?" I asked. "As in the Red Planet?"

Robbie nodded enthusiastically. I blinked. From my research, I knew Mars was a subject of great interest for him, but I had no idea what this had to do with the ACC or our ask. Jason gamely stepped into the breach.

"I think it's highly habitable," he said. "I'll bet in our lifetime, there'll be colonies."

Robbie grinned. "Right you are."

I glanced at Eleanor to see what she thought about this turn in the conversation. She sipped her wine, perfectly at ease.

I turned my head to look at Jason. Okay, mostly I was shooting daggers out of my eyeballs at him—why, oh why, couldn't that be an actual thing—but since he wouldn't make eye contact with me, he was missing it. Fine. If the boy wanted to play, I was all in. No one knew as much about Severin as I did. Not even Knightley.

I smoothed my expression and turned back to Severin. "With the advances made in constant-acceleration technology, such as ion drives and solar sails, the nine months that it takes to get to Mars could be cut down to just a few weeks. I can't speak for anyone else, but if that became the norm, I think living on the Red Planet would be a dream come true."

Jason finally turned to look at me. His gaze was wide eyed, as if he couldn't believe I'd gone there, but also amused, which warmed me. I turned back to Severin.

He favored me with an enormous grin that was surprisingly infectious, given that we were talking about living on Mars and all. "Tell me, how would you occupy yourself?"

Oh, shit. My bluff might have gone too far. I scanned my brain for viable employment. I suspected there weren't many jobs in the charitable fundraising arts in outer space. The thought of which terrified me, by the way, but I kept that tidbit to myself.

"Given the frontier-like nature of such a place, I assume I'd begin a career in agriculture," I said. My voice went up at the end as if it were a question. Ugh, upspeak. I was losing my way, but hey, I'd seen the movie *The Martian*.

"So you want to be a potato farmer . . . on Mars," Jason said. His voice was dry. He looked like he was trying not to laugh. Clearly, he'd seen the movie, too.

I met his gaze; his eyes were a soft flannel gray with a spark of laughter tucked in. He had to go to the potato. I knew we both knew that Severin proudly came from Idaho potato-farming stock. Now we'd see who'd done their homework.

"Potatoes—fascinating things, potatoes," Severin said. He glanced between the two of us as if issuing a challenge. "Eleanor, did you know that the average American eats about one hundred and twenty-four pounds of potatoes per year, while Germans eat twice as many?"

"I did not," she said. She turned toward him and pushed her glasses up on her nose, studying him with rapt interest.

"I once read that the potato is roughly eighty percent water and twenty percent solid," Jason offered. Severin's right eyebrow ticked up. Impressed.

"Fascinating," Eleanor said. She looked at Jason with approval, as did Severin. I could not drop the ball. Not now. As crazy as it was, I had the feeling our $10 million ask was riding on this conversation.

"The largest potato ever grown was eighteen pounds and four ounces," I said. Knowing Severin's personal history, I had recently read up on potato facts. It appeared Knightley had, too. He glanced at me.

"Did you know the Incas used the potato to heal injuries and they believed potatoes made childbirth easier?" he asked. He tipped his chin up ever so slightly.

Clearly, he was throwing down the potato-trivia gauntlet. Game on. I turned in my chair to face him.

"Potatoes have more vitamin C than an orange, more potassium than a banana, and more fiber than an apple," I said. Take that!

"There are over one hundred varieties of potato in existence," he shot back.

I could feel Eleanor and Severin watching us as if we were a potato trivia ping-pong match, and I didn't care.

"Potatoes are grown in all fifty states, with the biggest producers being Washington and Idaho," he continued.

Oh, you tricky devil, I thought, *giving a nod to Severin's home state*. I was going to have to bring it in for the win.

"Really?" I smiled, acknowledging his point. Then I went for the big-daddy factoid, linking our entire conversation together. "Interestingly, in 1995, NASA and the University of Wisconsin successfully grew the first vegetable in space, on the space shuttle *Columbia*, and it was . . . wait for it . . . the potato."

Severin grinned and pointed at me with his fork. "There you have it. Spuds could be your future."

"You never know," I said. But I knew it wouldn't happen in this lifetime.

"Well done, Martin. I can actually see you as a Martian potato queen," Knightley teased. His eyes were twinkling, and it irked me that he could be so adorable while joking at my expense.

"Don't worry," I said to him. "I see a bright future for you as my court jester."

Robbie and Eleanor watched us. Jason grinned. I mock glowered. Truthfully, I was impressed by Knightley's capability. I had never had a colleague match me in my exhaustive research on a donor's life and interests before.

"I'm sorry—that got a bit away from us," I said to Robbie. "While we're here, was there anything you wanted to ask us about the ACC?"

Robbie glanced between us. He gave us a considering look and said, "Truthfully, at the moment, I'm mostly curious as to whether you're the one who gave him that black eye or not."

My eyes went wide. Severin sounded like he was joking, mostly. Panic thrummed in my chest, as I was certain he could sense that things were strained between Jason and me. See? This is why they tell you not to get involved with colleagues. Once the line from professional to personal is crossed, there is no going back, and the potential for disaster is huge.

I glanced at Jason. He didn't look anywhere near as freaked out as I was. To my surprise, he actually laughed. It sounded genuine, and I forced myself to chuckle while hoping, praying, that the man had a plan.

"I'm sure I've given her a few reasons to want to be the one who popped me, but no, we treat knowledge like a blood sport. Speaking of which, this"—he pointed to his eye—"is actually a rugby injury."

"Rugby? I used to play. Are you in a league?" Robbie looked delighted.

I remembered from Severin's bio that he'd played rugby in college. Relief surged through me. All right, I had to give it to Knightley: the boy was quick on his feet.

"Yes, I'm in a local Boston league," Jason said. "This was from practice. I stopped my teammate's foot with my face." He shrugged. "It happens."

Severin laughed. "I know that play. What's your position?"

I clenched my hands in my lap. Did Jason really play rugby? I didn't know. Was he making this up because he'd read Severin's bio, too? What if he didn't know the positions? What if he couldn't bluff his way out? Then again, he'd certainly done his research on potatoes. I had to trust he'd been just as thorough with rugby.

"Fly half," Jason said evenly. "And you?"

"Hooker," Robbie said.

I glanced at Eleanor. Was this for real? I knew nothing about rugby. These positions sounded made up. I started to sweat.

"Tell me, Jason." Robbie leaned toward him with the same sort of scrutiny he'd given me about Mars. "Do you really think you have a black eye?"

"Well, it feels like a black eye and it looks like a black eye, so I'm thinking it's a black eye, or a dark-blue eye if we're being particular."

I glanced away, fearing I would laugh, knowing exactly how confused he felt by the question. I couldn't wait to see what Severin hit him with next. He didn't disappoint.

"But what if it isn't?" Severin persisted. "What if it's all a simulation?"

"A simulation?" Jason repeated. I could see him fighting to keep his face blank. "I'm afraid I don't follow."

"What if this, all of this"—Robbie gestured to the restaurant around us—"is just a simulation, the creation of a higher being, and we're all just players?"

Jason and I sat, speechless. From Mars to potatoes to simulations. This was not the dinner conversation I had expected. In fact, simulations had not been a part of any article I'd read on Severin. It must be something new. Oh dear.

Mercifully, the servers arrived at that moment and took our empty plates and brought the next course, gratinated onions, which were small onions flavored with Parmesan and truffle and filled with a liquid that reminded me of French onion soup. The artistic presentation of the nouvelle cuisine was so enticing. It looked like art and smelled delicious.

The flurry of plates coming and going gave Jason and me a second to regroup. He leaned close under the pretext of commenting on my food and said, "Help me."

His voice was so plaintive, I almost laughed out loud. Instead, I reached between our two chairs, caught his fingers in mine, and gave them a quick squeeze. We were two intelligent, hardworking people; surely we could handle this. At least, that was what I was trying to convey. When Jason's warm fingers squeezed back, I took it as *message received* and let go. He didn't. Instead, his thumb brushed over the back of my hand, making my breath hitch. I pulled away, breaking the moment.

Trying to regain control of the situation, I gave him side-eye and said, "I didn't know you played rugby."

This time, when he looked at me, his eyes were thoughtful. In a soft voice, he said, "I imagine there's a lot you don't know about me . . . yet."

Yet? What did he mean? And why, oh why, did my heart flutter at the sentiment? Was he trying to tell me we weren't done? That he would wait until I got back to Boston? That at the very least we'd be friends? The questions positively burned my insides, like hot lava trying to find a way out. I said nothing. Now was not the time.

As the servers departed, Robbie leaned forward again and said, "If the simulation hypothesis is true, then that black eye of yours is about as real as a unicorn."

Jason nodded. He leaned forward and asked, "Do you believe that we're living in a simulation, Robbie?"

To my surprise, Robbie laughed. It was a deep, hearty laugh that made me smile. He lifted his wineglass and took a sip. Then he met Jason's gaze and said, "Maybe. Definitely maybe."

"What makes you think that?" I asked. The words flew out of my mouth before I thought to check them. Damn it. I didn't want him to think I was being contrary, but I was curious. Believing that everything around us was fake, manufactured, as if we were living inside the movie *The Matrix*, was, well, weird.

"Because it makes the things that have hurt me in life, the pain I've felt, more manageable," Robbie said.

Eleanor, shockingly, reached across the table and patted his hand.

"Like losing your father?" Jason asked.

I choked on an onion. Oh my god. He went there. With Severin. Over dinner. I gulped some wine to clear my throat.

Severin glanced up from where he was pushing his food around his plate. He met Jason's gaze and said, "Yes."

A look of understanding passed between them, and Jason lowered his head with a nod. "That makes perfect sense to me."

Amazingly, Severin seemed to relax after that. There was a lovely rapport that existed between the four of us at the table, but I was darned if I knew how it had gotten there. The rest of the meal was conversationally just as random as the beginning. Severin rarely answered direct questions, but he fired out ideas and opinions that seemingly had nothing to do with the conversation at hand. We veered from the weather at the North Pole to how he lived in hotels and didn't ever reside in the many residences he owned. So much for sitting on the golden throne. This topic rolled into his dislike of material possessions and his collection of classic cars, housed in a garage in Los Angeles. He owned sixty-four luxury cars but didn't consider them possessions. Logical? No. It was mentally exhausting trying to keep up.

"Your gift is the largest we've ever considered," Robbie said toward the end of the meal while we enjoyed our pear sorbet. "While I like that you clearly understand that we would like to expand the company's exposure on college campuses, positioning us as a potential employer to some of the brightest engineering minds in the future, I'm curious as to what you think will be the most successful way to engage students?"

Aha, finally! Shoptalk. This was my wheelhouse. I gave Jason a look that said, *I've got this.* Then I carefully put down my spoon even though my sorbet called to me with an insistence that was hard to ignore. I smoothed the tablecloth with my hands and focused on the best way to answer his question. I fell back on my tried-and-true method of numeric persuasion.

Robbie listened and nodded as I quoted statistics and demographics for the campaign's optimum reach, but I got the feeling I was losing him. Panic made me talk faster as I pointed out that the Severin Robotics name would be attached to every bit of swag we distributed. That didn't work either. He still looked underwhelmed. I felt as if I were rearranging deck chairs on the *Titanic* while the ship slowly sank into the icy North Atlantic. I needed to get him enthused about how the ACC could use a partnership with Severin Robotics to raise money to fight cancer and give Severin Robotics the massive exposure he sought.

"Well, you've given me a lot to think about," Robbie said.

"Chelsea's being very modest about our ambitions," Jason said.

I looked at him and shook my head. He wouldn't.

"And she left out the part about the BattleBots." He did.

I was going to murder him. We'd talked about this. We were not going to pitch his insane robot idea.

"BattleBots?" Robbie asked. He dabbed his mouth with his napkin and leaned in. *In.* Instead of out, which was what he'd been doing when I talked.

"Yes," Jason said. "We had originally thought this could be something used for in-house employee engagement, but I think it could be much bigger. Picture this: each college campus that participates is in charge of building a robot—"

"That serves the community in some way," I interrupted. Jason looked at me in confusion. Too bad. If he was going to pitch this lunacy, I was going to make it the grown-up version with community involvement and not a death match between jacked-up old toasters.

"In what way?" Eleanor asked.

Jason shrugged. He looked as if he was grappling with my concept, but then he said, "That's up to them, but the college with the most badass—er, resourceful—bot wins the coveted tournament cup."

"There's a cup?" Robbie asked.

"Sure. Like winning a Stanley Cup but for robotics. It could become an annual event, and every year the team's name is inscribed, and it sits on display at their university for the year."

Robbie rubbed his chin with the back of his hand. "And you think this will increase awareness of the Severin Robotics brand as the premier employer for automation engineers?"

"Yes," I said. "It starts with getting them thinking about curing cancer and community needs—say, a drone that delivers medication to patients too sick to drive, or a companion robot who visits the homebound and keeps them company, or maybe it's a nursing robot who can take their vitals—the students will become invested in making a difference in other people's lives all in the name of fighting cancer. Plus, the most innovative robot will be declared the winner, giving the school and the students some seriously notable glory and giving Severin Robotics first dibs on the tech."

Jason gave me an assessing stare. I knew I had surprised him with my twist on his idea, which actually made me feel pretty good about the whole thing, especially since I had thought of it only right this minute. And yet I couldn't deny Robbie's instant interest or the obvious appeal of the proposal.

"I like it," Robbie declared. "It's smart and imaginative. Well done, you two."

"Thank you," I said. Jason echoed my words.

I smiled as I gazed down at my plate. For the first time all evening, I felt as if I could appreciate the exquisite meal. Christian Le Squer, the head chef, was clearly a genius.

"I'd like to talk more about this," Robbie said. "Are we still set for the wine festival in Italy next week?"

"Yes," I said. "My friend Marcellino DeCapio is looking forward to having you tour his vineyard, Castello di Luce. They specialize in Chianti."

"Excellent," Robbie said. "Jason, you'll be joining us, of course."

"Actually, I'm—" Jason paused. He looked at me and then at Robbie. "Really looking forward to it."

What?! What was he saying? Jason was coming to Italy? With me? While I reunited with Marcellino? I wanted to scream into my napkin. Instead, I turned to Jason.

"It would be great for you to join us," I said. "But I thought you couldn't miss that other business meeting in Boston."

I stared at him, right in his pretty eyeballs, trying to make my opposition to this change in plan obvious. Jason clearly had no feeling for his personal safety, as he took a casual sip of his wine, leaned back in his chair, and said, "I think I can reschedule."

"Excellent," Robbie said. He looked delighted. "Call Eleanor tomorrow, and we'll finalize the details."

It took everything I had not to show my distress. Instead, I smiled at Severin and said, "Great, this will be great."

I felt as if my smile was overly bright and possibly maniacal like the Joker's, probably because I was trying not to pick up my knife and shank Knightley with the stealth of a ninja.

He could *not* come to Italy with me. I had people to see—Marcellino!—and things to figure out, like where my happiness had been hiding all these years. Under a grapevine in Tuscany? Maybe. How could I clear my head of Knightley and his kisses if he was right there with me? Argh! This was a nightmare.

In my bewildered and panicked state, feeling as if my quest to find my old self had just been hijacked by a man who thought my future was farming potatoes in outer space, I wondered if my only recourse was to quit my job once and for all.

chapter twenty-one

WE LINGERED OVER our coffee, the conversation pinballing from favorite television shows to artificial intelligence to what superpower we would choose—as discussions with Severin seemed to go—and when we walked out of the restaurant, I was relieved to be able to mentally stand down for a moment. Mercifully, I found myself beside Eleanor as we made our way through the tables.

"Your presentation was smart," she said. "You had all the facts and figures that dazzled and wowed, but tying it into what the company actually does—robotics—was a solid closer."

"I wish I could take credit," I said. "The robotics portion was all Jason."

"Why do I suspect you're being modest?" she asked.

"I'm not," I said. "The robotics nerd, a.k.a. Jason, wanted to do BattleBots. My sole input was to make them community oriented."

"A brilliant suggestion," she said.

"Thank you, but it wouldn't exist without the original idea."

"Maybe. But Mr. Severin would still be interested in partnering with the ACC."

"I'm not so sure about that."

"I am," she said. "Mr. Severin took the loss of his father very hard, particularly because he believes it was preventable. He's a real advocate for early screening. Your name has come up several times in meetings as the person he would entrust a major gift to, and I'm pretty sure our dinner tonight just confirmed it."

She smiled at me, and I got the feeling it was something she rarely did. It felt like sighting a yeti or a mermaid, and it softened the unibrow that perched over the rim of her glasses. I felt the pitter-patter of optimistic feet trample through me. This was what I had lived for over the past seven years, raising awareness and money to fight the good fight. It felt wonderful even as I acknowledged to myself that I might be out of the game.

We paused in the lobby to say good night. Severin didn't shake hands with either Jason or me. Instead, he looked at us and said, "If you can, always be yourself, unless you can be Batman, then always be Batman."

With that, he turned on his heel and walked toward the elevator. Eleanor nodded at us once before she hurried after him.

Jason and I made our way through the revolving door and out to the curb. He pulled me to the side and doubled over. I bent down to get a look at his face. Was he sick? Choking? Having a nervous breakdown?

"Hey, you okay?" I asked.

"Be Batman," he wheezed. It was then that I realized he was laughing. A smile parted my lips, because yeah.

I chuckled and added, "Or a potato farmer in outer space, apparently."

He laughed harder and I joined him. "Don't mistake me," he said. "I like Severin—I really do—but oh man, he's—"

"Shiny!" I said. I pretended to have my attention drawn to something glittery in the distance.

"Yes." Jason stood and threw an arm around my shoulders. "I don't think I've ever had a conversation like that before. It was . . ."

"Mr. Toad's Wild Ride?" I offered.

He grinned. "I was thinking more like the Mad Tea Party teacups." He ran his free hand over his face. "My brain hurts."

"Come on," I said. "Let's go home."

It was almost ten o'clock, and I was exhausted. The hotel doorman immediately ushered us to a waiting taxi, and we climbed in.

Jason gave the driver our address as I slid across the seat to make room for him. As soon as the door shut behind us, he collapsed back against the seat. "We did it! Can you believe it? A ten-million-dollar major gift, and we nailed it."

"We don't have the money yet," I cautioned. I wasn't trying to be a wet blanket, but despite Eleanor's enthusiasm, I didn't want to get ahead of ourselves, as the disappointment if Severin changed his mind would be soul crushing.

"Oh, no, it's ours," he said. "Robbie told me just now that at the meeting in Tuscany next week, he wants to finalize his donation."

"Are you serious?" I asked. "I thought we had to present it to the board."

"*Yaaas*, I'm serious. The board presentation is a formality. That ten million is ours. Severin is eccentric, but I don't think he'll walk back his commitment to us."

I gaped at him for a heartbeat or two. Then I pressed my hand to my mouth. We did it! I was so overcome, I leaped on him, hugging him about the neck until he made a choking sound.

"Sorry, sorry," I cried. I let go of him and laughed, feeling equal measures of relief and joy surge through me, slamming the door shut on my doubts and sliding the dead bolt home. "I just . . . I can't believe . . . Aidan."

Then I started to cry. Thinking about how much this would mean to Aidan caused me to come undone. I buried my face in my hands and happy sobbed.

"Hey, hey. Chelsea, are you all right?" Jason's arm came around me, and he pulled me in close. I pressed my face against his jacket, letting his solid warmth enfold me.

"I'm fine," I said. I sniffed and took a calming breath. "I just really wanted this for Aidan, especially now."

"Yeah, I know what you mean." He pulled away and ran his hand up and down my back. "We should call him when we get to the apartment. It's still early in Boston. He might even be in the office."

"That'd be great," I said. My lips wobbled, and I pressed them together, realizing that phone call would be my opportunity to give my notice, and now that Severin was committed to the ask, it seemed more timely than ever. I couldn't keep getting sucked back into my career at the expense of finding myself. Decisions had to be made.

"You know, it's a damn good thing you lost your phone and I flew over. We make a hell of a team, Martin. This campaign is going to be huge. This could go even bigger than the hot-wings challenge. There is so much we can do to promote this. It's going to be amazing."

"I think you're going to be brilliant," I said.

He looked at me and his brow furrowed. "Don't you mean *we*?"

"No." I shook my head. "When we call Aidan about Severin, I'll be giving my notice, effective immediately."

His eyes went wide with disbelief.

"When you say 'notice,' you mean notice of how awesome your co-worker is, right?" he asked.

"No." I shook my head, trying not to smile.

The taxi stopped in front of Café Zoe, and Jason stepped out, holding his hand out for me. I noted how warm his fingers were, while mine were icy cold. Jason didn't let go while he paid our driver, forcing me to wait. I knew he was going to have more to say about me resigning and he probably didn't want me to get away. It was unnecessary; I wanted to clear the air before I called Aidan.

When the cab drove off, he turned to face me and I glanced up at him.

"Are you quitting because of last night?" he asked.

"No," I said. "I'm quitting because you don't need me for this anymore," I said. "And I have things I need to do, things that aren't about the ACC or . . . you."

"So if it isn't about last night," he said, running an exasperated hand through his hair, "is it because I punched the jackass?"

"No, it isn't," I insisted. "It's about me being on a journey to figure some things out and not being able to do it, because I'm a crazy workaholic who is still working when I'm supposed to be on leave and getting my life together."

"You just scored a major ask for the ACC. How much more together could your life be?"

"A lot," I said. I shivered against the evening cold. Jason immediately let go of my hand, shrugged off his jacket, and, ignoring my protests, dropped it about my shoulders. "Which reminds me, why the hell did you tell Severin you'd meet them in Italy with me? You know I have plans."

"Are you kidding?" he asked. "For his ten-million-dollar donation, I'd agree to meet him in the burning fires of hell with my body oiled in flame accelerant and wearing a grass skirt, or on a potato farm on Mars."

I tried not to laugh at the mental images and managed it, mostly. "You had no right," I protested.

"Maybe not," he said. "But if it means the difference between us getting the ask or not, I'd do it again."

Before I could respond, he took my elbow and escorted me into our building and up the stairs. He paused outside the door to my apartment while I searched for the key in my clutch bag. When my cold fingers grasped it, he took it and unlocked my door for me.

His voice was low when he said, "Listen, you don't have to quit. We can figure out a way to keep the work thing separate from your . . . quest."

I shook my head. "You know that's not how this industry works. It's all-consuming. I have to make a clean break."

We stared at each other. His head was tipped to the side, and he shoved his hands in his pockets in that slouchy way he had. His mouth tipped up on one side.

"Chelsea, you *can't* leave. You can't leave me," he said.

It reminded me so much of our conversation in my office just a few weeks ago that I smiled. He must have said it on purpose, because his lips twitched and he added, "I stand by it. Now more than ever."

"I have to," I said. I reached up to adjust my earring, but he caught my hand with his. He laced our fingers together, and I remembered that he'd noticed that was my tell when I was upset. I forged on, refusing to be charmed by him.

"You know, there's no guarantee you're going to be able to find the old Chelsea in Italy," he said. "This guy you're meeting could be married with kids."

"He's not."

"Or in jail."

"Nope."

"Or gay."

"Not gay," I said.

Jason didn't look happy about my certainty on that point.

"Chelsea, I understand that you need to do this," he said. At my look of doubt, he added, "I do, but I think we can figure out a compromise."

I lifted my eyebrows. I was willing to listen.

"Five days," he said.

I shook my head, not understanding.

"Take five days in Italy all by yourself," he said. "If you're going to find true love, your laughter, or the happy, carefree girl you used to be, you'll be able to find her within five days."

"That's pretty arbitrary," I said. "How do you know five days will do it?"

"Because both Ireland and Paris were resolved for you within two days," he said. "Good or bad, I'm betting Tuscany won't take any longer than that."

I opened my mouth to protest.

"If you need more time, we can arrange it," he said. "I'll stall Severin, or heck, I'll even take him to the wrong vineyard. Just don't quit, not now, not when you don't know how everything is going to play out."

"What are you going to do while I'm in Italy?" I asked.

"I'll fly back to Boston and get the paperwork and contracts for Severin's gift started," he said. "And I'll check on Aidan."

He had me hooked right there and he knew it.

I turned the knob on my door and pushed it open. "All right, Knightley, I won't quit tonight, but I reserve the right to change my mind."

His smile was blinding. "You're still in the game?"

"*Allora*, I suppose," I said, using the Italian word for "well then." I shook my head, thinking I must be crazy. "I'll see you in Italy."

He looked like he was going to step forward and hug me, but I could not allow that, because when it came to him, I had no common sense or self-preservation. Healthy boundaries were the only way to maintain my equilibrium. I slipped inside my door, and with a little finger wave, I shut it, but not before he sent me a knowing wink. Incorrigible.

AH, FIRENZE. WHEN I'd been here seven years ago, I'd spent my last hours before I departed curled up in a ball at the airport, awaiting my flight while clutching the tiny pocket prayer book with the title *ovunque proteggimi*, meaning protect me everywhere. No bigger than a matchbook with an embossed image of Saint Francis of Assisi on one side and his prayer for peace—or *pace*—in Italian on the other, I held it like a talisman that would get me back home to my mom as quickly as possible. I still had the prayer book. I kept it in the top drawer of my nightstand at home.

It occurred to me when I arrived in Boston after that desperate flight home how ironic it was to get the call about my mom while in a city and country that so revered the woman's role as a mother. The Madonna and child were by far the most prevalent images in the city to the point where I had begun to feel an affection for them, as if they were always watching over me.

My favorite representations were the ones where the mother looked affectionately exasperated with the child, who was usually depicted as a toddler in those poses. When I thought of my time in Italy, it was the ever-present Madonna and child that came to mind.

I reserved a room at a small hotel near the station where I would catch the morning bus to the vineyard, Castello di Luce, where I had worked with Marcellino. It was located about twenty miles outside of the city, nestled in the rolling hills of Tuscany. There was a small village adjacent to the vineyard, and I was looking forward to seeing what, if anything, had changed during my years away.

At the moment, I sat at a small wrought-iron table in the courtyard of the hotel, brooding over my espresso while admiring the massive terra-cotta dome of Il Duomo in the distance, which stood out above the city's skyline. I wished I had the energy to go browse the shops on the Ponte Vecchio, a bridge over the Arno River in the heart of town, but I hadn't slept well and I was exhausted. I knew there was nothing I could buy that would distract me from my current bout of self-doubt.

I breathed in the sweet air and tried to be present and enjoy the moment I was in right now instead of being full of worry about the unknown. It was a struggle, but I focused on my surroundings. There were exquisite tile mosaics on the walls, depicting, of course, the Madonna and child, and small orange trees were planted in enormous terra-cotta pots stationed all around the perimeter of the courtyard. On each table was a blue glass bottle with a fistful of daisies, a cheerful splash of color against the black tabletop.

Several other guests were enjoying the warm spring day, quietly conversing over their coffee or in some cases wine. It made me feel a sudden pang of loneliness I couldn't shake. I'd spent only a couple of days with Jason as my constant companion, but now it felt weird without him.

For the umpteenth time that day, I checked my phone. I didn't know what I was expecting. The man had flown out of Paris without so much as a "See ya later, *Mahtin*."

Zoe had been the one to break it to me. When I'd popped into the café for coffee and a pastry, she'd informed me that he'd left. I tried not to be hurt that he hadn't said goodbye, sent me a text, or even written a note on a Post-it. I wondered if it meant anything or if he was merely respecting my boundaries. I knew it was hypocritical to demand space and then complain when you got it. Still.

I tried not to dwell on why it disappointed me. I blamed my lack of sleep. Sitting at the table, I checked my text messages. Again. Nothing. I checked my voice mail. Nothing there either. Then I got angry at myself for checking and then checked again. Argh. I was losing my mind. I shook my head. No, I was just overtired. I never processed anything well when I was tired. I needed a voice of reason.

I opened my contacts and pressed the first name that came up.

Annabelle answered on the second ring. "Chels, where are you? Are you in Italy? Have you seen Marcellino yet? What happened in Paris? How was Jean Claude? Did you meet with Severin? What's happening?"

I smiled. Maybe it was the miles between us, but suddenly I missed my sister and her overabundance of exuberance more than I had in years. And just like that, I was in tears.

"Hey, Sis," I said.

"Oh no! Are you crying? Oh my god, why are you crying? *Ack!*

Wait! Are you having boy drama? Hallelujah! You never have boy drama," Annabelle said.

My sniffs turned into snorts. "I am not having boy drama."

"Yeah, right, why else would you be crying?" she asked. "So, catch me up. What's going on?"

Surprising myself, I did. To Annabelle's credit, she laughed only a little at the Colin-Aoife humiliation, fumed and swore at the Jean Claude disaster, and then grew very quiet as I described my time with Jason—yes, I even told her about the kiss, but just the one on the Eiffel Tower.

"Oh, wow," she said. "I have to say, I didn't see that coming."

"That makes two of us," I said.

"How did you end up kissing *him*?" she asked. "I mean, you hate that guy." She'd had to listen to many of my work rants before.

"*Hate* isn't the exact word I would use," I said. "And in all fairness, I might have been too hard on him in the past."

"Uh-huh." That was all she said. I had no idea how to interpret it. Was she uh-huhing me because she thought I was full of it, or was it a more nuanced response that meant she understood what I was saying? I had no idea.

"You're the one with the man experience, Annabelle. What do I do?" I asked.

My sister was quiet for a bit. I appreciated that she was giving the question due consideration. Usually, Annabelle went with her first, and worst, impulse. Then she said, "Well, I think the fact that you're in Italy means you've answered your own question. You must press on and go see Marcellino, regardless of how you feel about Jason."

"Whoa, whoa, whoa, I never said I felt anything for Jason," I said.

"Really?" she asked.

"Friendship," I said. "That's it."

"Friends don't kiss friends on the Eiffel Tower," she said.

"It was an accident," I said.

"Oh, yeah, my lips get stuck on my guy friends' lips all the time," she said. "It's such a silly mistake, like slamming my jacket in the car door or running the dishwasher twice."

"Are you finished?" I asked. "Because you're not helping. Forget Jason—what if seeing Marcellino, what if being in Italy, doesn't snap me back into my old self? What if this whole trip is a bust?"

"How can it be a bust when you've managed to score ten million dollars for the ACC?" Annabelle asked.

"That's just work," I said.

"I'm sorry, but who are you and what have you done with my sister?"

"I'm serious. I want more out of my life."

"Sunshine, you're in *Italy*," Annabelle said with a hint of exasperation. "So what if things don't go as you hope with Marcellino? Maybe he's like Jean Claude and not the man you remember. It doesn't matter. They have gelato there, which can cure anything."

I laughed, which was undoubtedly her aim.

"Chels, you have to remember, you're not on this quest to find a man or a relationship. You're on it to remember—"

"What it feels like to be carefree and happy and open to love. Yeah, yeah, I know." I sipped my coffee. "But it's been seven years. What if the new workaholic me has spackled on such a thick shell that I can't scrape her off?"

"You wouldn't be there if she had," Annabelle said. "You've got this."

"I hope so. If I could just not have my past bite me on the ass again, that would be helpful." I paused for Annabelle's chuckle and then asked, "How's Dad?"

"Worried about you," she said. "But not so much that he hasn't found time to go to cake tastings, florists, and the big wedding expo."

"Really?"

"Yup. Never in my wildest dreams did I think that mathematician Dad and I would have an in-depth discussion about tulle," Annabelle said. "It's weird."

"I can see how it would be, but it's also good," I said.

"Is it?" she asked. "Because he is full steam ahead on these wedding plans. We're at T minus two months now."

I felt ripples of panic begin to swell inside of me. My entire purpose for being here was to find the Chelsea that believed in love at first sight and happily-ever-afters. I'd found flickers of her in Ireland and France, but I wanted to *be* her again in time to attend my father's wedding with full enthusiasm and joy, no matter what outfit I was asked to wear.

"Yeah, I mean, it's good that Dad has you," I said. I tried not to sound forlorn. "You're the daughter he needs right now."

"We both are," she said. "And you'll get there. The Chelsea you're looking for is out there. I know she is."

"Right." I pushed the image of my dad marrying Sheri from my mind and finished my espresso, telling myself I could do this. Really, I could.

IT WAS LATE morning when the bus stopped at the entrance to the Castello di Luce vineyard. I climbed down the steps, hauling my bag behind me, trying not to notice how nervous I felt, but truthfully, my pulse was pounding so hard in my throat that I feared I'd choke on it. It had been seven years since I'd been here, after all.

Since I'd made my decision to revisit my year abroad, Marcellino and I had emailed and texted and shared one phone call, which had been hard to manage because of the time change. While I felt confident that seeing him again would be a pleasant experience, there was always the possibility that I'd be wrong. It had happened before—witness Jean Claude.

The vineyard was built on the grounds of a castle, thus the name, and as I stood looking up at the huge beige stone building dating back to 1173, I was filled with the same awe and wonder I'd felt the first time I'd set foot on the vineyard grounds. The squared-off ramparts and high watchtower loomed over the surrounding countryside just as they had when they'd been built almost a thousand years ago for a family who'd reigned over the area for over four hundred years before being stripped of their wealth and property by the Medici family.

I tipped my head back to take in the stone ramparts, which looked as if a battery of arrows or hot oil could come down on the unsuspecting people below at any moment. As always, the bloody history of Castello di Luce made me shiver. Meticulously preserved, the castle had been owned by a family, the DeNicolas, when I'd come to work here during my year abroad.

They'd lived in the upper levels of the castle, letting the vineyard and olive oil business take over the first floor. When I had checked their website, I'd seen Marcellino DeCapio listed as the owner of the vineyard. This didn't surprise me at all. He'd had a rare gift for working with the grapevines that covered the hills behind the castle. Mr. DeNicola had often said that Marcellino could sweet-talk the vines into producing more grapes than ever before. It hadn't been hollow praise. I had marveled at Marcellino's natural affinity for the winery business.

The vineyard had a gift shop and offered tours, which I'd led during my time there. The castle was a popular stopping place for tourists, and as I walked past the tour buses parked in the small lot, I almost felt as if I should be donning my Castello di Luce staff shirt and gearing up to give a tour of the grounds, the castle, and the vineyard.

Instead of following the other tourists into the castle courtyard, I went around the side of the building, where there used to be a rose garden belonging to Mrs. DeNicola. As soon as I stepped through the archway, the scent of the roses lured me in. The garden was still there, and while most of the rosebushes had yet to bloom, the overachieving Don Juan rose, a climber, was bursting with fragrant burgundy blossoms.

I left my bag by a stone bench and strolled through the garden, past the fountain in the center and out the opposite arch, which supported a heavily loaded lavender wisteria vine. I paused to look out across the rolling green hills, thrilled to see the red poppies just starting to bloom amid the lines and lines of grapevines, which had just begun to leaf. It was, as the Italians would say, *una bella giornata*, a beautiful day.

I soaked in the beauty of the landscape as the scent of the sweet air filled my lungs. I closed my eyes and tilted my face, letting the warm sun shine down upon me while a gentle breeze teased my hair. The memories of this place during that magical April and May, when the mornings were busy with tourists and the afternoons were spent sitting on the handlebars of Marcellino's bicycle while we rode into the village for gelato, were so thick and rich again, it felt as if I were stepping back in time.

"Chelsea?" A man called my name. "Chelsea Martin?"

chapter twenty-two

OPENED MY eyes. The sun was bright, and I blinked past the red haze, trying to bring into focus the man striding toward me. He was walking the narrow dirt path, coming up from the small grove of silvery-green olive trees, where I could see several workers scattered amid the orchard, pruning the branches.

The man was wearing a wide-brimmed brown canvas hat, which put his features in shadow, but I would have known that stride anywhere. Marcellino!

I wanted to shout. I wanted to say something, anything, but all I could do was nod—vigorously. That was all it took. Marcellino broke into a run. His hat flew off his head, and the sun lit up the copper strands in his dark hair. His smile was as big as the sky, and his eyes— oh, how had I forgotten those beautiful eyes—were shining as he sprinted toward me.

I couldn't wait for him to reach me. I started running, too, dashing across the uneven ground to get to him. It was like something out of a movie, a love story. My heart swelled. Everything around him faded into the background: the cypress trees standing in a tall line shielding the precious vines, the swallows and house martins twittering as they flut-tered past with twigs in their beaks, off to build their nests, and the people touring the vineyard, completely unaware of the epic moment that was unfolding before them.

I felt a lighthearted laugh build up in my chest. Was this what I'd been looking for? This place and these feelings? I wanted to believe it. I wanted to believe it so much that I didn't stop or slow down; instead, as soon as I was close enough, I launched myself at him.

Marcellino was tall and muscled from his long days of working in the vineyard, and he scooped me out of the air as if I were no heavier than a bouquet of wildflowers. He took my momentum into his body and spun me around, holding me up high. Then he slowed and hugged me close.

After he set me on my feet, he cupped my face, studying my features as if trying to convince himself that I was real. "I got your message and I knew you were arriving today, but still, I can't believe you're here."

"Hi," I said, feeling unaccountably shy.

He shook his head as if still registering that I was actually standing right in front of him. I understood. I was certain I was staring at him the same way. He kissed my cheeks and then hugged me again.

"So many times, I have imagined you standing right there waiting for me, just like you used to so long ago, and now here you are," he said. His deep accented voice curled around me like a hug. "I was so happy to hear from you, *dolcezza*."

I sighed when he called me sweetheart in Italian just like he used to when we were dating. "Oh, Marcellino, it's so good to see you."

I stepped back to study his face and was pleased to note he looked exactly as I remembered. Oh, sure, there were faint lines in the corners of his eyes, and the boyish softness had left his jawline, making it firmer and more chiseled, which only made him even more handsome. I liked that he had become a substantial part of the vineyard that he loved so much. I wondered how the rest of his life had worked out, but I wasn't sure how to ask.

"Come, let's get you settled," he said. He took my hand and laced his fingers with mine. He stared at me as if he was afraid I might vanish. "How long will you be here? Where are your friends? You mentioned being here with guests for the wine festival."

"They won't be here for a few days," I said. I leaned against him in a flirty way that was so *not* me—well, not me lately, but maybe the me who had been here seven years ago? Was that me then? Or was it me now? Because it occurred to me that I could totally see myself leaning against Knightley. I felt my smile waver as I realized I missed him. I shook my head, trying to be present. This was the moment I'd been working toward.

If Marcellino noticed that I was going banana balls right in front of him, he didn't remark on it. Instead, he said, "We must . . . how do you say . . . catch up, *sì*?"

"*Sì*," I said with a laugh. "I'd like that."

"*Bene*," he said. "Now come have lunch with me."

He grinned at me and put his hand on my lower back. Together we walked through the courtyard, retrieving my bag, which Marcellino carried as easily as if it were full of air, and into the castle through a doorway that was reserved for staff. Instead of taking me to the staff lounge on the first floor, where we used to spend time together, Marcellino opened a door to the right and took the spiral staircase that led up to the residential second floor.

I looked at him in surprise. "We're going up there? Isn't that where the owner—oh, wait. Are you . . . ?"

"Yes, when I bought the vineyard, it came with the castle," he said. He grinned at me as I put an embarrassed hand over my face. I knew he'd bought the vineyard, but somehow I hadn't really thought about the fact that it included the castle.

"This is so crazy. I always wondered what the second floor looked like." The previous owners had been very private.

"I hope you like it, *dolcezza*," he said. He sounded very invested in my response, which made me nervous even though I was certain I was overthinking it. Well, even if I hated it, I would pretend to love it, because that was just polite. Right?

We went through a doorway at the top of the stairs and entered the kitchen. It was completely modern with quartz counters, copper pots, and the latest appliances. Clearly, I was not going to have to fake a thing.

"Wow, this is beautiful," I said.

The interior of the medieval castle was the same blush-colored stone as the exterior, but instead of being cold and dark, it boasted floor-to-ceiling arched windows that looked out over the vineyard, plus enormous fireplaces that took up whole walls and were painted bright white, while track lighting illuminated the overbearing dark wooden beams that ran across the ceiling.

"How about a glass of Chianti?" he asked. He opened a small wine chiller, which kept the Chianti at an optimum sixty degrees, and pulled out a bottle. "I'll give you a tour after we eat. Do you like that idea?"

I did. I desperately did, but first I needed to gather some intel, things that needed to be asked in person.

"That would be lovely," I said. "But won't your wife or girlfriend mind that you're touring a former girlfriend around your home?" Yes, I asked just like that because I was the epitome of smooth.

He grinned. Then he shook his head. "I have no wife or girlfriend. *Sono single.*"

"How is that possible?" I asked. "I mean, look at you. You're gorgeous, and you're like the grape whisperer of the vineyard, plus you live in a friggin' castle. Are the women around here blind?" The words flew out of my mouth before I could stop them.

Marcellino laughed, and the deep dimples that had so fascinated me when I first met him framed the curve of his lips, making me want to press my thumbs into them.

"There is my Chelsea," he said. "So full of life . . . and questions." He tucked a strand of hair behind my ear, and his gaze moved over my face, taking in the changes the years had wrought. "Honestly, the vineyard is my wife, my mistress, my one true love. I am not the carefree boy you once knew."

"I'm not who I used to be either. I've changed a lot," I confessed.

"As we do," he acknowledged.

It was the perfect thing to say. Impulsively, I threw my arms about him and hugged him hard. Oh, I had missed him. He hugged me back and said, "We will spend time together, yes? And then we will talk about these changes, but first we eat."

We raided the refrigerator, which was amazingly well stocked for a bachelor. Marcellino made us sandwiches with thick slices of cheese and meat, along with fresh greens. He garnished them with olives and pickled asparagus and handed me a plate and a glass of Chianti. He then led me to a sun-filled terrace off the dining room.

We stepped through the French doors and walked to a tall café table with two stools. From here, we perched like gargoyles, looking down at the tourists who were walking from the vineyard to the basement below us, where the casks of Chianti were stored.

Marcellino watched the traffic for a moment, and then he looked back at me. He smiled as if he enjoyed seeing me there. Then he took an olive off his plate and popped it into his mouth. It occurred to me that he looked perfectly at home, just as the lord of the castle should.

I took a sip of my wine, savoring the robust flavor with subtle notes of tart cherry and letting it roll across my tongue, when he said, *"Dolcezza,* why did you wait so long to come back?"

I choked. I didn't mean to, but I inhaled some Chianti, and now it was caught in my throat, making me sputter and cough. I put my hand over my mouth to try to contain it, but my eyes were watering and my nose was running, because wasn't that a lovely picture for a guy who hadn't seen me in seven years?

"Sorry," he said. He leaped from his seat and patted my back, gently but firmly, until I had my coughing fit under control.

"No, it's all right," I said. "You just caught me by surprise. I didn't think we were going there right away."

"I've thought so often of the morning you left," he said. He gazed out across the hills before turning back to me. "The last thing you said to me was 'I love you.' It was the first time you'd said it to me, and my heart was so full of you all day I could barely work. I just wanted to be with you, but when I got back, you were gone. When I got your note, I understood your mother was ill, and when she passed, I knew you needed time. But as we kept in touch over the years, I always wondered why you didn't come back."

I picked at the thick crust of the sandwich bread on my plate. I didn't know what to say. Marcellino was the only person I'd kept in touch with from my year abroad. It had begun with me explaining my abrupt departure and then dwindled to Christmas cards over the past few years. He had always said I was welcome to visit, and I'd known he meant it, but I'd resisted.

I remembered my final day here so vividly. My father had called while I was working in the gift shop. When he told me about my mom, I fled. I knew that time was critical, so I raced to my room in the girls' dormitory on the vineyard grounds, packed my bag, and hopped on the next bus to Firenze so I could catch the first flight home. I had left Marcellino a note, but once I was home, the only thing I could think about was my mother, and after she died, well, I just didn't care about anything. My letters and emails were few and far between and then dwindled to just an annual card, which, if I was honest, was an afterthought.

"After my mother died, I just—" My words trailed off. I wasn't sure what to say.

"Stopped living?" he guessed.

"Yes, that." I felt my throat get tight. I took another sip of wine, picked at my sandwich, and then glanced up and forced a sad smile. "I wish I had been better about staying in touch. I wish I'd come back sooner."

"You're here now. That's what matters." Marcellino reached across the table and held my hand. "*Mi dispiace per la perdita di tua madre.*"

"*Grazie*," I said. His sympathy about my mother's death touched me. Possibly, it was hearing the words in Italian. I mean, I'd have to be made of rock not to respond. I squeezed his fingers with one hand and brushed the tears off my face with the other. I didn't want to dwell in the past. I wanted to live in the now. "*Basta. Mangia.*"

Marcellino smiled at me and let go of my hand. I could tell by the look of relief in his gaze that he didn't know what else to say to me about my loss. After Mom passed away, I got good at reading people and their emotions about grief. The people who were relieved when the topic went away were usually the ones who hadn't lost anyone near and dear and didn't know what to say to someone who had. They were uncomfortable when surrounded by someone else's grief and tried to avoid it as if it might be contagious.

I didn't fault Marcellino for it. I used to be jealous of people who had no experience with having their heart ripped out, and I'd wonder why me instead of them, but I'd grown as a person over the past seven years as I worked with people engaged in the fight of their life every day. Witnessing their losses along with my own, I wouldn't wish that misery on anyone.

"To your return," he said. He held up his glass, and I tapped mine against his.

I smiled. I was delighted to be here—I was. And if there was a tiny part of me that missed Jason and wondered what he'd make of all this—I could just see him taking in this castle—then I pushed it aside.

I was here to rediscover myself. Besides, Jason would be here in five—okay, four and a half—days, but who was counting? Not me.

THE NEXT TWO days were out of a dream. Marcellino was attentive and kind but restrained, as if he didn't want to push for more than I was willing to give.

We took long walks through the Tuscan countryside, which was ripe with wildflowers ready to burst into bloom. He showed me the improvements he'd made on the vineyard, and we ate every meal together and spent our evenings strolling through the small village, reading together on the couch in the living room of his castle, or simply savoring the beautiful spring evenings on the terrace while we drank wine and admired the stars. After Paris had gone so horribly awry, in just about every conceivable way, Marcellino was the perfect antidote.

Each morning, I awoke to a bouquet of handpicked flowers and a fresh carafe of coffee outside the door to the small cottage in which I was staying. On the second day, Marcellino fretted over my pasty office-worker skin and bought me a wide-brimmed bright-blue sun hat that was decorated with a bunch of silk daisies.

He cooked all our meals, tailoring the food to my tastes. Knowing my love of books, he gave me a stack of English novels to read when he had to tend to vineyard business. When a neighbor stopped by with a litter of puppies and I squealed over their roly-poly adorableness, Marcellino asked me if I'd like one when they were old enough to leave their mama. Not knowing what to make of that suggestion, I didn't answer. Was he thinking I'd be staying long enough to get a dog? I tried not to panic. This was what I wanted, wasn't it?

I was two and a half days into the five days Jason had said he'd give me until work required my attention again, and I was getting antsy. While I was enjoying my time with Marcellino immensely, I didn't know if what I felt was the same stirring of emotion I'd had with him before or if it was just the joy of being at the vineyard again. I didn't think I'd know for sure until we progressed beyond the hand-holding stage, but I wasn't sure how to get us there.

My opportunity came that evening, when Marcellino invited me for a stroll through the olive orchard. He wanted to check on the pruning to see that it was finished, and asked if I'd join him. I hoped it was his way of trying to take us to the next level. I was all in.

Twilight in the vineyard was magical, with a full moon rising over the hills, illuminating the silvery leaves of the olive trees and giving them an ethereal glow. No doubt about it—it was a wonderful backdrop for falling in love. *Come on, Marcellino*, I mentally cheered him on.

Like every moment of the past few days, it was perfect. A perfect view shared with a perfect man in a perfect place. It was almost more perfection than I could stand. And yet he still didn't make a move. Damn it.

I wondered if Jason was right; maybe Marcellino was gay. I mean, not that he had to be with me to prove that he wasn't. Oh no, maybe that was it. Now that I was here, maybe he just wasn't that into me. Ack, I was feeling the stirring of emotion right now, but it wasn't a good one. Was I in for another humiliation from a former boyfriend?

No! I refused to accept defeat. Marcellino had been a perfect gentleman during the past two days. That didn't mean he wasn't interested; he was just respectful. Wasn't that what every woman wanted these days? A man who treated her well? Feeling better, I decided it was do or die, right here on this vineyard hillside. I turned to him.

"Thank you, Marcellino," I said. I moved closer.

"For what?" He tipped his head and watched me. He didn't back away, so I took that as a good sign.

"For being you." And then I made my move. I slid my hands up his arms and pressed up against him. I met his gaze and tried to will him to lean down and kiss me. He hesitated, putting his hands on my hips as if he was undecided as to whether he should pull me in closer or hold me away.

A rustling noise from the bushes startled me, and I jumped, dropping my hands from him. I turned to see a wild hare sprinting away through the trees. I laughed and put my hand over my heart to calm its frantic beating. I tried not to dwell on the fact that my heart raced harder from the bunny scare than it did from being held by Marcellino.

The sound of an engine ripped through the quiet. By the light of the moon, I could see a motorcycle tearing up the dirt road toward the castle, leaving a cloud of dust in its wake. I assumed it was one of the vineyard workers coming back from an evening in town, but I noticed Marcellino was frowning in concern. Clearly, this was not someone who worked here.

He took my hand, and we left the grove and hurried up the hill to the parking lot beside the castle. The man pulled up in front of us, parking next to the cars belonging to Marcellino and resident staff. He cut the engine on the bike, put down the kickstand, and lifted the dark-blue helmet off his head. I blinked twice and then I gasped. *Jason?!*

chapter twenty-three

K NIGHTLEY, WHAT THE hell are *you* doing here?" I asked.

"You know this man?" Marcellino asked. His frown eased.

"Yes, we . . . um . . . work together," I said. "This will just take a minute."

I let go of his hand and marched forward. I was furious. He was two days early! How dare he come here without warning?

Jason lifted his leg over the bike and planted his helmet on the back. He looked at me with a sparkle in his eye that made my insides thrum. It was just rage, I assured myself.

"Well?" I asked. I crossed my arms over my chest in a clear signal that I was shutting him out completely. I hoped his ass was already hurting from a long ride on that motorbike, because I fully intended to send him away on it, and I hoped his backside was blistered by the time he landed far away from here tonight.

"There was a change of plan," he said. "Plus, it occurred to me that I'm your wingman. You need me, Maverick."

"No, I don't." I glared at him.

"Sure you do." He looked past me. "Is that the guy?"

"None of your business." I was so furious I thought my head would explode. When I spoke, my words came out with the trajectory of bullets. "Why. Are. You. Here?"

He put his hand on the back of his neck and stretched while he said, "Severin's trip to Milan was cut short. They're on their way here, arriving tomorrow, in fact."

"What? But you said you'd stall them," I protested.

"I tried." He shrugged. "But Severin is a force of nature."

"What am I supposed to do now?" I asked through gritted teeth. I didn't say it out loud, especially to Jason, but that attempted kiss with Marcellino had been a bust. Still, I wasn't sure I had really given it the old college try. And now with Jason here and Severin arriving soon after, I was feeling very pressured.

"Introduce me to the boyfriend," he said. He wagged his eyebrows at me. "I like the dress, by the way. Sexy."

I glanced down at my deep-blue sundress. It did not help my frame of mind to remember that when I'd bought it at the boutique in the village, I had thought it was a perfect match for Jason's eyes when they were their bluest blue. I had then promptly chastised myself for having such a ridiculous thought and bought the dress anyway. And now here he was, as if I'd conjured him. Argh!

"You need to go," I said. "I don't care what excuse you make, but you need to get back on that bike and ride off into the moonlight and give me the two more days you promised. Meet up with Severin at another vineyard."

"Yeah, that's not going to happen," he said. He raised his hands in a *what can you do* gesture, which made me think he wasn't sorry at all.

Why was I surprised? This was Knightley! He'd been a thorn in my behind from the day he'd come to the ACC. In a flash, "the incident" from our first corporate ask flitted through my brain, and I was furious all over again.

"This is so like you," I snapped. "I should have known you'd do whatever you wanted, just like with Overexposure Media Group."

Jason rolled his eyes. "I thought we made peace over that."

"And I thought you read up on workplace personalities and knew I was a guardian while you're a pioneer," I said. "And yet here we are with you changing the plan without checking with me first. This is not how a guardian works." I raised my hands in the air in exasperation.

"Would it help if I apologized for the Overexposure Media Group debacle?" he asked. "That disaster was one hundred percent my fault, and I truly am sorry."

That gave me pause. A contrite Knightley was an attractive object to behold. I shook it off. It did not help with this situation at all, however.

"Apology accepted," I said. "But I can't do this right now. I'm supposed to be figuring out my own stuff."

"I feel for you," he said. His gaze was soft as he studied my face in the moonlight. "I really do, but Severin is on his way. I have all of the paperwork." He patted the saddlebag on his bike. "We're doing this. I'm sorry if it interferes with your timetable—honestly, I am—but according to Eleanor, you are the only one Severin trusts, so it's imperative that you're involved until we get it signed and sealed. Besides, I would think you'd want to see it through."

Okay, Eleanor had said as much in Paris. And he made a fair point. I had done all the groundwork on this ask. It did mean a lot to me.

"I'm sure if you explain it to your boyfriend, he'll understand," he said. There was something in his tone that was off. I frowned.

"He's not my—" I began, but Marcellino interrupted.

"Is everything all right, *dolcezza*?" he asked.

I sighed. I looked at Jason's face and knew there was no way he was going to budge on this. If our positions were reversed, with this contribution to the cause to fight cancer on the table, I'd be just as stubborn.

"Yes, sorry," I said. My voice came out strained, so I forced a smile. "Marcellino DeCapio, this is my colleague Jason Knightley."

Without hesitation, Marcellino held out a hand to Jason. "*Piacere di conoscerti*," he said.

"Nice to meet you, too," Jason said.

"You speak Italian?" Marcellino asked. He sounded pleased.

Jason shrugged. "Mostly just enough to order wine and ask where the bathroom is."

Marcellino laughed. "In life, what more do you need?"

I glanced between the two men. Both handsome, both smart, both charming, and I felt as if my worlds were colliding. It was unpleasant.

"If you could just point me in the direction of a place to stay, I'd appreciate it," Jason said. He was looking at Marcellino with his most charming smile.

"Of course, but any friend of Chelsea's is welcome to stay here," Marcellino said. "You must take one of the guesthouses."

"No!" I cried at the same moment Jason said, "Thanks."

Marcellino glanced between us as if unsure whom he should listen to. I wanted to demand that he listen to me and encourage Jason to find lodging in the village. I couldn't even imagine trying to sort out my feelings for Marcellino with Jason around, but then I glanced at Jason's face and saw the dark circles beneath his eyes. He'd clearly been going all day and was on the brink of exhaustion. Fine, he could stay here, but only because Severin was on his way. Damn it.

"I'm sorry," I said. "Yes, absolutely, Jason, you must take one of the guesthouses."

He gave me a suspicious look with one eyebrow raised. "Are you sure?"

"Positive," I said. I glanced at Marcellino, who was looking at me with approval. "Shall we walk him down?"

"Of course," he said.

We waited for Jason to retrieve his small carry-on from the back of his motorcycle. He fell into step beside us, looked at me, and asked, "And where are you staying?"

"In another guesthouse," I said. "They're vacant because they're about to be remodeled. We have two others set aside for Severin and Eleanor."

"And you live on the grounds as well, Marcellino?"

Marcellino opened his mouth to answer, but I spoke first.

"He lives in the castle," I said.

Jason made a choking noise, and Marcellino looked at him in concern. "Are you all right, Jason?"

"Yeah, I'm good," he said. "Swallowed a bug." He gave Marcellino side-eye and pointed to the stone building looming over us. "Castle, huh?"

"Yes," I said. "He owns the castle and the vineyard, as well as an extensive olive orchard."

Jason glanced at Marcellino as if reconsidering him. "Impressive."

Marcellino ducked his head in humble acknowledgment and said, "Not really. Making Chianti and olive oil are the only things I know how to do."

"But you own a castle," Jason said.

Marcellino shrugged as if it was no big deal. He stepped ahead of us to open the door to the vacant guest cottage and went inside to turn on the lights.

Jason looked at me and asked, "Is this guy for real?"

"Yes," I said. "Very much so."

"Dang." He gave me a tired smile and said, "You'd better watch it. I may make a play for him myself."

That surprised a laugh out of me, and Jason's eyes moved over my face with warmth and affection. It hit me then that I'd missed this. I'd missed him. It was on the tip of my tongue to tell him I was glad he was here, but Marcellino called from the doorway.

"Come, *dolcezza*. We should let him settle. Jason, I hope you will be comfortable here," he said.

Jason turned away from me and entered the adorable cottage. It was exactly like mine, small with one bedroom, a full bath, a tidy living room and kitchenette combo, and a small veranda that overlooked the vineyard. Done in pale shades of blue with a wooden-beam ceiling and modern furniture, it reminded me of a mini version of the castle.

"I'm so tired I could sleep out in the field," Jason said. "But this is infinitely better. Thank you."

He held out his hand, and Marcellino shook it warmly. It was different from their first handshake. This one felt as if Jason was sincerely offering his respect, and Marcellino was accepting it. I had the feeling that in another place and time, these men would have been friends.

"We will let you rest," Marcellino said. "Please let me know if you need anything during your stay."

"I will," Jason said. He stood in the center of the room, watching as I followed Marcellino outside. At the door, I said, "Good night."

" 'Night, Martin." Then he gave me a little finger wave and a smile.

I shook my head in amusement as I shut the door.

"Are you all right?" Marcellino asked.

"Yes, absolutely," I said.

"Is there anything you want to tell me about Jason?" he asked.

"Such as?" I asked. I could feel my face get warm and was grateful for the cover of darkness.

"There's a tension between you two. Was he your boyfriend?" he asked.

"No," I said. "Nothing like that. We were work rivals, but now we have a very big corporate donation that we're working on together, the largest I've ever tried for, which is a challenge for both of us."

Marcellino considered me for a moment before he looked up at the moon, and then he smiled down at me as if he understood more than I was saying. I wanted to protest or try to explain more, but things were so new between us that I didn't want to mess it up by saying the wrong thing. In silence, we made our way back to my cottage, which was three down from Jason's. At my door, Marcellino kissed my forehead, as if I were his sister, before leaving me. Hmm.

I WAS ENJOYING breakfast on the second-floor terrace of the castle when I felt someone watching me. I glanced up to find Jason leaning against the doorjamb. He looked rested, wearing jeans and an untucked pale-yellow dress shirt with the sleeves rolled back on his forearms. He had clearly just showered, as his hair was damp and his body radiated the scent of the locally made lemon-verbena soap that Marcellino stocked in all the bathrooms on the vineyard.

I glanced at him over the rim of my coffee cup. Marcellino had left a little while ago to meet with the cellar supervisor. They were planning a large batch of Chianti Riserva, which aged much longer than the more affordable classic Chianti.

"That is a spectacular view," Jason said.

I glanced over my shoulder at the vineyard behind me. The hills were cut into patchwork squares in variegated shades of green. The day was already sun warmed and somnolent with the buzz of insects, the twitter of birds, and the muted voices of tourists walking the grounds below us.

"It really is," I agreed. I turned back around and met his gaze.

"I was talking about you sitting there," he said. "You look pretty in the Italian sunlight."

I felt my face get hot. "Thank you, but—"

"Inappropriate?" he guessed.

"Yes," I said. I refused to acknowledge any sort of flutter I might be feeling at his words.

"Doesn't make it not true, Martin," he said. "I ran into Marcellino downstairs. He sent me up to see you. He thought you might want to give me a tour of the place."

"Shouldn't we be preparing for Severin's arrival?" I asked.

"They won't be here until later," he said. "We have plenty of time."

"Define 'later.'"

"Later today or possibly tomorrow," he said. "Robbie said he'd be in touch."

I chewed on my lower lip and frowned. "It's a three-and-a-half-hour drive from Milan. Are they driving? Or is Severin going to arrive in some golden flying car type of thing?"

"That would be memorable," Jason laughed. He took the seat across from me. "Martin, relax. I have all of the paperwork. We'll trot Severin around the vineyard, give him some bottles of wine at the festival, and all will be well."

I stared at him, feeling a barrage of scenarios hammer at my brain. I forcefully shut them down. Jason was here. He had just as much skin in the game as I did. We weren't going to mess this up, and besides, I had other things I needed to focus on. Namely, getting Marcellino to kiss me so I could figure out if there was anything there.

"Coffee?" I offered.

"Does this mean we're friends again?"

"No."

"Aw, come on," he cajoled. "You have to be a little happy to see me."

"No, I don't," I said. I picked up an unused mug and filled it with coffee. I pushed it toward him, across the tabletop.

"Not even a little?" He held up his thumb and forefinger.

"A smidge, maybe. Is there anything smaller than that?"

"A drop," he suggested.

"That sounds about right," I said. I pushed a plate of sweet bread and a jar of Nutella at him. "Brioche?"

"Thanks," he said.

I glanced away as he slathered the inside of a circular bun with the chocolate-hazelnut spread. I remembered the feel of those hands on my bare back as we danced. Lines had been crossed in Paris—there was no question—but I couldn't let that interfere with right now.

"Jason, about Paris—" I began, but he shook his head.

"We don't have to talk about it."

"Yes, we do," I said. "I need to be clear that we're operating in a professional capacity only right now."

He glanced up from his plate. "Because?" he prompted. He looked as if he was assessing my every word. I didn't want to debate it, so I tried to explain it in my most pragmatic here's-a-PowerPoint-of-why-we-shouldn't-be-together voice.

"I'm a planner," I said. He raised his eyebrows. This was clearly not news. I continued, "You were obviously not a part of my plan when I came to Europe, and things got confused after Jean Claude, and lines were crossed when we kissed, and I handled it badly, as I do with disruptions in my plans."

Jason's eyes went wide, and then he laughed long and hard. "Is that what I was? A disruption in your plan?"

I met his gaze. I thought about Marcellino and how perfect he was and how much I wanted to be the young woman I once was when I was with him, before I had this truckload of grief weighing me down, and I said, "Yes."

"I see."

"Do you?"

"Yeah, you think Marcellino is the key to finding yourself again, don't you?"

"He's more the key than the other two were."

"Because he owns a castle?"

"Do you really think I'm that shallow, Knightley?"

"It's a castle, Martin," he said. "I'd be disappointed in you if you weren't that shallow."

A sparrow flew onto the veranda and hopped sideways toward Jason, keeping its bright eyes on him as if it knew Jason was the keeper of the bread. It had a brown back and a white breast. It looked similar to the sparrows back home, but the brown was a ruddier shade, almost rust.

Absently, Jason broke off a bit of crust and tossed it in the air. The sparrow leaped for it, catching it in its beak before it flew off.

"I'm not here because he has a castle," I said. I felt the need to emphasize this point.

"I know," he conceded. "So he's available?"

"Apparently."

"No crazy ex-girlfriend?"

"Not that I've seen."

"And you're positive he's not gay?"

"I'm sure."

He looked at me in alarm. "How sure?"

"Pretty sure."

He relaxed a little and bit into his brioche, and I watched him eat with gusto. There was a manly man knuckle-dragger quality to Jason Knightley that I had to admit I found attractive. He wasn't a quitter, and when he went after something, he went all in. It made him good at his career.

"I do have some news from the office," he said once he'd finished his bun and washed it down with more coffee.

I felt my chest get tight. "Aidan?"

"Is fine," he said. "Don't worry. If there was any news, I'd have told you first thing. I won't ever hold back from you."

"Thank you."

"No, this news is about the Quarter Thief," he said.

I sat up straight. "Did they catch the person?"

"Yes, but only because he let them," he said.

"Who was it?" I demanded.

"Gary Welch," he said. He paused while I placed the name. I blinked.

"The security guard?" I asked. "The one who had a quadruple bypass last year?"

"That's the one," he said.

"Why? How?"

"Apparently during his retirement party, which happened while we were in Paris, he cut out a quarter of his cake, lifted it up, and dumped it on top of Michelle's head."

My jaw dropped. "Oh my god. But why?"

"Apparently, last year Michelle took it upon herself to cut his recovery time by a quarter," he said. "She went to his doctors, and even though they recommended another month of recuperation, she insisted that Gary come back after three months, or she was going to put a letter in his file that she assured him would impact the supervisory position he had applied for within the company."

"She's evil," I said.

"Yes, well, when it all came out, Aidan fired her," Jason said.

"What? I thought she was untouchable."

"Apparently this was the last straw. Aidan stormed the office of the VP who she's friends with and had it out with him. No one heard what was said, but as soon as Michelle had most of the cake out of her hair, she was told to pack up her office, and then she was escorted from the building."

"That is some primo, grade A, juicy gossip," I said. "I can't believe Julia didn't tell me when I checked in yesterday."

"I asked her not to, since I knew I'd be seeing you here and all," he said.

"Oh." And just like that, things felt awkward.

I wasn't sure what to say, so I finished my coffee and pretended to be watching the comings and goings of the vineyard even though I was hyperaware of the man across the table. I was so tuned into him I felt as if I could pick out his heartbeat in a room full of ticking clocks.

I wondered if he felt the same. I glanced at his face to find him looking at me, but when our gazes met, he glanced away, and I knew he was struggling to find his footing with us, too. We were colleagues, we were friends, and we'd had a brief flirtation. Things were jumbled and messy, but I knew if I kept the boundaries in place, we'd be able to get our bearings. And after Severin signed the papers, we'd go our separate ways. We could do this.

If I could have back that night in Paris . . . No, regardless of how things were now, I didn't want to give up the memory of kissing him on top of the Eiffel Tower. When I was old and in my rocking chair, I was going to take out the memory of that evening in his arms, hum "La vie en rose," and smile.

We finished our coffee and I stood, gathering the plates to bring them into the kitchen. Jason helped, carrying the coffeepot and a tray of leftover food. I put the food away, but Marcellino had a housekeeper, who'd made it pointedly clear that tidying up was her job and I wasn't to do it. I had to admit, it was an unexpected perk to castle life that given a chance, I could really get used to.

"Come on—I'll show you the winery from vine to bottle," I said.

Together we wound our way down the spiral staircase and out the door that was marked *Private*. I guided Jason through a side door and along a dirt path that led into the heart of the vineyard, where the grapevines were just beginning to leaf. The thick vines twisted their way up out of the rich earth as if reaching for the sun, air, and rain that they knew awaited them.

Jason paused by one of the plants. He studied the leaves and then looked out over the rolling hills, where lines of vines spread all the way to the horizon. "That's a lot of grapes."

I smiled. "To be labeled a Chianti, the wine has to consist of at least eighty percent Sangiovese grapes."

"Sangiovese?" he asked. "Not exactly the Cabernet Sauvignon and Chardonnay of Napa, is it?"

"No. The name comes from the Latin *sanguis Jovis*, which means 'the blood of Jupiter.'"

He looked at me. "Dang, Martin, you are full of wine trivia."

"I did give tours here for several months during my year abroad," I said. "I learned a lot."

"Enough to make it your life?"

I shrugged. "Maybe."

When I glanced at his face, his expression was blank. If he was holding out hope for us in any way, I didn't want to hurt him—truly, I didn't. I'd spent most of the previous night tossing and turning, thinking about building a life in Italy if the opportunity presented itself, and honestly, I could almost see it. It was grainy and fuzzy, like an old film reel, but maybe after all this time, this was where I belonged, with Marcellino.

The truth was, he was kind, funny, smart, and, frankly, hot, and when I was with him, I felt glimmers of the old Chelsea, the young Chelsea, the Chelsea who didn't know the pain of great loss, and I liked it. I liked her, and I wasn't ready to give up on her just yet.

THE SUN WAS warm, hot even, so Jason and I took shelter in the olive grove. We walked down the center line of trees, and other than the birds, we were completely alone. Jason paused to take in the towering expanse of the branches above us, and then he flopped down on the grass with all the loose-limbed enthusiasm of a golden retriever.

"What are you doing?" I asked.

"Enjoying the day," he said. "When was the last time you got to sit in an olive orchard in Tuscany on a workday?"

"This side of never."

"Exactly," he said. "Have a seat, Martin. Take a load off for a minute."

I heaved a sigh and sank down on the grass, knowing there would be no moving Knightley until he was ready. A soft breeze rustled the leaves in the trees, and the grass was cool beneath my fingertips. I had to admit, it was nice to take a moment to soak it in.

He turned his head and studied me until I felt compelled to ask, "What?"

He opened his mouth to speak, but his phone went off. It was an abrupt clanging jangle in the middle of paradise. He sighed and reached into his pocket to pull out his phone. The initial wallpaper was the Red Sox logo—not a surprise—but he tapped in his security code, and a new picture came up of a boy and a girl. Now, I really wasn't trying to see his passcode, I swear, but he might have picked something harder than the six numbers in descending order from the number nine. Honestly, did the man have no sense of security?

He swiped the screen to open the text that had just come in. He read it quickly but didn't respond. Apparently satisfied, he closed the texting app and tossed his phone into the grass.

I glanced down at the photo of the kids, who looked to be about age ten, making goofy faces at the camera. Adorable! The boy had his eyes crossed and his tongue out, while the girl had her thumbs jammed in her ears, with her hands out like antlers, her mouth hanging open, and her eyes wide. They looked ridiculous, and I laughed at their expressions.

Were they Knightley's kids? A niece and nephew, perhaps? It occurred to me that I didn't know that much about Knightley's personal life, which was weird, because I felt like I should know more. I mean, I'd made out with the guy. Three times! Shouldn't I know if he had kids in his life?

Mentally, I scanned everything I knew about him beyond the surface handsome face and charming—when he wanted to be—personality. He arrived at the office a few minutes late every day, everyone greeted him like he was their best friend, and he responded the same. He was always on board for shenanigans, betting pools, happy hours, and holiday parties. As far as I knew, he was single—at least, he'd said as much the night I'd called him in Boston and he was leaving his "bros" at the bar.

I scanned deeper. He'd mentioned his parents in passing at a few work functions. I hadn't really listened, because at the time I'd considered him a useless frat boy and my rival. I had not been interested. Thinking about it now, I was positive he'd grown up in central Massachusetts, as he'd never met a Boston team of which he wasn't a die-hard supporter.

Boggled that I knew so little about him, I decided it was time for a fishing expedition. I picked up his phone. "Cute kids."

A grin slowly unfurled across his lips, drawing my attention to his mouth. "What are you trying to ask me, Martin?"

"Nothing." I shrugged. "Just making an observation."

"So you think I'm cute."

"You?" I glanced down at his phone, but it had gone dark. I tapped the screen, and a prompt to enter the security code appeared. I held it out to him in silent question, and he tapped in the number. Again, I wasn't trying to see it, but seriously, way to make it easy to be hacked. I refrained from saying anything. His phone, his business.

Instead, I glanced at the photo. I studied the picture of him as a boy. Then I looked at the girl. She was a feminine version of him. I could see the same mischievous twinkle in her eye, the unruly dark hair, and the same irrepressible grin.

"Yup, that's me and my twin sister." His voice was gruff, and he tipped his head back and squinted through the leaves at the bits and pieces of blue sky overhead as if he were trying to fit them back together to make the sky whole. "She died of leukemia." He cleared his throat. "When we were twelve."

chapter twenty-four

FELT THE blood drain from my face. Shame made my heart pound, and I felt as if I might be sick. Given his frat-boy everything's-a-party personality, I had always assumed he'd been a communications major who'd fallen ass backward into working for the ACC. I knew he'd begun his career in community outreach, organizing events and such, until his crazy hot-wing challenge had gone viral, and then suddenly he'd had an office down the hall from mine. I had no idea he'd suffered such a horrific personal loss.

He'd had a twin? He'd lost her to cancer? And all this time I had thought he was one of those lucky people who'd never had so much as a drop of rain fall in his perfect life. I was such a jerk.

"I'm so sorry," I said. And I was, for more than he knew. Without hesitation, I pushed off the ground and put my arms around him in a hug. He stiffened at first, obviously caught off guard, or maybe he wasn't a hugger. Either way, I didn't let go until I felt him relax and move to hug me in return.

"Is this awkward yet?" I teased.

He chuckled. "I think we moved through awkward to friendly, but it could turn into something else really fast."

I pulled back just enough to see his face. His smile was a bit lopsided, his lips curving up higher on one side, as if he knew that the flip side to happy was sad, and this knowledge made it impossible for him to smile fully, knowing that there was a grim truth to every joke. How had I never noticed that before? I handed him back his phone.

"Tell me about her," I said. It wasn't that I wanted to poke at his sorrow. It was just that I sensed he wanted to talk about his sister.

"She was my first best friend," he said. He shifted and leaned back against the trunk of a tree. "We were always together. In fact, we were so inseparable that our names merged into one. The entire family called us JasonJess, sort of a Jason-and-Jess mashup. She was always Jess, not Jessica or Jessie, just Jess."

He glanced at me, and his voice was thick with memories. "She was born five minutes before me, and she never let me forget it. We grew up in Charlton, a small town in Massachusetts, and we ran wild. Jess could climb our favorite tree higher than me, catch fish bigger than mine, and there was no hill she was afraid to sled down. She lived life large and in charge."

I felt my throat get tight. Jason's love for his sister was evident in every word he said, and the sadness that shadowed his eyes made his grief palpable. It was as much a part of who he was as his quick wit or the strong line of his jaw.

"When we were ten, she broke her arm when she fell out of our tree because we were having a Nerf gun battle with the Davidson boys across the street. They were total buttheads. Looking back, I think Pete Davidson may have been crushing on Jess. She'd gotten his attention by punching him in the mouth when he took her skateboard without asking."

He grinned at the memory and I did, too.

"It was love at first knuckle sandwich?" I asked. "I take it she was not crushing on him in return."

"Yeah, no, Jess was full-on tomboy with no interest in kissing and all that gross junk. Poor Pete, he didn't stand a chance."

Jason lifted up his phone and studied the picture. I glanced at it, too. Now that I knew, the boy was clearly a younger version of Jason. I studied Jess. She looked to be a scamp. I could only imagine the chicanery these two had gotten into as kids.

"My mom has that picture framed and on the wall of the living room. It was taken a few weeks before Jess's fall," he said. The image went dark, and he tucked his phone into his pocket. "We didn't know anything was wrong with her. She was always so rough-and-tumble, she never slowed down, but then her arm wouldn't mend."

His voice caught, and he took a steadying breath. I knew he was reliving the exact moment when the bottom had fallen out of his life. I wanted to reach out to him, but I waited, not wanting to interrupt.

"When the doctors ran tests, they discovered she had leukemia," he said. "I didn't understand. I thought it was like a cold or the flu, and she'd just shake it off. I mean, she was Jess—nothing stopped her. But she kept getting weaker and weaker. I thought she was milking it to get out of school. I'd had to go without her, which sucked, and I didn't realize what was happening, how serious it all was, until I found my mother in the kitchen one afternoon. She was sitting on the floor, curled up against the cupboard, crying into a dish towel. It was then that I knew it was bad, really bad."

He swallowed hard. He blinked. And then he continued, "She was in treatment for two years, but her cancer was aggressive, and her body was so riddled with tumors that they couldn't save her." His voice was raw, and he ran a hand over his face. When I looked into his eyes, just a glance before he turned away, he looked broken.

"She was the person I loved most in the world," he said. His eyes were watery and his voice tight. "I wanted to die with her because in my mind, we were supposed to do everything together. We were a team, two halves of a whole, and I didn't understand how she could leave me."

I nodded. I knew how that pain felt. A tear coursed down my cheek, and I wiped it away. This time I did reach out to him. I took his free hand in mine and gave his fingers a gentle squeeze. When I would have let go, he turned his palm and laced his fingers with mine as if he wasn't ready to give up the comfort of contact just yet.

"I didn't know how to go on without her," he said. "In fact, I refused to celebrate my birthday—it was *our* birthday—for years. When the big life moments came up, I didn't want to participate in any of it. Graduations, proms, getting my driver's license—every event felt like something, or rather someone, Jess, was missing. I couldn't get past it."

I knew exactly what he meant. Grief. The bottomlessness of it had been what surprised me the most. Every time I thought the feeling of loss couldn't get worse, a birthday would roll around, or a holiday or a special event, and the realization that my mother wasn't there to be a part of it would send me spinning into bereavement like a drunk on a bender.

I was twenty-two when I lost Mom. It had always felt so young to suffer such a great loss, but Jason had been twelve when he lost his sister. If I had struggled, and I had, I could only imagine how hard it must have been for him to go through the process of grieving his twin at such a tender age.

"After a few bad episodes, I ended up in therapy," he said. He gave me a rueful look. "Not surprisingly, I couldn't manage everything I was feeling, grief and guilt and rage, and I tried to relieve my own pain by hurting myself. Small things, a cut here and a burn there. When my mom saw a scar on my arm, she flipped out. She was not about to lose another kid. Not on her watch." He paused, and his mouth curved up just a little on one side. "I went right into counseling, and my therapist helped me to understand what survivor's guilt is. It took me a long time to accept that it wasn't my fault that I lived and Jess died, a very long time, and sometimes I still wonder—"

"If she should have lived instead?" My voice was barely a whisper.

"Yeah." He choked out the word and rubbed his eyes with the heels of his hands.

I didn't know what to say. I knew what I wanted to say. My heart was exploding with it. That the world needed him, that I needed him, but I didn't say any of that. Instead, I took a deep breath and asked, "And what would Jess say if she knew you thought that?"

A surprised laugh burst out of him, and he said, "She wouldn't say anything. She'd kick my ass."

He turned to me with a small smile, which I returned.

"I'm so sorry," I said. My voice was tight. I cleared my throat, wanting to be strong for him. "That must have been just brutal."

"Yeah, it was," he said. "But I learned to keep moving forward even when I didn't want to."

I nodded. We were quiet for a while, enjoying the dappled sunlight, the gentle breeze, the companionable silence.

"Okay, Martin, your turn," he said.

"What do you mean?"

"Now you know why *I* work at the ACC, but why do you? What's your origin story?"

I snorted. Leave it to Jason to make a backstory sound more like a superhero's journey, but then again, maybe it was. I plucked a blade of grass and considered it.

"I told you my father was remarrying," I said. "But I don't know if I mentioned that he's a widower."

"Oh, shit, Chelsea, I'm sorry," he said.

"Yeah, that crushing loss I mentioned to you in Paris? It was my mom. Seven years ago," I said. "Pancreatic cancer. I was here, actually, working at the vineyard, when I got the call."

Our gazes met, and the look of understanding on his face, as if he knew exactly how devastating that call had been, almost undid me. I hadn't cried over the loss of my mother in a while, but his gentle sympathy almost brought it bubbling up to the surface. I shook my head and tossed the sliver of grass into the air and watched it pinwheel back to the earth.

"You know what was weird? When I got home, she seemed fine," I said. "She and Dad picked me up at Logan. My sister was away at college, but she came home shortly after I arrived, and we had a family meeting about our new reality. The thing I remember most was thinking that it had to be a mistake, because she looked totally normal."

Jason didn't say anything. He just listened. Given that most people tried to change the subject when the loss of my mother came up, Jason's acceptance was a welcome change.

"The disease moved swiftly, however," I said. "She was already stage four. The cancer had spread to other major organs when it was discovered, so it wasn't resectable, but she held on a lot longer than we thought she would. She was stubborn like that."

"How long?" he asked.

"We had a little over three months from the time I arrived home until she passed away," I said. "We tried to make the most of it."

He nodded, and I knew he understood how differently you start to view time when the grains of sand start dropping in the hourglass faster and faster and there's nothing you can do to slow it down.

"My mom was my best friend. I suppose that's odd, but we had a special connection. My younger sister, Annabelle, was a daddy's girl. If he was fixing a toilet, well, then she was right in there with him, handing him a wrench. But for me, it was all mom all the time. I was her shadow. Saturdays were our baking days. We both loved to bake elaborate cakes for all occasions. I remember one Christmas we made a cake that when you sliced it, a Christmas tree appeared in the middle.

"Then there was the time we made a peanut butter cake. After hours of being so good, our golden retriever, Sally, jumped up on the counter and bit into the cake." I laughed at the memory. "Sally bolted for the door with half of the cake in her mouth, and my mom ran after her. I have no idea what she thought she was going to do.

"Sally managed to eat that enormous chunk of cake while running, and there was my mom chasing after her with her apron flapping in the breeze for the entire neighborhood to see. It took her years to live that down. I always wondered why she chased the dog. Surely she didn't think the cake was salvageable. When Sally spent the night vomiting the cake back up, my mom told her it served her right, but then she slept on the floor and stayed by Sally's side all night, rubbing her belly so she'd feel better."

I smiled and Jason returned it, which was what I'd hoped for. It hurt me to see him hurting. I was humbled that he'd told me about Jess, and it felt good to tell him about my mom. So few people really understood, but I knew now that he did. There was an emotional connection between us that I'd never felt with anyone outside my family before. Maybe it was the bond of having survived great loss, or perhaps it was being in charge of such a major gift, or maybe it was a combination of the two. Either way, I was seeing Knightley differently, and I knew I could never dismiss him as just a handsome charmer ever again.

"You know what was the hardest part, outside of losing Jess, of course?" he asked.

I shook my head. It was all hard, miserably, awfully, brutally, wrenchingly hard. I'd never really broken it down into a hierarchy of pain.

"Watching her get smaller and smaller," he said. His voice was soft. "I used to go into her room when she was sleeping, and I'd put my fingers around her wrist to see if it had gotten any smaller. Some days I could convince myself that she hadn't lost any weight, but other days I couldn't lie to myself, and I knew she was shrinking, disappearing before my eyes, and there was nothing I could do to stop the cancer from siphoning off the rambunctious, loud Jess I knew and leaving this fragile little bird in her place."

Yeah, I remembered. My mom had always had feminine curves, as a love of cake will do to a gal, but when she got sick, the pounds had swiftly slipped off her, leaving her skin sagging around her bones and her eyes sunken in her bald head. It had been a struggle for my mom, who, while not vain, had always felt confident in her femininity. The disease had stripped her of that. My throat got tight at the memory of those last days with her, because even while knowing that she would be out of pain when she passed, I selfishly hadn't wanted to say goodbye.

"Sorry," I choked. I waved my hand as if I could wave away the emotions that were suffocating me. I rested my head on my folded arms, trying to breathe through it.

"Nah, it's okay," he said. "I get it." He put his hand on my back and ran it up and down my spine in a comforting gesture.

"My memories of Jess are so bittersweet," he said. "Bitter because there are no more, but sweet because they keep her alive in my heart and mind and I treasure that, even though it hurts."

That was it, exactly. I had never, not in all my years of working for the ACC, met someone who put into words what I felt so precisely. Never could I ever have imagined that the person most likely to understand me so completely would be Jason Knightley.

I lifted my head and turned toward him. He didn't move, so I leaned forward and put my arms around him. We had just shared so much grief and pain that I desperately needed to feel anchored to something or someone. I needed help to step back from the ledge of grief that made me want to jump and wallow in the darkness.

A shudder rippled through me as I tried to get it together. He pulled me in close and tight. We huddled like survivors after a storm, trying to assess the damage while getting our bearings. I could feel his heart beat in time with mine, our breath mingling. The amber-resin scent of him wrapped around me like an invisible cord, lashing me to him. I wanted to stay there forever, but I couldn't.

I pulled back, forcing myself to let go of him. He was a coworker. We had a major ask to nail down in the next few days. These were lines that couldn't be crossed.

"Sorry," I said. I fisted my hands and drew them toward my middle to keep myself from reaching for him again.

"Hey, it's okay. We shared some pretty heavy-duty stuff. It's perfectly normal to get caught up in the moment."

I turned away and drew up my knees, tucking myself into a little ball of self-containment. I had this. I could resist the urge to cling to him, to bury my face in the curve of his neck, to weep all over his chest, to place my mouth on his. Really, I could.

"So hugging the stuffing out of you is the normal reaction from women when you tell them about your sister?" I teased, trying to break the tension between us.

He leaned back. His eyes met mine, and I noticed they were as blue and clear as the sky above. "I don't know," he said. "I've never told anyone about Jess before, not even Aidan."

Whoa. I had no idea what to say to that, so I said nothing.

He stood and held out his hand. "Come on—Severin might be here soon," he said.

WE WALKED BACK to the castle, continuing our tour, maneuvering around a busload of visitors, who were gathered for a lecture by a staff member. We paused to listen for a bit before moving on.

"Can I ask you something?" Jason asked, following me into the cask room, which was in actuality a very barrel-crowded former dungeon.

"Sure," I said.

"Do you love him?" he asked.

I hissed out a breath. I knew I could lie and say yes and end this whole thing between us, but after he'd taken me into his confidence and told me about his sister, I simply could not do him wrong like that, not even for the greater good.

"I did once," I said. "And I think maybe I could again."

"You think? Maybe?"

"We haven't had much time together." I gave him a pointed look, and instead of looking abashed, he grinned. Classic Knightley. I tried not to be charmed.

"Has it ever occurred to you, Martin, that you were a different person on your year abroad and you loved men then that the person you are now could never love?"

"No, it hasn't," I said. "Because the whole point of this trip is to remember who I used to be, and that Chelsea was very much in love with Marcellino DeCapio. What's more, I liked her. She was fun and adventurous and bighearted." I rubbed my knuckles over my chest. "I miss her."

"Well, I can't weigh in on that debate, since I didn't know you then," he said. He put his hand on the back of his neck as he studied me from beneath his lashes. "But I can say that I like the Chelsea Martin who's here right now. I think she's pretty damn special."

He turned and walked away, leaving me staring after him as he strolled through the enormous oak barrels, which were stacked up to the ceiling. He liked me. Why did that make me feel all fluttery, as if I'd achieved something rare and precious?

I mean, it was Knightley. He liked everyone. But for the first time, I knew he liked me as a person, and it meant something to me—it meant quite a lot, in fact, especially now that I knew his past was so much like mine. I felt that we had a bond, and I realized I cared about him. I cared about him very much. I wasn't sure what to do with these feelings, but I wasn't going to pretend they didn't exist. That wouldn't be fair to either of us.

Instead of dwelling on this startling realization, I hurried to catch up, keeping my thoughts to myself until I knew exactly what I was feeling. I showed Jason the rest of the cellar, where the casks of wine were stored, and the bottling room—my favorite—where one big steel machine bottled, corked, and labeled all the wine. I used to love watching the bottles come out on the line and had often volunteered to help box them. Many were sold in the gift shop, but more were shipped to stores and restaurants all over Italy.

Jason picked up a bottle and studied it. Marcellino didn't use the traditional Chianti fiasco, a bottle whose rounded bottom was covered with straw. Rather, it was a regular dark-green bottle with a cream-colored label. In stylized script it read *Castello di Luce Chianti* next to an artist's rendering of the castle in shades of light brown and rose, the same color as the castle stone.

"Is it any good?" he asked.

"The best in the region," I said. I felt a surge of pride. I'd loved working here that spring so long ago, and I really believed that the wine was the best.

"*Grazie, dolcezza.*" Marcellino appeared in the doorway. "Your confidence in our wine warms my heart."

I felt myself blush. I wasn't sure why I was embarrassed. Because Marcellino had praised me in front of Jason? Or was it having Marcellino find me alone with Jason? That couldn't be it. He was the one who'd suggested I give Jason a tour.

"Your vineyard is beautiful," Jason said to Marcellino.

"Thank you." Marcellino moved to stand beside me and took my hand in his. "Chelsea, I was coming to see if you wanted to join us in tasting the Riserva?"

I glanced at Jason and explained, "The Riserva is the Chianti that has been aged for over three years."

"Join us, Jason," Marcellino said. "You will like it."

Jason looked mildly chagrined by Marcellino's friendliness but forced a smile and said, "That'd be great. Thanks."

As we walked back through the narrow corridor, we were forced to go single file with Marcellino in the lead, then me and Jason bringing up the rear. I was hyperaware of him behind me but tried to shut him out. He made it impossible, as he leaned forward and whispered in my ear, "He really is the perfect guy, isn't he?"

I glanced over my shoulder at him and met his gaze. I didn't know what to say. I believed there was a reason that of all the people I'd met and of the three men I'd fallen in love with during my year abroad, Marcellino was the only one I'd kept in touch with. What that reason was, I had no idea, but there was no arguing that he was a heck of a guy.

"He's handsome, successful, and really, really nice," Jason said. His voice was so low I could barely hear him when he muttered, "How's a guy supposed to compete with that?"

Again, I didn't know what to say, so I said nothing.

chapter twenty-five

THE FOLLOWING MORNING kicked off the first day of the week-long wine festival, which began with the *infiorata*, a flower festival held in the center of the village. I glanced out the window of my cottage and noted that the weather was so perfect it felt as if it had been specially ordered. The sun was warm and the breeze cool but so light that no petals from the elaborate works of art that decorated the town would be disturbed as the air gently moved through the narrow cobbled streets as softly as a whisper.

I dressed in a pale-pink sundress paired with a wide-brimmed straw sun hat decorated with silk peonies the size of my fist. I kept my makeup light and wore my hair loose. Comfortable brown sandals were the footwear of choice, as Marcellino had told me we would be doing a lot of walking.

As the owner of the castle and the employer to most of the town, Marcellino was expected to attend the festival and admire the floral works of art, talk to the residents, and basically be the benevolent castle dweller of their humble village. I, as his date, was expected to do much the same.

While I had visited the village several times during the past few days, I hadn't gone there as Marcellino's special lady friend, so being out in the public eye with him in this capacity felt like a very big deal, and I was extremely nervous. What if the locals rejected me? I wondered if it was too early for wine.

I stepped out of my cottage and found Marcellino waiting for me on the terrace. He looked devastatingly handsome in a lilac dress shirt, gray slacks, and casual shoes, with his thick dark hair brushed back from his face. His grin when he saw me made all my efforts on my appearance worth it.

"Will I do?" I asked.

"*Bellissima,*" he said. "You will more than do. You are perfection."

I felt my face grow warm at his words. So charming.

Yesterday had been spent anticipating the arrival of Severin. Unfortunately, it wasn't until late in the evening that Robbie texted Jason to tell him he and Eleanor had been delayed by an unexpected business meeting. They were now hoping to arrive at some point today but would keep us posted. I kept my impatience at bay by thinking of what an incredible boon their donation would be to the ACC.

Consequently, with Jason underfoot, Marcellino and I hadn't had any time alone. My desire to have him kiss me had been repeatedly thwarted, making me surly and frustrated.

I glanced around the terrace. There was no one here now. Pushing down all the anxiety screaming inside of me that this was not a great idea—*What if he doesn't want to kiss you? What if it's terrible? What if there is no spark?*—I stepped close to Marcellino and gazed up at him. I tried to make my signal that he was all clear to come in for a landing as obvious as the guys on the airport tarmac with the big orange flags, but still, he didn't move.

I decided to take the initiative. I slid my hands up his arms and around the back of his neck. I rose up on my toes at the same time I pulled his head down to mine. I put my lips on his, fitting our mouths together the way I remembered. Finally, his hands moved hesitantly around me. At last, we kissed fully and completely, and it was . . . *meh*.

When we broke apart, he leaned back and his face was quizzical, as if he were trying to detect the subtler notes in a glass of wine but couldn't quite place them. His expression of puzzlement was exactly how I felt, so much so that I laughed. To my delight, he did, too.

"That was—" I stopped, stumped for words.

"*Noioso*," he said.

"Boring?" I cried. Then I laughed harder, because it really was. Despite the fact that my potential romantic relationship with Marcellino had just gone poof, there was something so ridiculous about the moment that I couldn't help but be amused. What thrilled me the most was the realization that this, right here, was exactly how the old Chelsea would have reacted. Not with anxiety or upset but with genuine belly laughs at the ridiculousness of it all.

Marcellino thought it was funny, too, which made me laugh even harder. It became a contagious fit of the giggles that was unstoppable. Every time we looked at each other, we cracked up again.

"*Allora, dolcezza*, I think perhaps we are meant to just be friends," he said between chuckles.

"The best of friends," I agreed. Still grinning, I hugged him tight, and he picked me up off my feet, squeezing me hard in return.

"Hey, Martin, let's get this party started!" Jason called as he turned the corner.

He stopped short when he saw us, and Marcellino gently put me down. He adjusted my hat and said quietly, "But that one, I don't think it is friendship he feels."

I opened my mouth to protest, but Marcellino had already turned away to greet Jason. "*Buongiorno*, Jason. Have you ever been to a flower festival?"

"No, this is my first," he said. His gaze darted between me and Marcellino as if he was trying to read the room.

"I think you will enjoy it. The artists make intricate portraits and landscapes all from the petals of flowers," Marcellino explained. "And, of course, there is music and food and dancing with pretty girls."

"And wine," I said. I smiled at Marcellino. "Don't forget the wine."

He put a hand on his forehead in mock alarm. "How could I?"

As Marcellino walked down the path, leading the way, we fell in beside him. I glanced at Jason out of the corner of my eye and noted that he was dressed like an Italian gentleman, in beige slacks and a white dress shirt with brown woven loafers, no Converse high-tops. To complete the look, he was wearing a straw trilby with a dark-brown band around the crown. He was handsome in a suave, cosmopolitan way, like Cary Grant, and my inner Audrey Hepburn was crushing hard. As if sensing my interest, he turned and smiled at me, and I literally got dizzy.

My awareness of him as a man was as visceral as a punch in the gut, and I wondered if Marcellino was right. Was Jason still interested in being more than coworkers? He seemed to be—at least, he was very flirty and charming—but he had respected my boundaries and hadn't said anything specific since Paris, keeping it strictly business between us.

In all fairness, how could he do anything else? I had shut that shizzle down. But even if he was interested, there were issues. We worked together, after all. What would that look like? Even without Michelle in HR, the no-dating policy remained. Would one of us have to leave the ACC? Was I willing to do that for a relationship?

It was one thing to leave the ACC because I was going to take up residence in a vineyard in Tuscany. It was quite another to walk away from a career in the city to which I planned to return. I had worked so hard to get where I was, and now that it appeared my quest to find my old self was a bust, my career was the only thing I had. My brain shorted out at the mere thought of leaving it for a relationship that might or might not work out.

When we approached the festival, Marcellino was greeted by everyone we encountered, with Jason and me introduced as his guests. It was clear he was well liked, and I wasn't at all surprised. He was a good man. I did notice that some of the residents of the village were uncertain as to my relationship with Marcellino and how Jason factored into the equation. I knew exactly how they felt. I didn't know how Jason factored into my equation either.

The first *infiorata* at the entrance to the festival was an elaborate depiction of Castello di Luce. It was done in a carpet of thick petals, seeds, and grass, all in pastel shades. I caught my breath at the precision of the piece; each castle stone was done in exacting detail. I knew the artist had been working on it for days, and by the end of the day's festival, it would be gone.

"*Questo è magnifico!*" Marcellino said.

"It's incredible," I said.

"That's wicked awesome." Jason nodded.

A little girl who looked to be about four years old, in a darling white dress and wearing a wreath of blue delphiniums and baby's breath perched on her honey-colored curls with trails of blue and white ribbons dangling off the back, approached me with a flower. It was a rose, a single perfect pink rose. She shyly handed it to me and then ran and hid behind her mother's skirt. I held the flower up to my nose and called, "*Grazie, bambina.*"

And so it went with every stop we made to appreciate the elaborate works of flower-petal art done in the middle of the street; young children would come forward and give me a flower. I was charmed all the way down to my toes by them, and when we reached the center of the village, which was marked by a large fountain, my arms were full of the beautiful blooms.

The tiny town consisted of three-story stone buildings that housed businesses on the ground floors and residences above. There were all the usual shops—grocer, baker, butcher, leather goods, pharmacy, hardware—and even a small lending library tucked into a corner building. An enormous church resided on the far end of the main road, with a cemetery adjacent. I had walked through the cemetery before and had been awed to find headstones that dated back centuries, their epitaphs faded and covered in lichen.

Together, the three of us ate everything from arancini di riso, which were fried rice balls, to zeppole, a sort of doughnut without the hole. We drank copious amounts of Chianti, of course, watched people dance in front of the street musicians, and enjoyed the performance artists doing their skits and juggling and pantomime. It was a perfect, beautiful, amazing day that rolled into a gorgeous evening.

After a final walk around town, we paused at the fountain that marked the center of the village. It was lit up, accentuating the various parts of the life-size statue. It was a couple, mostly nude, in a passionate embrace with a sheet draped artistically around them while leaving their very accurately depicted gender-specific parts in view. The couple were staring into each other's eyes, and it looked as if they were about to kiss, but behind her back the woman held a lethal-looking dagger.

"*La tragica luna di miele*, the tragic honeymoon," Marcellino said as we paused to study it.

"So not a happily-ever-after?" Jason asked.

"No. The story is that Dante fell in love with Francesca, and even though she told him she would not marry him, he went to her father and got permission to marry her for the price of a flock of sheep. On their wedding night, she vowed to kill Dante and herself before she would submit to a man she did not love."

"That seems like overkill—pardon the pun," Jason said. "Speaking as a guy, a simple 'I'm just not that into you' would do it, no need for stabbing."

Marcellino laughed and clapped Jason on the shoulder, almost sending him into the fountain. "I agree, my friend, no stabbing required."

Being the only female present, I hoped they weren't indirectly talking to me. Did I seem like the stabby type?

"Marcellino!" A woman hurried toward us; she was young and beautiful and cast a quickly masked expression of resentment in my direction before she began to speak in rapid Italian.

Jason turned to me. "Damn it—I like him."

"It's impossible not to," I agreed. I glanced down at my flowers, which were looking sad after such a long day despite the wet cloth I had wrapped them in.

"He's handsome," he said.

"And charming," I added.

"Successful."

"Kind."

"He has a good sense of humor."

"He's also very intelligent and speaks three languages."

"Of course he does, and let's not forget he owns a castle," Jason said. He turned away silently, staring at the fountain. "I think this is where I leave you, Martin. Marcellino is clearly the better man. I hope you'll be happy. You deserve it."

My heart stopped. The thought of Jason leaving broke it clean in two. Two halves that couldn't function independently, leaving me to mourn what might have been if I'd just had the courage to reach for it. I tried, but my fear kept me stuck in place, unable to speak or move.

"What about Severin?" I asked. Work—I could always rely on work. "He'll be arriving anytime."

Jason turned and glanced at me. A hank of unruly dark hair fell over his brow, giving him a boyish appeal. "You don't need me for that. You were always what sealed the deal for him."

He raised his hand as if he wanted to touch me, but he let it drop back down by his side. He looked resigned, as if he'd tried his best but failed and now had to accept the loss. Just like when he'd told me about Jess, seeing him hurting caused me physical pain. I couldn't stand it. I turned away and stared into the fountain, then I cleared my throat until I felt him look at me.

"It's a shame, then, that Marcellino and I decided just to be friends," I said.

Jason went still, so still that I wasn't sure he was even breathing. His voice when he spoke was a gruff rasp. "Say that again, Martin."

I turned to face him, glancing at him over the flowers in my arms. "We're just friends."

His gray eyes flashed. The next thing I knew, he had my free hand in his, and he was dragging me away from the fountain, Marcellino, and the festival.

"Sorry," he called to Marcellino over his shoulder. "But we have to get these flowers in water before they die."

I saw Marcellino's mouth twitch, and I grinned at him. He gave me a slight nod of encouragement and then held his hand out to the beautiful girl beside him. Clearly, Marcellino was going to be just fine.

We slipped by the darkened windows of the shops to the outskirts of town. The lights of the festival, the music, the laughter, and the smell of the food faded as we found ourselves on a dark and deserted dirt road.

I started to walk in the direction of the vineyard, but Jason stopped me. He turned me to face him, cupped my face in his hands, and then lowered his lips to mine in a kiss that felt as if it had been waiting just beneath the surface for days. He sipped at my upper lip, lightly slid his tongue across the lower one, and fit his lips to mine so perfectly it was as if our mouths had been formed with the other in mind.

I couldn't get close enough to him, so I dropped my flowers and pressed up against him. His hands moved to my hips, drawing me in and holding me in place. I realized as his mouth wooed mine that this wasn't just a kiss; it was staking a claim. When my lips parted on a gasp, his tongue swept in, clearing out any capacity I had to think or reason. The taste of him, of us together, was the breaking down of the old and the rebuilding of something new. It was everything.

"Dance with me," he said, breaking the kiss so we could breathe.

I raised my eyebrows in surprise. I studied his face to determine just how serious he was. He was staring at my mouth in a way that made my heart kick into high gear in my chest.

"There's no music," I said.

"There's always music when you're near me," he countered. Then he began to hum "La vie en rose."

And just like that, I was back on the Eiffel Tower with him, listening to Edith Piaf with his warmth wrapped around me while we swayed back and forth. The scent of him, cardamom and mint, rose up from his skin while we danced, and I suddenly felt as if everything in my life had been stumbling toward this moment in time. It was too much. He made me feel too much. I stepped back from him.

He didn't let me go, however. Instead, he stepped close and cupped my face, tilting it so he could meet my gaze. His eyes were filled with purpose, as if he could sense that I was panicking and he wasn't about to let that happen. He pressed his mouth against mine. The kiss smoldered, and any thought I'd had of escaping incinerated on the spot.

The magic that I always felt when he touched me, the euphoria that started low and deep and fluttered up through me reappeared, and I could no more ignore it than I could break the kiss. Instead of shoving him away, I found myself clutching his forearms as if I'd lose my balance and tumble to the ground without him to hold me up.

We kissed and kissed and kissed some more until I felt the burn of his whiskers on my skin and my lips were puffy and all I could taste was him. He wrapped his arms about me and held me pressed against him. When he broke the kiss, he didn't let go but leaned down and pressed his forehead against mine while we struggled for breath.

"I'm in love with you," he said.

"Don't—"

"Too late." He gave me his crooked smile, and it about broke my heart. "I know you probably think it's too soon to say it, but I have to, because it's true. I knew it the first time I kissed you, and then I knew it for sure when you left for Italy, because I've only felt that sort of heartbreak once before. I. Love. You."

I felt as if I might faint. This was so much more than I was ready for. I shook my head, but he ignored me.

"I thought about it and thought about it, and I realized when I left Paris that it was always you. All of our animosity at work, it was me trying to keep you from getting under my skin, because I think I knew even then that you were the one," he said. "The very first time I saw you, I noticed you. How you walked with purpose, your hair pulled back at the nape of your neck, looking all business, the cut of your skirt, slim and sexy but utterly professional. No flashy jewelry and barely any makeup, as if you didn't want anyone to see you as anything other than a woman who got things done."

"You remember what I was wearing?"

"Oh yeah," he said. He grinned. The moonlight made it look like a pirate's smile, all roguish charm and mischievous intent, and I felt my insides melt. "Aidan introduced us, and when I shook your hand, your grip was cool and dry and firm. Then you looked me right in the eye and said, 'There aren't any hot wings here,' and then you walked away."

I cringed. "Oh man, I was such a jerk. I'm sorry. Truth? I was totally threatened by you and your success with that viral challenge and felt the need to establish dominance."

"I know," he said. "It was totally hot."

I burst out laughing. Then I sighed. What was I supposed to say?

"Working together makes this really complicated," I said. "This whole thing would be easier if I had fallen in love with Marcellino again."

He frowned. "But you couldn't, because even though Marcellino is the perfect man, he is not the perfect man for you. I am."

"How do you figure that?" I asked, both charmed and affronted by his arrogance.

"Because I fell in love with you on the other side of your greatest loss, your deepest grief," he said. "I fell for the strong, determined, driven woman who you'll always be, and I love you exactly as you are."

I felt my throat get tight. He cupped my chin, bringing my gaze up to his.

"Chelsea, you're trying so hard to be who you were before your mother died," he said. "But you can't be her. That woman died with your mom."

A tear coursed down my cheek, and he tenderly wiped it away with his thumb.

"That was the girl Marcellino and Jean Claude and Colin fell in love with, but you're not her anymore," he said. "You're a woman who has suffered tremendous loss and found the courage to keep going.

"That's what makes us perfect together. We understand that pieces of our hearts will always belong to those who are gone. For us, love and loss are forever entwined, making us love more cautiously but also more deeply," he said.

I was openly crying now. "I can't," I gasped. "I don't want to be the person on the other side of my grief. I want to be the person before the loss happened. I want to be her."

"I know, darling, but you can't. You've been fooling yourself that if you become that person again, you can slyly keep your pain tucked way down deep. The truth is you've been hanging on to your grief as if it's the last part of your mother that you can hold on to, and you can't move forward, because you're afraid if you let it go, you'll lose her forever."

It was true. I knew it, but I shook my head in protest. He ignored me.

"I'm telling you right here, right now, that you won't ever lose her," he said. "You can move forward and be the woman on the other side of loss. You can be her with me, because I understand it. I know this is true, because I was the same with Jess. You have to let the grief go."

"I can't," I cried. "I don't want to."

"Yes, you do. You're brave enough. I know you are," he whispered.

He smoothed the hair back from my face. "Trust me that it will be all right. I'll hold you through it. I'll keep you safe, I promise. Be with me, Chelsea. Tonight. Here and now, in this moment, let the past go and choose me."

It felt as if I were ripping a part of myself out, root and stem. On a torrent of tears and sobs that shook my shoulders and left me feeling weak, I reached deep inside of myself and felt the pain, the sadness, the anger, and the grief, all the emotions that I'd been hanging on to for so long, as if they would keep my mother with me. Jason was right: they didn't. But it still felt like a fresh loss.

With a moan of distress, I let it all go. I imagined my grief and pain soaring out of me up into the dark night sky to find a new home in the stars above. I expected to feel hollow, bereft, adrift without the anchor of sadness I'd been chained to for so long. Instead . . . I felt free.

With a gut-wrenching sob, I threw my arms around Jason's neck and pressed my face into his chest. Tears were running down my face, which was undoubtedly puffy and blotchy. I pulled back and used the skirt of my dress to wipe my face clean. My breath was coming in great gulps, as if I'd been held under water almost to the point of drowning and had just broken the surface and could breathe again.

Jason pulled me back into the circle of his arms. He rested his cheek on the top of my head and whispered words of comfort while he ran his hands up and down my back in a gesture meant to soothe. It didn't.

I slid my hands up the front of his warm chest. I pressed my palms against the nape of his neck and pulled him close so that I could press my lips against his. I kissed him, long and deep, with everything that I felt.

The kiss tasted of tears and loss but also of hope and joy. He clutched me to him, breathing me in and holding me with hands that shook. When he scooped me up into his arms, I didn't let go and I didn't stop kissing him, but let him carry me through the moonlight-soaked vineyard as if I was the most precious thing in the world to him.

The part of me that had been hollowed out by loss began to fill with lightness and love. I felt healed. And it wasn't because I'd found my old self but rather because I'd finally accepted myself for exactly who I was. Jason's love, his warmth, and his understanding had given me the courage to heal myself. When he set me on my feet outside the door to his guesthouse, he hugged me close and whispered in my ear, "Stay with me."

Unable to find the words, I nodded. Jason opened the door and led me inside. He didn't bother with the lights, but closed the door and pulled me close. He kissed me with one hand tangled in my hair, holding me still, while the other rested on my hip, pulling me close. He kissed me softly, slowly, sliding his lips along mine until he found the sweet spot where we fit perfectly. Then he deepened the kiss.

I parted my lips, inviting him in, swirling my tongue around his the way I knew he liked. He tasted faintly of wine. I leaned up against him. I couldn't get enough. I felt as if I were on fire and he was the only thing that could contain the heat.

I pulled at his shirt, tossing it aside, exposing his skin to my fingers. I trailed my hands up his sides, over his sculpted chest, to wrap them around his shoulders so I could bury my fingers in his thick hair. He groaned into my mouth and put both hands on my hips, pulling me up against him while he kissed me, breaking the kiss only so that he could run his lips down the side of my neck to the curve of my shoulder, where he gently bit down.

He grabbed fistfuls of my skirt and pulled the whole dress up over my head. I was in my underwear, and the night air was cold against my skin. Jason walked me backward toward the bedroom, kissing me the entire way. His hands stayed busy, taunting, teasing, tickling every bit of me he could touch.

When we reached the bedroom, he paused, letting go of me to light a candle in a pretty mosaic votive. It shot beams of purple and blue all around the room, and the candle smelled of lavender.

"I need to see you," he said, and then he pulled me close again. He held me still, seeming to savor the feel of my lips against his as he repeatedly fit his mouth to mine, kissing me deeply and then doing it all over again as if trying to memorize the way we fit together.

The aching need I felt for this man was becoming too insistent to ignore, and I broke the kiss and pulled him toward the bed. I wanted to feel the length of him pressed against me, his weight on top of me, and his warmth enfolding me.

I paused by the bed to help him out of his pants. We let them drop to the floor, and I climbed onto the bed and reclined against the pillows, beckoning for him to do the same. Instead, he took a minute to take me in. His gaze moved over my body as strong as a caress, and I got the feeling he was committing this moment to memory.

I could feel my face get warm under his scrutiny, but I didn't cover up or hide. Instead, I took the same moment to appreciate him and how beautifully he was made. But it wasn't just his handsomeness that drew me to him. His relentless optimism, his cheerfulness, his ability to put it all on the line when it was something he believed in, his commitment to his sister—it was all these things that made me love him. And I did love him so very much.

When I couldn't stand it any longer, I reached behind my back and unhooked my bra, pitching it over the side of the bed. My undies went next. Then I gave him a pointed look, and he shucked off his underwear, too.

When he straightened up, I held up my arms and said, "I choose you Jason."

With a hum of approval, he joined me on the bed, sweeping me into his arms and kissing me for what could have been minutes or hours or days. I had no idea. I was so caught up in him. The feel of his hands on my skin, his lips on mine, the way his breath caught when I touched him, as if he was surprised that I wanted him as much as he wanted me.

I tried to show him, but he kept me off guard. He flipped me over onto my stomach, and his hands kneaded my body from the crown of my head to my toes; every bit of me was caressed or massaged until I was limp and tingly and swamped by desire. When he turned me over, he began to lower his head to my nipples, but I was not having it. I pushed on his elbows, sending him down on top of me. Ah, that was better.

I allowed him just enough space to slip on some protection, then I settled him between my legs, right where I wanted him, and hooked my legs behind him, arched my back, and pulled him toward me. He tried to resist me, and I knew he was attempting to draw this night out as long as possible, but I simply could not wait another second to be joined. With a quick arch of my hips and tug of my legs, I felt him slide right into me, exactly where he belonged.

He stiffened at the contact, and I knew he was trying to get control of the situation, but the time for control was gone. I put my hands on his hips and used his body, which he had braced above me, to leverage myself against him.

He huffed out a breath and said, "You're killing me, darling."

Darling. I turned my head and smiled into his neck. The endearment made my heart squeeze tight. I wanted to be his darling more than anything else in the world.

But then he lowered his head and took one nipple in his mouth, biting down enough to make me buck up against him. We both groaned at the contact, and then he gave in. He reached below me and cupped my bottom, angling my hips so he could thrust into me as deeply as we both needed. It was everything.

I felt myself go hot, and when my orgasm hit, it spread through my entire body like shock waves. I clenched so tightly around him, I wondered if I'd hurt him, but with another thrust he was right there with me. I could feel him pulsing inside of me, and it felt as if we really had managed to merge into one being.

Sweaty, hot, and exhausted, we curled up in the soft sheets of Jason's bed with his arm anchoring me to him and my head tucked under his chin as if that space had been made just for me.

"Darling, can we go home now?" His voice was a soft whisper against my ear, making me shiver. His arm tightened about me, enfolding me into his warmth.

Home. I thought about seeing my dad and Sheri, and for the first time, it didn't hurt. In fact, I felt a burst of genuine happiness for him. I lifted my head and kissed Jason, surprising him. His sleepy eyes brightened, and he rolled me under him.

"What was that for?" he asked.

Looping my arms around his neck, I held his gaze and said, "Yes, I want to go home with you."

He grinned. It was a wicked grin, full of mischief and delight. Then he kissed me, and I forgot about everything except him.

chapter twenty-six

I T WAS THE sound of the songbirds in the trees that woke me, and I smiled. For the first time in as long as I could remember, everything was right with the world, because in deciding to spend the night with Jason, I had chosen him . . . but I had also chosen me. I was finally ready to embrace me.

What he had said last night was true. I had been clinging to my grief as if it were the last bit of my mother I could hold on to, and I was tired, so tired of being sad. But Jason understood. He knew that my joy would always have a flip side of sorrow, because he felt the same way. What an amazing gift it was to have a person who understood me so completely.

I stretched in the large bed and rolled over to see if he was awake yet. He wasn't there. The bed was empty, but the dent in the pillow where his head had been remained. I blinked. I heard the shower running and settled back down amid the soft, warm sheets.

His phone chimed on his nightstand, and I glanced at it, wondering if it was an alarm. I saw the screen display a message, and I leaned over to read it in case it was something urgent from Severin. Jason had said they were still detained, and I was hoping that everything was all right.

I lifted his phone and looked at the screen. Sure enough, an alert appeared saying there was a new text message from Severin—well, technically Eleanor, as I knew she did all his texting for him.

I wondered if they were all right. As erratic as Severin was, he was now two days late in coming to Tuscany. I had the horrible thought that something awful had happened. I glanced at the display. How wrong was it to look at Jason's phone? Total invasion of privacy? How pissed would I be if he looked at my phone when I was in the shower? Well, if he thought it was an emergency, I'd understand. Reassured, I tapped in the code I'd seen him use. Honestly, the man and I needed to talk about his security—from me, apparently.

I opened his text app and read the message, but it had nothing to do with Severin coming to Italy. Quite the opposite, in fact.

Eleanor: *Following up. When can we expect you and Chelsea in Boston to finalize the proposal?*

What the what? I slumped back in the bed. My sleep-deprived brain was sluggish, and I couldn't understand what this meant. Boston? But Severin was supposed to be coming here.

I hesitated for one second but then scrolled through the conversation. I refused to think of it as an invasion of Jason's privacy. It was work, after all.

The messages sent my heart plunging into my feet. Dated the same day we had left Paris was the first message from Eleanor.

Eleanor: *Sorry. Change of plans. Mr. Severin has been called back to Boston for an important meeting. Please let me know when we can schedule a meeting with the board upon your return. Thanks.*

Jason: *No problem. We're happy to meet wherever at Mr. Severin's convenience. I'll be in touch when I have dates.*

What followed was Jason and Eleanor trying to coordinate our schedules. Reading between the lines, I realized it was Jason who had been stalling until he had an exact date for our return. My return. I thought about our conversation last night and how he'd asked if we could go home, and my heart started beating hard in my chest in a panicked staccato that made me dizzy. Had I been played?

It was pretty clear. Severin wasn't coming to the wine festival, but he wanted a meeting with the two of us. Everything Jason had told me since he'd arrived at the vineyard about Severin arriving soon had been a lie. Why? Why would he have lied to me?

The bathroom door opened, and Jason stepped out in a plume of steam with a towel draped loosely around his hips. I stared at him. Shock. Denial. Hurt. Rage. They all battled to be the front rider in the four horsemen of the apocalypse of emotion I had surging through me. Rage won, and I threw his phone at him.

It missed him. Drat! It bounced off the wall by his head. He looked stunned. "Chelsea, what's wrong?"

I was too busy flailing my way through the sheets and blankets, trying to get out of the bed, to answer. I was so furious I couldn't even look at him. I grabbed my underwear and yanked it on. My bra straps gave me fits, so I didn't even bother and flung it away from me like I was tossing beads at a parade. I grabbed my dress and yanked it over my head.

Jason started across the room, looking concerned.

"Stop," I snapped. I finger combed my gnarled hair out of my face. "Do not come any closer."

"Okay, darling, what's going on?" he asked.

I glared at him. Darling, my ass. "Severin."

Just the one word and I knew from the tense look on his face that he knew that I knew that he had lied. He put a hand on the back of his neck and said, "I can explain."

"Not necessary," I said. "I figured it out."

His eyebrows lifted. "Did you?"

"Yes. This"—I gestured to the room as if it represented what had happened the night before—"was all just a way to hustle me home."

He shook his head. "Excuse me?"

"Severin wants to meet with both of us in Boston, but you knew I wouldn't leave until I finished my quest, so you seduced me into thinking that I should be with you, so you could get me on the next plane out of here to finalize the ask."

He rubbed a hand over his face. "What are you talking about?"

"You got a text from Eleanor this morning, trying to schedule a meeting with the two of us in Boston," I said. I pointed to his phone on the floor.

"Oh." He didn't deny any of it. I was devastated.

"So what happens when we get back?" I asked. My throat was so tight I could barely squeeze the words out. "We meet with Severin and then what? It 'accidentally' comes out that you and I had a thing in Paris and Italy, and then I'm in a whole lot of trouble, aren't I?"

"That's not—" he began, but I interrupted.

"Of course it is. Do you see how this looks? I'm just the idiot female who slept with her coworker. If company policy prohibits relationships, and it does, who do you think they're going to fire? No matter how you look at this, I'm the senior employee. I'm the one who should have known better. I'm the one who is going to get ousted, leaving you all the glory of nailing down the Severin ask. Well played, Knightley, really well played."

"Darling, you're freaking out," he said. He held out the hand not holding on to his towel in a placating gesture. It didn't work.

"You think?" I asked. "And don't call me 'darling.'"

"You can't actually believe that I came all this way just to manipulate you into returning to Boston to seal the deal with Severin," he said.

"Can't I?" I asked. My voice broke, which made me furious. "You. Lied. To. Me."

I didn't wait to hear another word from him. I shoved my feet into my sandals and stormed from his house, slamming the door behind me.

It was midmorning; the grounds of the vineyard were already swarming with tourists for the wine festival. I kept my head down as hot tears scalded my face.

My usually carefully contained emotions had kicked the basement door open and were now raging through me, smashing everything in reach. My heart was pounding. My hands were sweating. I was having a hard time breathing, and I desperately wanted to go find a quiet, dark corner to curl up in so I could cry myself dry in peace.

How could I have been so stupid? What if this whole thing from day one was just Jason using me to get to Severin? What if he hadn't meant what he'd said last night? What if he didn't love me? I sobbed. What if I lost my job over this? My career? Everything? It hit me, a straight shot to the heart, that of all the things I stood to lose, losing his love hurt the worst.

"Chelsea, wait!"

I glanced over my shoulder. My eyes went wide. Jason was coming after me, wearing only his towel and a pair of sneakers. I blinked as the morning sun glistened on his muscular frame, and I heard a woman nearby sigh, "Oh my."

Exactly! The man was not going to charm me again! I ducked into the rose garden adjacent to the castle. There were several tourists in here as well, but I ignored them in my quest for escape. I had just cleared the opposite archway and was in front of the main entrance when Jason caught me by the arm.

"Chelsea, wait," he said. He was panting. "You have to let me explain."

"There's nothing to explain," I cried. My own breath was short as I turned away from him. "I get it. I get all of it."

The sight of him hurt too much. His dark hair was disheveled, his blue-gray eyes were swirls of both colors, he had trimmed the scruff on his chin, and the only thing between him and complete nudity was the fist that held the towel presently wrapped around his hips. Well, that and his black Converse sneakers, the sight of which perversely made me want to cry even harder.

We were drawing a crowd—not a surprise—but I found I didn't

even care. Let everyone see how callously I'd been used. What was a little humiliation on top of such a betrayal?

"Yes, I lied to you," Jason cried in exasperation.

With a gasp, I turned to face him, ignoring the murmurs of the crowd surrounding us. "You admit it?"

"Of course I admit it," he said. He shoved one hand through his hair. "You were about to make the biggest mistake of your life—" He bit off his words, glanced past me, and said, "No offense, Marcellino."

I looked over my shoulder and saw Marcellino standing amid several staff members, clearly preparing for the second day of the wine festival. They all looked quite bemused, even Marcellino, who said, "None taken."

"Yes, I lied to you about Severin coming here," Jason continued. "I had to. We need you in Boston, Chelsea, raising money to fight the good fight and helping to save lives. It's who you are, it's what you're good at, and it's where you belong."

"So you lied to get me to go back to work for the ACC?" I asked. It shouldn't have stung so much that his primary motivation was work, but it did.

"Yes . . . no. Nothing at the office was the same after you left," he said. "When Aidan sent me to Paris to find you, I couldn't wait to get there, because I knew I was already half in love with you. When we kissed on the top of the Eiffel Tower, you finished me off for good. You said you went on this quest to find yourself, but you didn't need to go away to find yourself, Chelsea. You needed to go away so that *I* could find *you*." He paused, and his lopsided smile turned up one corner of his mouth. He looked at me from beneath his eyelashes in that way he had that charmed me stupid. I tried to stay strong.

I crossed my arms over my chest, trying to shut him out. He wasn't having it.

"To put it plainly, I came to Italy early and lied to you about Severin coming because I couldn't risk losing you." His gaze held mine, and it was full of such love and affection, for me, Chelsea Martin, just as I was, that I felt everything inside of me shift as it tried to lock into this new happy place. "You're it for me, Martin. I knew it the first time I laid eyes on you, and I know it now more than ever."

"But—" It was all I could get out.

"Everything I told you last night about what I feel for you is true," he said. "*Everything.*"

I stared at him. I wanted to believe him so badly, but the grief, the crippling, controlling sadness that had shotgunned any chance at happiness for me over the past seven years, sensed my vulnerability and was trying to throw a wrench of doubt into the works.

"I know what you're doing," he said. His eyes were soft. "And I know why."

I stood frozen, incapable of moving and barely able to inhale enough to stay conscious.

"You're terrified of this, and you've latched onto the first possible thing you can grab to save yourself from what you're feeling here." He gestured between us with his free hand.

I nodded. It was true. I was petrified all the way to my squishy middle.

"And that fear is telling you to push me away because I lied, but I'm not going to let you," he said.

"I don't think—" I began, but he interrupted.

"That's a good start—don't think," he said. He smiled his charmer's smile. "It's okay. I'm terrified, too. We'll be terrified together. Just don't leave me, Martin. Don't turn your back on this. Give me a chance. Give us a chance."

"If she won't, I will." I glanced over my shoulder to see two American tourists ogling my man. I frowned.

"What about work?" I asked. I couldn't help it. I had to know that he hadn't planned to oust me all along.

"I'll quit," he said.

"You'd do that?" I gasped.

He shrugged. "If it means I get you, the woman I love, then I'll happily quit right now." The look he sent me was so intense, I felt it crack my resistance like a blast of flame on a sheet of ice. He held out his free hand and called to the crowd, "Can someone give me a phone? I don't seem to have mine on me."

The tourists laughed. A pretty woman held out her phone to him, but I stepped forward and waved her away.

"You don't have to quit," I mumbled. I believed him. I had no choice, since he was willing to give it all up—for me.

"What's that?" he asked, cupping a hand to his ear.

"You don't have to quit," I said louder. "I believe you."

He frowned. Then he shook his head. "That's not what I want to hear."

Now I returned the frown. I met his gaze, which was positively wicked. Uh-oh.

"What do you want me to say?" I asked. Despite leaving claw marks on my insides, my doubts were ebbing as if being pulled out to sea on a riptide of desire that got stronger with every second I gazed at him. My man.

"I think," he said, "that it's your turn to tell me that you love me."

My face flashed scorching hot with embarrassment. I glanced around. There were at least thirty people watching us. I couldn't, not in front of all these strangers. I shook my head, and he made a tsking sound.

"You're leaving me no choice, Martin," he said. "You either admit that you love me, in front of witnesses, or the towel goes."

What?! He wouldn't! There were people here with phones. He'd go viral, for sure, and then his identity would be outed, and the ramifications for the ACC . . . He couldn't be serious! I met his gaze. He was! He would! Oh dear god!

The crowd started to clap and cheer. Half—mostly women, along with a few men—wanted the towel to drop. The other half, primarily men, were encouraging me, quite loudly, to speak.

I stared at Jason, who resembled a muscle-toned god, dazzling to the eye in the spring sunshine. I glanced back at Marcellino, but he was useless, as he was laughing and clapping along with the rest of them.

It was then that I felt her, or rather me, the old me. The one who would have thought this was hilarious and romantic and lovely. She would have been absolutely swept off her feet by this ridiculous display. I glanced down. My feet were on the ground, but my heart—my heart was soaring.

"Well, what's it gonna be, darling?" Impatient, Jason dropped the towel an inch. Eep!

"Fine. All right. Enough." I lifted my chin. I met Jason's gaze and said, "You are an ass."

He grinned, completely unrepentant. "And?"

"And I love you," I said. This was met with much approval and a smidgeon of disappointment by the crowd.

Marcellino, clearly sensing we needed privacy, offered free wine samples, and in moments, we were standing alone in front of the castle with Jason in his towel and me with a spectacular case of bedhead and no bra. A perfect pair.

"Say it again," he said as he took a step closer.

"I love you," I said. I moved toward him until we were inches apart. "Totally and completely."

A look of relief passed over his face, followed swiftly by one of pure joy, and I noted that this time when he smiled, both corners of his lips tipped up. He cleared his throat. "Chelsea Martin, just to be clear, are you saying that of all the men you've loved before, you choose me?"

"Yes, I choose you, Jason Knightley." I met his gaze, letting all the love I felt for him show on my face. "But you can never lie to me again."

He winced. "In the interest of full disclosure, I have to admit I totally saw your amazing rack the day of 'the incident.'"

"I knew it!" I cried. I would have taken a swing at him, but he swooped in and kissed me full on the lips, making me forget I was mad. When I pulled back, my brain was scrambled, but I managed to say, "Promise me, no more fibs, lies, or prevarications of any kind for any reason."

"Never again, I promise." He went to raise his right hand, and his towel slipped. I grabbed it, saving him from flashing an incoming busload of tourists.

"Knightley," I chastised him as he wrapped both arms around me, hugging me close.

"It's okay. I gotcha, Martin," he said.

And then he kissed me again, passionately, in the middle of a vineyard in Tuscany, and I knew the feelings were real. Because I'd finally, after so many years, released my grief and pain and let happiness in.

I'd done it. I'd found myself again. I'd found my laughter, and I remembered, oh, how I remembered, what it felt like to be in love. Because right now I was quite desperately in love with Jason with my whole heart. And best of all, he was in love with me, too.

epilogue

"Y OU DID WELL in the ceremony, Martin," Jason said. He was looking particularly dapper in a navy-blue suit with a light-blue dress shirt that made his eyes a deep ocean blue that I wished I could dive right into to escape this day. No such luck.

"And you're smokin' hot," he added. I snorted.

"Having fantasies about deflowering the flower girl, are you?" I asked.

"You know it," he said. He leaned close and whispered in my ear in a gruff growl that made my pupils dilate. "I can't wait to get you out of this dress."

I laughed, sending the big fat curls Sheri had requested bobbing across my shoulders. "That makes two of us, but I'm thinking for slightly different reasons."

The June day was warm, and the pink satin bodice of my flower girl dress was horribly constricting. Despite the itchy crinoline that puffed my skirt out a few feet, Jason held me close, keeping his arm around my waist as he led me to our table. Annabelle was already there with her boyfriend du jour, and when she caught sight of me in my matching dress, she lifted her wineglass in a toast. I knew it was her way of showing respect.

I had shown up, worn the dreaded dress, strewn the flower petals, and been the model of an accepting adult participating in her father's remarriage. The one thing that made it all bearable was looking at my father's face and seeing his big, goofy smile whenever he gazed at his bride. He was cuckoo bananas in love, and now that I fully appreciated how that felt, I sincerely hoped that never changed for him. He deserved every bit of happiness life could offer.

I glanced around the reception. I had to give it to Sheri. It was a beautiful wedding. Swaths of tulle and multicolored paper lanterns were strung above the tables and over the portable dance floor that had been spread out in front of the band. We were outside on the lush green lawn of a resort on Smugglers Beach in Cape Cod, with the ocean's crashing waves just beyond the high dunes that acted as a barrier.

Hurricane lanterns surrounded by bits of driftwood, sea glass, and seashells were the centerpieces illuminating the tables. The wedding service, performed on the beach at sunset, had been short and sweet, and once the vows had been spoken, the bride and groom had led the guests back up to the resort for the reception.

Jason pulled out my chair for me, and I sat. Other guests were settling into their seats, so I took a moment to talk shop with him. Thankfully, when we'd returned to Boston, Aidan had lobbied hard for the company policy about no dating to be changed. During Aidan's absence, Jason and I had been made co-general managers of the department. While our work styles didn't completely mesh—pioneer versus guardian—we were having a lot of fun figuring it out as we went along.

"Robbie Severin left me a voice mail this morning," I said.

"Did he?"

"He wants to start the rollout of the campaign by the end of summer."

Jason made a fist pump. "Did you tell Aidan?"

"I did," I said. "Even without hair, he was pretty stoked."

I was quiet, and Jason, so in tune to me and all that I was, said, "He's going to be okay, darling."

"I know," I said. "The prognosis is really good, but still . . ."

"Yeah," he said. He pressed his forehead to mine, and we both took a moment to remember the ones we'd lost. It was who we were and what we did. He leaned back and brushed my cheek tenderly with his thumb. "Jess would have loved you."

I grinned, because I knew this was the highest praise he could possibly give me, and I said, "And my mother would have adored you."

His smile deepened. We got lost in each other for a moment, as we sometimes did. Our love was so shiny and bright and new, it distracted. It wasn't until Annabelle reached over and tugged on my arm that I glanced away from my man.

"What?" I asked my sister. I tried not to grimace at the thought of what the two of us must look like in our pink—thankfully revised to a tasteful shell pink—dresses. I was still going to burn all the pictures of me in this dress, for sure, which was fine because knowing Annabelle, there'd be a life-size cutout made of us for my birthday. Because that was how she rolled.

"While I adore seeing you on cloud nine," Annabelle said with a grin, "it looks like something is about to happen." She pointed, and I glanced in the direction of the stage.

Standing in front of the band was Sheri Armstrong—excuse me, Sheri Martin. She had decided to take Dad's name. She was in a cream-colored dress with a delicate lace bodice and an organza skirt with a matching lace trim. She looked lovely, and my father hadn't been able to take his eyes off her all evening.

Even though it had caused me a pang or two, I knew I wouldn't have it any other way. I was happy for him—truly, I was. I'd made an effort to spend some time with Sheri over the past few weeks. I didn't know if we'd ever be super close, because I still struggled with her replacing my mom, even though I knew that was my issue and not hers. But I thought we could probably become friends, good friends, in time. At least, I was going to try.

"Ahem." Sheri cleared her throat. Her dark hair was up in an artful twist and held in place with pearl hair clips. "Can you hear me?"

Her voice boomed across the reception, making her start and then laugh at herself for jumping. She smiled at her new husband, and he grinned back.

"First, I want to thank you for attending our wedding," she said. Her voice was soft with genuine gratitude. "I am so pleased that you all could come." I wasn't sure, but I thought Sheri's gaze lingered on me for a moment. When I felt Jason's fingers squeeze mine, I knew I hadn't imagined it.

"But there is someone who isn't here today who I would like to take a moment to thank, because it's important," she said. Her hand was shaking, and her voice quavered with a bit of emotion. She held out her free hand to my dad, and he took it in his. Looking at him with love and tenderness shining on her face, she said, "I want to thank Christine Martin for teaching *our* husband to be the kind, loving, and patient man that he is. And I want her to know that I love him with all of my heart and will care for him, always, with all that I am."

Well, that was unexpected. I felt my eyes fill up and my throat got tight. Annabelle leaned over and wrapped an arm about me, bracing me. I noted that her eyes were watery, too.

"And I want to promise all of you who were lucky enough to have Christine in your life and to be loved by her that I will honor her memory all the days of our life together."

Dad hugged his new wife close, and I saw him swipe away a tear beneath his glasses. When he looked at Sheri, I saw him say, "Thank you."

In that moment, I realized I had been wrong about Sheri. Completely and utterly wrong. My dad had been right. She was special, and he'd been able to figure it out in just two weeks. Smart man. I glanced at Jason with a stricken face, and he nodded in understanding. He knew what I had to do, and he supported me. I kissed him quick and then stood up. I took Annabelle's hand in mine and dragged her toward the stage.

"Oh no, we're not making a scene right now, are we?" Annabelle asked. She sounded panicked as she hurried to keep up with me. "I mean, it was nice what she said, wasn't it?"

I didn't answer. I stopped in front of my father and his new wife. I gazed at the petite woman who was nothing like my own mother but who made my father happy nonetheless. I wiped the tears off my face, opened my arms, and said, "Welcome to the family . . . Mom."

acknowledgments

There are so many people to thank for the creation of this book, I hardly know where to begin.

Thanks to my son Wyatt. If I hadn't been waiting for you outside that Circle K on a cold December morning when we were late getting you to school, the idea might have flown right by me. Thanks, kid. And, yes, feel free to remind me of this when I get cranky that we're late.

Big gratitude to my amazing agent, Christina Hogrebe, who gasped when I threw the idea at her, quite randomly, and insisted I stop what I was doing and write this book immediately. You've been this story's champion from day one and it is much appreciated.

Huge thanks to my brilliant editor, Kate Seaver, who embraced this story wholeheartedly and offered invaluable input and insight and endless encouragement during the process, earning an editorial Medal of Valor for going above and beyond to make this story the absolute best it could be.

Much appreciation to my amazing team at Berkley: Brittanie Black, Jessica Mangicaro, Danielle Keir, and Natalie Sellars. Thank you, all, for your support, enthusiasm, and hard work on behalf of this book.

Many thanks to my plot group pals, Paige Shelton and Kate Carlisle, who cheered me on and helped me plug plot holes from the beginning to the end.

On a personal note, I am ever grateful to my beta readers, Alyssa Amaturo, Annette Amaturo, and Susan McKinlay. Your input, enthusiasm, and encouragement were invaluable.

Shout-out to my brother, Jon McKinlay. You gave me the nuts and bolts of the city you've built, Boston, and I couldn't have written about it without you. Thanks, bro!

Many thanks to my son Beckett. You were such a trooper to hike so many miles around Paris with me, and I really appreciate that you kept me from getting lost, repeatedly. I will treasure being on the top of the Eiffel Tower with you and your brother always.

Unending gratitude to Chris Hansen Orf, aka the Hub. Your support of my work means the world to me and I'm so glad I have you to talk it out when the words get stuck. You're the best!

Lastly, I want to acknowledge my family and friends, for your unflagging encouragement; my fellow writers, who've been so supportive; and my readers, whose enthusiasm is always a light in the darkness for me.

Every book is a journey and this one was a steep climb, but none of you let me fall. Thank you all so very much.

PARIS IS ALWAYS A GOOD IDEA

Jenn McKinlay

questions for discussion

1. When Chelsea discovers her father is getting remarried, she has a strong reaction—one that causes her to rethink the last seven years of her life. Could you sympathize with Chelsea's feelings and her decisions in the wake of her father's announcement?

2. Chelsea decides to revisit her past to move forward with her future. Have you ever considered or taken a similar journey in your life? What was it? Did you find it helpful?

3. What does Chelsea hope to achieve in revisiting her post-college gap year?

4. Have you been to Ireland, France, or Italy? Do you have a favorite foreign country you've visited or you'd like to visit? What about that place appeals to you?

5. Which of Chelsea's former three loves—Colin, Jean Claude, or Marcellino—is your favorite? Why?

6. When does Chelsea start to see her work rival, Jason, in a different light? Have you ever had a similar experience—where your relationship with someone unexpectedly takes on a new dimension? What spurred viewing that person in a new way?

7. How does grief play a role in both Chelsea's and Jason's lives?

8. How does Chelsea's relationship with her family change during the course of the book?

9. What does Chelsea discover about herself by revisiting her past? How is Chelsea different at the end of the novel from who she was at the beginning?

Photo by Jacqueline Hanna Photography

JENN McKINLAY is the award-winning, *New York Times*, *USA Today*, and *Publishers Weekly* bestselling author of several mystery and romance series. Her work has been translated into multiple languages in countries all over the world. She lives in sunny Arizona in a house that is overrun with kids, pets, and her husband's guitars.

VISIT THE AUTHOR ONLINE

JennMcKinlay.com

JennMcKinlayAuthor

Ready to find
your next great read?

Let us help.

Visit prh.com/nextread

Penguin
Random
House